Books by Kris N

Death

Deadly Vision
Deadly Obsession
Deadly Deception

Enchanted Lovers

Healing Hands

Anthologies

Into the Spirit

Single Titles

Keeping Faith
Centerfold

Deadly Vision

ISBN # 978-1-78651-888-0

Interior text design by Claire Siemaszkiewicz

Totally Bound Publishing

Published in 2016 by Totally Bound Publishing, Newland House, The Point, Weaver Road, Lincoln, LN6 3QN, United Kingdom.

Totally Bound Publishing is a subsidiary of Totally Entwined Group Limited.

Printed and bound in Great Britain by Clays Ltd, St Ives plc

1

'Til Death

DEADLY VISION

KRIS NORRIS

Dedication

To Kyle, Jared and Sydney for showing me how to see the world in a way I thought I'd forgotten. I'll always be your biggest fan!
And thanks to Chris for helping me realise a dream.
You're the best!

Chapter One

"Nine-one-one, do you need police, fire…"

"I need the fucking cops!"

Fallon bit back a curse, curbing her urge to hang up, as she spoke calmly into the phone. "Where do you need the police?"

She heard the man tell someone to shut the hell up as he breathed heavily into the phone. "There's a fucking fight going on here, so stop asking me questions and send the damn cops!"

"It's hard to send the police when I don't know where you are, sir." Fallon kept her voice cool and detached, knowing any increase in her tone would set the guy off even more.

"I dialled nine-one-one. I know you guys trace the fucking calls!"

"Only landlines. You're on a cell, so the only address I get is the repeater you're bouncing off of. So why don't you tell me where you are, and I'll send some help your way."

"Goddamn, son of a bitch…I said shut up already…just send the cops to Joe's Bar. They'll know where it is."

"What kind of…" The phone went dead. "Bloody typical." She released the line and dialled the number back, not surprised when the asshole's messaging system picked up. "Great. Just great." She typed a few lines onto the screen, shaking her head in disgust. Why the hell jerks like him called the police if they weren't willing to talk to the dispatchers never ceased to amaze her. Seven years on the job and she still hadn't figured it out. She let the sigh she'd been holding back tremble across her lips as she keyed up the radio.

"Bravo one and bravo two, dispatch."

The line hung silent for a few moments before a husky voice surged over the airwaves. "Bravo one. Go ahead, dispatch."

"Are you guys available for the usual down at Joe's Bar?"

"Bravo two's clear."

"Yeah, we're clear too, dispatch. Got any details for us?"

"Just the usual dead silence on the other end of the phone," she sighed. "But I could hear the music still playing in the background, so I doubt it's that out of control yet. Other than that, I've got nothing for you." She paused, listening to the men mutter under their breath. "Would it help to say my spider sense is tingling?" she added.

Laughter erupted over the radio. "Thanks, Fallon. We'll be sure to watch our backs."

"Don't forget to give me a shout when you're on scene, and I'll set the timer for you. Let me know if you big strong fellows need any more backup."

"And distort the godlike images you've developed for us? I don't think so, *darling*."

Fallon smiled as she cleared the channel and rubbed the bridge of her nose. She knew it wouldn't stop the headache from spreading, but it was all she could do until she slept the bugger away. Damn, she was tired. The dispatch centre had lost more than a few operators over the past few months, and she'd worked more overtime than she cared to count, tonight being no exception.

"Hey. Fallon. What are you still doing here?"

Fallon turned towards the voice, smiling at Jane's watchful expression. "You know me, Jane. I can't seem to get enough of this place."

Jane rolled her eyes as she set her purse down on the desk beside Fallon. "Fourteen hours again?"

"Try eighteen," she replied, answering another call over the radio. She heard Jane mumble beside her but chose to ignore it. Jane had a husband and a life to go home to. All she had was her mountain bike to keep her company.

"Roger, bravo two. Do you want me to leave the channel open or set a five-minute timer for you?"

"Timer's fine, Fallon. Just a few redneck boys duking it out in the parking lot. No weapons. I don't anticipate any problems."

"Speak for yourself, Jeff. I just had my nails done," moaned Ken.

Fallon couldn't stop her smile. "I'll chat with you in five, boys."

"Another fist match at Joe's?" asked Jane, clipping her headset in place. "That's the third time this week, and it's only Tuesday."

"Must be the lack of sunshine."

"More like the lack of willing females," she retorted. "I swear men get so worked up when they aren't getting laid."

"This coming from a woman who gets more than her fair share of sex," pointed out Fallon. She watched Jane's face flush a deep red. No doubt she'd made the most of her days off. "You about ready?"

Jane nodded, tapping her computer to life. "Why don't you go home and call it a day…and a night, for that matter." She sighed as three lines lit up at once. "And don't come back for a while, got it?"

"Believe me, nothing will be able to drag me back in here before I've had a couple of days off." She gathered her things, wondering how she'd spend the next forty-eight hours. "Call me later. Maybe we can catch a movie tomorrow?"

"Sounds good, hon. I'll talk to you soon."

Fallon forced a smile as she headed out to her Jeep. Jane meant well, but she seldom called once she left the office. *Too much sex,* thought Fallon, settling into the driver's seat. God, what she wouldn't give to be in Jane's place. She loved sex. She just wasn't getting any.

You could have some if you weren't still pining over Gil.

She cursed the irritating voice in her head. She wasn't *pining* over Gil. She was just having trouble moving on. It didn't mean she was, in any way, *pining* for him.

She sighed, imagining his fingers grazing her body. He knew where every erogenous spot was and took his time teasing each one in turn—from the hollow by her collarbone down to the delicate arch of her foot. He was a master at making her feel sexy and feminine, and tears pooled behind her lashes just thinking about him. She missed him. Missed the feel of his tongue between her thighs, swirling her juices around her clit until she screamed out his name with her release. Missed the hard thrust of his cock deep inside her as he possessed her like no man had ever tried. He'd been her every fantasy, her best friend.

"Stop it," she hissed, revving the engine in the growing darkness. "He's gone. It's over. Deal with it." She stepped on the pedal, spinning the tires as she squealed out of the lot and into traffic. All she needed was a hot shower and a good night's sleep, and everything would look better in the morning.

* * * *

"He's going to strike again," sighed Special Agent Wade Davis. "It's only a matter of time. He can't hide from us forever."

Special Agent Gil Grant looked up at the man. He'd been going over the records for hours and was so tired he was sure the lines had started melding together. He glanced over at the wall, eyeing the photos pinned to the board. Six women—all young and fit—all dead. He cursed, crumpling the paper he'd been writing on. "Time is the one thing we don't have. It's been two weeks since his last victim. He won't wait much longer."

"Maybe this time he'll leave something behind we can nail him with."

Gil held back the growl building in his chest. Wade was young and still too arrogant to see himself as anything other than bulletproof. He hadn't watched his fellow agents die in the name of justice, and maintained the belief that good always conquered evil.

But evil was far stronger than anyone wanted to believe. And it was going to take more than one lucky break to catch this guy. "I'd rather nail the bastard before he strikes again, if it's all the same to you."

Wade merely shrugged. They both knew the chances of tracking the guy down before his next victim was found mutilated and marked was pretty slim, but Gil hated to give in to defeat. The thought of going over another bloody crime scene curdled his stomach. There was always so much blood.

Gil shook his head and closed the file. "Maybe he won't kill anyone tonight," he said, grabbing his coat off the back of his chair as he headed for the door. "I'll be on my cell if anything comes up. See you tomorrow."

Wade grabbed Gil's shoulder as he bridged the door. "I know I'm new and everything, but I want this bastard as much as you do. I know we'll get him."

Gil glanced back at Wade over his shoulder. "I sure hope you're right, Junior, or it's going to be a hell of a hard pill to swallow."

Wade winced and smacked him across the back. "Have a good night, old man."

Gil sighed and headed down the hall—a good night—now that would be a pleasant change. He hadn't had a good night since…

He shivered as thoughts of Fallon flitted through his mind. She'd been the best lover he'd ever had, and the only woman he'd truly loved. He could still feel her body against his. The soft press of her breasts in his hands as he massaged them with slow circles, teasing them until her nipples puckered against her skin. They were thick and hard, and he loved feeling them rasp against his teeth as he suckled them into his mouth. He could lave them for hours. Take her from one orgasm into another without ever touching her pussy. She was the most responsive woman he'd ever met.

He swallowed, forcing the moisture past the lump stuck in his throat. He couldn't think of her without his chest tightening and his breath hitching. She still haunted his dreams, and he wondered if he'd ever be able to move on... to forget.

"Ah, fuck," he cursed, feeling the rain dampen his face. The heavy clouds had been threatening all day, but he'd hoped to make it to his truck before the worst of the coming storm hit. Luck wasn't on his side tonight, and the steady rivulets of water were trickling down his back by the time he swung open his door and ducked inside. He leant back against the seat and closed his eyes. The metal pins in his left shoulder seemed to vibrate in the heavy air, sending tremors through his body as he tried to rub the damn ache away. But it wasn't any good. He was cold and wet, and so damn horny it hurt.

"Son of a bitch!" He banged his hands against the steering wheel, anger bubbling through his veins. It wasn't bad enough he couldn't get any kind of lead on the psycho stalking Washington state's women, now he was faced with another night of dreaming of Fallon, only to wake up to find himself alone.

* * * *

Fallon tossed in her bed, hearing the rumble of thunder echo across the sky. She'd been lying there for twenty minutes, but she just couldn't seem to fall asleep. She knew she needed it. Her eyes were heavy and dry. The muscles in her back ached, and her headache had blossomed into a migraine. But every time she closed her eyes, images of Gil raced across the darkness. She could see him clearly. The sexy little half-smile he gave her whenever he wanted to seduce her. Or the way his muscles flexed and bunched beneath her fingers as he pumped her full of his hot cum. He was dangerous, in every sense of the word, and it tore her apart to think she'd lost him. He'd just never been the same since...

A loud blast of music filled the room. Fallon jumped, grabbing her cell off the small table beside the bed. She flipped it open, fumbling for the right button as her breathing stalled in her chest.

"Nine-one-one..." She paused, staring down at the phone. "Ah crap. Hello?"

"Okay, you really need to get a life, Fallon, if you're starting to answer your cell that way!"

Fallon snorted into the phone, pulling the strap of her slip back across her shoulder. "Well, I'm sure you'd answer the same way if you'd just spent the past two days at work." She took a deep breath, hoping to calm the pounding in her chest. "So what's up? Don't tell me they want me to come back now?"

"Hell no. And I sure wouldn't be the one to phone you. I just wanted to ask you something." She heard Jane pause and wondered what her friend was up to. "You weren't sleeping yet, were you?"

"Not yet. You know how it is. It's hard to unwind sometimes." She bit at her bottom lip. "So what do you need to ask me?"

"I meant to ask you before, but it totally slipped my mind. Brad and I are having a barbeque on Sunday. I already checked the schedule. You aren't working. We were wondering if you'd join us?"

"Just me?"

Jane stammered on the phone, yelling something to another operator. Fallon could hear the nervousness in her friend's voice. "There may be another friend or two joining us."

Fallon smiled. So that was it. Jane was trying to set her up...again. "Okay, Jane. Spill it. What's his name?"

Jane huffed. "His name is Jackson and he's a new firefighter down at the station. Brad thought it might be nice to introduce him to a few people in town...so he doesn't feel lonely."

"And I, of course, was your number one pick."

"You need to move on. You've done nothing but work since you and Gil broke up. It's not healthy." Jane breathed heavily into the phone. "Okay, girlfriend. Tell me. When was the last time you got laid?"

Fallon nearly dropped the phone. "You do know these phones are recorded, right?"

Jane laughed. "Do you really think I'd call you on one of the regular lines? I'm using that old blue phone. You know, the one they used to get the old CB calls on. I don't think it's even hooked up to the system anymore. I've never heard the damn thing ring. And it was harder than hell to get through to your number. I had to press every freaking button on the damn thing. So no tapes. Now answer the question."

Fallon sighed. She hated talking about that part of her life. "You know damn well I haven't been with anyone since Gil, so don't go getting all smug."

"And what about those guys you went out with?"

"Oh, you mean the ones who showed up on my doorstep and said, 'Hey, sugar. Instead of going out to dinner, how about I make you breakfast?' Please. Give me a break. I may be needy, but I'm not desperate."

"Well if you ask me, it wouldn't hurt to give one of them a chance. A hot night of good sex would do wonders for you."

"And who says it'll be good sex?"

"Hey, when you aren't getting any, I'd think anything would be considered *good*."

Fallon chuckled. "That's why I've got toys. So I don't have to go looking for it."

"Toys are great, but they don't replace a flesh-and-blood man. Nothing compares to a good cock, I don't care what you say."

Cock. Great! Fallon cursed under her breath as more images of Gil filled her mind. Now there was a cock that deserved worshipping. Eight inches of pure steel that could take her from zero to sixty in a heartbeat. And the taste of him. Lord, he had a flavour that liquefied her body and gushed the cream from her cunt. She loved the way he stretched her as he pushed through her channel, plunging until he grazed her womb. He'd been the best sex she'd ever had.

No, he'd been far more than that. He'd been the best love she'd ever made.

"I'll manage, Jane."

"Fine, be a recluse if you want to. But will you come to the barbeque?"

"I'll think about it. You know I like to take long rides on my days off."

"So ride your ass over to my house. And don't worry about bringing anything. I've got it covered. Just wear one of those tight tops of yours and be sure to show a little leg."

"Why don't I just wear a sign that says, 'please fuck me', instead?"

"Sounds perfect. Okay, gotta run. This place is getting crazy again. See you Sunday. Two o'clock sharp."

Fallon listened to the line go dead before placing her cell back on the table. She knew Jane meant well, but *moving on* wasn't as easy as her friend thought. Maybe it was because she still didn't know why it'd all fallen apart. She'd always believed Gil had never really got over the shooting, but a part of her feared it was tied to their last night together.

She sighed and collapsed back on the bed. That memory was like a dream to her, and she sometimes wondered if it'd ever truly happened.

Chapter Two

Fallon tossed on the bed as the dream flickered in her head.

"Hey, baby. Where are you?"

Fallon smiled at the sultry sound of Gil's voice, feeling shivers tingle down her spine. "I just picked up dinner and was heading home. Is everything okay?"

"Fine, babe. I was just wondering if you'd mind if Charlie stopped by too? We've got a few things to go over before tomorrow."

Fallon smiled. Gil just couldn't let a case go once he got hooked on it. "Do you have my favourite?"

"A whole case of coolers…strawberry flavour."

"Then tell Charlie I'll see him soon," she replied, laughing at the sigh that rumbled across the phone. "Race you home, Gil."

Gil and Charlie were waiting in the driveway when she pulled in, a sly smile tilting both their lips. "It's cheating when you use your siren, you know," she scolded Gil, handing him the bags of food.

"Ah, you're just sore you lost. Now quit squawking and get inside. I'm starving."

Fallon leaned into the kiss Gil planted on her lips, letting her nipples graze against his shirt. He groaned and pressed harder, tasting the depths of her mouth before finally releasing her and heading into the house. Fallon smiled and turned, brushing a kiss across Charlie's cheek as he held the door for her. She headed straight for the kitchen, grabbing plates and forks from the cupboard before heading back to the coffee table. Gil already had the cartons spread across the table and barely waited until Fallon handed him a fork before digging into the food.

"Didn't you guys eat lunch?" she joked, watching the men devour the food.

"Only had time to grab a sandwich outta the machine," mumbled Gil around a mouthful of rice. He looked over at her, smiling slyly. "And as I recall, I was too busy this morning to get breakfast before I left."

Fallon blushed, remembering how she'd caught Gil in the shower. He'd been covered in soap, shampoo slowly dripping down the curve of his jaw as he'd turned towards the door, his eyes brooding. He'd watched her slowly step inside, the water washing down her body, trickling across her shoulders and down the valley between her breasts. His cock had lengthened along his stomach, pulsing with his increased breath, as he watched the water cover her stomach, finally soaking through the short hair covering her sex. She'd smiled at him and pressed her body against his as she'd licked the water rinsing over his neck. It'd tasted like him and she hadn't been able to contain her groan of pleasure. Gil hadn't even waited to see if she was ready before pushing her against the side of the shower and plunging his cock deep inside. She'd screamed out his name at the sudden intrusion, locking her heels around his tail bone as he pummelled into her, stealing her breath as he sent her into orgasm. He hadn't stopped at her convulsions but had merely hitched her legs higher, pulling her thighs farther apart as he'd slipped his finger around to the cleft of her ass, firmly thrusting his finger inside her tight pucker.

Fallon blushed even deeper, remembering the exquisite feel of his fingers up her ass. She'd never imagined anal play to be so exciting and was thinking about having him take her there tonight. It wasn't something they always did, but when the mood was right, it was one of the fastest ways to send her over the edge.

She smiled back at Gil, ignoring the hooded gaze he flashed her. "Is that a complaint, darling?" she teased.

"'Cause I can rein it in, if you're not"—she let her eyes travel down the length of his body, resting on his crotch as she continued—"up to it."

Gil's eyes darkened as she watched his erection bulge against his jeans. "Don't worry, Fallon. I'll show you later just how...up...to it I am."

Charlie cleared his throat, drawing their attention. "Should I excuse myself for a while?"

Fallon smiled, flashing Gil a provocative look. "It's okay, Charlie. We both know Gil won't have his mind on anything but the case until you guys have talked it all out. He just likes hearing himself talk."

Charlie laughed as she winked at Gil. He nodded at her, but there was an edge to his eyes she hadn't seen before. A dark promise of what he had in store for her. A shiver shimmied down her spine as she turned away, not able to hold his stare. He'd been acting different ever since he'd been handed the new case. Even Charlie seemed tense, as if he were holding some inner anger at bay. She'd tried to get Gil to talk about it, but he'd flicked her cares away, usually using an intense lovemaking session to make her forget what she'd asked him.

But she couldn't forget.

* * * *

"Damn. Look at the time," said Charlie, tapping his watch with a single finger. "Sorry, Gil. I didn't mean to stay so late."

"You're always welcome, Charlie. Besides, Fallon doesn't mind. Do you, baby?"

Fallon looked up from her book, catching Charlie's glance. "It's much better having him talk to you than listening to him talk to himself." She laughed as Gil squeezed her foot. She'd draped her legs over his lap after dinner, and he'd been touching them all evening. She glanced at the clock. "Why don't you stay, Charlie? The spare room's already made up."

Charlie looked at Gil and Fallon saw something pass unspoken between them. When he looked back at her, his eyes were dark, heavy lidded. "It's late," said Charlie. "But…"

Fallon swung her legs to the floor as she put the book down across the table. "It's settled, then," she announced as she rose to her feet, swaying slightly.

"Easy, babe," said Gil, rising up beside her. "I think you may have had one cooler too many."

She chuckled, feeling the room pitch as she tried to step forward. Her startled scream took her by surprise when her foot snagged the table and pitched her forward. Both men reached out, grabbing her before her head grazed the table. They pulled her upward and she came to rest against the hard panes of Charlie's chest. Gil moved in behind her, soothing his hands over her shoulder.

"Sorry, guys. I guess I have had…" Her voice trailed off when she felt Charlie's cock harden against her stomach, his hips bracketing hers. She held her breath, pulling away just enough to look up into his eyes. They'd darkened, hiding the light hazel colour behind the large black discs. The skin over his cheeks seemed taut and she could feel his breath raking through his chest. She went to step back when Gil's lips came down softly across the nape of her neck.

"Are you okay, Fallon?"

His voice was husky and raw, the same tone he used when he wanted to seduce her. She gasped at the erotic sensation, feeling his tongue trace the back of her shoulder. "Gil?"

Gil sighed, rustling the hairs on her neck. "I need you, Fallon." He paused then, brushing his finger down the curve of her breast before palming her stomach. "We both need you."

Fallon tensed as he pressed his chest into her back. She could feel his erection hardening along the cleft of her buttocks as his hand slowly unbuttoned her shirt. She looked up at Charlie. He was watching her chest, licking his lips with each inch of skin Gil revealed. The man was taller than Gil, with shoulders that could fill a doorway. He had sandy blonde hair cut close to his scalp, and a body any woman would drool over. But there was something in his eyes—a pain that never seemed to ease, even when he laughed—that had always made her keep her distance. And she wasn't sure she wanted to bridge it now.

"Gil? What..." Her voice cut off as he freed the last button, and moved back just enough to shed the garment from her shoulders, exposing her skin to the cool air of the room. It beaded beneath his touch as he smoothed his hand up her stomach, coming to rest just beneath her left breast. She turned to look at him when his lips slanted down over hers, claiming her mouth with a possessiveness she'd never felt.

She moaned, not able to keep her desire for him from bubbling to the surface. She tried to turn her chest into his, but he held her firm, his hand still perched on her ribs. It was then she felt Charlie's fingers between her breasts, tugging against the clasp of her bra. She wanted to pull back, confront the men, but Gil held her captive, plundering her mouth as if his life hung in the balance. He was stroking the velvety softness of her tongue, playing with it while the cups of her bra fell aside, revealing her pale skin.

"Damn, you have beautiful breasts," moaned Charlie. "So soft and round. I've always dreamt of touching them."

Fallon gasped, feeling Charlie's thumb graze her nipple. His touch was gentle but firm, and she couldn't stop her body from reacting to him. She whimpered against Gil's mouth as he finally released her, allowing her one deep breath before taking her mouth again, this kiss even more demanding than the first. His tongue brushed against the inner reaches of her mouth just as Charlie's lips descended upon her other nipple. She cried into the kiss, not sure whether it was anger or arousal pumping the blood through her veins. Charlie's tongue wrapped around her peaked bud, slowly drawing on it as if any hard motion would hurt her. He'd managed to strip off his shirt and the feel of his hot skin brushing against hers sent her pulse skyrocketing. Without thinking, she arched into his caress, silently begging him to take more of her breast. He responded with a low growl, lifting up her breast as he suckled more into his mouth.

Gil broke the kiss, holding up her right breast to Charlie's talented tongue. It seemed surreal as she heard Gil's shirt rustle to the floor, his skin now touching hers. His hot breath washed over her shoulder as he nibbled his way to her ear.

"Easy, Fallon. We won't hurt you, baby."

Fallon could only gasp in a quick breath as Charlie knelt down in front of her, his fingers working the buttons of her jeans. "I don't understand, Gil. You always said you'd kill any man who touched me."

Another sigh rumbled from Gil's chest, his lips feather soft against her skin. "This isn't the same, baby. Charlie's like a brother to me. I need you to do this for me. Just this once."

"Can't you tell me why?" she asked, more than aware Charlie was lowering her pants to the floor. "Please, Gil. I couldn't live with myself if you hated me for this later."

"Hate you?" His voice sounded stunned, as if her question had caught him off guard. "Fallon, I could never hate you. I'll only love you more for having the strength to give me this gift. Please, just trust me. I promise I'll explain everything later, once this case is over. But for now, I just need you to close your eyes and let us show you how much we love you, baby. Can you do that for me?"

She wanted to say no. To insist he was the only man she could ever be with, but the words lodged in her throat at the desperate quality of his plea. As if sharing her with Charlie was the one act that would save him from the fires of Hell. She chanced a glance back over her shoulder. His eyes were dark and smoky but edged with uncertainty. She knew he wouldn't take her without her permission, and he was scared she'd deny him. She drew in a long breath, feeling Charlie's fingers rim her panties. "I trust you, Gil."

A wide smile spread across his face, lighting the gleam in his eyes. He eased forward, gently taking her lips in his as her panties fell to the floor. His thigh moved between her legs, gently splaying them apart. Gil rested some of her weight against his chest, massaging her right nipple, plucking at it with just the right amount of pressure. Liquid seeped from her cunt, lightly coating the velvety skin of her labia. Gil groaned, moving his lips back to her collarbone.

"God, I love the smell of you, so sweet and warm. And the taste...it's like drinking some voodoo love potion."

Gil wrapped one hand around her waist while the other tracked down her body, caressing each inch of skin he could find. She tried to turn her head to follow his motion, but he stopped her with a gentle bite to her shoulder.

"Oh no. Just look at me. Just focus on me for now."

"Tell me what you're going to do. I need to know."

"We're only going to love you. There's no need to be scared. Just open yourself up and let Charlie taste that sweet little pussy of yours."

Gil had no sooner said the words than Charlie's lips brushed against her inner thigh. She held her breath, not sure what to expect as Gil's hand moved over her mound, softly drawing her drenched lips apart.

"Damn, you're wet. God, I love that you react like this. You're so responsive, baby."

"*Ohmygod.*" Fallon screamed out Gil's name as Charlie's tongue slipped between her delicate folds of skin, lapping at the juices flowing from inside her. He hummed his appreciation, vibrating the tightly knotted nerves of her clit, sending her careening skywards. God, it felt amazing. Gil's lips on her neck, his finger stroking her clit while Charlie dipped his tongue inside her vagina, drawing more moisture out before swirling it around her bud. She leaned into Gil, unable to hold her weight on her feet. Gil smiled against her skin as he moved her backwards until her legs brushed the edge of the couch. Then he lowered her down beside him, propping one leg over his thigh, the other over

Charlie's shoulder.

"Does it feel good?"

"Yesss," she hissed out, not able to keep the air from purging from her chest as Charlie plunged two fingers inside her.

"Goddamn, Gil. She's so tight. We'll have to go slow."

Charlie's voice rang through her head, but she pushed it away. If she thought too much about what was happening, she knew she'd freak out. Instead, she concentrated on Gil's body. It was pressed tight against her left side, his cock hot against her thigh. She reached down and encased it in her hand, loving the tormented cry that ripped from his throat. Gil surged forward, pressing into her hand, fucking himself in her firm grip. She looked over at him, overwhelmed by the pleasure on his face.

"Why don't you bring that up here and let me please you, too?" she rasped, amazed at the husky drawl to her voice.

Gil shook his head, growling as she squeezed her fingers down his length and back up, rubbing the bead of fluid around the tip. "Later. It's about you right now. Now reach down and touch that pretty pussy for us. Let Charlie see how beautiful you are when you pleasure yourself."

The blood rushed to her face, heating it. She didn't know if she was strong enough to do as Gil had asked.

Gil seemed to sense her nervousness and moved his face over hers, gently nipping at her bottom lip. "Don't make us punish you, baby. Now reach down and touch that wet pussy."

She shivered at the dominance in his voice, as Charlie whacked her ass with the palm of his hand. It was a warning, a sign of what would happen if she disobeyed them. She closed her eyes and lowered her hand, dancing it across her mound.

"Lower, Fallon." It was Charlie's voice this time, and she felt more liquid gush from her cunt at the husky sound.

"That's it," said Gil as she dipped her finger into her slit, swirling the cream around her clit. "Milk your clit for us.

Show Charlie how you want him to touch you, to make you come in his mouth."

Come. Yes, she needed to come, and somehow she knew they'd keep that sweet abyss away from her if she didn't do as they'd asked. She circled the bud again and then slid down, pushing her finger into her hole, arching up at the fiery caress. She moaned and pumped her finger in again, slowly fucking herself as Charlie's groan feathered across her skin. She looked down, unable to hide from the sensual heat searing through her. Charlie's eyes meet hers and she couldn't resist pulling her finger free and holding it up to his lips. His eyes burned as he bent forward, suckling the digit into his mouth, tasting the musky juice of her sex.

"Damn, you taste delicious. I think I'll have some more. Suck her breasts, Gil. She looks like she needs more stimulation."

Gil smiled and lowered his lips to her nipples, alternating between licking and biting the tips. Fallon's cry filled the room, but she didn't care. This is what she needed. Charlie sucking her pussy, Gil teasing her nipples. If they just kept the pressure up, she'd come in just a few more strokes.

"Oh no, baby. Don't come yet. Let us taste you for a while longer."

"It's so close, Gil."

"But waiting is half the fun. Charlie, give her a moment to calm down. Why don't you come up here and give her your cock. I bet she'd love to taste you, wouldn't you, my love?"

"Oh God, yes." She barely registered her own plea and wasn't surprised at the joint chuckles that echoed in her head. All she could think about was getting Charlie's cock in her mouth. He wasn't quite as thick as Gil, but damn if he wasn't tempting.

Charlie moved out from between her legs and she whimpered at his retreat. He smiled as he stood beside her, gently touching her face. His cock bobbed down from his stomach, heavy and glistening with fluid. She glanced at Gil, and at his nod, took Charlie's cock in both hands, pumping the length of his shaft. He groaned and moved closer, pushing the tip against her lips. She opened for him, allowing him to push his cock inside her mouth and against the back of her throat. He tasted salty and sweet and she sucked harder in hopes of getting another drop of his cum in her mouth.

Charlie wrapped his fingers in her hair, firmly pulling on the ends as she plunged his shaft deep inside her mouth. The added sting of his tugs only heightened her arousal, and she felt each pull echo in her groin. She moaned around his erection, wanting to feel his head swell as he pumped his cum down her throat.

"So good, darling," said Charlie. "Take me all the way in."

Fallon opened wider, allowing more of his cock to slip between her lips. He was as deep as she could take him now, and concentrated on teasing his skin as it slowly withdrew from her velvet heat.

"That's it, Fallon. Suck my cock real good."

She moaned at the erotic words, taking him deep again, feeling her throat constrict around his bulbous head. Charlie groaned louder, fisting her hair, thrusting firmly into her mouth.

"God damn, girl. Where did you learn to give head like this? No wonder Gil's always so damn happy." His voice grew harsher, his cock hardening further inside her mouth. He was getting close. She released one hand and traced his length until she reached his sac. It was pulled tight against his body and she felt his muscles clench as she massaged them softly with her palm before rubbing the skin just behind them.

"Do you like the taste of his cock, baby?"

Fallon eased Charlie's erection out of her mouth, flicking her tongue down the length of his shaft as she moaned a muted, yes, back at Gil. Gil only smiled, his finger teasing her opening as she suckled each of Charlie's testicles into her mouth. Charlie grunted, just as Gil plunged three fingers inside her cunt, stretching it. She hummed in pleasure, feeling Charlie react to the strong vibration. His back bowed and she could tell he was fighting not to come. She smiled and moved back up his shaft, nipping and licking before rolling her lips around his crown and taking him to the back of her throat.

"Damn it. I'm going to come, darling. Decide where you want my cum to go, but do it fast."

Fallon merely sucked harder, knowing she couldn't pull away. His taste was too exciting, too much like Gil's to abandon the delicious feast that awaited her. She bobbed down and took him all the way in, feeling the first jet of his cum shoot out from the tip, coating her tongue as it slid down her throat.

Over and over, he spurted, until his grip in her hair finally eased and he stepped back, pulling his still hard cock out of her mouth. She stared up at him, not sure how he could still be sporting an enormous hard-on after spraying five jets of sperm down her throat. Was he naturally this way, or had he taken something? He smiled down at her, his eyes red as he watched her lick her lips, wiping any stray drops into her mouth.

"Yummy," she whispered, eyeing his cock again. Maybe he'd be up for round two?

"You're dangerous, darling," he groaned, lowering his lips to hers. "Now let me taste my cum on your tongue."

Fallon opened for his tongue as he slanted his mouth over hers and dove inside. He tasted like beer and rice, and she couldn't stop the moan that erupted in her chest, caught in Charlie's mouth as he explored every inch of her, licking and tasting until her lungs burned and he finally pulled away.

"You're so beautiful, Fallon," breathed Charlie, his lips hovering over hers. "So damn beautiful it hurts my eyes sometimes. Gil's a lucky man, and I'll make sure he never forgets it."

Then he was moving, settling back between her legs, his

shoulders splaying her thighs apart. Gil still softly finger fucked her. Not enough to push her over. Just a slow rock in and out designed to keep her wet and hot. It was working. She could feel the silky slide of his finger, her channel so wet it accepted him easily. She turned to look into his eyes, still stunned by the passion in them. She'd never imagined he'd ever want her to be with another man, and she was still having a hard time believing it was actually happening.

"Did you enjoy that?"

She nodded, not sure she had a voice. He smiled at her response, brushing his lips over hers. She opened easily for him, taking his tongue deep, tasting the same beer on him as she had on Charlie.

"You taste delicious. And your lips are all pink and swollen from Charlie's cock. Damn, I love seeing you like this."

"I'd like to taste you too," she whispered.

"Soon, baby. But first you deserve a reward for sucking Charlie off so well. What do you think, Charlie?"

Charlie took Gil's cue and thrust his fingers inside her pussy, while clamping his mouth around her clit. She arched up, unable to hide her neediness. They'd set her on fire and she desperately wanted to come before her sanity went up in flames.

"Oh God. Please."

Gil chuckled against her skin, raking his teeth over her other nipple. "Soon, baby, soon. But we still have an area to attend to."

"Gil!"

His name was torn from her chest as Charlie sank one, cream coated finger into the hot depths of her ass, parting her tender tissues, as he slowly impaled her until his palm cupped her flesh. "So hot and tight," said Charlie, his lips feathering his breath across her clit. "God, I can't wait to take you here."

Fallon would have cried out at his declaration if Gil hadn't picked that moment to sink two fingers into her cunt, pushing against the thin wall separating his hand from Charlie's. She bucked against the intrusion, sinking Gil's fingers even further. Her body was racked with pleasure so exquisite, arcs of light speared across her vision, bursting into white hot flames that seared through her body, gathering in her womb. She could feel her orgasm building, warming the muscles in her stomach from the inside out. Her thighs clamped around the hands that stroked her higher, daring them to withdraw, to abandon her. She felt the rush of pleasure wash over her. So close. So damn close, but still lingering just out of reach.

"Gil!" His name was a plea. A rough entreaty on her lips as her desperation grew to bone-crushing levels. "Charlie!"

Gil moved his face over hers, brushing her lips with his. "Now, Fallon. Scream for us now!"

Gil covered her lips as Charlie's tongue, once again, latched onto her clit. The world exploded into shards of bright light, as her orgasm raced over her. It fanned out from her stomach and speared through her ass and into her pussy, sending her vaginal walls into spasm. Charlie sucked harder, catching every drop of honey that seeped around Gil's fingers, all the while probing her tight nether hole, stretching it for the invasion yet to come.

Minutes passed before her breathing relaxed, her body still shaking on the couch. Hot hands still possessed her body, but she couldn't tell who they belonged to. They were strong and comforting and she was content just to feel the pleasure of their touch.

"You're amazing, darling."

Fallon opened her eyes. Charlie stood over her, looking down at her with heavy eyes. She hadn't felt him move out from between her legs, and felt more liquid gather along her lips at the sensual smile on his face. Remnants of her release glistening around his mouth, and the thought of it quickened her pulse until her breath came in short pants. Gil still stroked her thigh, teasing her with small caresses to her pussy. She smiled when she saw the pain had lifted from Charlie's expression, a new hotter emotion replacing it. She reached up and touched his face, drawing him back down to her.

His kiss was harder this time, expending some of the tension she felt in his shoulders. She allowed her hands to rove over his body, touching the hard angles of his chest and abdomen. He was firm, like Gil, but on a larger scale. She shivered at the thought that he must outweigh her by at least a hundred pounds, and for a spilt second, she questioned her body's ability to take both men. Either was intimidating, and considering the size of both their cocks, she wasn't sure she'd be able to give them what they wanted.

"Charlie..."

"Easy, Fallon. We won't do anything to hurt you, I promise. Just try to relax, and let us show you how beautiful this can be."

Charlie kneeled down beside her as Gil shifted on the couch and eased his body between her thighs. He looked intent on taking up where Charlie had left off, and just the thought of his lips touching her clit gushed the cream from her body. God help her, but she was ready to explode for them again.

"You're even wetter than before," noted Gil, running his finger between her drenched lips. "I think you enjoyed having Charlie make you come with his mouth."

He looked at her, his eyes warning her to reply. "Yes," she moaned, feeling him make another pass.

"Would you like to come again?"

"Yes." The word was torn from her chest before she could even think about it. Even though she could still feel the last tingling of her orgasm along her spine, the need to come again was already clouding her head with a red, fuzzy haze. She wasn't sure where the vixen inside her had come from, but she wasn't about to question the neediness coursing through her.

"Good, 'cause we aren't nearly through with your sexy

little body yet."

Fallon looked down at him, knowing the night had just begun.

Chapter Three

Gil shifted over, allowing Charlie to kneel beside him, both their heads lodged between her thighs. Charlie smiled up at her, angling her ankle over his shoulder, opening her up even wider. It was obvious he was a visual lover, like Gil, and enjoyed seeing her spread wide for them, her body completely at their disposal. He licked his lips, as if remembering the taste of her release in his mouth, and then lowered for one quick swipe through her cunt.

"Mmm. It's like eating candy," he moaned, whispering his breath across her sensitive tissue.

Gil murmured his agreement, lapping at her juices, the soft sounds of his wet thrusts floating through the air. She arched into him, the familiar feeling already moving through her groin.

"Getting close already?" asked Gil, flicking his tongue against her clit.

"Please."

"Soon, baby. But first Charlie needs to get you ready."

Fallon stilled as she felt the cold press of lubrication against her ass. She didn't know when Charlie, or Gil, had got out the tube of gel, but Charlie was busy spreading it around her hole, softly slipping it inside. She moaned, low and primal, feeling her body relax to let him inside.

"That's it, darling," said Charlie. "Just lie there and concentrate on Gil, and let me touch this pretty ass of yours. Oh, it's going to be so good. Gil fucking your sweet pussy while I fill this beautiful ass. You'll never want us to stop."

Fallon groaned at his words, not sure if it was desire or fear beading her skin with small bumps. She'd never experienced double penetration and wasn't sure what to expect. She looked down, watching Gil sip at her clit while Charlie pushed two fingers inside her. Her body was hanging again, and if Gil would just press a bit harder, she'd come.

Gil glanced up at her as if hearing her thoughts. He pulled back, her juices coating his face. He smiled at her, watching Charlie press slowly in and out of her ass before adding two fingers to her pussy.

"Oh God."

The words sprang from her lips, her body twisting beneath them. Gil seemed to take that as his cue to move and curled his tongue back around her clit as the two men fucked her body with their fingers. Heat infused her nerves, her body so full she didn't see how it would ever accommodate their cocks. But she didn't have time to worry as Gil nipped at her tightly knotted nub and sent her careening over the edge. Her body contracted, trapping Charlie's fingers in her ass and Gil's in her cunt. Both men groaned in unison, revelling in the steady beat of her pulse through the thin walls separating them. She fell back to earth, her limbs going limp at her sides.

"Gil." His name came out as barely more than a whisper. Her voice felt raw, like her body, and she didn't know how to say what she felt inside.

"I'm here, baby."

His voice was equally as raw as he stepped up beside her, the long length of his cock stretching towards her. She didn't wait for his permission. She took his cock in both hands, licking the precious fluid from the tip, taking it deep inside until it grazed the back of her throat. Gil's harsh wail filled her head, mixed in with the sound of her heartbeat. She lost herself in the sheer pleasure of his taste. How his skin moved back and forth along her tongue, so soft she often feared she'd scratch it. He was her wet dream come to life and she wanted nothing more than to hear his roar of release echo in her ears.

"Oh God, Fallon. You're too damn good at that, baby." Gil thrust into her mouth again, his growl filling the room. "Damn. If you don't stop, darling, I'm going to come."

"So come," she whispered, swallowing another drop of fluid.

Gil seemed to hesitate, before thrusting forward again, giving Fallon every inch of his shaft. She took it, opening her throat, pushing the huge head against the back. Gil groaned and stiffened, increasing his thrusts, fucking her mouth with strong, steady strokes. She gloried in his pleasure, still aware Charlie was working her ass, pressing three fingers inside until he could separate them and stretch her tight muscles. Sensations bombarded her, layering on top of each other until all she could feel was Gil's cock in her mouth and Charlie's fingers in her ass. There seemed to be nothing between them and she knew that when Gil filled her mouth, she'd come again.

"Now, Fallon. Open up real wide for me, 'cause I'm going to shoot my cum down your throat, baby."

She did as he asked, taking him deep, allowing him to drive into her until his cock exploded and hot fluid cascaded down her throat, burning her with such fiery essence a sharp contraction stole through her ass and into her womb.

"You've got her coming again, Gil," moaned Charlie. "Damn, she's a little minx."

"Just wait until you feel how good her ass is," Gil tossed back. "It's like sinking into a hot, velvet vice."

Fallon moaned at the words her lovers said, still sucking Gil's cock. Like Charlie's it was still rock hard, and she questioned, again, how it could stay so rigid. But if they'd taken some kind of erection drug, then that meant they'd been planning this threesome all along, and she wasn't sure how she felt about that. She was just going to ask, when Gil's voice whispered in her ear.

"Fallon."

She opened her eyes as he pulled his erection out of her mouth and knelt down beside her. His chest was heaving, and she could see the fiery need in his eyes. She reached out and touched his face, just as Charlie rose to his feet. She shot both men a heated glance as they reached for her, pulling her gently from the couch. Gil cuddled her against his chest as Charlie threw the cushions onto the floor. She tried to stem the tremors shivering through her body as Gil laid down with her, bringing her body over his.

"Nice and easy. We'll take it real slow."

Fallon bit at her bottom lip as Gil spread her legs over his thighs, lodging the head of his cock at her weeping entrance. She'd never needed to be fucked so badly before, and she nearly cried at the slow sweep of his crown through her slick juices.

"Please, Gil. I need you."

"We have to go slowly. I don't want to hurt you."

"But I need..."

Her voice ended in a strangled wail as he pushed the thick head inside her, wedging her tender tissues apart. He felt harder than ever, his cock pulsing with every metered thrust, as he slowly took possession of her body. Inch by inch, so damn slow she wanted to pound her fists on his chest. Her vagina convulsed again, threatening to explode with one hard stroke, if he'd only give her what she needed.

"So tight. God, you feel amazing."

Fallon answered his declaration by lowering her weight, taking his cock another inch inside her before his hands tightened around her hips.

"Goddamn, Fallon." He held her firm, resisting the strong twisting motions of her hips. "I won't be able to keep my control if I take you like that. Just trust me, baby. We'll give you more than you ever dreamed of."

Fallon cursed at the strength of his hold. She was no match for him in bed and finally had to relent to his approach. Gil eased his grip, allowing her to slowly sink down until his shaft was fully seated inside her.

"Better?"

"I need you to go harder, faster. Please, Gil."

"All in good time. Now lean forward and give your lover a kiss."

Fallon sighed at the feel of his fingers in her hair, loving the intimate gesture as she bent down over him, brushing her sensitive nipples across his chest. She didn't bother to hide her satisfaction when a low growl vibrated from his chest, his lips rising to meet hers. She moaned into his mouth, jousting her tongue with his, needing him to give her the strength for what she knew was coming.

"I love you, Gil." She whispered the words, nuzzling into his neck as Charlie's fingers caressed the soft skin of her ass.

"I love you, too, Fallon. Now let me show you just how much."

Her breath hitched as Charlie traced the long hollow between her cheeks, once again probing his finger inside. It felt so much tighter this time, the width of Gil's cock squeezing the walls of her anus shut.

"You've got such a pretty ass," said Charlie. "So round and firm. Relax onto Gil, darling, and let me inside."

Fallon closed her eyes, trying to relax the muscles in her ass as Charlie eased her cheeks apart, gently opening her tight little pucker. He took her slowly, pushing against the small opening, thrusting softly until the head was clenched in her tight ring of muscles. She cried out, not sure she could stand the pleasure and pain that ripped through her body, threatening to drag her into the darkness. She whimpered against Gil's neck, clenching on his shaft as Charlie sank deeper inside her anal channel, until his sac pressed against her flesh.

"Oh yeah, baby. Tighten on me," rasped Gil, pulling out until the only the tip was still inside her before plunging back in. "Milk my cock, Fallon."

Fallon's back bowed in pleasure as both men began to move. It was like a well-choreographed dance that picked up speed until their twin shafts were pounding into her, sending her from one orgasm into another. She didn't know if it was the anal play or the way Gil grazed her G-spot, or both, but she was dying and she didn't want saving.

"Damn, you're so hot and tight," moaned Charlie, slamming his cock into her ass. "I can feel every move Gil makes."

Fallon could only whimper, trapped between pleasure and pain as both men filled her body. Every stroke Gil made filled her with pleasure, quickly followed by the pass through her ass, adding a bite that was driving her insane. It was too strong, too intense, too…something.

"Gil! So much… Oh God… Now, now, now!"

Her screams filled the room, mixed with the sounds of wet thrusts and male groans. Like a symphony, it rose, gathering strength until the very walls vibrated with the heady sounds of sex. The room dipped and swayed, suspending her on the verge of consciousness, when Charlie roared out behind her, spurting the first hot jet of semen into her ass. It coated her anal walls, heating her already enflamed tissues.

"Charlie! Oh God, yes!"

Her cry of release was followed by Gil's, his ejaculation filling her channel until the excess seeped out around his cock, coating her thighs and his stomach. Darkness merged with light, fire swept through her body as her final orgasm shook her to the core, clenching the muscles in her groin so tight both men stopped, held prisoner by her body. She could hear them groaning, trying to push through the last of their release. She opened her mouth for one last soundless scream before collapsing on Gil's chest, her body totally spent.

"Damn it. I've never come so hard in my life. You're amazing." Gil brushed his hand down the curve of her back as he pulled her even closer. "Just breathe, Fallon. Everything's okay."

The words came from far away, as if spoken from another room. She tried to open her eyes but nothing seemed to work. She sighed, content to let the men move her once they were done.

"Thank you, baby." Gil's words seared through her heart,

the love in them overwhelming. His lips were soft against her ear as he kissed her gently. "I'll always remember this night."

Fallon mumbled something against his chest, too exhausted to form words. She felt Gil smile at her attempt, smoothing his hand down her hair and across her shoulders. The last thing she heard was Charlie's groan of pleasure as he pulled free from her body and kissed her on the cheek, whispering his thanks, his devotion. Then the world faded into Gil's heartbeat and hers.

Fallon opened her eyes as the scene shifted around her. Suddenly she was standing in a warehouse, the smell of decay and urine heavy in the air. She looked around, hoping to see the way out, when the sound of gunfire filled the air. She screamed, ducking behind a large box as more shots and a loud blast echoed through the empty space. Men shouted in the distance, their feet thudding against the floor, followed by cries of pain and more shots. She covered her ears, needing to dull the sharpness of the pleas. She'd never heard men beg for their lives, and the sound tore through her chest. It seemed never-ending.

Shots. Screams. More shots. She waited until a bleak silence fell over the warehouse before she turned to leave. She twisted behind the box, crawling towards the rear of the building, just as two men moved in front of her, one carrying the other across his shoulders. They were dim against the shadows, their faces blurred into the surroundings. She edged forward, fear holding her captive, as the smaller man placed the other man on the floor, catching his head before it hit the dusty wood.

"Damn it, Charlie, don't do this to me."

The man cursed as he shook his friend by the shoulder. She moved closer, needing to see the man's face.

"You promised we'd always be partners. Now wake the fuck up!"

Gil! Her heart slammed into her chest as she recognised

the man kneeling over the other. His chest was covered in blood, a black patch burnt into the left side of his shoulder. He was coughing up blood, desperately trying to rouse his partner. She looked down, nausea washing over her as she stared at Charlie. His skin was white and his face was frozen in a grimace. She could tell by the way his head lolled to one side he was dead, but Gil wasn't giving up. He pressed down on the wounds, too many to count, and breathed his own laboured breath into Charlie's mouth.

"Live, damn you!" he yelled, pumping down on Charlie's chest, making the blood run from his body.

Fallon stepped forward, unable to look away, needing to share in Gil's pain. But they moved with her, always staying a step away.

"No! Please, Gil!"

Sirens blared in the distance, rain fell against a grease-smeared window, as Gil battled against death. Slowly his body succumbed to his injuries, until he lay beside his partner, his eyes open, but unseeing. Fallon sank to the floor, unable to move. Tears fell, sobs wrenched from her chest as she watched her lover slowly dying. She felt his pain, his regrets, knowing even if he lived he'd be lost to her forever. She put her hands to her head, trying to block out the sudden blast of music in her head.

Fallon bolted upright, clawing at the images tumbling across the darkness. Gil, his body shuddering in the cold, blood slowly leaking from his shoulder. Charlie, lifeless, splayed out on the floor as thick pools of blood gathered around him. She could taste the metallic scent, hear the desperate gasps, feel the guilt pour through her as her hand lunged out, grabbing the annoying object off the small table. Words collided in her head, as she flipped the phone open, mumbling the first line that popped into her mind.

"Nine-one-one, do you need police..." She stopped, unsure of what to say. She didn't know where she was, or what time it was. A man breathed on the other end, and for a moment, she thought it was Gil.

"Aren't you going to ask me what I need?"

The voice was deep and dark, like the sound of evil clawing up from the depths of Hell. She felt her body tense, a cold shiver shimmy down her spine. "What?"

There was a moment of silence before the eerie words wavered over the line. "I said, 'aren't you going to ask me what I need'?"

Fallon pulled the phone away and stared at it for a moment, finally registering where she was. Home, however dismal and empty, she was home, tucked into her bed. She placed it back beside her ear, not sure what was happening. "What do you need?"

A rough cackle filtered through the static and she cringed at the menace the sound carried. "Well, it's a little late for the ambulance, but I'm certain the police would love to stop by and take a look at my work."

"And what work is that?" she asked, staring into the darkness, afraid the sound might be coming from one of the shadows.

"I save sinners from their sins. I restore their faith and free their soul."

"And how do you do that?"

The man sighed, a hint of remorse edged in his voice. "I purify them."

A wave of heat flashed through her, but she pushed the dizzying feeling away. She needed to keep focused. Somehow this psycho had dialled the wrong number and she needed to get as much information as possible to give to the police. "Okay. I'll send the police your way. Where are you?"

"Where…195 Mortimer Street. It used to be the old gospel church. It's on the right."

"And what's your name?"

He laughed then, a grating sound that seemed to echo off her bedroom walls. "You can call me *the Priest*."

Fallon frowned into the phone. *The Priest.* Couldn't he

have come up with a better code name than that? She shook her head, ready to ask her next question, when he spoke to her again.

"What's your name?"

"I go by operator number. Would you like that?"

He chuckled and she knew the bastard was smiling. "I'll just call you, Angel. Goodnight, Angel. And don't worry, we'll talk again real soon."

Fallon listened to the phone disconnect, the empty air loud in her ear. She went to press her recall button when the image slammed into her head, the picture so bright, so clear, it knocked her back against the mattress. She screamed out, thrashing against the visions filling her mind, as they pulled her into another place. An altar, dotted with candles, centred on the sculpture of Christ. A woman's body spread across it, her limbs hanging lifeless towards the floor. She was young with blonde hair that melded into red, the ends still dripping blood onto the smooth wood. Her body was slashed in long strips that seemed to spiral out from her abdomen, ending at the tips of her fingers. Her eyes were open and dull, staring up towards the heavens. Fallon looked closer at the girl's chest. Just above her left breast was an intricately carved cross, the edges curved and sculpted. She'd never seen anything like it before. Her eyes followed the lines, tracing their path until they stopped at the woman's groin.

Fallon turned away, unable to look at what the monster had done. God, there was so much blood it ran in rivulets down her thighs, collecting in the toes of her high heeled shoes. She couldn't imagine what he'd stuck inside her, but it'd shredded the woman's cunt. She tried to cover her eyes, when a dim silhouette moved in the distance. She drew her hand over her brow, shielding herself from the glare of the candles, just as a man opened the door. He was large, with blonde hair sprinkled with grey and a long black coat. His hand hung down by his side, absently twitching a knife against his leg. He paused for only a moment, his back to the altar, his head tilted to one side before stepping into the rain, his outline vanishing into the night. Fallon moved to follow when a pain ignited in her temples, dropping her to the floor. The room began to sway, dipping first right, then left. She heard the phone tumble to the floor, saw the lightning flash outside her window, a moment before her eyes rolled back in her head, pulling into oblivion.

Chapter Four

Fallon pried her eyelids apart, squinting at the bright light casting long shadows in her room. She was lying on the floor beside her bed, a blanket crumpled at her feet. She pushed herself up, only to fall back down at the pain that speared through her temples. A muted moan feathered from her lips as she tried to remember how the hell she'd got on the floor.

"Oh God." She closed her eyes and pressed her hands against her head as images flip-flopped across the darkness, blurring together memories from the previous night. Gil, his tongue curled around her nipple as Charlie stroked his along the velvety skin of her soft inner lips. Twin cocks thrusting inside her, shattering her sanity as she climaxed over and over before falling asleep on Gil's chest, Charlie's whispered thanks following her into the darkness. The shooting. Both men covered in blood, lying beside each other as sirens echoed through the building. A man's voice, dark and hushed, calling to her in the dead of night. A woman…

"No!" Fallon forced herself up, ignoring the way the room dipped and swayed as she searched for her phone. She found it buried beneath the blanket, the lid still hinged open. She pressed the buttons, searching the call history, needing to see what number belonged to the bastard from her dream.

"What?" It didn't make any sense. The only number that had called her cell was an old number from the office. She frowned, remembering Jane's call. The room circled again and Fallon closed her eyes, grabbing the table to stop the rotation. She touched a button on her cell without opening her eyes.

"Radio communications, Colleen."

"Colleen, it's Fallon."

"Hey, Fallon. How are you? I was surprised they hadn't called you in yet."

"I need a day off. Hey, do me a favour? Look at last night's history and see if there were any calls to…" *Damn, what was the number?* "The one-hundred block of Mortimer Street."

"Sure thing, Fallon. Hey, is everything okay? You sound… different."

"I'm fine." She paused as she listened to Colleen typing on the keyboard. "Well?"

"Sorry, Fallon. I don't see anything on Mortimer Street. Not for the past few days."

"Damn." She bit her bottom lip, wondering what to do. If she let it go and the call had been real, then the police would never catch the guy. But if she'd only dreamt it? "Hey, Colleen. Do you think you could send a unit over there, say to maybe one-ninety-five, and have them take a look around? You could say you got an anonymous call about a suspicious male hanging around there last night."

"If you think there's a need." Colleen paused and Fallon knew the woman was more than puzzled.

"Look. I took a drive that way last night and I'm not sure if I saw something or not. And I'd rather not have the guys tease me about it for the next few weeks if it turns out everything's okay."

"All right, Fallon. I'll send Ken and Jeff that way. They're just hanging at the coffee shop anyway."

"Thanks, Colleen. I owe you one."

Fallon hung up the phone, still staring at the number flashing on the screen. No evidence the guy had ever called her, but there was something about the dream she'd had of the woman. She'd only ever had two other visions like that and they'd both…

"Stop it!" she hissed, picking herself off the floor. "I'm not crazy and I'm not having visions again. It was probably just a dream. I'm just working too much." She nodded as she headed for the closet. A long ride down a hard trail was just the ticket to clear her head. And erase the images, especially the ones of Gil. Damn, she could feel the slick slide of juices along her velvety lips as she remembered the dream, and the last thing she needed was to get herself so damn horny even a session with her vibrator wouldn't stem the need. She sighed. Jane was right. She needed a man, even if it was just for sex. Maybe she'd go to Jane's barbeque after all.

24 Hours Later

"Goddamn. He struck again!" Gil slammed down the phone and grabbed his coat off the back of the chair.

Wade looked over at him, his lips pulled tight. "Where?"

"Some obscure church over on Mortimer Street. Looks like the girl's been dead for close to two days already. Seems they locked the damn thing up on Tuesday night and didn't check back in till this morning." He wrinkled his nose as he pushed his arms through his sleeves. "I can't imagine how bad it's going to be in there."

"Want me to check it out alone?" asked Wade, zipping his jacket as he followed Gil out the door.

Gil shot Wade a knowing glare over his shoulder as he ducked out into the rain and headed for his truck. "Thanks, Junior. But we both need to be there. Let's just hope the bastard left something behind this time."

Wade nodded, climbing into the passenger seat. "He can't evade us much longer. We'll get him."

Gil sighed as he revved the engine and pulled into traffic. "Keep on saying that. Maybe you can make it come true."

* * * *

"Hi, Fallon. I thought you had another day off?"

Fallon shrugged her shoulders. She'd intended to take a few days off, but the dream had got her so worked up, she'd figured the best way to kill the images was to immerse herself in work. So she'd accepted another overtime shift. "Just doing my part to help out."

"Well it's crazy over in the southwest precinct. Seems they found another body."

Fallon stiffened. She'd called back the other day, but her address had turned out to be a beauty salon, minus any dead blondes. "What body?"

"You know, that serial guy…what's the press calling him…the minister or something? He's killed a bunch of women in Olympia and Tacoma. I guess he's moving north. Seems he killed another girl over on the south side a couple of nights ago. Boys said the scene was pretty gruesome."

Fallon felt her stomach heave and the blood drain from her face. "Where? Where did they find her?"

"On Mortimer Street. Nine-fifteen, I think…an old gospel church. Hey, Fallon, are you okay? You don't look so good. Maybe you should take the day off after all?"

Fallon heard the words, but couldn't seem to speak. Nine-fifteen. She'd mixed up the numbers, or he had. Either way, the image had been real. She backed away from the desk, panic rearing inside her. This couldn't be happening, not again. The visions…

"Fallon? Aren't you going to sign in? Fallon…"

Fallon muffled a scream as the scene played in her head again. The woman draped across the altar, her hair matted with blood. Spiral lashes covering her body, dripping blood onto the dark wooden floor. And the cross…it was so intricate. All curves and whirls. It must have taken hours to carve into her skin. Had the girl still been alive?

She covered her ears, a ragged cry echoing in her head. She didn't know if it was hers or the woman from the dream, but it was the last thing she heard before she hit the floor.

* * * *

"No. You aren't coming into work for a week, and that's final!"

Jane's voice was strong and firm, and Fallon knew there'd be no debating it. "I'm fine, Jane, really."

"Oh, is that so? First you answer your cell as nine-one-one. Then you start calling in anonymous tips, and now you pass out at the desk. I don't quite see how that measures up to *fine*."

"I had a headache and stood up too fast, that's all," insisted Fallon.

"Nice try, girl, but I know for a fact you never even sat down."

"Technicalities." She paused. "Hey, wait. How did you know about the tip?"

"I have my ways," said Jane, with a tone so smug Fallon wanted to reach through the phone and wipe the woman's smile right off her face. "Look, you're one of our best operators. But if you don't take some time for yourself, you're going to burn out, and then where will I be?"

"Glad to see you're so worried about *my* future."

"You know what I mean. Take a week. Go out on a date. Get yourself laid…and not necessarily in that order." She paused, and Fallon wondered what her friend was thinking. "Um, Fallon? That tip you called in. Wasn't it on Mortimer Street?"

Fallon tensed. She wasn't sure how she was going to explain that to anyone without ending up locked up on the psychiatric floor of Harborview. "Yes," she said, trying not to sound too nervous. "I believe it was."

"Wow. That's the same street they found that girl. Kind of creepy if you ask me."

"Look, Jane…"

"Sorry. My mind is made up. I don't want you anywhere near the station for at least a week. I'll check in with you on Wednesday and see how you're doing. Oh, and don't forget the barbeque on Sunday. Brad brought Jackson by last night. The guy's hot. And he's into all those extreme things you do, so you guys would be a great match. But it might be wise to get a bit of sex beforehand, so you don't come across so needy."

Fallon shook her head. And here she was worried about explaining the tip she'd called in. "Thanks. I'll keep that in mind. Talk to you later."

"See you Sunday."

Fallon hung up before the other side disconnected, and stared out the window. It was raining again. Lightning flickered across the sky, followed by the deep rumble of thunder. She moved from the kitchen towards the living room, cradling a cup of tea in her hand. With any luck, there'd be a half-interesting show on, and she could spend the next hour curled up on the sofa, immersed in someone else's life. She flicked on the TV and scanned the stations, finally settling on a movie she'd only seen once. She needed the distraction. If she thought too much about the murder, she'd drive herself crazy. She didn't know how to explain what had happened. The visions were one thing, but how had the guy called her number without it even registering his call?

She cursed and relaxed back against the cushions. Everything would be all right as long as it didn't happen again. She'd done her part. Now there was nothing left to do but get some sleep and try to figure out the rest of her life…without Gil.

Gil.

Damn. Just the thought of his name brought back more images of her dream. It'd felt so real, and she hadn't been able to sleep since. Every time she'd tried, she'd woken up thirty minutes later, aroused and wet. She'd resisted resorting to her toys, knowing the release she'd get would only make her need hotter, but it was getting so bad any relief was a welcome thought.

Fallon eased off the sofa and headed to her room, removing a few select toys from the small side table beside her bed. She looked at the soft mattress but decided against lying on the bed. She needed a different place to fulfil her needs, and the couch where she'd shared her body with Gil and Charlie seemed the perfect choice.

She padded back to the living room, dimming the lights and the sound on the TV. The woman on the screen was kissing her lover, giving Fallon just enough visual to set up her fantasy. She placed the toys on the coffee table, then shimmed out of her clothes, leaving them in a rumpled pile on the floor. Then she relaxed back on the couch, resting her head against an oversized pillow. She took a soothing breath, caressing her skin lightly with the tips of her fingers. It'd been months since she'd found release, and her body was already humming with the thought of what was to come. Her breath whispered across her skin and she closed her eyes, imagining Gil's lips on the soft curve of her breast. Feeling the slow progression of his kiss stealing ever closer to her peaked nipples. Her body shuddered as one hand grazed over the tight bud, puckering it against her skin. She'd always loved the way he'd touched her breasts, pulling and twirling until the juices seeped from her pussy and coated her inner thighs.

Her fingers imitated Gil's touch and she couldn't stop the moan of pleasure from filling the room. She tweaked again, elongating the hard tip between her fingers. God, it felt so good. Just hard enough to take her to the edge of pain, but not over. She pulled again, and cried out at the sharp contraction in her womb. Damn, if she didn't stop, she'd go over without using the toys.

Fallon sat up and grabbed the tube of lubricant and the anal plug off the table. Ever since Charlie had fucked her up the ass, while Gil had filled her cunt, she'd longed to experience the sensation again, only with Gil and a well-placed toy. But the fantasy had never materialised, and she'd been forced to live with nothing, but longing.

"Not tonight," she whispered, squeezing a long line of gel down the edge of the toy. It wouldn't quite be the loving she'd envisioned, but it'd fill the void…for now. Her blood pounded in her veins as she smoothed the slick lubricant around the surface, ensuring every inch had a thick coat. Then she held her breath as she placed it against her anus, swirling some of the gel around the outside of her nether hole.

"*Ohmygod,*" she moaned, feeling her muscles clench as she pushed the tip of the plug inside her ass. Nothing had penetrated her there since Charlie had eased his large cock inside her, and the sensation felt new again.

She paused, leaving only the tip inside, until her muscles relaxed slightly, and she was able to inch the plug deeper, pushing steadily against the base until it was seated fully inside her. Her ass felt stretched, the sensation bordering on pain, as fiery waves spread through her body. She moaned, removing the plug until the tip reached her tight ring of muscles before plunging it back inside, lighting a deeper fire along the tight channel.

"Gil."

His name whispered across her lips before she could stop it, the sound sparking deeper emotions inside her. God, what she wouldn't give for one more night with him. One more taste of his love. A tear tracked down her cheek as she reached out for her vibrator, feeling the cool shaft rest against her palm. She pulled it close, twisting the base until a hushed hum filled the room. Her breath stalled in anticipation as she brought the device to her flesh, brushing it across her clit.

"Yes."

Her hips bucked up, pressing against the cool tip of their own accord. Fire raced through her veins, driving her need higher, as more nerves flashed to life, carrying the waves of pleasure throughout her body. She made another pass, feeling the building orgasm start to move through her stomach.

"Not yet."

She moved the vibrator away from her clit, inching it inside her pussy, feeling it push against the plug stuffed in her ass. The pressure was incredible and she had to thrust firmly to fill her channel with the shaft.

Fallon groaned, no longer able to keep the need at bay. It'd been too long, too lonely. She pulled out the toy, plunging it home again with a hard twist of her wrist. Gil's name echoed off the walls as she started to fuck herself, thrusting in and out as fast as her hand could go. She could hear the wet sounds of her juice along the smooth shaft as it left her channel only to burrow back inside, filling the void. Pleasure swept over her body, beading sweat along her skin. She reached down with her other hand, pinching her clit between her fingers. Light erupted in the darkness, and she didn't know if it was from her growing orgasm or outside, but it drove her forward. She moved her finger across her clit, rubbing it with the same rhythm she worked the vibrator, edging her closer to the abyss she knew awaited her.

Minutes passed, thunder rumbled, and just when she didn't think she could stand another pass of her fingers, her body exploded, shattering the silence with a scream so primal it felt like the walls shook. Fallon's hips ground against the toy, pressing it deeper, needing it to fill her channel like Gil always did. Her vagina pulsed, sending vibrations back to her ass, which had clamped around the plug the moment her orgasm had ripped through her. She couldn't breathe, couldn't speak, as her body slowly descended back to earth, finally collapsing against the couch.

More tears filled her eyes as the emptiness returned, even stronger than before. Damn, Gil. No man should have that much effect on a woman. She was strong, independent and worth far more. Surely she could find another man to fill her life with joy. Someone she could love. But even the soothing words couldn't stop the steady flow of tears. She needed Gil. Needed to feel him beside her, chasing away her demons. Needed to watch him smile as he told her about his day, knowing she cared about his job as much as he did. She needed to love him.

Fallon let the sadness ease down her cheeks as she pulled the toys from her body and dropped them on the table. She'd clean them up tomorrow, when things looked better. When her body didn't ache for the one thing it couldn't have.

* * * *

A ripple of lightning shattered the darkness as Fallon woke to the sound of music vibrating the table beside her. She reached for the phone, jumping as a loud crack of thunder erupted overhead. "Hello?"

She cringed at the broken rasp of her voice, so thick with sleep she barely recognised it as her own. She heard a man curse quietly on the other end, his voice mixing in with the play of thunder. "Is anyone there?"

"Aren't you supposed to answer nine-one-one?"

Fallon nearly dropped the phone. It was him. The same tone, the same dark menace in his voice. He was calling her again, and that could only mean one thing. "Is there an emergency?" Oh God, her voice was so meek and timid she nearly cried. He'd got to her, and he hadn't even told her anything, yet.

He chuckled. It sounded evil, but…familiar. "I wouldn't call it an emergency…*Angel*. I've taken care of that, myself."

Bile rose in her throat and she had to force it back down. He'd recognised her voice, and she wasn't quite sure what that meant. "What did you take care of?"

"I think you already know that, Angel. We talked about that last time. You do remember, don't you?"

"You think you're saving them," she whispered.

"I *know* I'm saving them!" he roared. "What's the matter, Angel? Don't you believe me?"

"Yes, yes, of course I believe you. You're *the Priest,* after all, right?"

His voice soothed and sighed into the phone. "So you do

understand," he replied. "I'm only doing what's best for them, before they hurt others with their virtue. They do that, you know. Use their pretty little bodies to get men to believe in them...to trust them. But it's all an act. In the end, they show their true nature and good men suffer for it." He paused, another sigh trembling across the line. "It's the only way."

"But..." Fallon shrieked as another clap of thunder shook the house, rattling her mug on the table. She tensed, nearly dropping the phone before catching it in mid-air.

"What's the matter, Angel? Afraid of the thunder?" Fallon shook her head, unable to form any words. "It's okay. It'll all be over soon. Send the police to the abandoned church on Mission Street. I don't know the address, but I'm sure they will. And this time, Angel, get it right. I don't like waiting to see my work on the news."

Fallon listened to the phone disconnect, the dull whine barely registering. She could feel the vision coming. Feel her body drifting, the room washing into another, brightly lit by candles. This church was darker than the other, with debris scattered around the small space. Pews were turned on their side and most of the stained glass windows were broken. She turned around, taking everything in—the door hanging off its hinges, the tilted cross standing beside a faded picture of Mary. The altar was off to her left, kept dry by the last bit of ceiling still holding together. It was raised several feet off the floor, and all she could see were the limbs of the dead woman hanging still in the heavy air. Blood dripped down from her fingers and toes, making small rivers across the floor.

She walked towards the body, whether by choice or intervention, she didn't know. But each step brought her closer to the girl...to death. She stopped at the bottom step, her face level with the alter. The same markings adorned the woman's body, another cross carved above her left breast. Fallon reached towards the woman's face when the door opened behind her. She spun around, daring the bastard to look at her, to see her. But he was turned away, his hand supporting the door from falling to the ground. He turned his head slightly to the side, as if sensing her presence, and then left,

Fallon cursed and rushed the door, needing to see the man's face. But as she grabbed the handle, the door fell forward, knocking her to the floor. She hit hard, expecting to bounce on the hard wood, but found herself sinking through the floor instead. She screamed and clawed at the surface, trying to stay in the church, but felt her body falling farther and farther down until the darkness closed in around her, and she lost herself in the abyss.

* * * *

"Oh, God." Fallon grabbed her head, wondering what the hell she'd done. Light streamed through the window, bathing the room with a cheerful yellow glow. She was lying on the couch, naked, the TV playing quietly in the background. Her phone was tossed on the floor beside the shattered pieces of her favourite mug, and the toys she'd played with last night were still resting on the table, the scent of her sex still lingering in the air. She sighed, feeling the blood pound through her veins. "Maybe Jane's right. I need a vacation."

She swung her feet to the floor, ignoring the throbbing that pulsed across her temples, and gathered her things off the table and floor. A flash across the screen caught her attention. She moved to the TV and turned up the volume.

"The young woman's identity has not yet been released by police officials, but they have confirmed this is another victim in the series of killings which began over two months ago, just south of Olympia. A passer-by saw a suspicious vehicle leaving the area and called police late last night. Nothing has been said about the murder other than it's under investigation..."

Fallon stared at the TV, her body frozen, as she listened

to the reporter repeat the broadcast. It was the church she'd seen in her dream…her dream.

"No." She backed away from the screen, shaking her head. It couldn't be happening again. Not now. The visions only came when she was connected to the people involved. Her sister. Gil. But she didn't know the women the bastard killed. How could she be connected?

Maybe your powers are getting stronger? Evolving?

"I don't have powers!" she scoffed, heading towards her bedroom. "It's nothing but a bloody curse. I can't control them and they sure as hell don't come soon enough to help, so how is that a power?" She stalked into the room and stared at her reflection. Her eyes were red and she could see the dark rings that rimmed her cheeks. "Damn." She'd been passed out for hours, and yet it looked like he hadn't slept in weeks.

Fallon sighed and sat down on the edge of the bed. There was no denying the signs. The visions were back. And she had a bad feeling they wouldn't stop until the city's newest serial killer was caught.

Chapter Five

"I'm really sorry, Fallon. I'm sure it won't be too much longer."

Fallon looked up at Detective Trevor Watts. He was a large man with dark skin and gentle eyes. She'd known him since she'd first started working at the station, and had been more than relieved to find him still heading the homicide unit. He'd listened patiently as she'd mumbled out the story she'd rehearsed in the car, nodding his head and writing down notes. Then he'd offered her a drink and told her to wait on the small couch while he notified the men in charge of the investigation. Now he stood in the doorway, his hands stuffed in his pockets as he kicked his toe against the floor. She forced a smile, knowing he was more than aware she was anything but happy. "That's okay. I've only been waiting about four hours. That's barely enough time for them to finish their coffee and doughnuts."

Trevor chuckled, but Fallon noticed the smile didn't reach his eyes. He was anxious. "Why don't you rest for a while? You look like you could use it. Jane told me how much overtime you've been working. You really should try to take more time for yourself."

Fallon shrugged her shoulders and settled back against the cushions. So he'd called Jane and checked some of her story out. She supposed she couldn't blame him. He wouldn't be much of a detective if he took everything at face value. But just thinking about how she was going to give them all the information she knew without mentioning her visions made her skin crawl. It just wasn't the sort of thing you mentioned without fear of getting locked up in the psycho ward. "I'm fine. Besides, I get out on the trails a lot."

"I heard you're training for that big endurance race a few months from now. Some of the guys said it's a really nasty ride. Pretty hardcore."

"Just the sort of thing a girl loves," she joked.

Trevor rolled his eyes, giving her the first genuine smile all day. "I've never met anyone quite like you. Now close your eyes and get some rest. I'll wake you before the boys get here."

Fallon nodded as the door closed behind him. Maybe an hour of sleep was just the ticket to prepare her for the questions she didn't know how to answer. She closed her eyes and drifted to sleep.

* * * *

"Want to tell me, again, why we're heading over to the southwest precinct?" asked Gil. "We really don't have time to *chat*."

Wade shot him a sideways glance, a hint of a smile curving his lips. "Apparently the chief of homicide wants to talk to us."

"Who?"

Wade shook his head, shrugging as he turned to look out the window. "A Detective Watts."

"Trevor Watts?" asked Gil.

"I don't know. I didn't catch his first name."

"Must be Trevor," sighed Gil. "He's the only cop there that would bother calling us while we're at a scene." Gil glanced over at Wade. "Did he say why he needed to talk to us?"

"He said he couldn't say too much over the cell. He was worried it wasn't secure. All I know is that he's got someone at his office who has some information for us."

Gil snorted, glancing down at his watch. "That was five hours ago. What are the chances the guy's still there?" He shook his head, turning onto Weber Street. "Probably some psychic wannabe who thinks the killer is communicating with them. Damn. Sometimes I really hate this job."

Gil was still cursing as he parked his truck and wove his way through the halls to Trevor's office. He'd known Trevor for years but hadn't spoken to him since Charlie's death. Hell, he hadn't talked to anyone since then. But...

"So what's this Watts guy like?" asked Wade, drawing Gil from his thoughts.

"He's hard, demanding and rarely smiles..." Gil grinned at Wade. "But he's a good man, and a straight cop. In my opinion, that's more than anyone can ask for."

Wade nodded as they stopped in front of Trevor's door. Gil knocked twice before pushing the door open and stepping inside. "Hey, Trevor. What's—"

Gil stopped dead, not even flinching when Wade crashed into him. Wade muttered under his breath before following Gil's gaze over to the couch. She was curled into a ball, her head resting against the arm of the sofa. Someone had laid a small blanket across her waist, hiding her legs from view. But it did nothing to hide her beauty.

"Fallon."

He wasn't sure if he'd breathed the word or heard it echo in his head, but the sound of it sent shivers tingling down his spine. He took an involuntary step forward, unable to halt his need to get closer to her. Her hair was loose around her shoulder, the red hue shimmering in the harsh light. She was dressed in a tight shirt that clung to the firm curves of her breasts. Gil felt the blood drain from his head and pool in his groin. God, just the sight of her had his cock at full attention, so tight in his pants he wasn't quite sure how he was going to walk. She was sleeping, her chest rising gently with the steady rhythm of her breath. He could just see the smooth swell of creamy skin above her breast, where her top plunged into a deep vee. What he wouldn't give to lick every inch of her silky skin. To taste her sweet feminine scent on his tongue as he drew her nipples slowly into his mouth.

A low growl rumbled through the small room before Gil realised he'd made his way over to the couch. He was standing in front of her now, his hand reaching out to her shoulder. She sighed when his fingers wrapped around her flesh, snuggling deeper into the cushions.

What the hell was she doing here? He hadn't seen her for six months, not since he'd walked out of her life without so much as a note, and now definitely wasn't the time to deal with the past.

"Fallon." He said her name too loudly, too sternly, shaking her shoulder with more force than he'd intended. He winced as a moan feathered from her lips and a small frown creased the lines of her mouth. She tilted her head towards him, her eyes slivering open just enough to see his face. He nearly creamed his pants at the dreamy smile that graced her lips as she stared up at him with those deep blue eyes that seemed to turn his will to mush.

"It's still early, Gil. Just let me have five more minutes." Her voice was raspy and low, and she barely got the few words out before her eyes drifted shut again. She turned back into the couch, pulling at the soft blanket. "It's cold, darling. Come back to bed and warm me up."

Gil's throat closed around a large knot as he watched her fade back to sleep. He'd expected every reaction but that one. He managed to catch himself just before he'd climbed onto the couch next to her, wanting nothing more than to grant her request.

"Damn it." He inched his body back, hoping to hell Wade hadn't heard her. "Fallon. Please wake up."

Fallon shrugged his hand off her shoulder, huffing out a breathy little whimper as she forced herself up, her legs finding the floor. She looked at him again, her eyes glassy and large before her senses seemed to slam back into her head. Gil knew the moment she realised where she was. Her eyes rounded in shock as her body went rigid with surprise. She scooted sideways on the couch, her gaze never leaving his as she tried to stumble to her feet. Gil saw her foot snag on the blanket an instant before her startled gasp filled the room and she fell to the floor, landing on her ass with a dull thud. He chuckled as she cursed under her breath, taking a small step towards her.

"Hey, Fallon. I think the guys should be here any moment, so you'd better..." Trevor's voice faded into a surprised grunt as he marched through the door and stared at Gil. He mouthed Gil's name just as he caught sight of Fallon flailing on the floor. "Damn. Are you okay?" He lunged towards her, grabbing her arm with his large hand as he pulled her up. She popped off the floor and seemed to teeter for a moment, swaying right then left, before the momentum sent her tumbling forward. She slammed hard against his chest, her breath whooshing out with another curse. He smiled at the feel of her body pressed against his and couldn't stop his hands from curling around her back as he drew her into a firm embrace.

"Jesus, Fallon. I'm sorry." Trevor moved towards them, stopping an arm's-length away. "Are you okay?"

Gil felt Fallon relax against him, her curves hugging his torso. God, she felt so right in his arms. The way her breasts pressed against his chest, raking her turgid nipples across his ribs with every breath. Or how her hips cradled his erection, rubbing the length just enough to keep it hard and hot. He groaned into her ear, knowing she could feel his cock lengthening even further along her stomach. She rocked her hips twice against his before stiffening in his arms and pushing herself away. She pulled her arms tight across her chest, whether to hide the hardness of her nipples or to give herself strength, he didn't know, but the act only made his pulse race more. He flashed her a heavy-lidded half-smile, loving the way her breathing hitched and a deep flush laced down her neck and across her upper chest. Seemed he wasn't the only one feeling needy today.

"I'm fine, Trevor. Just fine," she finally replied. Gil smiled. Her voice was husky and thick and he could tell by the way she flinched at the sound of it, she knew he'd caught the lusty edge in it.

Trevor stared from her back to him, his lips drawn tight. Gil could see the uncertainty flare in the man's eyes before he removed all emotion from his expression. "Gil. Nice to see you. It's been a while."

Gil stepped forward and shook the man's hand, adding a healthy slap to Trevor's back. "Too long. How's homicide treating you?"

"Ah, you know how it is. The same shit, just different locations." Trevor looked over at Wade. "So what brings you gentlemen by?"

"Hey, you were the one who called us." Gil motioned towards Wade. "You told my colleague you needed to talk to us. Said you had some information about the case."

Trevor's mouth opened in surprise and he shot Fallon a desperate glance before returning Gil's stare. "I didn't realise the feds were involved yet. I thought it was still a state matter."

"We linked the bastard to an attack in Portland a few weeks ago," said Wade, stepping forward to shake Trevor's hand. "That makes it FBI business. I'm Wade Davis, Gil's *colleague*."

Gil scowled at Wade, not amused by the tone in his voice. "Sorry, Wade. Trevor Watts, Wade Davis. Wade, Trevor."

"Pleased to meet you, sir," said Wade, turning to look at Fallon. He smiled at her, pushing Gil aside as he stepped in front of her. "Special Agent Wade Davis, at your service, ma'am."

Fallon blushed even deeper as Wade lowered into a graceful bow. A growl rumbled through Gil's chest, as he pushed Wade back. "Easy, Junior." Wade mumbled something under his breath, but Gil was pretty sure he knew what the man meant. "Wade, this is Fallon Kinkade. Fallon..." He paused, resisting the urge to sweep his gaze along her body. "Wade Davis."

Fallon shuffled on her feet, pulling her arms tighter. "Nice to meet you," she replied, her voice more relaxed.

Gil glanced at her, wanting to gauge her reaction. Wade was several years younger than him, and it was obvious he had a way with the ladies. More than one assignment had ended with a pocketful of numbers buried in Wade's pants. But Fallon barely glanced at the handsome man. Instead, she looked over at him, holding his stare for a few moments before turning away, but not before he saw the wounded edge in her eyes. He sighed and raked a shaky hand through his hair. "So what information do you have for us, Trevor?"

Trevor motioned to the chairs at the side of his desk before taking his seat. "It appears your serial killer has decided to add a new twist to his game. He's called in the last two killings."

"What!" Gil stomped to his feet, anger twisting his fists at his side. "The bastard's called the centre and you're just telling us now!"

Trevor waved his hand in the air and calmly stood up. "He didn't call the centre, Gil, or we would've notified you sooner."

"So who the hell did he call?"

"Me."

Gil turned towards Fallon, her soft voice drawing him to her. He looked into her eyes, nearly buckling at the pain and fear he saw in them. "What? Fallon..."

Fallon stopped him with a wave of her hand. "Look. I don't know how or why, but he's called my cell twice now. I think he believes he's calling nine-one-one, but I don't see how that's possible. All I can tell you is that he calls me whenever he's...finished."

Gil watched her face pale, a glassy film covering her eyes. He moved closer, not really sure why, but needing her to know he was there for her, even if he couldn't say it. "What did he say?"

"Just that he's *the Priest,* and that he thinks he's saving the women he kills. He said he purifies them." She shook her head and stared down at the floor. "He wouldn't tell me anything else, just rattled off their location."

"So why didn't you call us sooner?" asked Wade, stepping up beside Gil.

"I tried calling in the first location to the centre, but either he messed up the address or I did. It came back as a beauty salon, so I thought maybe I'd dreamt the whole thing. But after he called again…"

"But some passer-by called that one in," interrupted Wade. "Why did you wait so long?"

Fallon looked up at them and Gil saw the nervousness in her expression. "I wasn't able to call right away and it was too late when I finally got the chance…but I'm here now and isn't that what matters?"

Wade shot him a puzzled look before nodding his head. "I suppose so," he said.

"Okay, Fallon," said Gil. "Let's sit down. I want you to tell us everything he said, and with as much detail as you can remember. Mention everything, no matter how insignificant you might think it is."

Fallon nodded and sat down. She spoke slowly and quietly, as if the sound of her voice might hurt her somehow. Gil watched her closely, noting every shift in her eyes, every twitch of her lips. She kept her hands clasped firmly in her lap, her eyes diverted to the side. She seemed more than frightened, and he couldn't help but think there was more to her story than what she was telling them.

"Did he give you any hint as to who might be his next target?" asked Wade, looking up from his notepad.

"No. Just what I told you."

Wade sighed and closed the book. "Well, at least we have a connection. Fallon? Would you mind if I took a look at your cell?"

Fallon shook her head and dug through her purse, finally handing the small unit over to Wade. "I've already checked. His number doesn't even register on my phone. That's why I thought maybe I'd imagined it that first time. I don't understand how he can call without leaving any trace at all."

"Maybe he's got something on his end that blocks it," suggested Wade. "I'll check it out."

"What if he calls again?" she asked. "He might get upset if I don't answer."

"Do you think he's targeting you?" asked Trevor. "I can post a unit outside your house if you're worried."

Fallon shook her head. "No, I don't think it's like that. He feels comfortable talking to me. I just think I might be able to get more out of him if I get the chance."

"I'll return your phone later today," said Gil. "He never strikes during the day."

He watched Fallon's face pale. "I'm going riding. I won't be by the house till later."

Gil smiled at her. "I know how to find you. I'll make sure you have it, one way or another."

Fallon sighed and stood up, turning towards Trevor. "Thanks, Trevor."

"No problem. I'll see you out."

She nodded and turned back towards Gil. "I suppose I'll see you later. Nice meeting you, Wade."

Wade gave her another charming smile as she brushed past both men. She tensed as her shoulder raked Gil's chest. He barely contained his groan at the heat that passed between them. Despite everything, they still had a connection neither could deny. He wondered just how far he'd delve into it.

"I'm sorry," said Trevor. "If I'd known Gil was on the team…"

"You'd have played it the same way," she interrupted.

Trevor sighed and touched her on the shoulder. "Are you going to be okay?"

"He's heading the investigation. I don't see how I can be any other way. Besides, with any luck, the bastard won't call again, and I can bow out." She smiled at Trevor's nervous twitch. "I'm a big girl, Trevor. I'll be fine."

Trevor patted her shoulder as she turned and headed for her Jeep. She walked quickly, hoping her anxiousness was hidden in her stride. It wasn't until she was seated behind the wheel she released the tight rein she had on her emotions, allowing the stray tears to tumble to her cheek. Six months of putting Gil behind her ruined by one look into his eyes. He was just like she remembered. Thick dark hair, stunning blue eyes and a smile that could make her knees weak. His hands were just as firm as they'd held her close to his chest, his fingers locked around her waist. His muscles were firm and tight, and she thought he'd been spending more time at the gym. His shoulders were slightly broader, his chest more pronounced. But his hips. Damn, they were just as lean, just as tight as when they'd last made love. She'd nearly melted into a puddle at his feet when she'd felt his cock harden against her stomach. Even through two layers of fabric she'd sensed it flaring in response, and she knew, if she'd pulled away the clothing, a shiny bead of seminal essence would have been covering the thin slit on his crown.

Fallon felt her body heat even further. She'd been in an instant state of arousal the moment their bodies had collided, gushing the silky cream from her body until the slide of juices had dampened her panties. She'd tried to keep her distance, hoping Gil wouldn't catch her scent, but had cringed when he'd glanced at her and given her body a long, slow sweep. The man was more than dangerous, and if she didn't watch her step, she'd lose more than her heart this time.

"Stop it. Just stop it!"

She shouted the words, hoping the sound of them would bring some sanity back to her head. He was only there on business, nothing more. And it didn't take a psychic to sense the walls he'd built around himself. The same walls he'd use to hide from her after the shooting.

"Damn." She let her breath whisper out in a long sigh as she laid her head against the steering wheel. There was no way she'd be able to spend any amount of time with him without wanting more. He may have left their home, but it was clear he still held her heart.

Fallon cursed and started the Jeep, slamming the small stick into gear. At least she'd had the good sense to strap her bike on the back before she'd left. A few hours of grinding her frustrations away on a trail was her only hope right now. Gil could wait until she was good and ready to give her back her cell. *I know how to find you, Fallon.* Damn, he was arrogant. Let him drive around trying to find her for a while and he'd see just how easy it was to track her down. A sly smile touched the corners of her mouth as she pulled into traffic and headed for the hills.

* * * *

Gil stood in Trevor's office, listening to the man escort Fallon down the hall. He tried to ignore how her voice had changed as soon as she'd left the room, the tension easing from her shoulders once she'd brushed by him. He curbed his need to growl, directing his anger inwards.

"So," said Wade. "That was interesting. Didn't realise I'd be the odd man out here."

Gil looked over at him, his brow pulled into a distinct vee. "What the hell are you whining about?"

"Oh nothing. Just because you all seem to be fast friends didn't bother me any, especially since I'm only your *colleague*."

Gil huffed out his breath, shifting his hand through his hair again. "You knew Trevor and I were friends before we arrived. And technically speaking, the Bureau doesn't use the term *partner*."

"Maybe they don't, but every other agent does, so it wouldn't kill you to use it every once and a while. Besides, I had no idea you knew that lovely creature sleeping on the couch." Wade raised his eyebrow. "How long were you two lovers?"

Gil sneered at the man. He'd obviously heard every word Fallon had mumbled. "Nearly two years. But it's over."

Wade laughed, not even bothering to hide the cocky smile Gil immediately wanted to smack off his face. "If you believe for one second there's nothing between you two, then you're a worse investigator than I thought. You *were* here when she practically drooled all over your shoes, weren't you? And you weren't much better. I heard you growl...twice." Wade's smile widened. "Besides, the girl must be spoken for when she didn't even give me one '*baby come here*' smile."

"Maybe not every girl is lured by your charm, Junior," countered Gil. "Or maybe she belongs to someone else," he said, hating the sound of the words the moment they left his lips.

"Oh, it wasn't my charm she was preoccupied with, *partner*. It was your body, or didn't you notice her physical reaction to you. Man, if my girlfriend had nipples like that, I'd never leave the damn house."

Another growl trembled through his body before Gil had the sense to stop it. Wade merely smiled at him. "I burned too many bridges to get her back. Besides, now isn't the time to get distracted."

"Buddy. When a lady looks that fine, anytime is a good time to get...distracted."

Gil chuckled. "Just do us both a favour and get up to the communication's centre. Get Jane to show you which phone she called Fallon on. It must be the key to why she's getting the phone calls. I'll go over to the medical examiner's office and see if there's anything new on our latest victim. I'll be back in two hours to get Fallon's cell back."

"I'll have it ready, not that you're anxious to see her again, or anything."

"Just figure out the connection, Wade. This might be the one lucky break that blows this case apart."

"Or at least ends up with Fallon blowing you," he teased. "Either way, it's a win-win scenario."

Chapter Six

Fallon ripped down the trail, skipping over logs and dodging trees as if the bike were an extension of her body. She'd never felt so in tune with her surroundings and almost wished today had been the race. She'd already conquered two sections of the run that normally threw her to the ground, and she was quickly edging up on the third.

"Son of a bitch. Thinks he can waltz into my life and look at me like some victorious predator..." She skidded across some rocks, spraying a layer of mud across the path. "Well, it'll be a cold day in hell before I give him so much as a fucking smile."

She barrelled forward, cursing Gil with every breath. "Who needs him to fulfil my fantasies? I can get laid any time of the week if I so desire. Who says I haven't moved on?"

Fallon felt the bike hit the lip of the jump and pulled up the wheel without even thinking. It shuddered through the air, dropping her several feet down the trail, nearly shaking her against a tree. She veered right, skimming the bark with her arm as she skidded to a halt. "Damn it!" She looked back up the trail. She'd never tried the drop before and was stunned she'd gone over it without even thinking. "See. I'm way out of his league," she snapped. "He never would've taken that jump."

She pressed forward, stopping once she'd reached a clearing near the bottom of the ride. It was her favourite spot to regroup and rest before the drive home. The air was thick and cool, the promise of rain gathering in the clouds. She could feel the charge building on her skin and knew they were in for another storm. A familiar shiver danced along her spine. It'd been raining the last two times the bastard had called, and she couldn't help but wonder if he'd strike again. If the storm didn't set him off somehow.

"Doesn't matter. Gil still has my phone, so I won't be the one answering it this time."

The words sounded promising, but a part of her refused to believe Gil would let her off that easily, not when she was connected to his case. She nodded, knowing he'd do whatever was necessary to solve the case, even if it meant being around her. "A sacrifice, I'm sure," she sneered, tossing her helmet on the ground. "As long as I'm not the only one suffering." She forced a smile and braced her foot against a large boulder just as someone grabbed her from behind and knocked her to the ground.

* * * *

Gil pulled into the gravel lot, eyeing the red Jeep parked beside a stand of trees. This hadn't been his first stop, but it also hadn't been as hard as he'd hoped to find her. Seems she hadn't made that many changes in her life since he'd left, which made him wonder if Wade had been right. Was Fallon still in love with him as much as he was with her?

He shook his head, stepping out into the cool air. He'd hurt her too badly to expect she felt anything other than revulsion for him. He was sure she'd only been polite at the station, not wanting to embarrass him in front of Wade. So did that mean she was seeing someone new? He cursed the thought, trying not to picture another man spreading her thighs wide, watching her pretty pink lips quiver as he drew his finger along her crease, tasting her sweet cream.

"Fuck!" He'd always been a possessive lover, never wanting her to so much as hug another man, and it seemed surreal to him that their last time together had been shared with Charlie. But then Charlie had been special. He'd owed the man his life, and it'd seemed the only action fitting of the sacrifice Charlie had made for him.

Gil sighed as he wove his way up the trail, watching for signs of Fallon's bike. He wouldn't put it past her to run him down if he gave her the chance, and was relieved when he made it to a large clearing without having to dodge into the bushes. He looked around, wondering where she was, when he saw a flash of her through the trees on the ridge off to his left. He'd been on that trail before and remembered how close to the edge it came as it rounded the bend, allowing anyone in the clearing a clear view. His blood pressure soared as he watched her race down the path, veering right and left as if the bike were part of her body. She'd always been good, but this display was nothing less than stunning.

"Okay, baby, you did good. Now stop and walk it down the drop." He smiled at her skill, expecting her to pull the bike up, but felt his heart stop dead when she took the jump at full speed, flying through the air until she landed several feet down the trail. He saw the bike wobble and shift, brushing her against a large tree before she swerved and skidded to a halt.

"Jesus Christ, Fallon! You could've killed yourself!" He was yelling at no one, but he didn't care. He watched as she surveyed her accomplishment before heading back into the trees. He shook his head, trying to calm the shaky rhythm of his heart. "You'll pay for that, sweetheart," he promised, imagining a proper punishment for taking ten years off his life. Then a smile found his lips and he darted into the brush before Fallon barrelled into the clearing.

Gil pressed his back against a tree, watching Fallon as she tossed her gear on the ground, stretching her arms up. Damn, he loved when she did that. The way the motion jiggled her breasts, making her nipples arch higher on her chest. He could almost taste the sweet fruity perfection of her skin, mixed with a hint of salty sweat. Even that turned him on. It reminded him of all the times she'd collapsed on top of him after fucking him for over an hour. Her body would be hot and slick, the smell of sex and sweat lingering on her skin. God, it'd been paradise.

"A sacrifice, I'm sure."

Her voice drifted along the breeze as she threw her helmet on the ground and shrugged her CamelBak off her shoulders. He smiled. She was pissed, and that made his plan even easier. He snuck out, keeping his body low as he moved towards her. She was huffing out her breath and running her fingers through her hair. She never once looked over her back as he straightened up behind her.

"As long as I'm not the only one who suffers," she began, but her voice shuddered into a gasp as Gil grabbed her by the shoulders and pulled her to the ground. He did his best to cushion her fall, rolling his body on top of hers. But he hadn't even caught her gaze before she bucked her hips underneath him and threw him over her shoulder. His back hit the hard dirt a moment before she pounced on top of him, holding a small Swiss army knife to his throat. He watched as her eyes went wide, and her grip weakened.

"Gil?" was all she got out before he broke her hold and rolled her over, pinning her beneath his heavy body. She cursed as her shoulders hit the ground, knocking her breath out in a loud huff. She growled at him and immediately raised her hips again, but Gil was ready this time and shifted his weight, locking her in place. She fought against his hold for a few minutes, trying every technique he'd taught her before finally stilling beneath him, her chest rising sharply against his.

"Fine, Gil. You win. Now get off of me."

Gil smiled at the reluctant tone of her voice. She hated admitting defeat and had injected just enough anger into her voice to make him think she was serious.

"Are you conceding I'm the more skilled warrior?" he asked, knowing the question would boil her blood.

Fallon grunted, giving one more attempt to best him, before snorting out her breath. "You only won because I let my guard down when I realised it was you. Don't think for a moment I would've done that with anyone else."

"A true warrior knows how to take advantage of any mistake," he noted.

Another irritated sigh rumbled through her chest as she stared up at him. "Fine. You're the better warrior. Now can you get off me?"

Gil shook his head, lowering his body closer to hers. His smile widened when he felt her breathing hitch and her nipples harden against his chest. "Not yet, sweetheart. First I want to know what in the hell made you try a stunt like that?"

Fallon fought for breath as she stared up at him, her eyes already darkening. He knew she could feel his cock hardening even further against her stomach, and he didn't try to hide his amusement at her reaction. "What are you talking about? What stunt?"

He rubbed his cock across her stomach, revelling in the breathy whimper that escaped her lips before she could pull them into a tight line. "That jump back there. What in the hell made you think it was a good idea to try it?" He lowered even farther, keeping her arms pinned above her head. "You scared ten years off my life, darling."

Fallon watched him for several moments, her tongue moistening her lips in a slow sweep across her mouth. He groaned, wishing she'd do that to his lips. "I've been practicing. And in case you didn't notice, I landed it perfectly."

Gil growled and shifted both her hands into one of his before pulling down on the neckline of her shirt until the upper part of her right shoulder was exposed. Even in the dull light the cuts made on her skin by the bark of the tree she'd nearly collided with were visible. "And what to you call those?" he asked, raising his eyebrow in challenge.

Fallon smiled at him, a wicked gleam in her eyes. "Love bites," she whispered, grinding her hips against his erection. He couldn't stop a groan from tearing from his chest. Her smile widened. "Are we finished now, Gil?"

Gil stared down at her, unable to look away. Her eyes were almost black now, just a hint of the blue rimming the edges. He could feel her body warming against his and he knew the sweet scent starting to mingle with the breeze was the proof of her arousal. She wanted him. He just needed to show her how much.

He bent down, brushing his lips across hers, catching the startled gasp that purged from her lips. "Finished?" He looked down between their bodies, noting how closely she pressed herself against him, before catching her gaze once again. "Darling, we haven't even started yet."

With that, he took her lips, slanting his over top of hers, taking advantage of her surprised yelp to slip his tongue inside her mouth. It was soft and warm, and he had to hold himself back from ripping her clothes off and slamming inside her before her tongue even played with his. She was hesitant at first, just brushing the tip across his, allowing him to explore her mouth without really returning his passion. Then her willpower seemed to vanish, and she latched on to his tongue and suckled it, dipping into his mouth when he finally retreated. She tasted fruity and sweet, and he dipped his head for another kiss once they'd both grabbed a quick breath.

"God, you taste good," he moaned, moving his lips to her neck, nipping at the delicious hollow near her shoulder. Fallon arched into the bite, her moan joining his. "Does that feel good, baby?"

"Yes," she whispered, her voice so soft he wasn't sure she'd even answered him.

Gil glanced up at her, his body tensing. Did she really want him to make love to her, or was she just humouring him to the breaking point before dismissing his actions? He lowered his chest, rubbing it against hers. He could feel her nipples through her shirt, so hard he could almost see the small holes in the tips. She was panting, her eyes dark, her skin flushed. He held her gaze, his lips suspended above hers, every inch of their bodies touching, looking for any hint of regret in her expression. He didn't want to stop, but if she gave so much as a dart of her eyes that suggested this wasn't what she wanted, he would, even if it killed him. She watched him, tugging against his hold, waiting on his move until her patience must have waned and she arched her pussy against his cock, rubbing it along the full length of his erection.

"Gil."

God, he nearly creamed his pants at the soft plea of her voice. All thoughts of stopping vanished with that one word, and he smiled down at her victoriously. "Yeah, baby. I feel it, too. But I don't want to rush through this. I want to savour you."

Fallon moaned again as he brought his lips back to her neck, nipping and licking at the soft skin. He loved the way she whimpered with each new sensation, whispering his name out with her breath. He moved down to where he'd left his mark, soothing the mild hurt with a series of soft licks. Fallon moaned even louder.

"Gil."

Gil glanced up at her, smiling at the pout gracing her lips. "Yes, darling?" he replied, grazing his free hand across one hard nipple.

Fallon arched against his hand. "Let go of my hands. I can't touch you like this."

"Soon, baby. Once I've finished tasting all of you." He chuckled as she continued to pull against his hold. "Impatient little minx, aren't you?"

"It's not fair…"

Gil laughed again when her voice keened into a sharp cry as he latched around one turgid peak and drew it into his mouth. Even through the fabric of her shirt he could feel it thicken and harden. "Damn, I love your nipples. They're so hard and thick. But you've got way too many clothes on for me to do this properly, darling."

"So release my hands, and I'll undress for you," she tempted.

"Nice try, baby. But I like to open my own gifts."

Gil reached between their bodies, slipping his fingers around the zipper of her shirt. The first layer was easy. One quick tug and the zipper slid to her waist, revealing the tight tank underneath. He wanted to lift it over her head and see every inch of her pale skin, but that would mean letting go of her hands, and he wasn't prepared to do that just yet. Even though she'd given him every indication his actions were welcomed, he couldn't quite bring himself to give up control.

Fallon gasped as Gil grabbed the small knife still poised in her hand and placed the tip against her shirt. He didn't waste time explaining, just simply cut down the centre of her tank, peeling it away to reveal the creamy swell of her breasts. His cock pulsed at the sight before him. Her breasts were full and firm, the nipples hard points thrusting up from the middle. Each breath raised the sweet buds closer to his mouth, making him ache with need.

"So pretty. You've got such pretty breasts."

He eased down, and circled his tongue around her nipple, getting as close as he could without actually touching it. Fallon arched into him, twisting in an attempt to move him to where she seemed to need him the most, but he shifted with her, bringing her closer to the edge. Then he moved to her other breast, teasing it with the same slow swipe of his tongue.

"Gil."

Gil looked up at her, his tongue still circling her nipple. Her voice had been strong and hard. She was getting desperate. He grinned at her, knowing it'd only frustrate her more, before taking her nipple into his mouth and sucking it.

Her wail vibrated through his chest, making his balls pull tight against his skin. He moved his free hand over to her other nipple and tweaked it between his fingers. Fallon tossed her head from side to side, softly chanting his name, bucking her hips up against his stomach. A new sheen of sweat broke out on her skin, flushing it a dark pink.

"Oh God. Please don't stop."

Gil sucked harder, flicking his tongue against the hard tip, making her back arch off the ground. He switched sides, drawing the bud deeper, taking more of her breast into his mouth. She was nearly crying now, thrashing against his assault. He worked quicker, moving between breasts until she stiffened in his arms, a primal growl erupting from her lips. He smiled, knowing her sent her into her first orgasm without even touching her pussy. But he could smell her. A strong sweet musky scent that filled the air around them, making him feel dizzy and weak. He moved upwards teasing her lips with a soft flick of his tongue. "Better?"

Fallon flitted her eyes open. They'd softened slightly from the intensity of her orgasm, but he knew when she came like that, it only made her pussy ache more. "I'd be better if you'd give me what I need instead of teasing me."

"Does that mean you didn't enjoy yourself?"

She sighed out a long breath and smiled. Nothing pleased him more than sparing with her. It made him hot and hard, and he suspected it had the same effect on her. "You're too smug for your own good, you know that?"

"Oh, but you like how good I am, baby. And now that I've taken the edge off, I'll treat myself to a taste of your sweet pussy. I can smell it from here, all hot and wet. Perhaps it's a good thing I missed lunch today."

"But what about my hands?" she said, pulling against his hold again. "I need to touch you, too."

Gil hesitated, not sure why he was so reluctant to let her go. He wanted to believe it was his need to dominate her. To keep her so hot and wanting she wouldn't have the breath to tell him to stop. But if he was honest with himself, he knew it was out of fear. Fear that once she'd touched him, he'd never be able to live without her. And he didn't know how to bridge the hurt he'd caused. How to show her how much he still loved her.

Fallon snorted and pulled against him one last time.

"Damn it, Gil! Either let me touch you, or get the hell off me!" She'd made her tone strong and sharp, showing him the seriousness of her claim. And while she wanted him to touch her, to lick her, she'd be damned if he did it while she was bound and unable to explore his body as well. It'd been too long, and just having his cock wasn't going to be enough. She needed him. Needed to touch and taste, stroke every inch of his skin until she'd memorised each dip and curve of his body.

Gil looked away for a moment and she watched him fight against some inner demon before finally sighing out his breath and slowly releasing her hands. He traced his fingers down her arm, gently caressing her face, as he stayed poised above her, a worried crease across his brow. She left her hands above her head for a moment, wanting him to know she was still submitting to him, before easing them down and placing them on his shoulders. Tension bunched his muscles, so she squeezed them, smiling as the action was mirrored in his hips. They punched forward, giving her an even better feel of his cock. God, he was hard. Hard and long and, damn, she remembered how thick. She felt a momentary flicker of panic when she wondered if she'd be able to take him inside her after so many months of nothing but emptiness, but it quickly receded, replaced by a hunger so primal, she knew any pain she felt would feel so damn good she wouldn't care.

Gil seemed to sense her momentary apprehension and smiled down at her, grinding his cock into her pussy again. "Don't worry, darling. I'll still fit."

She whimpered against the delicious sensation, loving the feel of his thick shaft gliding through the folds of her pussy. Even clothed it brushed across her clit, sending shards of pleasure coursing through her veins. She arched into him, wishing he'd let her wrap her legs around his hips, but he held himself still, encasing her thighs with his knees. She sighed, knowing she was powerless to fight against him. He'd always dominated the bedroom, and it didn't look like things had changed.

"Easy, Fallon. I know you want me inside you, but I'm not finished playing with your pretty little body. I let your hands go, but I'll take you when I'm ready to, and not before."

Fallon huffed at his declaration, not bothering to hide her irritation. It seemed to only make him that much more determined, and he pulled away when she leaned up to kiss him. His eyes glowed with pride, but she reached her hands around his neck and savagely pulled him down, finally claiming his mouth with hers. She could feel the strength in his muscles as she squeezed his neck, dancing her fingers across the broad bands splaying out across his shoulders. He was letting her kiss him, but the thought didn't bother her. She was touching him, and that was a grand victory in her eyes.

"You've been working out," she whispered, trailing her tongue along his neck. "I can feel the difference."

Gil smiled, but a sadness crept into his eyes, as if talking about their previous relationship hurt him. She lowered her eyes, not wanting to see the rejection in his. Did he wish he'd never started this seduction, or was he sorry he ever let the relationship slide? She eased back, giving him a chance to pull away, to leave her hot and wet, but he didn't move. Instead he took her departure as his signal to move down her body, and he wasted no time capturing one of her nipples in his mouth.

"Oh God, yes." The words vibrated through her chest, so deep and sultry she felt shaken from the inside out. He'd already made her come once without touching her cunt, and she knew if he kept it up, she'd come again.

Gil laughed at her words, drawing back so only his tongue brushed across the tip. "Oh no, baby. I'm not going to let you come again until I taste that sweet pussy of yours. Damn, your scent is so strong I can already taste you on my tongue."

Fallon moaned at his words, the anticipation of having

him lick her burning the blood in her veins. She arched into the hand that travelled down her stomach, slowly inching inside her tights. Her skin felt singed by his touch and she looked down, expecting to see tiny tendrils of smoke rising up off her body. Gil was watching her, a sly smile on his face. She knew he liked it when she watched him, and the look in his eyes was warning her it would be wise not to turn away.

She held his gaze, unable to look away even if he hadn't silently forbidden her. The moment was too surreal, like a page out of one of her fantasies, and she feared if she lost contact with his eyes, the dream would fade and she'd be left feeling empty and hollow. Gil shifted his weight, still holding her tight between his legs, but allowing enough room for his hand to rim the top of her mound. He froze.

Fallon bit at her bottom lip, trying to wiggle him lower, but he stayed poised on the edge of her sex, only one finger grazing the vee of her pussy lips. His eyes looked distant, like he was trying to figure out a complicated puzzle, before he turned a heated gaze on her. He growled and pulled down her tights, stripping them from her body and ripping the seam in his haste, as he stared at her bare lips. A strangled moan escaped his mouth and he couldn't seem to stop himself from running his fingers along her skin, testing out the smoothness of it.

He looked back up at her, fire raging in his eyes. "You're bare."

She nodded, not trusting her voice. There was a lump stuck in her throat and she didn't know if she'd be able to talk around it.

Gil looked back down, as if needing to see her mound again to believe the change he'd discovered. "Who did you shave yourself for?"

Fallon heard his words, but she was too distracted with the slow sweep of his fingers along the edge of her pussy to respond. If he'd just move over a bit, he'd be touching the wet folds of her sex. Gil grunted and she forced her eyes to meet his stare. "What?"

He growled again, and grabbed both her hands, pining them to the ground beside her hips. "I said, 'who did you shave your sweet pussy for'?"

Was that jealousy in his voice, in the gleam of his eyes? She shook the thought from her head, convincing herself she'd read more into his question than there was. Surely he wasn't being possessive after leaving her without so much as a note. "No one."

"Don't lie to me. I want to know who's been fucking you." He drew back slightly and seemed to catch some control back before he continued. "I don't want to hurt him, baby. I just want to know who you've been fucking. One of those pretty boys down at the station?"

Fallon shook her head, not sure he'd believe her words. Except for her escapade with the vibrator the other night, she hadn't found release in months. He stared at her and she knew he wanted her to answer him out loud. "I haven't been with anyone, Gil. Jane shaved herself and told me to give it a try. That if felt so sexy to be bare. So I did."

"And you haven't had sex with anyone else? Not even let a guy touch you?"

She saw the possessiveness in his eyes and fought to keep the air in her lungs. Damn, it was like they'd never been apart. "I haven't so much as kissed another man since…" She let her voice fade.

Gil's lips curled up into a sexy half smile. "Have you touched yourself? Made that pretty little pussy shake and shiver with your fingers and your toys?"

God, how could he know? She nodded again, heat flushing her face.

"Did you like it?"

"Yes." Then she pressed her pussy up against his thigh, smiling at his groan, as she added, "but not near as much as when you make me come."

"Then I'll enjoy being the first man to lick your bare pussy. To feel that soft skin moist and hot beneath my tongue, surrounding me as I slide inside you. Do you want that?"

She nodded as the word, 'yes', hissed through her teeth. God, she wanted that and more. She wanted him deep inside her forever. "Please, Gil."

The anger disappeared from his expression and the tension in his shoulders eased. He gave her one last glance before releasing her hands again and lowering his body. His knee nudged her thighs, urging her to open her legs, to allow him access to the core of her need. She moved willingly, easing her thighs apart until his shoulders were wedged between them. Then he reached his hands around to the backs of her knees, pushing her legs even wider.

"That's it, baby. I want you spread wide for me, so I can see every flicker of your clit when you come. You know how I like watching you." He teased the joint of her lips with the tip of his tongue. "Umm, so tasty. Play with your cunt for me. I want to see how much you enjoy your new fashion statement."

Fallon's cheeks flushed further at his command. She'd never quite got over the embarrassment of touching herself while he watched, but was too caught up in the erotic words to stop her hand from inching down her stomach and skimming across her skin. She was surprised when a low rumble filled the air and she discovered it was her voice, not Gil's. She moved down, dipping into the slick crease, pinching her clit before thrusting her finger inside her.

"Damn, I love watching you touch yourself. It's so beautiful." He bent down and lapped at the juices spilling along her hand. "Push inside again and bring me more of your sweet honey."

Fallon complied, pushing her finger inside her pussy, coating it with the warm liquid that oozed out of her, before drawing it out and spreading it around her clit.

Gil licked the cream away as fast as she collected it, and by the time she was close to climaxing, she was sure he'd eaten every drop from her cunt. She pressed up into his mouth, slipping her juice-coated finger into his hair. She was done giving into his commands. Hell, he still had all his clothes on.

Gil didn't seem to take notice and continued to lick at her clit. She tried to pull his shirt from his body, but the collar caught on his neck, refusing to move. She huffed and gave one last mighty tug. The seams gave a moment before she heard the cotton separate, tearing partway down the neck. Gil looked up, the sound apparently interrupting his task. He smiled at her startled expression, bending his head so she could pull the torn garment over his head, taking the T-shirt he'd worn underneath with it. Then he grabbed the edges of the shirt he'd cut open and shoved it down her arms, baring her upper body. She shivered as the cool air breezed across her damp skin, making her flesh prickle and bead.

"Cold, sweetheart?"

"Not for long," she tossed back, curling her body against his, feeling his heat seep into her. Gil pulled her close, rubbing his skin on hers. He felt like fire in her arms and she couldn't stop from relaxing against him, allowing his arms to encircle her. Damn, she'd missed him.

"Better?"

She whispered her thanks into his neck, not sure she could talk without crying. Gil smiled against her hair.

"Well, now that you're warm again, sweetheart, I've got some pussy to eat."

Chapter Seven

Fallon moaned as Gil pushed her gently to the ground. She wanted to resist, to insist he give her time to explore his body. But she could tell by the firmness in his touch, playtime was over.

"I suggest you get comfortable. You're going to be lying there for a while."

Fallon moaned, not just from his words, but from the way he pushed her legs apart, baring her to his heated gaze. She looked down between her legs, held captive by the way he watched her as he licked his lips, tasting some of her juice still clinging to his face. Then he smiled and dipped down, tonguing her clit.

"Oh God."

Gil hummed his reply, vibrating her clit while he teased her channel with just a hint of his finger. She arched into him, hoping to sink it in farther, but he moved with her. He'd told her he'd take her when he was ready, and she had a feeling he was holding true to his claim.

"Need something, baby?" he teased, sinking one knuckle inside her.

"More," was all she could say, her breath lodged too tight in her chest to form more words.

"Don't worry, baby. There's more."

Gil thrust forward, sinking his finger completely inside her, rubbing her walls as he teased the digit back and forth in her slick juices. She arched into him, feeling the emptiness disappear, replaced by a hunger so strong she knew she wouldn't be able to move until Gil had fucked her senseless. She needed him filling her, thrusting his thick cock back and forth, driving into her so deep she'd forget her name as she screamed out his. She opened her legs wider, clamping them around his shoulders as she pushed her cunt up against his mouth.

"That's it, baby. Just go with it. Let me feel you come in my mouth while I finger-fuck your pretty little pussy." He lapped against her clit. "So sweet, baby. Damn, I could eat you for hours." He laughed as she shuddered at the thought. "Umm. Do you like the sound of that, baby? Want me to eat this hot pussy of yours over and over?"

"Yes, oh God, yes."

She couldn't stop the words from spilling from her lips any more than she could stop the juice from gushing from her cunt. Even though her mind told her this was nothing more than a quick fuck, a convenient meeting that wouldn't go any further, her body wanted more. Wanted him tasting her night after night, licking her from one orgasm into another. Wanted his shaft buried deep inside her, his hot cum coating her walls and her thighs. Even more, she wanted to taste him, feel his cock thicken in her mouth until his control shattered and he came with a roar, pumping his semen down her throat.

"Oh, yeah. You like the sound of that, don't you? But you don't just want my mouth. You want my cock filling you. You want me to come inside that sweet little pussy."

"Yes, Gil. Please."

Gil licked at her, but not enough to make her come. "Tell me what you want," he whispered, his breath feathering across her clit, making it pucker and twitch. Gil groaned.

Fallon snagged her bottom lip and gripped it between her teeth, trying to resist the need to answer him. If he just circled her clit a few more times…

"Tell me, or I'll make you want so bad you'll have to beg me before I let you come."

Fallon cried out, so hot with need she felt as if her body were burning from the inside out. She fisted his hair in her fingers and tugged, knowing the slight pain would only strengthen his resolve. She looked down at him, catching the steely look in his eyes, and threw her head back, practically screaming out the words he needed to hear. "I want you to lick me until I come. Damn it, I want you to fuck me until I can't stand up!"

Gil smiled against her flesh. "Your wish is my command, darling."

Fallon held her breath, the anticipation making her head spin. Gil shifted between her legs, opening her wider, repositioning her thighs over his shoulders. His finger was still lodged inside her, but he was holding it still, making her ache until she wanted to scream.

"Ready, baby?"

"I can't wait..."

He moved. His fingers—two now, or was it three?—thrust inside her pussy just as his lips clamped around her clit, milking it with strong, steady pulls. Fallon arched off the ground, fire racing through her body and into her groin. It flamed higher, dancing black dots across her vision. The ground was swaying, shifting the view over his shoulders. Trees. Sky. The dark brown of his hair. She twisted to get closer, to grind her pussy so far in his mouth she'd feel as if he'd climbed inside her. She was close. So close.

"Don't rush it. Make it take you, baby. Fight as long as you can. I want to eat you forever."

Fallon cried at his declaration, wishing they were more than hot words spoken in the moment. She wanted to come, but fighting made the release that much hotter. He pulled out his fingers and thrust his tongue inside her, fucking her deep and strong. The feeling faded around her clit, and she knew he was tormenting her. Prolonging her pleasure until her body went over of its own accord. He lapped at her, the wet sound making her want soar. Damn, she needed to come.

"Gil. Now. Oh God. So close. Just a bit more."

Gil hummed against her cunt, replaced his tongue with his fingers again and suckled her clit, sending her over the edge and into bliss. She screamed his name, not sure if the sound was only echoed in her head or if she'd shaken the ground with the vibration of it. Gil only sucked harder, inching his fingers deeper, drinking in the liquid that seeped around his hand and slipped down her thighs. She felt something soft around her fingers and slowly realised her hands were still speared through his hair. It took several tries before the message got through and she released her hands, letting them fall boneless by her sides. It'd been so long since she'd come that hard, and her body needed a chance to regroup.

Gil moved, a soft whimper accompanying her breath as he eased free of her body and moved over top of her. She was still panting, her eyes squeezed shut.

"Can your toys make you scream like that?"

She forced her eyes open. He looked roguish and sexy, and she couldn't help but smile. "Not even close."

Gil seemed surprised by her honesty but only paused for a moment before widening his smile. "Good answer, sweetheart." He leant down and licked her lips. "Ready for the main course?"

Fallon answered by arching her hips up and slipping the first few inches of his hard, hot shaft inside her.

Gil's head snapped down and he gazed at the vee of her mound, where their bodies were now joined. He pulled back and she knew he was watching his cock slide back out, part of the length now covered in her thick cream.

"Like what you see?" she taunted, grinding him inside again.

Gil moaned and looked back down at her. "Do I like seeing my cock covered in your juice as it slides in and out of your hot little pussy? Oh yeah, baby. I like it a lot. But I like the idea of fucking you until you can't stand up even more."

Fallon closed her eyes as he punched his hips forward, driving his cock deep inside her weeping channel. She wanted to scream, but the air hissed from her lungs as the pleasure tore through her body. He was hard and thick, and the sharp entrance he'd made had been a fine line between pleasure and pain.

Gil stilled, his sac lodged against her flesh, his cock brushed up against her womb. His mouth was pulled tight, his eyes heavy with lust. "You okay?"

She nodded, not able to speak the words aloud. She was stretched tight, but after months of emptiness, she wasn't about to complain.

Gil lowered down over her, rubbing his chest against hers. "You're tighter than ever. I'm sorry, baby. I shouldn't have entered you so quickly."

Tears stung her eyes, but she blinked them back. He sounded so sincere, so damn loving it was almost as if the months of separation had been some kind of bad dream. She reached up and nibbled at his ear, whispering his name in the low, sultry tone she knew he loved.

"Nice try, darling. But I know you're feeling it. We'll take it slow for a while. Let you adjust to me again."

Gil moved slowly, dragging the heavy length of his cock through her sensitive tissues, making her back arch and her legs tighten around his hips. God, he was so thick, so filling, she swore she felt every inch of his shaft as it left her body, leaving only the bulbous head still clenched inside her. She tightened on him, feminine power surging through her at the husky groan that tore from his chest.

"Tease," he breathed, pushing back in, forcing his cock through the tight walls of her pussy. "That's it, baby. Squeeze me. Tighten on me real good."

He locked against her flesh, giving her a few moments to adjust to his width before pulling out again and slowly thrusting back in. He didn't pause this time, but his pace stayed easy, his hips pumping gently against hers.

Fallon traced the muscles in his back, not quite sure when he'd lost his pants. She remembered tearing his shirt, but then he'd attacked her clit and everything had blurred into his tongue, his hands, and how they touched her body. She could feel his skin against hers, his muscles bunching beneath her fingers. She traced his back, dipping into the hollows as he flexed his muscles, following the sleek lines up to his shoulders and along his arms. She could see the scars on his left side and avoided them, not wanting to give him any reason to pull away from her. Their need was intense, but she wasn't convinced he'd stay if she reminded him of why he'd left in the first place.

"Feeling better?" he asked, increasing his thrusts slightly.

She arched her hips up, taking him deeper. Her juices were slick and wet, allowing him to penetrate her easily now. She nipped at his bottom lip, licking away any hurt she'd caused. "Faster, Gil. Go faster, darling."

He smiled down at her, pressing harder, taking her deeper. She moaned and met his thrusts, levering off his back, using her heels to keep her channel aligned with his shaft. Another orgasm started building in her stomach, flowering outward and threatening to pull her under.

"You're so beautiful. I can't wait to watch you come again for me." He rocked faster, pumping his hips more firmly into hers. "I can feel it building, baby. The way your cunt tightens on me as it starts to pulse. And your skin gets all pink. Damn, it's amazing." He laughed at her gasping cry. "Oh yeah. Don't fight it. Come for me, Fallon. Come for me, now."

Fallon screamed, his finger suddenly stroking her clit, adding another layer of sensation to her body. The heat punched through her stomach, spiralling upwards, sending sparks of fire into her womb. She felt the orgasm stall, hanging her on the edge for one glorious moment before the dam gave way, and she exploded in Gil's arms.

"Oh, Fallon. You're so beautiful. So damn beautiful. God, I love seeing you like this."

Fallon moaned, too lost in the pleasure to say anything. He hadn't climaxed with her and she knew he was just waiting for her to fall back to earth before sending her over again.

"Gil." Her voice was weak and distant, and she wasn't

sure if she was speaking or just thinking his name.

"I'm here, baby. Just breathe."

"More," she moaned. "I need more, Gil."

"Oh, there's more. Let me show you just how much."

"Yes!"

The word was ripped from her chest as Gil pounded into her, filling her with every inch of his cock. Hard, fast, deep. Over and over, pulling up on her hips, stretching her, filling her. She heard her voice shatter the air, Gil's name joining with the thunder that played in the sky. Gil thrust again, relentless in his pursuit, fucking her like a man with nothing to lose. Her body pulsed again, teetering on the edge, needing just one more push.

"Yes!"

Gil's roar filled her head, sending her over, blinding her with hot flashes that filled her vision. He pulsed inside her, spilling his seed as he came over and over, his body stiff against hers. She held on, her fingers digging into his shoulders, her legs clamped around his back. She wasn't sure how she managed to breathe as he pulled her close, dropping gentle kisses across her hair.

"Oh, baby."

He seemed like he wanted to say more, but the rest of his breath sighed out against her hair as he lowered his body onto hers, allowing some of his weight to press into her. She smiled and let his body cover her, a warm contentment settling inside.

Gil felt Fallon melt against him, her small body protected within his, and had to fight back the tears that burned in his eyes. He could feel his chest tighten around the heart he'd hidden from her months ago, and knew he'd been running from the truth. The only question that remained was how long could he continue to hide?

Fallon nuzzled against his neck, gently biting his jaw. He chuckled and eased back enough to gaze into her eyes. They were soft and bright, and so damn blue it was as if she'd captured the brilliant hue of the ocean inside them. His chest constricted again, and he closed his eyes against the rush of emotions smothering his senses. She made him feel alive, and he wasn't sure if he was ready to feel anything.

"Gil?"

Her voice was soft and timid but edged with the same fear he felt rising inside him. He forced himself to meet her gaze, his best smile curving his lips. "Still hungry, darling?"

Fallon's face flushed a deep red, and he could tell she was fighting the urge to hide against his neck. His cock was still inside her, not as hard as when he'd fucked her, but enough to let her know he wasn't finished just yet. She shifted her body beneath his, a low moan trembling from her lips as the motion pressed his groin against her clit and his cock just a bit deeper inside her. He smiled.

"It's okay. I'm hungry, too. See?" He punched his hips forward, thrusting his crown against the end of her channel. She arched into him, more cream flowing from her body to cover his shaft. The warm juice spilled along his cock and across his sac, and he lost the tentative hold he had on his control. "Knees, baby. Now."

Fallon moved, whether by her volition or his he wasn't sure, but before a drop of her cream could fall off his cock, he had her turned, the pale skin of her ass glowing in the dim light. "Spread your legs wider, baby. Let me see how bad you need me." He smoothed his hand along her hip, whispering more demands as she inched her knees apart, baring her ass and lips to his view.

"Very nice. Now let me see how wet you are."

Fallon moaned as he slid his fingers through her crease, dipping into her heat and spreading the moisture around her clit.

"Oh, baby. You need it real bad, don't you? Once wasn't enough, was it?"

"Oh God. Now. Fuck me now, Gil!"

"Demanding little vixen." He moved his hand up, circling her tender nether hole. "Too bad I'm not prepared to take you here," he moaned, sliding his finger slightly into the tight pucker. "You know how much I love fucking your ass."

"Yes."

The word came out as a plea and he felt his cock throb as she pressed back against his intrusion, sinking it completely inside her.

"Damn it, Fallon. Don't test me, or my need might outweigh my good sense. I don't want to hurt you, baby. Just my finger right now. You're too tight for anything else. I need to prepare you."

She moaned her disappointment and reared back on him, thrusting his finger inside her ass again.

"Damn, you're intoxicating. Just relax and feel what I can do for you."

Fallon's breath hissed from her chest as he pumped her ass with his finger, keeping the rhythm steady and strong. He'd spent months dreaming of touching her like this and wasn't about to rush the sheer pleasure of seeing her body under his spell.

"More. Pump me harder."

"How about I give you something else to think about?" he countered, brushing his swollen head through her glistening folds. "Ready to feel me inside you again?"

She arched back, catching the head inside her hole.

"I'll take that as a yes. Now put those pretty breasts down lower, so I can see more of you."

Fallon moved, her ass pushing higher as her breasts grazed the dirt. Gil thought about offering his shirt to her, but he didn't think he could spare the time to look for it. She'd tossed it away after practically ripping it off his back, and he didn't want to spend one more second without his cock inside her.

He smiled as he scanned the vision before him. Fallon's hair had pulled loose from its clip and now hung in long waves around her shoulders, the red hue shimmering against the white of her skin. Her back was long and lean with just enough muscle definition to look feminine and sexy. He followed the line down to her waist, loving how it dipped in before splaying out at her hips. She wasn't skinny or thin, but athletic and curvy, soft and strong, in an alluring paradox that made him want to jump inside her skin.

"That's much better," he whispered, easing forward, pushing just a bit more inside her. "Now I can see that beautiful ass of yours as I fuck it with my finger." He pressed in, rubbing against the edge until he felt the head of his cock through the thin barrier of skin. "And here... damn, I can feel my cock begging to go deeper, baby."

"Gil, you're killing me. Please, just fuck me. I need you driving hard and fast."

"Is this what you need?"

Gil thrust deep, claiming her sex in one hard movement. Fallon screamed his name as her pussy clenched around his cock, holding it inside, daring him to deny her the pleasure, the fucking she needed. Her ass felt like a vice as he moved his finger forward and reclaimed the hot hole, causing her back to bow and a primal wail to shatter the heavy air. She was gripped with pleasure, and he knew the time for teasing was over.

He pulled back, one last slow drag of his cock through her swollen tissues before slamming back in, slapping his sac against the soft flesh of her clit. Her body shuddered beneath him, his quick thrusts already sending her into orgasm. Somewhere in the back of his mind he heard his little voice warning him, telling him to go gently, slowly. To make it good for her, but it seemed lost amidst the pounding of his blood and the driving urge to have her submit to him. To acknowledge his claim over her regardless of whether he could say the words she needed to hear.

"Damn. You feel so good."

He moved in perfect rhythm, claiming her cunt with his cock then sinking his finger into her ass. She rocked against him, countering his thrusts, driving him deeper. Her hips were high, angling his shaft over the rough patch of skin he knew drove her crazy as he worked her higher, determined to see her explode again before he gave into the fire burning up his spine, pulling his balls so tight he wondered if they'd tucked inside him. She was close, but so was he.

"Come for me, Fallon. I want to see you come one more time before I pump my cum inside your pretty little pussy."

"Oh God. Yes."

Her words filled his head, shattering the last of his control. He pushed into her, once, twice, three times and them he came, his back bowing, his hand gripping her hip so tight he knew he'd see marks later, as he spurted inside her, filling her with his sperm, his mark. She clawed the ground, convulsing until her strength seemed to fade and she went limp in his arms. He grunted through the last of his release, pushing into her three more times before the tension eased from his body and he followed her to the ground, dragging her into his chest with a possessive curl of his hands.

She shuddered against him, moulding into the natural curve of his body. She looked tired and content, like a woman well pleasured, and he smiled knowing he'd given her the rosy glow and half-lidded eyes.

"Think you can stand up?"

She laughed and looked back at him over her shoulder, stealing a few soft kisses as she shook her head in reply.

"Me neither," he breathed, relaxing, content to just hold her in his arms. She was so warm and soft, despite the cool air and damp ground, and he realised he was holding everything that mattered to him in his arms.

He bounced the thought around in his head, trying to determine how to act on his revelation, when Fallon nudged him in the ribs.

"What's that noise?"

Gil pulled her closer, his body primed, when he heard the faint sound of music vibrating in the air. He listened, finally recognising the song he'd earmarked for Wade. "Damn, it's work."

He rolled away, hating the loss of her heat the instant his body left hers, and picked through the scattered items on the ground. He found his pants a few feet away and dug through the pockets. "Here." He tossed Fallon her phone, loving how she was still sitting naked. She seemed confused and he felt a flicker of panic cool his skin. He couldn't ignore the call, but their little meeting was far from over.

"I have to get this," he warned, holding up his cell. "Why don't you get dressed and warm yourself up. But stay put. Once I'm finished with Wade, you and I are going to have a chat."

Gil turned away, feeling the need to give her a touch of privacy as he flipped the phone open. "This better be important."

"What's the matter, Gil, did I interrupt something? Busy giving it to Fallon—I mean, the phone to Fallon?"

"Cute. Now what's up?" he asked, tugging his jeans up over his hips. He had to bite back a groan as the material brushed against his cock, pumping more blood into the shaft. Damn, now was not the time for another hard-on, especially if he was going to have to talk to Fallon. He didn't need her to see how badly he really needed her.

"Nothing much. I just single-handedly figured out how our friend, *the Priest,* is calling your girl."

"It might be wise if you didn't let Fallon hear you describe her in those terms. Not if you want to keep all your body parts intact..." Though he had to admit, he liked the sound of it. "So what's the story with the phone?"

"Well it seems that in the olden days...you know, when *you* first joined up with the Bureau...and cell phones weren't quite the fashion statement they are now, they had a phone designated for CB calls. Anyone who had one could tune in a certain frequency and ring this phone in the centre. Of course, that technology is pretty old school, and most truckers and the like all have cells now, so they just dial nine-one-one instead. But according to the records, the phone's still connected as a backup measure."

"That's very interesting, and I appreciate the history lesson, but what has that got to do with Fallon? She's using a cell, not a CB."

"I was just getting to that part. Geez, Gil. Don't take all the fun out of this. Anyway, it seems when Jane called Fallon that first night, she used the old CB phone to make the call. She said she didn't want their conversation to be recorded. I took that to mean they were talking about sex. But apparently, in her efforts to get the damn thing to dial out, she inadvertently forwarded the line."

"So when Fallon picked up…"

"Any incoming calls for that phone were sent on to her cell."

"Wade, are you trying to tell me our serial killer is calling Fallon using a CB radio?"

"Maybe not a CB exactly, but some type of handheld transmitter tuned to the old emergency frequency. Quite brilliant, really. Not only is his call not recorded, but it's harder than hell to trace, especially now that it's being forwarded to a cell. It'll jump off a few repeaters in the process."

"Damn."

"Yeah. I just thought you'd want to know, so you can decide where we go from here."

"Where we go?"

"Yeah, you know. Whether you want me to cancel the call forwarding so the calls come into the centre instead of going to Fallon's cell."

Gil frowned. He hadn't really thought about that. It seemed more logical, but then his reason for seeing Fallon would disappear, and he'd have to face the reality of his feelings for her. Damn, it wasn't a fair decision. He cursed under his breath and glanced back at Fallon over his shoulder just in time to see her ride into the trees, her bike barely visible in the growing dark.

"Damn it, Fallon! Fuck."

"Everything okay?"

"What? Ah, shit." He raked his fingers through his hair, scanning the ground for his T-shirt. Instead he found her cut-up tank and his ripped pullover. *Great, she took my T-shirt.*

"Hey, Gil? You still there? Do you want me to change the phone?"

"Just leave it the way it is. There's no one at the centre better qualified to take the calls than Fallon, anyway. Besides, the bastard might not be too pleased if we make him talk to someone else. Better to keep Fallon on it. At least she'll keep us in the loop."

"And give you a reason to keep close tabs on hers... sounds like a good plan to me."

"Wade..."

"Easy, Gil. I'm only teasing. I've heard nothing but great things about *your girl* since I got here. I was going to suggest we keep her involved as well."

His girl. Damn, he wished that were true. But he had a bad feeling she was going to be even less thrilled to see him next time. Maybe he needed to work on his technique, though he'd thought she'd been more than happy with his performance.

"Okay. I'll head back over to the precinct and pick you up."

"What, no plans?"

"Oh, I've got plans. Plans of heading back to the office to go over the new crime scene photos. We can pick up some Chinese on the way."

"We?"

"I'll be there in forty minutes. Don't keep me waiting."

Gil slammed the phone shut and stared at where the trail wove down to the parking lot. If he hurried, he might be able to catch her before she drove off. But if he caught up with her, they'd have to talk, and he didn't quite know what to say...yet.

"Okay, Fallon. I'll let you go this time, but don't think you'll escape so easily the next time I've got you beneath me." He smiled at the thought. "And there will be a next time, darling."

Chapter Eight

Fallon sat by the window, watching the rain streak down the glass. She'd managed to strap her bike on the back of her Jeep and jump behind the wheel before the sky had opened up and poured the tears she'd refused to shed. Even now she sat silently in the dark, her heart numb, her fingers clenched together on her lap. She tried to lose herself in the rhythm of the rain, knowing if she thought about Gil her control would snap, and she'd end up weeping on the floor. Or worse, she'd call his cell and beg him to fuck her again.

"Damn you," she snarled, fighting the urge to throw the mug at her feet across the floor. She'd banished herself to the back window bench once she'd showered and paced the living room floor until she was sure she'd worn a path in the wood. What the hell had she done?

She sighed and leant her head against the glass. She'd spread her thighs wide and practically begged Gil to fuck her.

I want you to lick me until I come… I want you to fuck me until I can't stand up.

She cursed the taunting voice in her head. Okay, so she'd begged. Either way it didn't change the facts. She'd slept with him—*twice*—thrust her pussy into his mouth, felt his fingers stroke her ass, cried out as he'd pumped his cum inside her over and over…

Fallon gasped and sat up, kicking the mug across the cold wood. He'd come inside her, and he hadn't used a condom.

"Oh God."

She felt the world spin as the realisation rocked through her. She panicked, not sure how she found herself staring at the calendar on the fridge. Somehow she'd moved, but she couldn't remember the path to the kitchen. She frowned at the insignificant thoughts, brushing them away with a flick of her wrist as she scanned the dates. She'd had her period…

"Fuck!" She shook her head, counting the days again. "Great. Just fucking great!" Her voice bounced off the cabinets, but she didn't care. She needed to yell, to scream at the injustice her life had become. For two years she'd taken the pill, faithfully ensuring their lives weren't disturbed by any mistake either of them would end up regretting. But shortly after Gil's departure, she'd developed headaches and had stopped taking the damn thing at her doctor's request.

At the time, it hadn't seemed to matter. No sex, no problem. But now here she was, up the proverbial creek without a paddle. Sure, she wanted kids, and the thought of carrying Gil's child inside her made her knees weak and her stomach flip-flop. But they weren't *together*. One romp in the hay, or two on the ground, wasn't a relationship, and she sure as hell wasn't going to use getting pregnant as a way of getting him back.

She sank down in a chair and tried a deep, soothing breath. Maybe she was one of those women who'd have to try for years to get pregnant? Maybe Gil and she weren't a good match, genetically speaking? Maybe…

The feeling came upon her in a sudden rush of grey. It moved through her, extinguishing all thoughts and feelings. She fell forward, her hands instinctively bracing her fall, as the invisible cloud surrounded her, drawing her into its elusive mist. She struggled at first, scared at what images would greet her on the other side, but finally relented when the fog blurred into solid form, the outline of an altar appearing before her. She knew where she was, even if she didn't know which church it was. And she knew who had summoned her.

Fallon closed her eyes, hoping it was all a dream. She

didn't want to see another woman mangled and bloody, knowing any information she discovered would come too late to stop the woman's blood from running in tiny rivulets along the hard wooden floor. She didn't want the knowledge that even as she watched the scenes rush past her, she was helpless to change them. That she'd never see the man's face. Never stop the bastard from claiming his prey.

"Yes. Take it. Take all of it."

The words caught her by surprise and she forced her eyes open. She hadn't expected to see him until he'd opened the door, seeking his escape, as in her previous visions. But this one seemed different. She couldn't place what was out of sorts, but something was…missing.

"Let me cleanse the wickedness from your soul."

Fallon turned. A familiar sound echoed through the dark space, vibrating off the silent walls. She looked around, noting the intricate stained glass windows and arched walkways. This wasn't a broken-down building, like the last place. It was regal, and worthy of whatever God its clergy prayed to. The pews were polished, shining in the wavering light cast by the candles, and she could almost hear the soothing tones of a children's choir singing from behind the pulpit.

"Can you feel me?" the voice asked.

Fallon tensed as her gaze settled off to the right, where the altar had filled her vision upon her arrival. It was hidden in the shadows and she found herself inching towards it, hating each step but needing to see what was happening. The sound grew stronger, wet slick sounds that made the hairs on her neck tingle. She recognised it now for what it was—someone was fucking. A male groan rumbled through the air and the wet sounds grew faster.

She cringed, not sure why she was here. She'd expected to find a woman spread across the hard wood, her body carved, her eyes dull, unseeing. Perhaps this was a dream?

"Yes. You want it, don't you?"

She stopped, unable to turn away from the scene before her. A man, his pants pushed down to his thighs, his ass pumping steadily back and forth. He held the woman's feet around his waist, keeping her open for him, her knees bent against her chest. His face was turned away from her, but she could tell by the grey hair laced amidst the blond, it was him…*the Priest*.

Fallon stepped closer, but no matter which way she moved, his face was never visible. It was part of her curse. She'd never been able to see anyone's face except the victims. And those haunted her dreams.

She stopped moving and watched the man rape the woman, his cock sliding in and out of her pussy, glistening with the woman's cream, as it left her body before plunging back in. The woman's eyes were open, but they were dull. Not dead, but not seeing. He'd drugged her, or tortured her to the point she'd retreated inside herself, already gone but still breathing. Either way, it eased some of the fear from Fallon's chest. At least the woman wouldn't die knowing she'd been used in such a manner. The man didn't seem to care. He watched only her cunt, commenting on the wetness of it and how warm and plump it was as he cleansed the demons from her soul. Fallon watched as his thrusts increased, a tension bunching the muscles in his thighs. He was close.

"Yes. Take my seed and let it purge the evil from your soul!"

Fallon flinched at the righteousness in his voice, as if he truly believed he was saving the woman. His body went rigid, his hips grinding into the woman's pelvis as the air hissed from his chest in steady pants. He was still coming and Fallon only wished she could strike now, while he was most vulnerable. But all she could do was watch the images flow around her, alternating between their solid and semi-transparent forms. Her presence here was tentative, and she wondered how long she'd be able to stay.

"Now, you're clean." He pulled out and sighed as he

tucked his cock back inside his pants and fastened them around his waist. Then he took his knife and placed it at the woman's throat. "Rejoice in your purity as you move from this world to the next."

Fallon screamed and backed away, unable to draw her eyes away from the steady stream of blood flowing from the woman's neck. He hadn't sliced it open or mutilated it, but simply put a small hole in one side. The woman's body jerked once, and then stilled, her eyes still open, still staring at the ceiling.

"Oh God."

Heat fused through her, circling the room right, then left. Her body moved, and she knew she'd fallen to the floor. She thought she'd heaved, but only knew the feel of the wood beneath her hands, the rough play of fabric across her knees. She was crawling, but she didn't know where she was heading. A loud crack filled the room, dropping her to her stomach. The sound rolled through her head, pulling her down, sparking pain so fierce she heard her own cry fill the heavy air. She was dying. It was the only answer. The vision was killing her, as surely as the man had killed the woman. She reached out and wrapped her hands around a thin spindle as the world shifted again and launched her into the air.

"No!"

* * * *

Fallon moaned and grabbed her head, her stomach lurching as the floor dipped one way and then the other. Her phone blared off to her left, the music filling the empty air. She pulled herself over, not sure why she needed to answer it, only knowing she did. Somehow she found the strength to lift her body up and grab the small unit off the table. She opened it, her mind already aware of who was on the other end.

"Nine-one-one."

That's all she could say before the kitchen swirled again, threatening to throw her to the floor. She didn't know how she kept her body upright. It was unusual she was even conscious, always losing herself for hours after her visions. But somehow she held on, clearing her mind, fighting to keep the air flowing into her chest. She heard a man breathe into the phone, and tensed.

"Hello, Angel."

She cringed at the sexual tone to his voice, as if they were lovers. And while she'd never seen his face, she knew the smile that curved his lips. It was smug, but with a hint of regret, like killing the woman had taken a toll on his soul. But he'd done it just the same. She tried to pull herself up, inject some authority into her words, but any motion set off fireworks in her head, and it took all her strength not to moan. "Priest."

He chuckled as she spoke his name. The sound sent a cold shiver down her spine. "I love that you know the sound of my voice, Angel. It's like we're connected."

Fallon's stomach heaved again, and she had to beat the feeling down. She wouldn't fail the woman…not again. "I'm sure you'd feel that way with whoever answered the phone. I suppose I've just been lucky."

The Priest growled, and for a moment, she thought she'd made a mistake. "I told you before that you're destined for this, *Angel!* It's your voice, so soft and deep. It's like listening to the heavens sing. I won't talk to another, Angel. Only you."

Her throat constricted around her next breath, and she had to force herself to inhale through her nose. She wanted to talk to him, but the grey feeling was returning, threatening to draw her back into his world. She closed her eyes, willing the vision away.

"What's the matter, Angel? Don't you want to talk to me?"

She nodded, forcing a hushed, "Yes," from her lips.

"Good. You know, it's funny. I feel as if I know you, like

I've seen you before. I can imagine your eyes, so full of compassion and understanding. I bet they're blue, Angel. Am I right?" He laughed, the sound cold and calculating. "You don't have to answer me. I'll know…in time."

"What do you mean?"

"Nothing. Don't worry, Angel."

"But it sounds as if you think I need to be…cleansed." She struggled around the word, hoping he wouldn't hear her revulsion. She needed to keep his trust until Gil could catch his sorry ass.

He paused, the sound of his breath the only noise filling her head. "But then who would I talk too?"

His question sounded real, sincere. But there was something in his voice that made her wonder if there'd come a time when he wouldn't *need* someone to talk to. And then what? She tried to ask him, but only a faint whimper came out.

"I like talking to you," he continued. "You soothe me. Help me hold off the need…at least for a while. I—I don't *want* to hurt you."

But he would, if his demons demanded it. She could hear it in her head as surely as if he'd spoken the words aloud. She forced herself to swallow, hoping the saliva would ease the dry feeling in her throat. "I don't want that either. I like talking to you, too." It was a lie, but she hoped maybe the idea would *soothe* him further. Maybe keep him from killing another woman for a few more days.

"Then I'll have to call you again. But first, you need to know where to send the police. It's by the river, southwest district, very ornate. I think you'd like it. She's waiting there for them. Until next time, Angel…"

"Wait! Can't we talk a bit more? I'd like to know more about you."

"All in good time. But I've lingered too long as it is. And I wouldn't want you to give me any reason to change my opinion of you, Angel." He grunted then. "I don't like to be betrayed."

Fallon listened to the words followed closely by the whine of the phone. He wanted her to advertise his work, but he didn't want her to give any information that might get him caught. He was hanging on the edge, and she feared his desperation to cleanse his own demons was strengthening.

She disconnected the line and stared at the phone, watching it blur and shimmy against her hand. The visions were still pulling at her, but she focused on dialling the number, pressing each button in sequence. She couldn't let them take her, not until after she'd talked to Gil. Her stomach rolled in protest and she sucked in a deep breath to keep the bile from rising in her throat. They were hovering just outside her reach, but she was managing to keep them there, a first for her. That's when it hit her.

"Oh my God."

Now she remembered why the vision had seemed different. It'd happened before the call, before *the Priest* had any connection to her. She closed her eyes and concentrated on the ringing sound. She wouldn't admit what was screaming in her head. Their link was gathering strength. Her powers were emerging.

* * * *

Gil sat at his chair, staring down at the pictures he'd arranged on his desk. Eight women now. And if *the Priest* had his way, more would join their ranks. Gil cursed and pressed his head against his palms. He'd been staring at the damn things for hours, ever since he'd picked up Wade at the precinct. And the fact he hadn't touched them in the last fifteen minutes was just another indication his mind wasn't on his job.

Fallon.

Her name filled his mind, echoing through him until all he could see was the image of her face. He'd stopped on the way to the station for a quick shower and a change of clothes, not wanting Wade to throw more lewd comments about his relationship, or lack of, with Fallon. And showing up with the scent of her juices clinging to his jeans, and his shirt ripped down to his chest, was not the sort of action that would keep Wade off his back. The man seemed relentless. Even now Gil could feel him staring at him, trying to figure out what demons Gil was fighting. Or what ravenous thoughts he was conjuring up.

He didn't need any help thinking about Fallon. She was all he'd thought about since she'd scurried off like a frightened rabbit. While he didn't mind playing the part of the big, bad wolf, the least she could have done was call him to let him know she'd made it home okay.

Yeah, like she's going to call you. All she thinks you want from her is a quick, hard fuck.

He huffed at the thought, ignoring the way Wade's eyes flicked in his direction. He'd never been really good at vocalising his feelings. Sure, he could toss out an 'I love you,' at a moment's notice, but really telling someone how much they meant to him was about as easy as catching this bastard was turning out to be. His chest just got too tight, and the words seemed to get stuck in his throat. He'd always relied on Fallon's sensitivity to read into his actions what he hadn't been able to tell her.

But all that had changed the moment he'd walked out their door and never returned, leaving only his set of keys as any explanation as to what had happened. She'd called his cell a few times after, but those had stopped quickly when he'd chosen to ignore them. Fallon might have loved him, but she'd known when to back away, and he knew she'd never show him how much he'd hurt her. She was far too stubborn and proud for that.

He sighed, wishing to hell he knew what to do. He wanted to call her, but he knew she'd hang up on him, if she even bothered to answer the phone. And somehow dropping by her place didn't seem like a good idea. He'd be able to smell her again, and he knew what would happen if he got even a whiff of her scent. He'd ruin another one of her shirts when he ripped it from her body, along with whatever she had on the bottom. God, he hoped she'd be bare on the bottom. Nothing would stop him from dragging her to the floor and pressing inside her soft, wet heat until the emptiness left him and he rode her until neither one of them could walk this time. He obviously hadn't drained enough of her strength if she was able to ride her bike down the trail, though he'd noticed how shaky she was on it.

Yeah, he'd certainly screwed things up. Now all he could do was sit there and trace the inside of his mouth with his tongue, searching for the lingering flavour of her creamy juice. He'd often dreamed of tasting her again, and now that he had, he was obsessed with having more. Always more with her. He'd never been able to get enough, and his hunger was only becoming stronger.

"Why don't you just call her?"

Gil shook his head and turned towards Wade. He'd heard the man's voice but hadn't a clue what he'd said. "What?"

Wade chuckled. "You're not going to accomplish anything here when your mind's a thousand miles away. Or at least thirty miles away. Why don't you just call it a night? And call Fallon while you're at it."

"Who says I'm thinking about her?" he challenged.

"Partner, you've got it so bad for that girl, I can see her name inscribed on your forehead." Wade smiled and leant back in his chair. "Stop worrying about your pride and make the first move. I'm sure with a little grovelling and a lot of sweet words, she'll be back in your bed in no time."

Gil snarled. *She's already been back in my bed,* he thought, trying not to show Wade he'd been too close to the truth. Only it hadn't been his bed, it'd been the damn clearing on the trail, and he couldn't quite remember saying, 'I'm sorry', let alone anything remotely sweet.

Push inside again and bring me more of your sweet honey.

Okay, so he'd mentioned her pussy was sweet—a number of times—but he didn't think that held the same weight as telling her how pretty she was, or how much he'd missed her. Or better still, the truth.

Something rattled in his coat, but Gil ignored it. He was too caught up remembering the sights and scents of Fallon's body. How her nipples had puckered against her skin, pointing straight out from her body. Her breasts weren't overly large, but they were firm and responsive and he never got tired of licking and suckling them. It was like sipping ripe, smooth berries into his mouth. And her skin, he'd never felt anything as soft and smooth. Every inch was creamy white and felt like fine silk beneath his fingers. Even her pussy was like that now, and he had to bite back another groan when he remembered how she'd declared no other had touched her, fucked her, since he'd left. He'd been the first to touch that smooth cunt, running his tongue up and down the plump lips until her taste was all he knew. Until his cock got so hard he'd thought the damn thing was going to explode in his pants.

"Hey, Gil."

He had to have her again. Needed to know she wanted him as much as he wanted, no needed, her. Damn, Wade was right.

"Gil!"

Gil turned and scowled at Wade. Didn't the man ever give up? "What?" He didn't bother to hide his irritation. His cock was hard again—still—just thinking about Fallon, and he wasn't quite sure how he was going to convince the little vixen she was the only one who could give him the relief he sought.

"Aren't you going to get that?"

Gil's scowl deepened. He had no idea what Wade was talking about. "Get what?"

Wade's expression turned slightly serious, like he was suddenly worried about Gil's mental state. Well good, because Gil was worried too. His unexpected reunion with Fallon had knocked most of his good sense right out the window and left nothing but the need to claim her behind.

"Your phone. It's rung three times already."

As if to prove Wade's claim, the phone rang again. Gil cursed and stuffed his hand into his pocket, fishing the damn thing out. He couldn't imagine who'd be calling him. He was already at work, for God's sake. It rang again and he stared at the number, feeling the air leave his lungs.

Fallon.

Even if it hadn't flashed her name across the screen, he'd have recognised the number. Her number, the one they'd shared. He flipped it open, not sure how to answer the call. "So, darling, are you finally getting tired of playing hide and seek? Or were you calling to give me a hint?" He smiled as the words popped into his head. He didn't want her to think he'd been sitting around pining for her.

Gil listened but could only hear her breathing on the other end. He sat up, a tingle of fear prickling down his spine. "Fallon?"

She whispered his name, a low moan following the sad sound.

"Fallon? What's wrong? Are you hurt?"

"Gil." He heard her sob once before she sighed into the phone.

Gil stood up, his jacket grasped in his other hand. Wade scraped his chair back and Gil knew the man was already heading to the door. "Just stay put. We're on our way."

"No, Gil. Wait." She sobbed again, but he couldn't tell if she was in pain or just sad. "*The Priest*. Another woman... Oh God, my head hurts."

"Fallon, honey, I need to know if you're okay. Did someone hurt you?" Fear gripped him as new images sprang to life. "Oh, God. Did *he* hurt you?"

"No. I'm...I'm fine. The girl... Oh Gil, there was so much blood. She was alive, but then..."

Her voice trailed off and Gil fought the urge to stomp his foot on the floor. Fallon was obviously overwhelmed by her last conversation with the creep and he needed to stay calm if he had any chance of helping her. "Just talk slowly, darling. Where is the woman?"

"A church. Southwest side, near the river. Lots of stained glass… He killed her. I…"

Fallon broke into another sob followed by a loud moan. Damn, Gil didn't know what was going on. She sounded hurt, but she'd said she was fine. "Fallon. Are you okay?"

"My head hurts. Just find her." Her voice faded again, but she returned. "I'm fine. I have to go."

Gil cursed as the phone went dead in his ear. "Damn it!" He headed for the door, pulling on his jacket as he went. "The bastard struck again. Some church over by the river. We'll have to call dispatch and see if they can give us some possible locations."

"Is Fallon okay? Do you want me to have them send a unit over to her house?"

Gil shook his head, dodging the puddles as he ran for his truck. "She insisted she's fine. We'll stop by after we check out the scene." He heard a chuckle and was surprised to discover it'd come from him. "Fallon doesn't like people codling her. She has this image that she's bulletproof. If I send anyone over, there'll be no reasoning with her later. And I have a feeling we need to have a long chat with her. She's hiding something from me, and I plan on finding out what the something is."

Chapter Nine

Fallon woke to a loud pounding in her head. She closed her eyes and willed the damn thing away. She needed to sleep, but the noise kept banging. Her eyes fluttered open again, adjusting to the dark, when she realised she was sleeping on the kitchen floor. She sat up, feeling the room sway as the noise sounded again.

"Damn it, Fallon. Open the damn door!"

She flinched and glanced at the clock. It was just past twelve. Three hours since she'd called Gil and sent him in search of the woman she'd watched die. But she felt as if she'd only been resting a few moments. The intensity of the visions was getting stronger, and she seemed to need more time to recover after each one.

"Fallon!"

She sighed and forced herself up, hoping she didn't face plant onto the floor, and slowly made her way to the door. Gil was still pounding on it when she released the lock and swung it open, using its strength to hold herself up.

"What the hell took you so long?" Gil's voice was dark and deep, and Fallon recognised the tone. He was angry, and maybe a bit scared.

She sighed and stepped back, knowing he'd push past her if she didn't make any space. "I was sleeping."

Gil and Wade walked through the doorway, stopping several feet inside. "You were always a light sleeper, Fallon. It's not like you to sleep through the noise."

She shrugged, ignoring the heavy weight of his stare. He looked hungry, but not for food. "Things change." She swayed a bit as the room flip-flopped once and then settled.

Gil grabbed her arm but released it when she tensed in his hold. "It's pretty late. Shouldn't you guys be trying to get some sleep?"

"You sounded hurt on the phone. I wanted to make sure you were okay."

Fallon hid her surprise. Why should he care how she was when he hadn't for the past six months? "I just have a bad headache." It wasn't a lie. Her head felt like someone had used it as a chopping block. "Did you find the church?"

Gil's face paled slightly, and Fallon felt the room sway again. She knew what he'd had to face when he'd walked inside that place. She'd already been there. "Yeah. We found it." Gil stepped back and leaned against a small table. "We need to ask you about the call. It might help the investigation if we knew exactly what this guy says to you."

Her stomach dropped as she closed the door, once again leaning against it in the hopes of staying on her feet. While she didn't feel the vision trying to pull her under anymore, the memory of seeing the girl die was still vivid in her mind. She didn't want to remember that. "I'm really tired. And my head still hurts. Couldn't we wait until morning?"

Gil's eyes narrowed as he gave her a long, slow sweep. If it'd been anyone else, she would've sworn he was merely assuring himself she was okay. But the way Gil did it—with half-lidded eyes and a small tilt to his lips—she felt as if he was assessing her stamina. Trying to determine if she was up to a hard night of fucking. "If we wait until morning, you might forget some of the details. And right now, we need all the help we can get." He moved a step towards her, his eyes once again lingering on the length of her body. She watched him pause at the vee of her thighs and again at her breasts, dampening the inside of his lips as he finally looked up and met her gaze. The fire she saw in his eyes purged whatever breath was left in her chest. "It won't take that long."

Fallon stared into his eyes. He'd spoken again, but she was too caught up in the way his mouth moved when he talked to really hear his words. His lips were perfect. Full and pink and she remembered how they'd felt on her breasts and between her legs. God, what she wouldn't give to feel them there again. Have them wrapped around her nipples, sucking with just the right amount of pressure so that she'd feel every motion mirrored in her pussy, making it weep with joy. Then he'd move lower and kiss each plump lip of her sex in worship before driving his tongue inside her and lapping away her cream.

She shifted, vaguely aware of the slick slide of her lips against her pants. She'd thrown on a pair of sweats after her shower, and the lack of panties was brushing the soft fabric against her engorged cunt, sending sparks of pleasure into her core. She still had on Gil's T-shirt, having grabbed it instead of the ripped tank, and could feel her nipples pushing against the thin lace of her bra. They were hard and thick and she knew the men could see them pressed against the thin cotton.

Fallon took a deep breath, startled by the way Gil watched her chest rise and fall. His breathing seemed laboured and she couldn't help but notice the way his hands were fisted at his side. She chanced a glance at his groin, but his shirt was loose around his jeans, hiding any evidence he was as aroused as she was. But just the thought of his cock hard and thick beneath the denim made her mouth water. He hadn't allowed her to taste him, or hell, even touch him, and she wanted nothing more than to slip her lips around his shaft, feeling it pulse and thicken in her mouth. It'd seemed like an eternity since she'd savoured the sweet, salty musk of his cum, and she had the sudden urge to drop to her knees and take what she'd been denied. He'd always loved the way she'd sucked him, and she was confident she'd have his instant attention once her mouth was wrapped around his flesh.

"Fallon?"

She gave herself a mental shake. He'd asked to talk and was waiting for her answer. But she knew she had to put off his questions until tomorrow. If he stayed any longer, she'd just as soon push him to the floor and ride him into oblivion as give him the answers he sought. Even the thought of Wade watching her didn't stem the need building inside.

She sighed and walked past the two men, stopping near the kitchen door. She really was tired, and her head still throbbed from her vision. Surely Gil wouldn't insist on staying if she made him understand how bad she felt. "I'd love to help you guys out, and I promise I won't forget a single detail, but I really am tired and I think I'll be able to give you a better account of the conversation once my head clears. So if you don't mind..."

She waved at the door, hoping they'd get the hint. Wade glanced over at Gil, and then back at her. "I understand how disturbing this must have been for you, but..." Wade didn't get to finish as Gil stepped forward, his arms crossed over his chest.

"All right, Fallon. What's going on?"

Fallon flashed him her best innocent smile. "What do mean? Nothing's going on. I'm just tired and would like to get rid of this headache before we talk."

Gil shook his head taking another step closer. "Nice try, darling, but I'm not buying it. You're way too stubborn to use an excuse as lame as being tired. And pain's never stopped you before. So why don't you cut the act and just tell us what's going on?" He narrowed his eyes on her. "I know you're hiding something."

Fallon felt her face flush but ignored it. Why the hell he'd chosen now to be so damn observant she had no idea, but two could play that game. "I'm not hiding anything. What gives you the right to question my motives?" She crossed her arms beneath her breasts and straightened her shoulders. She was several inches shorter than both men, but she wasn't about to let them intimidate her. "Now if you don't mind..." She turned to go.

"Running away again?" taunted Gil.

Fallon stopped and spun around. "Running away? You

actually have the audacity to stand there and accuse *me* of running away? This from a man who left his keys on the table and took all his stuff while I was at work, all because you didn't want to have to talk to me!" Her voice had risen into a yell, but she didn't care. If Gil wanted to fight, she was more than up for it. "At least I answered the damn door, which is more than I can say for you!"

Gil clenched his jaw and stuffed his hands in his pockets. She could tell he was holding himself back, but it didn't matter. She'd crossed the line and there was no turning back. He took one step towards her. "Okay. I get your point. You're angry. But do you really want to talk about this now? It's not exactly the best time." He nodded towards Wade, making the man shuffle his feet.

Fallon ignored Wade and faced Gil head-on. "That's the problem, Gil. It was never a good time to discuss anything with you. Every time I tried, all you ever did was pull back and hide behind your job." She took a deep breath and said what she'd been thinking for six months. "Charlie died, Gil. But it might as well have been you, because you've been dead to the world ever since."

Gil stared at her, the vein in his temple pulsing with each beat of his heart. She thought for a moment he was going to turn and leave, but then he sighed and raked a shaky hand through his hair. "So you do want to talk about this now." He crossed his arms and pushed his shoulders back. "All right, Fallon. Let's talk."

Fallon snorted and threw her hands up in the air. He just didn't get it. "You know what? There's really nothing left to talk about. I got your message loud and clear when you left without a word and refused to even pick up your cell. Not to mention the couple of times I went to your apartment only to discover you weren't home." Oh, he'd been home, he just hadn't answered the door. "You wanted a life without complications. Where your job was the only thing you gave a damn about. Well, it looks like you got it. But sue me for not sharing in your devotion."

Oh, and the next time you want to fuck, go fuck yourself!

The words filled her head and she had to snap her back teeth together to keep from blurting them out. While a part of her wanted to hurt him with them, she knew they'd be a lie. She'd been more than willing.

Fallon glared back at him, channelling her anger into her stare, a triumphant smile touching her lips when she saw him flinch. "And for the record, you owe me a new cycling shirt." She turned but stopped before she'd taken a step, glancing back at both men over her shoulder. "On second thought, forget it. I've learnt to live through disappointment."

Gil watched Fallon storm into the kitchen, grabbing a handful of bottles out of the fridge before slamming it shut and stomping her way out to the porch. The air was cold and damp, but he had a feeling she wouldn't even notice it.

"Feisty little vixen, isn't she?" said Wade, his voice tinted with humour. "Damn, Gil. You sure pissed her off. Wouldn't want to be in your shoes tonight."

Gil could only shake his head. He didn't really want to be in his shoes either. "I'd be real careful with what I said right now, if I were you, Junior. Fallon won't hesitate to launch any handy object at anyone who ventures through that door, so don't think she'll pull any punches just for you."

Wade sauntered up beside him, still staring at the door Fallon had nearly slammed off its hinges. "Couldn't help but notice she's wearing a shirt exactly like the one you had on earlier." He looked Gil in the eyes. "Don't tell me you went straight for the nasty before grovelling at her feet and begging for forgiveness?" Wade moaned when Gil raised his eyebrow in challenge. "Gee whiz, Gil. Haven't you learnt anything hanging around a chick magnet like me?" Wade shook his head. "At least tell me you made it good for her."

"I don't see how that is any of your business, *partner*. But I'll have you know, she screamed my name so loud the fucking earth shook."

Wade smiled and it was all Gil could do not to smack the grin off his partner's face. He wasn't one to brag, but Wade's taunting was getting to him. Maybe because the man understood Fallon better than he did. And that thought alone was enough to ignite a blaze in his chest. He didn't know how to handle Fallon, or this…thing…they had between them. Great sex was one thing, but he knew she needed more. And he didn't know if he was capable of giving that to her. She was right. He'd been dead ever since Charlie had died.

Gil sighed and leant back against the table. He hadn't expected Fallon to get so emotional, and he wasn't quite sure how to proceed. It hadn't helped that she'd been wearing his shirt. Just watching her breasts press against the cotton had made his mouth water. He'd suckled those breasts just a few hours ago, and his cock had only got harder at the sight of her perky little nipples poking out at him. Thank God he'd had the good sense to leave his shirt hanging loose to hide his growing erection. The last thing he needed was Wade teasing him about having a hard-on.

"So what do we do now?" asked Wade. "She may be small, but I wouldn't want to face her in a showdown."

Gil smiled. He'd always loved Fallon's passion, even when he was on the wrong end of it. "We go and talk to her. Just try not to say anything else to piss her off. I meant what I said before. She's a wildcat."

"Don't worry about me. I plan on keeping my mouth shut until you've taken the brunt of her anger. I may be younger than you, but I'm not stupid."

Gil glared at him as he walked through the kitchen. "Just look sincere and be ready to make a hasty retreat if she grabs one of those bottles."

Chapter Ten

Fallon was curled up on a patio chair, chugging a cooler, when the sliding door opened. She sneered into the bottle, wondering if she should just throw the damn thing across the porch, before deciding against it. Knowing Gil, he'd sent Wade out first in the hopes the man might soothe some of her temper. But there was little chance in that. Arguing with Gil had brought back all the months she'd spent agonising over what had gone wrong. Why Gil had refused to talk to her, to share his pain. Why she'd promised herself she'd never get involved with him again.

So I guess fucking him doesn't count as getting 'involved'.

She cursed the voice and knocked back another gulp. Maybe she could get drunk and forget the whole thing?

"Fallon? We need to talk."

Damn. Gil hadn't sent his partner in ahead. He'd chosen to face her, and she wasn't quite sure what he was up to. She glanced at him over the edge of her drink but said nothing.

Gil sighed and took a step forward. He looked reluctant to get too close to her. *Good!* She didn't want him close. He was too tempting in his faded jeans and cocky half-smile. And she'd already caught the scent of his cologne on the breeze drifting through the trees. It was a mixture of spice and pine, and it was all she could do to keep her ass in the chair instead of pouncing on him like a hungry animal. Even angry and hurt, she wanted him. But it wasn't just the sex. She needed to confide in him. Share her secret. But he'd only laugh, or worse, turn away. And she didn't think her heart was up to another disappointment.

"Fallon."

"There's nothing to say," she said, tipping the bottle up, needing to drown her pain in the cold liquid.

Gil moved forward and placed his hand over hers, gently lowering the bottle. "The alcohol won't help, darling. Believe me. I've tried."

Fallon stared at where his hand touched hers, trying to ignore the heat that flowed between them. It was as if her body was tuned to his, always accepting and ready. He simply needed to touch her, and her juices collected along her slit, preparing her body for his penetration.

She pulled her hand away, spilling some of the drink on her arm. "I believe I asked you to leave."

She watched Gil sigh, stepping back from her. "We need to know what *the Priest* said to you. Just tell us about the conversation, and we'll leave."

"Don't you think I'd tell you if he'd given me anything remotely useful? Do you really think I enjoy being part of his little masquerade?" The image of the bastard raping the woman flashed in her head and she turned away. There were aspects she hadn't shared, but she knew they'd never believe her.

Gil stepped back over to her and knelt down. "No. And I know you wouldn't hold back anything you thought was important. But we've got nothing to go on. And sometimes the small details are the ones that mean the most."

"Meaning…"

"Meaning, maybe you know more than you think."

Fallon huffed and stared out at the night. The rain had passed, but the clouds were still thick and dark. "What do your profilers think?"

Gil shrugged and stood back up. "Nothing other than the usual. Caucasian male anywhere between twenty-five and forty. Sexually assaulted as a kid, probably hates his mother and is trying to make his mark as a man by carving up women."

"That's it?" she asked.

"It may be slightly transparent, but it's all we've got."

Fallon shook her head and took another drink. The Bureau was so far off on this guy, it was no wonder they didn't have a clue how to track him down.

"What's the matter?" asked Gil. "Disagree with the profile?"

She snorted and looked up at him. "Other than you've got it all wrong, not really."

Gil smiled at her and crossed his arms over his chest. "Think you can do better?"

Fallon rolled her eyes and looked away. "Let's start with the fact that the guy is much older, say mid-fifties, and that this has nothing to do with his mother."

"Is that so? And what makes you so sure?"

Fallon sighed, so damn tired she blurted out the truth before she had time to consider the consequences. "Because most psychos don't rape their victims if they think they're their mother."

She barely had time to gasp before Gil crossed the small space and lifted her from the chair. He locked his hands around her shoulders, giving a firm shake that made her head spin. "How do you know that? Did the bastard tell you?" Her head bobbed again as he shook her even harder. "Damn it, Fallon. What the hell is going on? First you talk about all the blood at the scene and how the church has stained glass windows. And now you know he rapes his victims before he kills them. How do you know all this?"

"Easy, Gil." Wade was at Gil's side, trying to pry his fingers off her shoulders. But she could only glance at him before Gil shook her again.

"Answer me, Fallon!" Gil shouted. "We didn't tell anyone outside the Bureau. So how do you know?"

"I…"

"He told you over the phone?" prompted Gil.

"No…I…"

"How?"

Tears stung her eyes and fell down her cheeks before she could blink them away. She'd never seen Gil so upset, other than the first day in the hospital when he'd regained consciousness and realised Charlie hadn't made it. Her shoulders felt numb where he'd clenched his hands around them, and her head was still spinning. She met his stare, watching something flicker across his expression as she drew a deep breath. "I saw him."

Gil released her, whether because she'd answered him, or he'd finally noticed she was crying, she didn't know. But as soon as his hands fell away from her shoulders, she backed up, putting as much space as she could between them.

Gil watched from the edge of the porch, his expression unforgiving. "What do you mean, you saw him? You were at the scene?"

"Yes, no." She sighed and crossed her arms around her chest. She felt cold and vulnerable and didn't want Gil to see how badly her hands were shaking. She looked up at him. "You won't believe me."

"Whether I believe you or not isn't the issue here. Now explain what you meant by, you saw him."

Fallon huffed and couldn't resist stomping one foot on the floor. "What good is explaining everything if you think I'm crazy? Can't you just accept what I tell you without questioning it?"

"You know I can't. Now quit stalling."

Another tear tracked down her skin, but she didn't have the strength to wipe it away. She took a deep breath and stared at the floor as she spoke. "I was at the church, but not in the way you think. I have...visions."

Both men stifled moans, and she could only close her eyes. She'd known they wouldn't believe in her ability. Hell, she sometimes wondered herself.

"You have visions?" asked Gil.

Fallon nodded and forced herself to meet his glare. She could see the uncertainty in his eyes, his doubt mirrored in the twitch of his hands. "Yes, Gil. I have visions." She held up her hand, stopping any questions before he had a chance to speak. "Look, I know what you're both thinking, but I'm not crazy and I'm not making this up. I've had them before, but never this intense. Or with someone I don't know. They've always been with people I've had a personal connection with." She shook her head and stared at the floor again. "I don't really understand why it's happening."

Gil stood on the porch, silently watching Fallon toe the floor as she huddled against the wall. She looked lost and scared and he would've gone to her if she hadn't completely unnerved him. Visions? What the hell was she talking about? They'd been together for two years and she'd never mentioned anything about having visions.

He shifted his feet, not sure what to say to her. "Fallon."

Her head snapped up as his voice seemed to fill the night air. It'd sounded suspect in his own head, let alone how it must have sounded in hers. She glared at him and palmed her hips. "Don't even start with me," she sneered.

Gil took a step back, not sure what she thought he was intending to do. Hell, he was far too confused to think of anything remotely intelligent to say. He cleared his throat and hoped to hell he could sound convincing. "I wasn't going to *start* with you. I just don't quite understand what you're trying to tell us. Exactly what do you mean by *visions*?"

Fallon just snorted and shook her head, her eyes blazing with heat. If he didn't know she was furious with him, he'd have sworn she was aroused. She'd had the same black rage this afternoon when she'd begged him to fuck her. He sighed, wishing her intentions were more along those lines. Fucking he could deal with.

"Don't patronize me, Gil. It doesn't suit you."

"I'm not..."

"Visions!" she yelled at him, her hair bouncing across her shoulders as she stomped her way towards him. "Good, old-fashioned, full-fledged, lock-you-up-in-a-padded-cell visions! You know, the kind of stuff that makes you cringe whenever some lunatic saunters into your office and claims they've *seen* where the body is buried, or where some bastard has taken a kid. Those kinds of *visions*, Gil!"

He watched as she crossed her arms again and dared him to question her. Shit, she was mad. If it wasn't for the sick feeling rising in his stomach, he would've shoved her down and fucked her until she'd channelled all that energy into him. Lord knows he could use the distraction right now. But he could tell from the glint in her eyes, fucking him was the furthest thing from her mind.

Gil raised his hands, palms forward, compelled to show her he wasn't trying to fight with her. It seemed an inane gesture, but some of the tension eased from her brow and she lowered herself to the chair again. He stepped in front of her, keeping an arm's length away. "So you're saying you get images of the dead women?"

She looked up at him, exhaustion replacing the anger in her expression. "Not images. It's more like…" She paused as if searching for the right metaphor. "I'm watching a movie. I can see, hear and even smell, but I can't change anything…or help anyone," she added quietly. "I feel like a ghost."

"So you've seen the killer?" asked Wade.

Fallon jumped and turned her head towards the man. Her lips pulled tight, as if she'd forgotten the other man was still in the room. "No. It's part of the curse. I only get to really see the victims." She looked pleadingly at Gil. "But I can give you a more accurate description. He's tall, with blond hair and large shoulders. He seems to be in his late fifties…"

Wade nodded, though Gil could see the uncertainty in the man's face. "But you can't identify who's doing this?" interrupted Wade. "You've never seen his face?"

Fallon sighed and shook her head. "No."

The answer was soft and distant, and Gil knew Fallon had seen Wade's scepticism. Gil reached out and brushed his fingers along her shoulder. "Why don't you get some rest, and we can discuss this more tomorrow?"

"I'm not crazy. I know you both think I've lost it, but everything I've told you is true."

"I never said I didn't believe you." It wasn't a lie. He'd never said the words out loud, and he didn't think she could hear his thoughts. "I'm sure there's a reasonable explanation for everything you've experienced."

Fallon huffed and stood up. "Believe what you want." She grabbed the remaining bottles off the floor and headed to the doorway. Her shoulders sagged as she stopped and glanced back at him. "I've told you everything I know. I can't make you act on the information, but at least I'm not hiding it anymore. I can tell you that he told me talking to me helps him quiet his demons, so you should get a day or two reprieve." She looked over at Wade. "Gil knows the way out. Lock the door behind you."

Gil watched her leave, a tight feeling gripping his chest. He didn't know if it was the desolate look in her eyes or the pain that seemed to radiate from her body in visible waves, but the image of her small frame stepping through the kitchen door slammed a stake through his heart, resurrecting the love he'd buried. He'd forced her to reveal a secret she'd kept hidden for years, and then done little to soothe her fears.

"Well?" asked Wade, stepping over to his side. "What do you make of her claim?"

Gil shrugged his shoulders and stared at the empty space. "To be honest, I'm not sure. It's not like Fallon to make shit up, but…" But he didn't believe in psychics or mystics or whatever you called them. He'd always believed they were usually just desperate, lonely people who needed to feel valued. But Fallon?

Gil turned to Wade. "Let's let her rest until morning. Maybe she can explain it better then." He dug into his pocket and pulled out his keys. "Here. Take my truck and get some sleep. I'll call you in the morning for a pick-up."

Wade took the offering, a knowing smile kicking up the edges of his lips. "You're going to stay? You're braver than

I thought."

"I just don't think it's safe for her to be here alone. This bastard seems to be getting pretty attached to her, and I'm not convinced he'll be satisfied with just talking to her." He motioned towards the door with his hands.

Wade nodded and stepped into the kitchen. "Just do me a favour? Make sure you apologise before you seduce her this time, or I'll be the one getting visions," he crooned. "Of your death."

Gil sneered at his partner as the man bolted for the doorway and left the house. And while he'd never admit it to Wade, the man was starting to grow on him. Gil sighed and stared at the hallway off to his left. Fallon was probably tucking herself into her bed as he spoke—that or plotting his murder—either way, the image flickered in his mind and he smiled at the clarity of it. He could see her, his shirt still draping her body, only she'd be completely bare underneath. Her hair would be soft around her face and her skin would shimmer in the pale light filtering through the window. She'd smell warm and womanly, the faint trace of her perfume still lingering on her skin. She'd slide into the sheets, not bothering to pull the shirt down as it rose over her hips, exposing the curve of her buttocks and the vee of her thighs.

Bare.

He still couldn't believe she was bare. He'd loved that she'd kept her pubic hair short before, but having none at all was more than he'd hoped for. Feeling every inch of that undiscovered flesh with his tongue had been like opening the sweetest gift.

Gil felt his body move and had to grab the doorframe to stop himself from stalking down the hall and into her room. She needed space, and after all the times he'd pushed her away, it was the least he could do. He took one last glance and moved over to the couch.

Chapter Eleven

It was just past four as Gil lay on the couch, listening to the wind pelt rain against the window. He'd been trying to sleep for hours but just couldn't seem to quiet his mind long enough to drift off. He'd even found himself standing in the hallway a few times, staring at Fallon's closed door, but couldn't bring himself to open it. He kept remembering the pained look in her eyes when she'd asked them both to leave. Regardless of how he felt about her confession, he knew his reaction had hurt her.

Visions. He still wasn't sure what to make of it. Was she really serious? He sighed and closed his eyes, willing his body to relax. But it didn't work. His muscles clenched along his back, straining up his neck until he was forced to snap his teeth together. He was tired and frustrated and sporting an erection that just wouldn't die. Ever since he'd stepped into the house and sensed Fallon's sweet, womanly scent, he'd been hard and thick. Based on the ache between his legs, it wasn't going away any time soon.

"Maybe I should call nine-one-one," he jeered, squeezing his shaft in hopes of finding some relief. "Tell them I'm in need of emergency medical attention because my cock won't get soft."

He smiled, thinking about how the operators would deal with him, when a soft sound penetrated his haze. He straightened. There was a hushed shuffling noise followed by a gentle click.

Fallon's door.

Gil held his breath, waiting. The house was silent. He cursed, knowing she'd returned to her bed when a loud creak echoed down the hall, followed by a muted curse. Gil chuckled. The door had needed oiling several months ago, and it seemed Fallon hadn't got around to it after he'd left.

He eased his body back against the cushions, listening to the soft pad of her feet across the wood. She paused at the hallway, her startled gasp floating across the room. She'd obviously expected him to leave with Wade and hadn't planned on finding him sprawled out on her sofa.

He angled his head over and watched her lean against the wall. He smiled when he noticed she was still wearing his shirt, just as he'd envisioned. It hung just below the tops of her thighs, allowing him to see every inch of her legs but nothing of the bounty that awaited him beneath. He swept his gaze upwards. She'd crossed her arms beneath her breasts, pushing them against the fabric. Either she was cold or the sight of him on the couch had aroused her, because even several feet away he could see her nipples pointing out from the shirt. They looked long and hard, and he had to clench his fists into the cushions to keep from launching his body forward and ripping the damn shirt off her body. One taste was all it'd taken to renew his addiction and he had every intention on fulfilling his cravings.

Fallon sighed, drawing his attention to her face. She looked confused, and when she turned, he could see tears glistening in her eyes. He clenched his jaw and called to her as she turned to leave. "Trouble sleeping?"

She stopped, her hand resting against the wall, as she turned back to face him. "I thought you'd left with Wade."

Gil tried not to smile at the relief in her voice. She hadn't wanted him to leave. He pushed himself up and ran his fingers through his hair. "I didn't want to leave you here alone."

Fallon snorted and leant back against the wall. "Since when are you worried about my being alone? You left months ago and never looked back."

Gil sighed and kept his teeth locked shut to keep from blurting out anything rash. She had every right to be angry with him, and it appeared she wanted to pick up their discussion where he'd left it earlier. He swung his feet to the floor and stood up, hoping to use his height to his advantage. "I see you still want to discuss this, darling," he said, taking a step towards her. "Just tell me where you want to start."

"Where to start?" she snapped, cringing as a tear cascaded down her cheek. She wiped it away, daring him to challenge her, and Gil knew he'd made another mistake. Fallon pushed her shoulders back and took a deep breath. "Why don't we just start with goodbye?"

Gil cursed as she marched into the kitchen, her back stiff, the muscles in her shoulders bunched. She'd brushed him off earlier, but he wasn't about to let her walk away so easily this time. He took a fortifying breath and followed her through the door.

She didn't turn to look at him but just stood in front of the window, staring into the darkness. Her arms were wrapped around her chest, as if she was trying to keep herself warm. He paused to look at her silhouette. Her hair hung in waves down her back, the red hue barely visible in the light reflecting through the window. Her shoulders were slightly hunched, making her look small and fragile, though he knew she'd laugh at such a thought. Her legs looked long and sexy beneath the hem of his shirt, which accentuated the curve of her ass, and he couldn't help but smile at her perfect little feet shifting on the floor. She was a temptress, and his weakness.

"Fallon." A small shudder raced through her body at the mention of her name, as if his words had been a caress to her skin. She didn't face him, electing to shift some dishes in the sink instead. He stepped closer. "Fallon, darling, it's hard to explain everything when I don't understand it myself. I was in a bad place and I didn't know how to get out of it." He sighed and raked a shaky hand through his hair. "Hell, until I saw you in Trevor's office, I hadn't even thought about trying."

"But you're not trying," she whispered, her back still to him. "You've got walls all around you that clearly say, 'keep out'." Her shoulders sagged a bit further. "I...I think it'd just be best if..."

"No." Gil lunged forward and spun Fallon around to face him. More tears glittered on her cheeks and he could see she was about to break down. He brushed her face with his thumb as he pulled her against his chest. "Don't think. 'Cause if you do, you'll find a thousand reasons why I should walk out that door." He eased her back until her eyes met his. "I don't want to leave, darling. And I sure as hell don't want to spend the night on the couch, either." He slipped his hand around until he cupped the back of her head. "I want spend the rest of this night loving you. Tasting your sweet cream, feeling your skin surround me, drinking your release as you make the walls shake with your screams." He lowered his face until his lips brushed against hers. "I want to fuck you all night then hold you until we can do it all over again in the morning."

Fallon's body melted at his words, and she knew she'd be powerless to turn him away. Her treacherous heart had leapt for joy when she'd found him camped on her sofa, his head cradled in one large hand, his legs bent to fit the small space. His eyes had been encased in shadows and she hadn't realised he was awake until he'd called out to her.

Trouble sleeping?

Was he suddenly psychic, or did she have insomnia written on her forehead? It didn't matter that her body was exhausted. All she'd done was lie in the bed, remembering how it felt to have Gil touch her. Use his fingers and tongue, caressing and licking until she'd collapsed into a limp heap beneath him. It'd taken every ounce of strength she'd had this afternoon to pull on some clothes and grab her bike. Hell, she'd nearly fallen off the damn thing twice on the way to the car. Now here he was, his lips hovering above hers, his eyes daring her to look away. She could say no.

He'd leave. She could read that in his expression, but she'd have to say it while looking him in the eyes. He wasn't going to let her lie her way out of his arms. God knew she couldn't.

Gil tipped her back, arching her over the counter as he ran his tongue along the rim of her lower lip. "Well, darling? What's it going to be? Do you want me to leave?"

Fallon's stomach dropped and her mouth went dry. She parted her lips just enough to swipe her tongue slowly across them, touching Gil's tongue as he made another pass along the edge. She moaned at the sudden contact, unable to hide the exquisite feel of his warm, wet flesh against hers. He smiled at her breathy whimper, flicking the tip of his tongue against hers before pulling back.

"I want to hear you say it, so there're no misunderstandings tomorrow. Tell me whether you want me to stay or go."

Gil pressed his chest tight against hers, his eyes never wavering. One hand was fisted in her hair, the other grazing her hip, making small circles at the hem of her shirt. His weight had her pinned to the counter, holding her still as he rotated his groin into hers. She moaned at the sensuous feel of his cock hard against her stomach. Images of her kneeling before him, her mouth stretched around his thick shaft, returned, and she couldn't stop her body from grinding into his, seeking the sheer joy of feeling her pussy mould around him. He groaned and punched his hips forward.

Fallon took one more moment to savour the steamy look in his eyes before giving him the only answer she could. "Stay."

"Stay," he echoed.

The sly smile that curved Gil's lips made her wonder for a moment if she'd made a mistake, but then all thoughts vanished when he slanted his mouth over hers and thrust his tongue inside. He tasted spicy and hot, and he swallowed her whimper of lust as he traced every contour before finally easing away, his lips still touching hers. His breath mixed with hers, his hand inching up her thigh. This wasn't going to be a fast, hard fucking, like they'd shared this afternoon. Just the way he brushed his hand over her skin told her he was primed for a long night full of pleasurable torture. She knew he had every intention of teasing her to the point of coming before backing off until the tingling sensations subsided and he could begin again. But Gil wasn't in charge tonight. If he was going to stay, it was going to be on her terms.

"Mmm. I knew you'd be bare underneath," he breathed, massaging the curve of her hip. He'd scooted his fingers up her thigh without getting too close to her groin. "Such an inviting gift."

Gil moved just enough to free their bodies, in the hopes, Fallon knew, of removing her shirt. But she rotated with him, spinning out from the counter in a quick motion that pushed him forward, effectively changing their positions. He grunted as his back bumped into the wood, but she already had her hand pressed against his chest.

"Not so fast, darling," she crooned, keeping her body back. "You've had your turn. Now be a good boy and let me have mine."

"Fallon..."

"I mean it," she said, injecting just enough authority into her voice so he'd know she was serious. "You barely allowed me to touch your back earlier, let alone anything else. Now either you let me pleasure you, or I'll go back to my room...alone."

Again she watched Gil fight against some inner decision, as if allowing her to touch him scared him. He gave her one long sweeping look before easing back, his hands gripping the lip of the counter. "You know, there was a time when you wouldn't have challenged me, especially in the bedroom."

Fallon smiled and slipped one of the buttons of his shirt free. "This isn't the bedroom, Gil, and I've grown to appreciate my independence." She smoothed her hand down a few inches, flicking at the next clasp. "Besides, you're not the only one who likes to get his own way."

Gil watched her face as she released the buttons in sequence, his jaw tightening with each inch of skin she revealed. She tried not to smile victoriously when the pulse in his throat quickened, fluttering beneath his skin. She could tell by the set of his jaw, he wasn't about to show her how aroused he was, how badly he needed her to kneel at his feet and wrap her lips around his cock. She'd won the first battle, and she knew how much Gil hated to lose.

But what a pleasurable loss.

Fallon opened the last button and watched the two halves fall open, revealing the muscled planes of his chest and the tight ridges across his stomach. He was lean and strong, and she couldn't stop from scratching her nails down his skin to the top of his jeans. He grunted, his muscles contracting in sequence, his cock pushing up against the fly. Fallon gazed at his groin, wondering how he survived the tight pull of fabric across his shaft. The bulge was massive, pulsing outwards towards her fingers. She inched closer, needing to feel the heat radiating off his body, as she pushed the material from his shoulders, watching as it pooled around his wrists. He was still gripping the counter, only now his fingers were clasped so tight his knuckles had gone a pale shade of yellow.

A smile curved her lips. Gil was strong, a warrior of sorts, but here, in this moment, she held the power. Her. Measuring in at half his weight and a full head shorter. She could reduce this prime alpha male into a trembling pillar of lust, so consumed by his need for her, his body quivered beneath her gentle touch.

Fallon eased her fingers back up his chest, palming his pecs as she moved her mouth close enough for him to feel her breath skim across his skin. Small bumps erupted beneath her lips, and she couldn't stop from lightly kissing them.

"Good God, Fallon."

Gil's voice was husky and deep, edged with a tension she felt throughout his body. His arms were rippled with the strain of keeping his hands away from her, and his stomach was bunched so tight, she half expected him to keel over in pain. She smiled against his skin, allowing him to feel the subtle movement. His nipple hardened at her touch—a tiny pale pebble amidst a light dusting of brown hair. She inched her lips forward and kissed the small bead. Gil's jaw clenched, and she could tell it was only with measured control he kept his hands from ripping her shirt off.

"You're tense, Gil," she murmured, licking at the hard, tight prize perched beneath her lips. "You need to relax more."

Gil growled above her as she drew his nipple into her mouth, nipping at it. She didn't need to look up to know he had his eyes clenched shut. His chest was pushing against hers, his breath heavy pants in the still air. A small moan erupted from his mouth when she released one side and moved to the other. "Darling..."

His words echoed into a hiss as she pressed her breasts against his ribs, her groin against his erection. He couldn't seem to stop his hips from punching forward, as if his cock were leading a revolt. There was no question he wanted to mount her and fuck her hard and fast, but she knew his pride would hold him bound to the counter until she'd verbally released him.

"Need something?" she asked, roaming her hands along his arms. His biceps flexed as she smoothed her fingers across the tight muscles, scratching lightly at his skin.

"You can only push me so far," he warned.

"That sounds like a challenge, baby," she sighed, slowly kneeling between his legs. "And you know how much I love a good challenge."

She looked up and met Gil's gaze. His eyes were dark and hard, and she could see his jaw tensing. She flashed him a smile as her fingers found the button of his jeans and gently flicked it open.

"This is a dangerous game you're playing, darling," he said. "Are you sure you want to continue it?"

Fallon raised her eyebrow at him, answering his threat by slowly lowering his zipper, revelling in the loud hiss of metal as the sides of his pants fell open. She could see the tip of his cock bunched against his briefs, the slit making a small wet circle in the fabric. She leant closer, inhaling the warm scent of man and musk. He smelled even spicier than she remembered, and she knew she wouldn't be satisfied until he'd pumped his first climax down her throat.

"Do you know how long it's been since I've tasted you?" she asked, looping her fingers around his jeans and tugging them down. His cock pulsed out at the movement and she nearly climaxed just watching it. "How many nights I've dreamt of licking you, feeling you thicken in my mouth, all warm and wet?" She clawed at his briefs, trying to remind herself not to hurt him as she fought to free her precious prize from the thin material. "You denied me this afternoon, but I won't be denied tonight."

Fallon's head spun as she ripped off his briefs and stared at the gift before her. His cock was massive, the head swollen and dark, shiny with the proof of his desire. It fell towards her face, bobbing with the weight of the blood coursing through its length. She would've purred aloud at the sight of it if she'd had any air left in her lungs to make more than a desperate squeak. Gil tensed at the soft sound and clenched his thighs, making his penis rise swiftly towards his stomach. Fallon watched, breathless, as it wavered there, seemingly suspended in mid-air, before it slowly descended again, coming to rest directly in front of her mouth.

Her control vanished.

She grabbed his thick shaft with both hands, pumping it up and down in a frantic, disjointed movement. It was almost as if she were watching another set of hands cover his hard flesh, drawing drop after drop of pearly white fluid from the tip. Gil groaned at her rough play, thrusting his hips forward, clenching the counter so hard she was certain the thing cracked. But nothing seemed to register past the red haze of desire pounding through her veins. Even the knowledge that she was going to make him come before she ever got a chance to wrap her lips around him and take him deep to the back of her throat didn't seem to stem her hands from surrounding him, taking him as if her life depended on the outcome. It wasn't until she actually saw the bulbous head flare, the thin slit widening to twice its normal size, that she was able to pull herself back and ease the death grip she had on him.

A deep rumble filled the heavy air, and it took Fallon a few moments to realise Gil was chuckling. She chanced a look at his face, smiling at the heat and desire flickering in his eyes. His jaw was clenched, making the muscle in his temple dance, and he was breathing roughly in what she suspected was an attempt to keep from spurting all over her hands.

Fallon sighed, loving how her breath fluttered across his cock, making him tense. "Sorry," she whispered. "I didn't intend to be so…rough."

"A proper apology requires a kiss," he rumbled.

Fallon's lips kicked up in an amused half-smile. Seems he'd enjoyed her uncontrollable burst of desire and was hanging on the edge but wasn't going to admit it to her. She looked back up at him, swiping her tongue across her lips. "Just a kiss?" she asked, bending forward to place a dainty little peck on the tip of his cock.

Gil moaned and thrust forward, but she moved with him, keeping her contact light. "Fallon." He released the counter and slid one hand into her hair, fisting it around his fingers. "No more teasing."

"Tell me what you want," she challenged, knowing her delay would push him further over the edge. He'd made her scream out her desires earlier, and she'd make him do the same. She looked up at him. "So there won't be any misunderstandings later," she added.

Gil grunted, and she was sure she saw him weighing his decision. He wanted her to suck on him, but did he want it bad enough to ask? She waited, her lips barely touching his smooth skin. His grip tightened, a strangled hiss of air purging from his lips. "Take me deep."

Fallon hid her smile and leant forward. Though he'd been fairly explicit about his needs, she wanted to lick all the fluid she'd pumped from him first. She moved slowly, distending her tongue so he'd anticipate her actions. The muscles in his stomach contracted as she nudged the flared head with her mouth, tasting just a hint of what she'd coaxed from him. Gil groaned above her, moving his other hand into her hair. He kept his grip firm but didn't try to force his way between her lips.

Fallon hummed in delight, savouring the spicy musk on her tongue. She'd always loved the flavour of him, but it seemed so much more delicious after going without for so long. She opened wider and slipped the head inside her mouth.

"Oh God, Fallon. So good, baby. Damn, I love seeing you like this."

Fallon glanced up at him, bobbing as he watched her through lowered lids. His eyes were dark and glassy, and he dropped his head back as Fallon took him deep into her throat.

Mine!

The word echoed in her head, and she only kept from screaming it out by lodging Gil's cock in her mouth. He wasn't hers, not in the sense the voice wanted, and if she didn't stop thinking along those lines, she'd lose her sanity when he left this time.

"Oh, darling," Gil moaned above her. She looked up at him, repeating the deep penetration with her mouth. "Man, one minute in your hot little mouth and I'm already fighting it off. You're far too good at this."

Fallon pulled back, drawing on his shaft as she eased away, finally releasing him. He growled and punched forward, but she only licked the tip. "I think you need a break, baby," she crooned, dipping down to swipe her tongue across his sac, lingering long enough to take each one gently into her mouth. The muscles in his buttocks tightened, proof he was fighting as hard as he'd claimed.

Gil pulled on her hair just enough to add a slight bite to her scalp. "Like I said, darling. This is a dangerous game you're playing."

"But isn't waiting half the fun?" she asked.

Gil stopped and stilled, and Fallon knew he was remembering all the times he'd tossed those same words out at her. She smiled victoriously. He was hers.

His breath sighing out of his chest was her signal to continue. She'd played the one card he hadn't counted on, and now all he could do was lean back and try to trick her into giving him what he wanted. She would, just not on his schedule. Who knew if, or when, she'd get another chance to taste him, and she didn't want this time to be over too quickly.

"You taste divine," she said, licking her way back up his shaft, as she cleaned away more fluid from the tip. "I could do this for hours."

Gil cupped her head in his hands, gently stroking her hair. "I'm willing to wait, darling. But take too long and you'll find our positions reversed."

She smiled up at him. "Is that a threat, or a promise?"

He grinned at her, pushing his cock back into her mouth. "Your time is coming, baby. Just remember I warned you ahead of time."

Fallon heard him speak, but his words got lost in the rush of blood pounding in her head. All she could concentrate on was the slow penetration of his shaft in her mouth. Somehow Gil had taken over and was gently fucking her, pushing deep then retreating back until only his crown was captured within her lips. Her little voice warned her to seize back control, but there was something about the way Gil groaned, clenching her hair in his fists, that left her feeling powerful and sexy. He'd lost control and that knowledge alone made her want to give him the release he needed.

"That's it, baby. Let my cock slide between those sexy lips. God, you look so fucking beautiful this way."

Fallon opened wider, allowing him to increase his thrusts. He brushed the back of her throat, pushing so far she had to fight to keep from gagging. But she couldn't find the strength to ask him to stop. Feeling him move, hearing the strangled moans wrenched from his chest spurred her on. She could feel his sac pulling tighter against his flesh as she started pumping the bottom part of his cock with her other hand. There was no use trying to stem off his release now, not when she knew he was only moments away, and she wanted him to scream her name with the intensity of it.

"Fallon. Damn it, darling, I'm going to come. Decide..."

The rest of his words were lost in a heated growl and his hips moved quicker. She knew his orgasm had taken over, and she allowed him to set the pace, thrusting hard and fast until he yelled her name, spurting the first hot jet of semen down her throat.

"Fuck, yes!"

His words echoed in her head, mixing with the sensual feel of his cock exploding in her mouth. She swallowed every drop she could, keeping his shaft buried deep inside. He was panting out loud, his legs trembling, as the last of his release washed over her tongue. She smiled as she slowly pulled back, finally allowing his cock to ease from her lips. His hands were still clenched in her hair, keeping her close. She kissed his thigh, nuzzling the base of his shaft until he softened his hold and pulled her to her feet.

"Fallon, I..."

He pulled her hard against his chest, wrapping her tightly in his arms. He seemed unable to convey his thoughts, as she listened to his heart gradually calming. She smiled, content to just have him hold her.

"You're amazing, darling," he finally whispered. "Beyond compare." He paused and then smiled against her forehead. "But I'm afraid you've worn me right out," he said, though she could feel his cock still thick against her stomach. Not hard, like before, but not soft either. "Perhaps you should've thought about the consequences before you sucked me dry."

Fallon chuckled. Did he really think she was buying his act? She pulled back and stared up into his eyes. "That's okay. I got what I wanted." She darted her tongue out and licked at a stray drop of his cum still clinging to her lips, loving the husky growl that erupted from him. "And as for the rest, I've got my hand to keep me company. I'll just go back to my room and..."

She squealed as Gil picked her up and tossed her over his shoulder, giving her ass a firm smack with his right hand. He took a step forward, leaving his shirt and pants in a puddle on the floor. "Like hell you will," he said, marching through the house, bobbing her head against his back. "By the time I'm finished, you'll be so damn exhausted, you won't have any strength left to sass me."

Chapter Twelve

I've got my hand to keep me company.

Gil scoffed. As if he'd leave her wet and wanting, even if his cock had been finished for the night, which of course it wasn't. Hell, he was already hard again, or maybe still. Either way, there were a number of ways he could please her, all of which would far surpass *her* hand.

He turned down the hall and kicked open her bedroom door. He thought she giggled, but the sound was lost in the ringing in his head. Desire and need unlike any he'd ever felt pounded through his veins, and just making it to the bed seemed an incredible act of control. His body was energised, every movement an exaggeration. He nearly jumped when Fallon's hair brushed over his back, his skin so sensitised it felt as if she were digging her nails into his flesh.

He took a deep breath and focused on easing her to the bed instead of simply throwing her down and jumping on top, not that she'd probably mind. He'd already caught the fragrant scent of her arousal, and he knew she'd be more than ready for him. But he'd taunted her with his stamina, and laying her down and thrusting inside her before the shirt he was too close to ripping off her fell from her shoulders was not exactly the way of holding true to his claim.

Gil stepped back and stared at the beautiful woman nestled on the bed. Her hair was fanned out across the pillow, like a thick blanket of auburn silk. He could still feel the softness of it as he'd fisted it in his fingers, anchoring himself as she'd taken him deep in her throat. Even now his hands cried out at the sudden loss, urging him to wrap the strands around his fingers again and never let go.

"Christ, you're beautiful."

The words slipped from his lips as he swept his gaze down her body. He loved every inch of her, from her long, pale neck to the delicate arch of her foot. Her legs were bent at the knees, lifting the hem of her shirt until it grazed the vee of her thighs. Not enough to see the fullness of her mound, but positioned perfectly to hint at the wetness he knew covered her smooth lips. He moaned and pressed his tongue against his upper lip. He'd licked her earlier but needed more to remember the sweet flavour of her juices.

"You're looking incredibly sexy yourself. Especially the naked part."

Gil smiled. She couldn't hide her excitement, and the way her eyes seared a path to his groin told him everything he needed to know. She wanted him, and he wasn't about to disappoint her.

Gil knelt down in front of the bed, caressing one ankle as he dragged her towards the edge. He tried to remind himself to go slow, to get her close several times before letting her go over, but his thoughts got mixed up with the sound of her breath. She was panting quietly, her chest rising against her shirt with every inhalation. He wanted to rip the damn thing off her, reveal the soft skin of her breasts, but just getting her body in position seemed to take an unreasonable amount of time, and his hormones were too revved to wait any longer.

He lifted her ankle and placed a gentle kiss just above her bone. God, she felt incredible. "Your skin is so soft. I love touching it." He kissed her again, higher, as he draped that ankle over his shoulder, opening her legs. "Damn." He couldn't help but stare at her naked mound. It was so smooth and pink. It amazed him with its beauty. He'd always found a woman's pussy to be attractive, but seeing Fallon this way overwhelmed him. The lack of pubic hair allowed him to see every pulse and flicker of her lips as she tightened and relaxed her muscles. He'd never noticed how her skin was a deeper pink there, or how her arousal made her lips appear plump and thick, much like his cock.

Gil reached forward, drawing a single finger along the edge of her sex. He kept his touch soft and gentle, not wanting to damage the perfection of her skin. "So pretty, Fallon." He made another pass, slightly deeper. "So pretty and soft I'm afraid I'll catch your skin on my calluses."

Fallon laughed, a deep breathy sound that made his cock peak and his breath hiss out through his teeth. "I'm not fragile." She shifted her ankle farther onto his shoulder, opening herself wider. "You don't need to treat me like a porcelain doll. I can take anything you dish out and still beg you for more."

"Can you now?" he said. "Why don't we put that challenge to the test, darling?"

Gil leant forward and breathed in a mixture of aromas. He could smell the floral scent from the freshly washed sheets woven in with the fruity fragrance of Fallon's perfume. There was a hint of pine and rain on her skin along with the sweet heady musk of her sex. It amazed him how all the scents mixed together to create one perfect aroma that infused her image into his mind. How he knew he'd think only of her when he smelled any part of the mixture.

You are such a goner.

He smiled at the thought, too caught up in the moment to care about the repercussions of his actions. Fallon was his. For how long, he didn't know, but he'd make the most of their time together and worry about figuring the rest out later.

"You're extremely wet, darling," he said, dipping his finger between the soft folds of skin. "Did you enjoy tasting me?"

A muted 'yes' hissed from her chest as he sank one finger inside her channel. It was tight and soft, and just the sight of her skin parting around him made his cock jump. "You're so warm and tight. Damn, I love touching you."

He eased forward, teasing the top of her mound with the tip of his tongue. Fallon moaned and pressed her hips up, slipping his mouth farther down her sex. He knew she wanted him to dive in, lap the juices flowing from her body, but he didn't want to rush it. Just watching her body react to his touch was fascinating. Every movement of his tongue was echoed by a contraction of her muscles. Her stomach clenched and her thighs tensed. Her hands twisted the sheets as she desperately tried to anchor herself. He smiled when her back arched off the bed as he flicked her tightly knotted clit, slowly lapping at it with his tongue.

"Umm," he moaned. "I can't imagine anything tasting better than you, baby."

"That's because you've never tasted yourself," she tossed out.

Gil chuckled against her flesh, loving how more contractions rippled along her stomach. "There's no way I taste better than this sweet cream. So warm and tangy." He pulled his finger slowly out of her channel, still watching her skin move around him. "Here," he said, holding it up to her lips. "Taste how delicious you are."

Fallon looked at him, a devious smile curving her lips as she slowly distended her tongue and tickled the tip of his finger. Then she leant forward and ran it up and down the side before finally slipping it between her lips and bobbing down its length as she'd done to his cock only minutes earlier.

"I see you want to continue with your dangerous game, darling." He shook his head in feigned disappointment. "Not a wise choice when your body is so obviously pleading to come." He pulled his finger free of her mouth, groaning at the suction she applied to it. "Now you'll have to take your punishment for being such a naughty girl."

Fallon raised an eyebrow. "And just what are you going to do?"

Gil smiled at her. Apparently she thought he was joking. He could tell by the way she gave his body a slow sweep, lingering on the increasing thickness of his erection, that she didn't think he was in any shape to prolong his needs, let alone hers. But if she thought he was going to let her off without any kind of pleasurable torture, she was wrong. She'd challenged him more than once tonight, and he was going to make sure she knew what happened when she decided to take control of their lovemaking.

Gil moved back slightly, caressing her thigh with his fingers. "There's only one punishment fitting of your sass tonight." He moved his hand up to her waist. "Turn over, baby."

"Why?" she asked, stretching her foot up to his chest.

Though he tried, he couldn't help but look down and watch the way her plump lips rubbed against each other, opening slightly as she traced small circles across his chest with her toe. The motion seemed to inflame her need higher and he moaned as more juice spilled out and down the soft skin of her inner thigh. It was enough to make his cock flare in protest.

Gil didn't even realise he'd moved until Fallon's startled gasp filled the room and he found himself poised on the edge of the bed, her body draped across his lap. Her muscles bunched and flexed as she wiggled around, trying to make the position more comfortable, but his firm grip across her thighs kept her from moving away.

"Damn it, Gil! What the hell are you doing?"

She moved again but only succeeded in rubbing her breasts against the outside of his legs. He smiled and slipped a hand under her chest, rolling one nipple between his fingers. Fallon stilled, a breathy whimper fluttering across his skin.

"I told you, darling. You're going to be punished for sassing me and thinking you could challenge me in the bedroom." He lowered his head so his breath whispered across the back of her neck. "And we are in the bedroom now, baby."

Fallon's whimper hissed into a moan as he moved his

hand to the other side, taking that nipple between his fingers. She arched up slightly, giving him just a bit more room. "It's only fair," she whispered. "You didn't let me touch you earlier and it's been so long..."

Her words broke off at the first firm slap across her buttocks, replaced by a quick gasp of air. "I control the bedroom, baby. I always have and I always will." He smoothed his hand over her ass, massaging the slightly red area. "The sooner you remember that, the better."

"But..."

A second slap purged the air from her chest, and she hissed his name as he timed the spank with a firm pull on her nipple. "Still sassing me, baby? You are dangerous, aren't you?" He smoothed her skin again, this time tracing the curve down to her pussy. "Open your legs, Fallon, and let me feel how wet you are now."

Gil waited, but Fallon only shifted on his lap. His smile widened. She wanted more. He raised his hand, holding it in the air for several seconds before landing it smartly on her ass, loving how her entire body clenched at the action. But this time he only gave her a few moments to recover before repeating the motion, spanking her several times before smoothing her skin again. "So soft and smooth, baby. And now such a pretty shade of pink." He drew his finger down the cleft of her buttocks, gently probing her anus before moving back to her pussy. "Let's try this again. Open your legs and let me feel how wet you are."

Fallon moaned as she shifted her legs apart, giving him access to her drenched folds. He hummed with satisfaction as he sank two fingers inside her sex, amazed at the creamy dew that saturated his skin. "Oh God, Fallon. You're practically dripping. Did you enjoy your spanking?"

When she didn't answer, he pulled out his fingers and swirled the juice around her clit, making her moan. Then he stopped and gave another firm slap to her bottom. "Answer me, sweetheart, or we'll keep this up all night. And I know just how to touch you to make you want without going over."

"No, please."

The words were soft and low, as if speaking them took every ounce of strength she had. He eased down and kissed her shoulder. "Then tell me what I want to hear."

"Yes."

"Yes, what?"

Fallon snorted and shifted again. "Yes, I enjoyed my spanking. Now please, make me come."

Gil placed another gentle kiss on her skin, following it with a quick flick of his tongue. "That's much better. But I'm not ready to let you come just yet." He moved his fingers back to her sex, dipping them inside her again. "I want to feel how much you want me. How badly you need me to give you your release. Then I'm going indulge myself and eat every last drop of honey from between your thighs, until you beg me to finish you off. Then, maybe, I'll let you come." He eased his fingers up to her clit, circling it slowly. "How does that sound, baby?"

"It sounds like it'll take all night," she said, pushing her bud harder against his fingers.

"That's my plan," he agreed, moving with her so his touch remained soft. "My pace, my schedule. After all, it's only fair after you had your way with me in the kitchen."

"But I let you set the pace at the end. I didn't make you wait."

"Like I said this afternoon. A true warrior knows how to take advantage of any mistake." He pressed inside her again, rubbing her G-spot. "And I promise, the waiting will be half the fun."

Chapter Thirteen

Pleasure erupted in her groin and Fallon closed her eyes as a red haze slowly smothered her. Gil's fingers were rubbing her inner channel, making the ache in the pit of her stomach tighten and grow. Damn, he was good. He hadn't been bragging when he'd said he knew just how to touch her to keep her wet and wanting without going over. He'd done it before. Made her wait for hours before allowing her orgasm to destroy her. And it would. She remembered a few nights when she'd climaxed so hard from hours of his torment, she'd had to sleep for an hour just to have enough energy to make love to him. If Gil had his way, tonight would be a repeat of those nights.

"Feel good?" he asked, pressing a bit deeper. "Would you like more?" She moaned her reply, trying to push her hips back, but he held her tight. "Naughty little minx," he rasped, drawing his finger out to place a lighter smack on her ass. "Let's get you right side up so I can finally have a taste of my prize."

The room dipped and swayed as Gil eased her up and flipped her over, cradling her body against his. She snuggled into his warmth, drawing in a deep breath of man and musk. She savoured the aroma, smiling at the delicious scent of him. It was spicy and hot, and she couldn't wait until he'd rubbed that scent all over her body. She opened her eyes and nibbled at his chin as he stood up and twisted around, dropping her back down on the bed. She gasped at the sudden jolt, having only enough time to look up at him before he'd pounced on top of her, his weight crushing her into the mattress. She shifted beneath him, her legs already spread around his hips, when she felt the head of his cock slide through her silky folds, spreading more moisture around her clit. Her moan vibrated through her chest and she couldn't stop from punching her hips up, hoping to push just a bit of his shaft inside her.

Gil chuckled as he worked her clit with the tip of his cock, undulating just enough to keep the head from penetrating her channel. She grabbed at his shoulders, arching into him as the fire grew inside her.

"Soon, baby, soon. But not before I get a taste."

Fallon nearly cried as he slipped down her body, leaving her cold and empty. She wanted him inside her, filling her. Pumping her so hard she'd beg him to finish. But she could tell by the clench of his muscles, he wasn't planning to give her any part of his cock until he'd had his fill.

"Gil, please. You tasted me this afternoon. Can't you take me first and taste me later?"

Gil glanced up at her, a sexy smile on his face. "Yes I did taste you this afternoon. But it was hardly enough to sate my hunger, darling. You know how much I love to eat you."

Fallon watched as he distended his tongue and gave her slit a long, slow lick. Her stomach fluttered and a warm tingle raced down her spine.

"Umm. Delicious. I think I'd like some more." Gil dipped down and Fallon couldn't stop another moan from slipping from her lips. Gil smiled against her skin, lapping again at her sex. "See, darling. Playing is half the fun." He nodded towards the wooden side table. "Do you still keep your toys in the drawer?"

She glanced over at the small table, a sense of anticipation building inside her. "Yes," she replied slowly, locking her eyes back on him. "Why?"

The grin that lit his face told her everything she needed to know. "Well, darling. I can't truly play without toys, can I?"

Fallon barely blinked before Gil had propelled himself off the bed, grabbed the items out of the drawer and reclaimed his spot between her legs. Then he pushed her knees farther back, opening her even wider.

"That's it, baby. I want you spread nice and wide for me. You know how much I like to watch you."

"What are you going to do?" she asked, hoping the nervous twitch in her stomach didn't radiate into her voice.

Gil smiled up at her. "I'm going to make you scream." He held up her anal plug and a tube of lubrication. "And these are just the right tools for the job."

Fallon felt the air leave her lungs and the blood heat her face. Anal sex? No one had touched that part of her since Charlie…

Gil continued, seemingly unaware of the new tension in her muscles. "You went wild when I put my finger in there earlier. So let's try something slightly bigger."

Fallon watched, spellbound, as Gil held up the plug and applied a long, thick line of gel down the length. Cream slipped from her pussy, tickling the inside of her thighs as he prepared the toy, ensuring every inch was covered with the gel. When their eyes finally locked, she could barely breathe past the tightness in her chest.

"Ready, baby?"

She nodded, not able to speak without whimpering at the images racing through her mind. She'd often dreamed of having Gil touch her that way again, but she'd never thought he'd actually want to.

"Lie back, Fallon, and try to relax. This plug is pretty large and based on how tight you were this afternoon, I'll bet you haven't been using it too much."

She shook her head. Except for her exploits on the couch the other night, she hadn't used the anal plug since Gil had left.

"I didn't think so." He nodded at her and she relaxed back on the bed. "Now take a deep breath and push the air out slowly."

Fallon tried to breathe, but the air just stalled in her chest when she felt the cold press of the plug against her anus.

She squeezed her eyes shut, whimpering as Gil eased the toy inside her, surging it forward until the base locked against her skin.

"Damn, that's a beautiful sight." He pulled the plug out, leaving only the tip inside before plunging it home again. Her moan echoed in the room, but it seemed so far away. Every sense was already honed to the movement of the plug through her body. The way Gil pumped it in and out, igniting every nerve in her ass... She arched up, needing a release from the pressure building inside her.

"Feel good, baby?"

"Gil..." Her voice shuddered into a wail as he thrust two fingers into her channel, countering the thrusts to her ass. She bucked against him, taking him deeper, twisting the sheets in her fists. Fire swept through her ass and into her stomach, pluming outwards as her climax drew closer, sending shivers up her spine. Her skin beaded with sweat and her clit start to pulse.

"Do you know how beautiful you look right now?" asked Gil, pressing the plug back inside, the tip pressing against his fingers through the thin barrier of skin. Fallon snapped her head up, locking her eyes on his. Her body was swaying on the edge, ready to explode with just a few more strokes.

"Damn it, Gil. I need..."

"I know what you need. But I've already told you. Not until I've eaten my fill."

Fallon screamed at the touch of his tongue against her clit. Her nerves were raw, overstimulated, and the hard flick of his mouth was more than she could stand. She reached down and wrapped her fingers in his hair, giving it a firm tug as he lapped at her flesh, making her body twitch. Gil moaned at the movement, but continued to lick the juices spilling around his fingers, making it more than obvious her tactics weren't going to distract him into giving her what she wanted. She cried out, falling back on the bed as the orgasm began to build again. It was deeper this time, a warm ball in the pit of her stomach that rolled outward, consuming every inch as it flowed through her body. Gil seemed to sense the impending rush and began moving his fingers again, licking every drop of juice he pulled from her body.

"Okay, Fallon. No more teasing. Time to come for me, baby."

Fallon fought the sensation, knowing she'd be screaming by the time it finally hit, but unable to stop the steady ascent. It pushed her higher, filling her head with a dull pounding sound as the blood seemed to throb in her ears. She felt one last suckle of Gil's lips against her clit before the world exploded, releasing the fire inside her. It swept across her skin, tingling her fingers as it raced through her body, ending in a harsh cry of Gil's name.

"That's it, baby. Feel it. Let it take you."

Fallon twisted on the bed, unable to pinpoint the source of her pleasure. Heat pulsed through her ass, into her womb and then back again, blurring any single point of reference. Her ass clenched around the thick plug as her channel gripped Gil's fingers, trapping them inside her. His breath feathered over her clit, making it twitch and his head was lodged too far between her legs for her to close them and squeeze some of the feelings away.

"Gil. Oh God." The words got jumbled in her head, and her tongue seemed too big in her mouth. She shifted beneath him, but only succeeded in driving his fingers even deeper. A moan filled her chest, but it came out as little more than a sigh.

"Now that was an orgasm," he said smugly, slowly pulling his fingers from her body. Fallon tried to close her legs in protest, but he held them firmly apart. "Don't worry, baby. There's more."

She opened her eyes just as Gil came down over her, covering her body with his. He was hot and just the smell of him pulsed the blood in her veins. She needed him. No more games. Gil seemed to acknowledge her need and made no protest when she wrapped her legs around his thighs and pushed the crown inside her, rubbing it against the plug. She looked up, her eyebrow marking her question.

Gil shook his head, pushing his cock another inch inside her. "I want to leave the plug in, darling. So you'll be nice and loose the next time. I told you I wouldn't take you there until I'd prepared you, and this is part of it."

Fallon bit at her lip as he pressed farther inside her. He felt incredibly large with the plug still lodged in her ass and every inch he claimed seemed to take an eternity. She dropped her knees a bit, opening herself wider, hoping to give him more room. Gil took her gift and surged forward, filling her with his thick shaft.

"You feel so good. So warm and wet." He dragged the heavy length of his cock back through her tissues, teasing each nerve as he withdrew from her body. "I could stay inside you forever," he moaned, slowly pushing back inside, rotating his hips as he locked himself in place. "Spend every moment filling this sweet paradise." He pulled back and thrust again. "Live on your taste, your smell."

Tears burned behind her lids and she fought to blink them away. Gil had always expressed himself during sex, but she knew better than to believe his words. They were spoken during heat and fury, when blood pounded in his veins and the sound of their hearts beating in his ears crushed out the rest of the world. She wouldn't allow herself to think he meant them.

Fallon pushed the unsettling thoughts away, concentrating on the easy strokes of Gil's cock through her channel. He was still going softly, his hips just rocking gently back and forth, as if giving her a chance to gather herself before the real onslaught began. She smoothed her hands across his back, feeling his muscles contract and release with each stroke. It was like touching liquid steel. She moaned, the warm feeling returning.

"I feel it too, darling. Ready for more?"

Fallon pulled her head from his neck and smiled at him. "I told you I could take anything you dished out and still beg for more," she teased, punching her hips up, meeting his next stroke. "So stop worrying and take me."

Gil's eyes narrowed for a moment, then widened as a slow, sly smile spread across his face. He lowered down and licked her lip. "As you wish," he whispered, kissing her gently before rising up on his hands. Then he hitched his thumbs behind her knees and planted her ankles on his shoulders. She gasped at the new angle, loving how it drove him deeper, but knowing the intensity would leave her screaming.

"Damn, you're tight," gasped Gil, pushing through her channel. "Tight and wet and all mine."

"Faster." It was all she could say without crying. And if he didn't start thrusting into her, she knew she'd lose herself in the sensuality of his rhythm, and she couldn't afford to do that.

Gil seemed to pause for a moment, as if reading her thoughts, but then picked up his tempo, filling her with strong, steady strokes. His crown thickened inside her, pulsing against her womb, igniting each nerve in sequence as it advanced and retreated. The vein on the underside pushed against the plug through her thin membrane, sending shards of fire into her ass. She arched back, anchoring herself on his arms, twisting her hips to meet his strokes, fighting against the climax already building.

"You're getting close, aren't you, darling?"

Fallon stared up at him, watching the edges of his jaw clench. She tightened around him, loving the way his eyes narrowed and a muted moan tore from his chest. "So are you," she tossed back.

Gil smiled, lifting her legs slightly higher. "True. So why don't I give us what we both want."

And then he was driving into her, plunging fast and deep, claiming not only her body, but her soul. She cried out, clenching her hands around his arms, digging her nails into his taut flesh. Her release surged through her, catching her by surprise, stealing what strength was left in her body.

She screamed his name, felt her body shatter around him, and then darkness.

Gil shouted as Fallon's passage clamped around him, gripping him so tightly his orgasm stalled, robbing him of his breath until her muscles weakened, and he came in one hard spurt. He could feel the steady contractions of her pussy along the length of his shaft, coating it with warm, slick juice. He yelled her name, pouring his seed into her channel, knowing her body would take every drop. She was limp beneath him, a contented smile touching her lips as he contracted again, spilling more cum from his cock. His body was locked over hers, his muscles clenched so hard he had to force his arms to relax, allowing him to collapse on top of her. She sighed out a hushed breath, rustling the hairs on his neck as she snuggled into his warmth, seemingly unaffected by his weight on her. Gil smiled, but then frowned. What the hell was he doing?

Hurting the only woman you'll ever love!

He growled at the righteous voice in his head, kissing Fallon's forehead as he slowly pulled free of her body. He watched a small pout crease her face before she shifted again and drifted into a deeper sleep. God, she was so damn beautiful he nearly cried.

Gil cursed and eased off the bed, stumbling his way to the bathroom. He needed to clean himself up and bring a washcloth back for Fallon. Though he knew she'd sleep the night away in his arms, he didn't want her to be uncomfortable with his seed drying between her legs. And for some reason, her comfort seemed more important than anything else. He shook his head, warming a cloth under the tap, when he stole a look in the mirror. His hair was spiked up across his head and there was a small red blemish on the left side of his neck.

He tilted his head, examining the small bruise. His little vixen had taken quite a chunk out of him. Seems she'd been unable to control herself. He smiled with a sense of male pride and made his way back to the bed. Fallon had rolled onto her side, fanning her hair across her shoulder. He brushed it back from her face, loving the soft feel of it against his fingers. She pressed against his hand, another soft sigh feathering across her lips.

"Shhh," he hushed, lifting her leg just enough to ease the cloth between them and soothe the flesh beneath. He moaned as he gently removed the plug, loving how her body clenched around it, begging him to give her more. Even asleep she responded to him. Her nipples tightened as a soft red flush spread across her skin. His cock tightened, but he quickly quelled the growing ache. He'd already come twice. She needed to sleep.

Somewhere in his mind the voice was taunting him about fucking her all night, but it faded as he climbed in beside her, rolling her onto his chest. She moulded perfectly against him and the lump in his throat returned.

Gil closed his eyes and listened to the soft sounds of Fallon sleeping. How many nights had he lain in his dismal apartment, wishing he could have her just one more time? And yet, as he wrapped his arms around her, he knew he'd never be content with just one night. Hell, a lifetime of nights didn't seem long enough. But that meant admitting his feelings for her—not only to himself, but to Fallon as well. And he wasn't quite sure how she'd react. He'd sensed her caution, and he couldn't blame her. He'd hurt her in more ways than one and trust wasn't something she simply gave away.

"Damn."

The word was soft and low, but it sounded loud in his head. How could he tell her how he felt when, in her eyes, all he was after was a good hard fuck? She'd been right. He wasn't trying to break down the walls. And as much as he loved her, he'd only allowed her to scratch the surface of his emotions. Pleasure was easy, but would he let her see more? Pain? Trust? Fear?

Fallon whispered his name in her sleep and he couldn't

help but draw her closer. She seemed so small and fragile in his arms, and he was reminded of how she'd looked earlier when she'd confessed her darkest secret to him. He sighed and relaxed into the bed. He'd figure it out in the morning, but for now, he'd hold her.

Chapter Fourteen

Fallon sighed and rolled over in the bed, snuggling beneath the covers. The bed seemed cold and it took her a few moments to realise Gil wasn't beside her. She pushed herself up, not caring how the blanket slipped down to her waist as she gazed around the empty room. Gil's shirt she'd been wearing last night before he'd yanked it off her had been hung across the back of a chair and Gil's clothes were folded across the seat.

"Gil?" She listened for a reply and only then recognised the distant sound of the shower through the door.

She tossed the blankets aside and padded over to the closed door, pressing her ear against the cool wood. The steady spray of water filtered through, accompanied by the deep rumblings of a man lost in his own conversation. Fallon smiled. Seems Gil still insisted on talking everything out with himself. If she hadn't spent the last few days lost in her visions, she would have found the idea of him babbling away to himself amusing. But not now, when the line between psychic and psychotic was growing smaller by the second.

Fallon sighed and leaned against the wall. She knew Gil would demand more answers today, and she wasn't sure how to make him believe her. It wasn't like she could grab his hand and drag him into a vision with her. And she knew anything short of physical proof wouldn't be enough to sway his judgement. He didn't believe in psychic powers, plain and simple. She doubted even their relationship would be enough to convince him otherwise.

Relationship. You mean a night of hot sex!

The cold reality of the statement sank into her soul, even as she turned the handle and eased open the door. It was safer not to allow herself any emotions other than physical pleasure until she figured out if Gil was planning on more than just a quick reunion fuck—a way to help him through the stress of the case. And if he left once the case was solved, then she'd just go back to her life and…

"Oh my."

The air rushed out of her lungs and the blood drained from her face and into her sex as she caught her first glimpse of Gil in the shower. He was leaning against the wall, water cascading down his back and across his buttocks. His head was pressed into the tiles and she could see the tension in his muscles. The steamy glass was just starting to blur the edges of his silhouette, but not enough that she couldn't take in every detail of his body and how it moved beneath the spray. A familiar red haze surrounded her as she moved forward. She walked to the open panel beside the glass partition and stepped inside.

Gil leaned against the shower wall, his mind lost in thought. He'd spent the better part of an hour lying in the bed, holding Fallon's gentle weight on his, trying to persuade his body to get up. He needed to talk to the Medical Examiner and go over the crime scene again. Wade had taken his camera back to the office to download the images, and Gil needed to get more information from the CSI gurus before another body was found. *The Priest* was becoming more violent with every attack, and based on the rash of bodies, it wouldn't be long before it became a nightly occurrence.

He told me talking to me helps him quiet his demons, so you should get a day or two reprieve.

Fallon's words had settled with a thump into his chest and he'd pulled her tighter against his body. He still didn't know how he was going to broach the subject of her *visions*, and wondered if leaving before she woke up was a better option. Of course, it wouldn't go a long way to getting him back into her bed again tonight, but then arguing with her wasn't going to accomplish much either. He knew from experience she wasn't going to be very cooperative about the case, not after the way he and Wade had reacted to her confession.

He'd sighed and finally eased her away, tucking the blanket around her shoulders as he'd stood beside the bed. She'd looked like a vision herself, and it'd taken more willpower than he'd imagined to drag his ass to the bathroom and turn on the shower. He'd even gone back for one more glance after he'd gathered his clothes from the kitchen and stacked them on the chair. But common sense had finally won out and now he was standing in the shower, the warm water easing a bit of the tension from his shoulders. Just another few minutes and…

A swirl of cold air drew him from his thoughts. He turned just as Fallon stepped into the shower, her hair flowing around her shoulders as she moved in behind the spray and leaned against the far wall. A fine mist collected along her skin, making it bead beneath the small droplets. Her nipples tightened from the cold, turning a deep shade of purple near the base and then fading into a dark-hued pink. His tongue swiped across his lips as he followed the movement of water down her body, covering first her stomach and then her thighs. Her sex glistened in the pale light, like a beacon calling him home. The lips seemed a cooler pink beneath the light wash of water, though he could tell instantly she was aroused. Even cold, her labia were engorged, giving her mound an almost pouting appearance. He smiled and looked back up at her.

"Good morning," he rasped, taking a step towards her.

Fallon reached out and touched his chest, scraping her nails across his skin in small circles. The rumble that filled the small space brought a devious smile to her face. "Morning." She nodded at the steady stream of water. "Still using the shower to talk to yourself, I see."

Gil couldn't help but smile. She knew him better than he knew himself sometimes. "Saves me from having to worry about people listening in." He took another step forward, ducking his head beneath the spray. "But then you never were one for allowing others their personal space."

Gil watched Fallon's smile pull tight and turn down into a small pout. She obviously wasn't in the mood for teasing, though the heat in her eyes told him she was definitely in the mood to play. She shifted and straightened her shoulders. "If you'd rather be alone..."

Gil caught her arm as she tried to push past him, and pressed her against the tile. She gasped and arched her back, fighting his hold until he pinned her body to the wall, locking her hips in his. Heat punched through his stomach and into his groin, straining his erection into her belly. She stiffened for only a moment and then relaxed against him, her hips grinding into his. He lowered his lips and blew a warm breath across the soft shell of her ear, stealing a heated moan from her chest. "I'd rather be inside you making you scream. Feeling your hot wet cunt clench around my cock as I fill you so much it feels as if I crawled inside you." He punched his hips forward, sliding the crown through her slit. "I'd rather fuck you until you can't remember your own name but can't stop screaming mine."

Fallon didn't give him a chance to pull back, locking her hands around his neck and lifting her legs until she'd straddled his hips and crossed her heels behind the small of his back. "Then love me," she whispered.

Gil's chest constricted around his next breath. *Love her?* Were his feelings that obvious, or was she just toying with him? He dismissed the thought as Fallon arched her hips forward, slipping the first inch of his shaft inside her. Heat fused through his body, raising the small hairs on his neck as a fiery tingle raced down his spine. Hell, just one small taste of her tight sheath and he was already dying to pump his cum inside her. But she needed more, especially if he was going to sate her enough that she wouldn't argue with him later when he questioned her about her *visions*.

He eased forward, inching inside her, taking her slowly in the hopes of binding her to him. He could feel her body stretching. Curving around his shaft as it parted her tender tissues, forcing them to accommodate his width. She was even tighter this way, and it took all his strength to push inside, finally locking his sac against her soft skin. He forced in a deep breath, his hands cradling her buttocks, his weight holding her against the tiled wall.

"Better?" he asked, licking the small droplets of water off her neck.

Fallon purred in his ear, tightening her sheath around him. "Much," she moaned back, clenching around him again.

He fought back a moan, biting at the cords of her neck.

"But I need more."

Gil nodded, feeling her body tremble in his arms. He wanted to go slowly. Make every moment last a lifetime, but he could tell by the desperate quality in her voice, she was past the point of gentle lovemaking. She needed something wilder. Something hard and possessive. And he didn't have the strength to deny her.

"Hold on tight, darling."

Her arms tensed as she pulled herself harder against him, her fingers digging into his shoulders. He waited to see if she'd squeeze her legs tighter, but she kept them steady, leaving him enough room to move freely. She moaned as he pulled his cock back, raking her channel, sending small pulses through her pussy and into his shaft. Male pride clouded his thoughts. He'd only just started and already she was on the verge of climaxing. He smiled at the thought, lifting her butt higher, spreading her legs just a bit wider.

"Ready."

It hadn't been a question, and when her reply was little more than a hushed whimper, he didn't waste time worrying. In one hard, quick thrust he was buried again inside her, his crown flaring across her womb. She trembled and cried out, but he was too lost in the tight hot feel of her to hear. Her channel clenched around him, holding and massaging his cock as if it were some great treasure. He could feel the tissues warming him, welcoming him, and he only paused a moment before drawing back and thrusting again.

"Oh, God. Gil!"

Her voice echoed in his head, the sensual sound a caress to his soul. He moved faster, wanting to bring her more pleasure. Feel her body shatter around him. Watch her skin flush a deep pink as her body surged into orgasm. It was as if his pleasure relied on hers. It wasn't enough to simply fuck her. He needed to please her. To know the smile on her lush lips and the swagger in her step was because of him. That, even if just for a moment, he'd battled her demons and banished them, giving her a peace he suspected she hadn't felt in months.

"Please. Now. I need you now."

"Just enjoy it, baby. I'll give you what you need."

And he would. If it took all day, he'd hold off until she'd come.

"Yes!"

Her voice echoed off the walls and he felt the tight pull of her pussy along his shaft as her body exploded around him. Her nails bit into his skin, her legs clamped around his hips, locking him deep inside. Her teeth bit into the taut muscle of his shoulder as her body convulsed in his arms. He moaned at the steady contractions down his cock and pumped into her one more time before releasing his hold, and filling her with his seed. She whimpered with each ejaculation, pulling herself closer until not an inch of skin was left untouched. Gil bowed his head against her neck and pressed into her, using his weight to keep her suspended. The tension eased from their bodies, replaced by a warm contentment that made his eyes lull shut and his heart swell.

Fallon sighed, her head notched in his shoulder, her arms

bound to his neck. He peppered her with soft kisses, needing her to share the immensity of the emotions swirling inside him. He longed to tell her he loved her. How his world was incomplete without her, but just stealing a breath seemed to take all his strength. Somehow she'd broken down his defences, and now all he could do was hold on and pray for a gentle ride.

"Well, you little vixen," he teased, patting her ass as he drew back and smiled at her. "It's a good thing we're still in the shower, as it seems I'm in need of another one."

Fallon smiled at him, clenching his softening cock one last time before releasing her legs and swinging them to the floor. A small frown momentarily creased her face as his shaft slid free of her pussy, and he took a step back. "A small price to pay," she said, sweeping her gaze down his body until she was staring at his cock. "Here. Let me help you with that task."

Gil chewed at his bottom lip, squeezing his eyes shut as she reached out and gently cupped his shaft, running her fingers slowly up the underside and back again. Already more blood was surging through his groin, threatening to make him hard again. He moved his hands to her shoulders, determined to pull her close, to stop her from acting on the gleam in her eyes. But as his fingers brushed against her smooth skin, all thoughts of stopping her vanished, replaced by more erotic images. What was it about her that made common sense a passing thought? Made him forget duty and responsibilities?

Fallon smiled at him, her hand still caressing his shaft. She seemed to sense his indecision, and squeezed down the length as if to hedge his decision. He grunted and tightened his grip on her shoulders only to watch her kneel down, her head even with his groin.

"Fallon..."

His voice trembled into a growl as she placed a delicate kiss on the tip of his cock, humming her appreciation. Damn, she was so sexy he couldn't halt his need to see her pleasure him. The way her lips stretched over his shaft, straining to take it deep. Or how she moaned around his erection, feasting on it as if it were the greatest delicacy she'd ever known. He stared down at her, brushing the hair back from her eyes.

"Darling. I'm not sure I can come again. Even if I can, it may take a while."

Fallon merely laughed, licking at the drops of water covering his cock. "Then I'll just play for fun," she said, sucking at the tip. "Besides, I don't have too much on my agenda today. So just relax and let me taste you."

Gil clenched his teeth, trying to fight the rising need. He had obligations. Aspects of the case hovered at his consciousness, demanding his attention. But as Fallon looked up at him, her eyes sparkling, her body glistening beneath the spray of water, he knew he was lost. He closed his eyes and gave her control.

Gil's head lolled back against the tile and she knew she had him. A surge of feminine power coursed through her veins, making her feel sexy and alive. She knew Gil needed to get back to work, but the fact he'd been unable to fight his own desires made her purr with pleasure. She looked at his cock. It wasn't rock hard, but already it'd grown in width, filling more of her hand as she teased the sensitive flesh beneath the hood. Gil groaned above her, his body tensing.

"Do you know how much I love touching you like this?" she asked, squeezing his flesh as she made another pass up and down his length. "Your skin is so soft and warm here." She bent down and lapped at the tip. "And you taste so good." She looked up at his face, loving how his gaze was locked on hers. "I could spend hours touching you this way."

Gil's mouth kicked up into a sexy half-smile as his fingers slipped into her hair. "Be careful, darling, or you might spend the entire day on your knees before me."

Fallon merely shrugged. "Sounds like a perfect Sunday to me," she said, bending forward to ease his cock inside her mouth. She hummed at the mixture of flavours. His salty musk with a hint of her sweet juice all tempered by the swirl of water was enough to gush more cream from her pussy. She clenched her knees together. Her release would have to wait. She hadn't expected Gil to acquiesce to her wishes, and she wasn't going to waste the chance she'd been given.

Gil shifted, using the wall to support more of his weight. His cock was harder and thicker, and she loved to feel it come to life in her mouth. She knew from experience he'd be fully erect within minutes of her oral stimulation, and she couldn't help but moan at the first taste of pre-cum that slipped from the tip and coated her tongue.

She pulled back, ignoring how the water beat across her skin, spraying small droplets into her eyes. She needed to see him. Drink in every detail of his body as the pleasure inside him grew. The way his sac contracted tight against his groin, or how his stomach rippled and flexed as he fought each new sensation. She could see the bands of muscle straining along his shoulders, pulling at the tendons in his neck, making the muscles of his jaw twitch. Every inch of him responded to her touch, and she knew, when he came, his entire body would convulse with the effort to purge every drop of seed from it.

Fallon leant forward, teasing his crown with just a touch of her tongue. Gil moaned and she couldn't help but smile as his cock bobbed up and his hips punched forward. He was on the verge of losing control.

"Fallon, darling."

His voice was soft, but she heard the underlying warning. Either she gave him what he needed, or she'd find herself pinned to the wall again with his shaft buried to the hilt. She looked up and met his heated gaze. His eyes were dark and stormy, like a predator watching a fallen prey. She lowered her lids, hiding her satisfied smile as she leant forward and wrapped her lips around his shaft, taking it deep to the back of her throat.

"Good God, baby."

Gil moaned above her, stroking her hair, keeping the spray of water off her face. She paused for a moment, his cock lodged in her throat, then slowly withdrew, mindful to keep her tongue pressed against his ridge so she could tease the sensitive flesh around his hood. Gil moaned louder, his body twitching as she pulled back, leaving just the tip encased by her lips.

"No more teasing, darling. Please."

His words tugged at her consciousness, but they seemed to come from far away. She was too immersed in her delicious task to pay attention to them. It seemed as if her entire world had narrowed into Gil's body and how she could bring him the most pleasure.

Fallon bobbed down again, feeling his fingers press against her scalp and his thighs tense beneath her hands. She didn't stop this time but continued to move up and down his length, swirling her tongue and lapping at the drops of fluid that eased from the tip. All sense of time faded. She knew only her need to taste Gil's climax on her tongue as he echoed her name off the walls. Somewhere in the haze she realised the water was cooling off, her skin beading beneath the cold spray. But it didn't matter. Gil was moving with her now, rocking his hips, plunging his shaft deep then retreating. She held on to his thighs, anchoring herself as he fucked her mouth harder. She let him set the pace, knowing it would take time for his body to reach the edge, but wanting to give him the freedom he needed. He'd already pumped a week's worth of sperm inside her, and she was amazed he still had enough strength to attempt another orgasm.

"Now, Fallon. Suck harder, darling. I'm going to… Oh God…"

His words were disjointed, his voice a mixture of pleasure and pain. His body was strung tight, every muscle clenched beneath her touch. Fallon glanced up as she increased the pressure of her mouth, loving the way he threw his head back and moaned her name. His fingers clamped around her head, the tips trembling as if he were unsure whether to pull her closer or push her away. She closed her eyes and slowly drew his cock to the back of her throat, keeping her lips sealed tight around his skin. Gil's thighs buckled slightly and his grip tightened a moment before he shouted her name and she felt the first spurt of cum purge from the tip and ease down her throat.

"Lord have mercy."

Gil's words were hushed against the steady beat of water as Fallon felt another stream of fluid flow into her mouth. She swallowed quickly, tugging at his shaft in hopes of getting one more taste. Gil groaned and slid a few inches down the wall.

"Sorry, darling. But I've given you all I can."

A small pang of disappointment fluttered through her chest. It wasn't until now she realised she'd been hopeful he might be able to take her against the wall again, and the unfortunate reality that the loving she'd been looking forward to wasn't coming left a hollow feeling in the pit of her stomach. Not that she should complain. Gil had brought her more pleasure in the past twenty-four hours then she'd had in six months. Still, she couldn't help but wish for more. She wanted to make the most of their time together, before Gil shut her out again.

Fallon sighed and slowly pulled back, careful to keep Gil's cock in her mouth as long as possible. Gil's body shuddered when she finally allowed his shaft to pop free of her lips and ease down between his thighs. She placed one last gentle kiss on the base before he lifted her up and pulled her tight against his chest. His breath raked through his chest, the harsh pants cooling the water already beading on her shoulder. A small shiver shook through her body and she instinctively curled closer into his heat.

Gil sighed and turned off the water. "You're shivering, baby. Let's get you out of here and warmed up."

Fallon wanted to protest, but the chattering of her teeth blocked any attempts at speaking. She followed him out, wrapping the towel he handed her tightly around her shoulders. Gil didn't seem to notice the cold and barely flicked the water off his skin before tying the towel around his waist. She smiled at the sexy image he made. His hair tousled, his broad shoulders still covered in a dusting of water, making the light in the room gleam off his skin. She loved how lean his hips were, the pale colour of the towel accentuating the slight bronze tone of his skin. She licked her lips, wondering if she'd get another chance to taste him.

"You know, darling, if you keep looking at me like that, we'll never leave the damn washroom." He stalked towards her, brushing his fingers along the bottom edge of her towel, making her skin tingle and bead. "Besides, I believe it's my turn to eat."

Fallon gasped as Gil picked her up and carried her back to the bedroom, planting her ass on the edge of the bed. Then he was kneeling between her legs, pushing the edges of the towel apart until her plump inner lips glowed in the pale light.

Gil inhaled, a look of pure male heat fussed in his eyes. "Mmm, you smell delicious. Just what I fancied."

"Gil…" Her words broke off into a hiss of air as he lowered his lips to her mound and swept his tongue through her narrow slit. Bolts of pleasure tore through her body. She hadn't realised how aroused she was until the tip of his tongue circled her clit and she had to fight back the orgasm.

Gil hummed against her skin, adding another level of sensation. "You can fight it all you want, baby. But I'll taste your release before we're done."

Fallon cringed at the sound of his voice and wished she had the strength to wipe the smile off his face, but her hands were woven through his hair and she couldn't bear the thought of releasing him long enough to make a stand. Instead she arched into him, grinding her clit against his teeth.

"Yes. Now!"

She thought Gil chuckled at her demands, but he didn't pull back. Instead, he pulled her ass closer to the edge and opened her legs even wider as he slung the closest one across his shoulder. Then he slipped two fingers inside her channel and began pumping her weeping flesh to the rhythm of his tongue. Heat plumed in her stomach and punched through her body, spreading like a fire out of control. She had one last moment of clarity before everything exploded and she was left gasping for breath as a symphony of coloured lights danced across her vision. Gil was humming softly against her flesh, pausing periodically to lap at the juice she knew was dripping from her sex, his fingers still lodged inside her. The soft sound of music played in the distance, but she was too tired to figure it out. She relaxed back, content to just feel Gil connected to her.

"Damn it."

Gil's voice caught her by surprise and she managed to push herself onto her elbows just as he slipped his fingers free and grabbed his pants off the chair. He wiped the traces of her juice off his mouth as he dug through his jeans, a small scowl etched on his face. She frowned and went to speak when he pulled out his phone and flipped open the lid.

"As I recall, Wade, I said I'd call *you* when I needed a lift."

"What's the matter? Did I interrupt your interrogation of Fallon?" Wade laughed. "I sure hope you weren't giving her too *hard* a time."

Gil stood up, yanking on his pants. It seemed a harder task than usual and somehow the clothes didn't feel right. "Not half as hard as I'm going to give you, *partner*." He paused as he punched his fists into his shirt. "What's so important it couldn't wait another hour?"

Wade sighed and Gil felt the hairs prickle on the back of his neck. "I just got a call from the Medical Examiner.

Seems there's nothing new he can tell us about our guy. This victim's the same as all the rest, except..." Wade paused for a moment as if gathering his strength. "Except our vic was a couple months pregnant."

"Fuck!"

"Yeah. Anyway, the good doctor wants us over there to pick up the forensics so he can release the body. Says he won't give the stuff to anybody other than you."

Gil nodded and stuffed one hand in his pocket. "Fine. How soon can you be here?"

Wade chuckled into the phone. "I'm standing on Fallon's doorstep as we speak. I tried knocking, but..."

He let his voice trail off into another chuckle and Gil had to still the urge to run to the door and slap off the smile he knew graced the other man's face. "Not funny. I'll be out in a moment."

"Sure thing, *partner*."

Gil sighed and closed his cell, slipping it back in his pants. His shirt was still open and he hated the thought of buttoning it up and heading outside. He'd hoped to spend a few more hours with Fallon before the real world intruded on his fantasy. He turned back to the bed, but she was already gone. "Fallon?"

She walked out of the closet, dressed in tights and a cycling jersey. The clothes clung to her hips and breasts and he took an involuntary step forward before he seized back control. Damn, she was a tempting sight. "Going somewhere?"

She merely shrugged as she sat down on the chair and pulled on some socks and her cycling shoes. "It's Sunday. I always go for long rides on my days off. Since Jane has banned me from the office for a week, I might as well make the most of it."

Gil frowned at the casual tone to her voice, as if his presence were an interruption to her schedule. "What about the investigation? I've got another body in the morgue and this time the woman was a few months pregnant!"

She didn't turn to look at him, but he noticed a tremble

wash over her. Either she was nervous or irritated. "I'm sorry about the woman, Gil, really I am. But I've told you everything I can. Until he calls again, I don't see how I can help you any further."

"You can explain what the hell these visions are you say you're having." Gil cringed at the judgmental tone to his voice, but he was too damn tired to care. It was as if she'd forgotten they'd just spent the better part of the past twenty-four hours with his cock inside her. And now he had Wade waiting outside for him like some kind of chaperone. "And why you never mentioned them before," he added for good measure.

Fallon's back stiffened. She pulled the last lace tight and then stood up and turned to face him. "I can't explain something I don't understand, and I never mentioned them because I know how you feel about psychics."

Her voice was too calm and he hated the fact she knew him better than he did himself. "Oh, so now you're a psychic?" he said, throwing his hands in the air. "Can you read my palm as well?"

Fallon's lower lip trembled and, for a moment, he thought she might cry. But then a different emotion washed across her expression. "See!" she yelled. "That's the exact reason I never told you about this. You won't consider anything you can't see, touch or smell. It's as if the entire world is broken up into 'what Gil believes in,' and 'what he doesn't.' You don't consider anything out of the ordinary, and this is so far outside your comfort zone, you can't even imagine what it must be like."

"I can imagine there must be a logical explanation for all this, other than the idea you *see* what happens to these women."

Fallon huffed and stormed to the door, not bothering to look back at him over her shoulder. He growled and followed. They were far from finished. "Come on, Fallon. We were together two years and not once did you claim you *saw* anything crazy like this."

"It's not crazy, and neither am I. I don't just *see* things. It's only happened twice before and they were both very personal incidents."

"Like what?"

"Like when my sister was abducted and killed when I was twelve." She paused as if considering what to tell him. "And the day Charlie died."

The air hissed out through his teeth and he felt the room dip once before it straightened. "What?" he demanded. She'd never mentioned anything about having a sister, let alone Charlie's death before, and just the possibility that she'd seen…

Gil grabbed the edge of the small table in the foyer and steadied himself. A cold shiver washed over his body. He couldn't afford to get distracted right now, despite the nagging feeling that there was more to Fallon's claim than he wanted to admit. A memory that he'd blocked out. He needed answers, and mystic voodoo wasn't the sort of evidence that was going to lock this psycho away.

He looked over at her. "Explain."

Her skin paled and she glanced at the door as if she wanted to make a run for it. She'd obviously told him more than she'd intended and seemed to realise her mistake a moment too late. She took a deep breath and squared her shoulders. "Look. None of that matters right now. All you need to know is that I can't control it. The visions just come."

Gil matched her step and took another in hopes of blocking her in. She looked ready to bolt and he didn't want to let her out of his sight until she'd given him more. "That's not an explanation, Fallon. I need you to tell me what happens."

Fallon threw up her hands and stomped her foot. "Haven't you been listening to what I've been saying?" she bit out. "I don't know how or why it happens. One moment I'm talking to the bastard on the phone, the next the room shifts and I'm inside the church. I never know how long I'm going to stay, just that it seems to vanish when he leaves." She looked away and for the first time, Gil saw the fear she was trying to hide. "It's nothing but a curse."

A shiver shuddered through her body. She looked lost and scared and he didn't know what to do to help her. He just couldn't see how it all worked out. He sighed and leaned against the table, picturing the scene in his head. He didn't have a clue about her sister or Charlie's death, but maybe he could find a reasonable explanation for her present situation.

"So the *visions* happen after you talk to him?" he asked, careful to keep his voice more neutral. He didn't know why he was so upset. Where the hell had all his soothing tones and calm demeanour gone?

Fallon looked over at him and he was certain he saw something flicker in her eyes before she simply nodded.

"Okay. So he calls you in the middle of the night…usually waking you up…and tells you he's just killed a woman."

Fallon snorted and put her hands on her hips. "I know what you're thinking, Gil, but I didn't imagine all those details from the crime scene."

"I never said you did. I just think you're overlooking another possibility."

Fallon smirked at him and shifted her hands lower on her hips. "And what's that?"

Gil took another step towards her until he was close enough he could've touched her. "I think this creep calls you in the dead of night so he can catch you by surprise. Then I think he tells you—in vivid detail—everything he does to those women." Gil stepped closer, forcing Fallon back until she was trapped between him and the door. "I think he describes how he touches them, rapes them and mutilates them. I think he taunts you with his sick desires until your sanity is stretched so thin your body just shuts down." He reached out and touched her cheek. "I think these visions you're having are just images your mind creates when it tries to cope with the stress of having to listen to this monster's ranting." He forced a smile. "Having witnessed this guy's handiwork first-hand, I can only imagine what it must be like to have to talk to him. It's only natural your mind..."

His next words were cut off by a loud knocking sound at Fallon's back. Fallon jumped, banging into his chest as she spun around and yanked the door open. Wade stood on the porch, his hands stuffed in his pockets.

"Sorry to interrupt, but..." He tapped his watch and gave them both a sheepish smile.

"Damn it, Wade. I told you..."

"No!"

Fallon's voice was loud and almost a full octave higher than usual. Gil felt the tension shift in his body, tightening his chest and making the blood pump loud in his head. She looked ready to fight and he had a bad feeling he knew exactly who her anger was going to be directed at. He took a step back, hoping his brief retreat would soothe the raw emotions swirling in her eyes.

"Fallon."

"Don't." She raised her hand and shook her head, grabbing her keys off the table behind him. "I have nothing left to say. I can't make you believe me. I can only tell you what happens." She stalked forward, pushing Wade aside as she headed for her car. "I'm going riding. I'll be gone for four or five hours. I have my cell. You know the number if you need to reach me." She stopped and turned to face him. "I'll call you if the bastard calls again. Lock up when you leave." She moved to turn but then stopped and glanced back at him again. "While I appreciate the gesture, I won't be needing a babysitter tonight."

Gil cursed as Fallon stalked down the driveway, jumped in her SUV and peeled off, the front tire of her bike spinning in the wake of the car. *I won't need a babysitter tonight.* Damn. Of all the things he'd wanted to do, pissing her off wasn't one of them. But she'd been so calm and removed, he'd lost sight of his intentions and simply reacted on instinct.

"So tell me," said Wade, turning to smile at him. "Is Fallon angry again...or still?"

Gil scowled and grabbed his jacket and a set of keys off the table, not bothering to look at Wade as he brushed past the man and headed for his truck parked at the kerb. "Did you download those photos onto the laptop yet?"

"First thing this morning. And I made a set of prints for you as well." Wade followed him to his truck and jumped in the other side. "Once we pick up the evidence from the morgue, we can see if there's anything new, though I doubt it." Wade sighed. "This guy's good."

Gil nodded, but his mind wasn't on the investigation, or Wade. All he could think about was the sudden change in Fallon's attitude. As soon as he'd asked her about the case, she'd shut him out—not that she'd been too forthcoming before. But something he'd said had obviously bothered her.

He sighed and revved the engine, pulling onto the quiet street. He'd have plenty of time to figure it all out while she was gone. But she was crazy if she believed they were anything close to finished.

Chapter Fifteen

Fallon rode along the trail, lost in thought. She'd already tumbled over the handlebars twice because she hadn't been paying attention, but she still couldn't seem to focus on her ride.

This time the woman was a few months pregnant!

Gil's words were stuck in her head and she couldn't get the image of *the Priest* raping the girl out of her mind. Had the monster known she was pregnant? The woman had obviously been too early in the pregnancy to be showing, but…

She stopped the bike and ran her fingers gently over her stomach. Pregnant. That word had sent a shiver straight to her soul and she'd been unable to deal with Gil after that. Every word he'd spoken had just seemed a reverberation of *that* word, and she'd barely been able to breathe past the lump in her throat. She'd allowed Gil to come inside her, again. More than once! Even though she'd known she was in the middle of her cycle and that it was the perfect time for *her* to get pregnant. Yet, somehow, all that knowledge had vanished as soon as he'd touched her, and she'd taken everything he'd offered her.

That had been the real reason she'd been so angry this morning. Hell, she'd never expected Gil to believe her outright, not without a bit more proof, but she'd lashed out at everything he'd had to say because she couldn't stop thinking about her own mistakes. The kind that stayed with you for a lifetime.

"Damn."

Fallon sighed and grabbed her CamelBak, soothing her

dry throat with a sluice of water. The liquid swirled along her tongue, rekindling images of Gil in the shower, his body covered in droplets. How he'd groaned at her touch and climaxed so hard she could still feel the indents of his fingers in her scalp. She'd never tasted a man as delicious as him, or as dangerous. She knew he'd return, despite her candid declaration, and she was going to have to deal with that. Her only question was whether she'd be strong enough to turn him away.

"Assuming he wants me," she reminded herself. Besides, the more times she played with fire, the more likely she was going to get burned. And if she asked him to wear a condom, she'd have to tell him she wasn't on the pill anymore. And that was a conversation she definitely wasn't up to having just yet.

Fallon glanced at her watch and cringed. Jane had called her cell twice to see if she was going to come to the barbeque, and she'd finally had to agree just to get the woman off the phone. Right now anything was better than sitting at home, wondering if she was going to be a mother. She could only hope all the stress in her life would mess up her periods and she'd escape with little more than a few weeks of worry. But even as she thought the words, an image of a small baby, wrapped in blue, hovered at the edges of her mind, as if daring her to deny what was already happening inside her.

"Come on, Fallon. Suck it up and get going." She scowled, hoping the rough tone in her voice would motivate her. There was no use agonising over what she couldn't change. She'd know soon enough, and then she'd make her choice. She nodded and kicked the pedal forward, launching herself into the trees.

* * * *

Gil sat in his truck, listening to what sounded like the same song waver across the radio. He'd arrived at her house twenty minutes ago, but Fallon still hadn't returned from her ride. He huffed as the music changed, the new melody strangely similar to the one before. He hated waiting around outside her house like some college frat boy who was so desperate to get laid he'd follow women around waiting until they were vulnerable before descending on them. But right now, his options were extremely limited. He'd gone to all her usual places, only to find the lots empty. Apparently she'd found a new place to ride, and he didn't have time to scour the countryside looking for her. So he'd executed the only alternative left. He'd driven to her house and parked by the kerb just down the street.

He could've waited inside. Though he'd followed her wishes and locked her door behind him, he'd also snagged the spare set of keys she'd left hanging on the hook by the door. But somehow it didn't feel right going inside without her. It was *her* house now, and he felt a strange desire to be invited in.

"You're losing it, Gil ole boy," he muttered, wondering if this was the first inkling of approaching insanity. He sighed and considered investigating the thought further, when a flash of movement caught his attention. He glanced up the street just as Fallon's Jeep came into view, merging out from beside a parked truck. She didn't seem to notice his truck as she turned into her driveway and pulled to a halt, the front tire on her bike still spinning as it'd been when she'd left. She jumped out and turned to survey her bike. She seemed to be considering whether to take it off the rack or not, before her shoulders slumped and she headed inside. Even a fair distance away he saw a rip in her tights down by her ankle and the mud splattered across her face spoke volumes.

She'd pushed herself. Hard.

Gil sighed and opened his door, scanning the streets as he made his way to her door. He still had this uneasy feeling that their serial killer wasn't going to stay satisfied with merely talking to Fallon, and he didn't want to risk her life because he was too caught up in his own thoughts to do his job.

He paused at the door long enough to try the handle. It swung open without a sound and he barely had the good sense to crush the curse on his tongue before stepping inside. Didn't the woman have any sense? Leaving her door unlocked was a careless mistake she couldn't afford to make. One he'd make sure she didn't do again.

"Fallon?"

Her name seemed to vibrate in the silence as he stepped farther inside the room. The air was heavy and still and except for her mud-caked shoes tossed over to one side, there was no indication anyone was in the house. He walked over to the small table, fingering her set of keys, when something on the floor drew his attention. He knelt and ran a single finger through the watery drop, holding it up to the light. The redness of it shimmered, making his skin look sickly in comparison. He looked up and saw more drops trailing down the floor towards her room.

"Fuck!"

Gil drew his gun and edged his back against the wall. More than a few images of what he might find flashed through his mind, but he pushed them away, forcing himself to concentrate on his movement. Every footstep was hushed, every twitch was calculated until he was standing outside Fallon's bedroom door, gun poised beside his face, his chest tight with fear. He toed open the door and swept the room with his gun, ignoring the line of blood heading to the bathroom. He darted over to the closet, clearing the room first before stalking to the bathroom. The sound of running water was suddenly loud against the silence, and he only paused for a second before he kicked the door open and burst inside, his gun aimed straight ahead.

Fallon dabbed at the wound, securing the first few strips across the opening. She'd miscalculated the last section of trail and had landed on a log when her bike went in one direction and her body the other. She'd used some bandages to hold the bleeding at bay, but it'd opened up on the drive home and left a bloody trial from her front door to her bathroom.

"Damn it!" Now she was going to be even later getting to Jane's, a fact the woman wouldn't let her forget. While Fallon appreciated her friend's concern, the constant matchmaking was driving her crazy. Jane just didn't seem to understand her reasons for staying single.

You just want Gil back.

She cursed at the thought, wishing her head would just shut up. Gil was only interested in her because of the case. They had a history. That made jumping into bed easy. But she was sure he'd find an excuse to let it all slide once the case was over, if he even bothered to say goodbye this time.

She winced as she tightened the last strip, not sure if it was the cut or the thought that hurt. She had enough in her life right now to worry about. She sure as hell didn't need Gil added to that list. And what happened if she was pregnant? Would she keep the baby? Would she tell Gil?

She moaned and lowered her leg to the floor. It was all happening too fast. She never should've let Gil back in her life, even for a night of hot sex. Her heart just wasn't able to distinguish between pleasure and love. And she definitely loved him.

Tears gathered in her eyes a moment before her bathroom door crashed open, banging the wall as it bounced back off the hinges. She screamed, dropped and rolled, tossing the can of disinfectant at the man who'd just burst into her bathroom. The bastard grunted as her aim hit home, and she used the distraction to grab the toilet brush off to her left. Though she'd only got a glimpse of the gun in his hand, she knew if she hit his arm just right, the gun could be knocked loose, giving her a chance to defend herself. She cocked her arms and lunged to his left, swinging the brush in a graceful arc that connected hard against his knuckles, knocking him into the counter. She moved with him, determined to hit him again, when he turned sharply and grabbed her arms, pushing her back against the wall.

"Jesus, Fallon, it's me!"

She fought against his hold, not willing to go down without a fight, until he pressed his body against hers and yelled her name again. She looked up, finally breaking through the panic, and stared into Gil's blue eyes.

"Easy, baby. It's just me."

Her breath came in hard pants, the fear making it difficult to get any air. He held her tight for another second and then slowly eased his grip, stepping back as he took the brush from her hand and tossed it on the floor. She forced herself to swallow, not sure how her legs were still able to hold her when they were trembling so bad she felt as if her teeth were chattering.

Gil held her stare as he slid his gun back into the holster under his left arm. Then he leaned against the counter and crossed his arms. "That was...inventive."

Fallon snorted and groped her way over to the toilet, plopping herself down when her legs finally gave out. She ran a shaky hand through her hair, hoping to hell he couldn't see how badly she was trembling. "Damn it, Gil! You scared me half to death! What the hell was that all about?" She waved her hand at the Glock nestled by his chest. "What did you think you were going to find in my bathroom that required your gun?"

Gil's expression changed and she saw the flash of fear register in his eyes before he quickly hardened his expression. "I wasn't sure, that's why I had the gun out." He straightened his back and flicked his head towards the door. "Did you know there's a trail of blood from the doorway to your bedroom? Or that you left your front door unlocked?" He crossed his arms again and tensed his jaw. "There's a serial killer loose, Fallon. I wasn't sure what I was going to find."

Fallon huffed and forced herself up. "I cut my leg riding, and I guess I was just more preoccupied with fixing it than remembering to lock the door."

Gil growled and took a step towards her. "Well starting now, that's a mistake you can't afford to make. Either you lock your door, or you don't stay here alone."

His statement was followed by his 'this isn't open for discussion' look, but Fallon wasn't buying it. "Like I told you before. I don't need a babysitter."

Gil only grunted as she pushed past him and propped her leg back on the counter. The cut she'd just finished bandaging together had started bleeding again.

"Good God. That's not a cut. It's a bloody gash." He moved in beside her. "You'll need stitches."

Fallon merely shrugged and applied pressure. "A set of butterfly bandages will do the same." She looked up and glared at him. "As long as no one makes me roll across the floor again."

Gil sneered back but didn't move. "It needs more than a few bandages." He reached out and caressed her leg just below the wound. "Besides, if you don't get it stitched, it'll scar."

"So?" she countered, trying to ignore the heat searing through her body where his fingers grazed her skin.

"You have beautiful skin, baby. I'd hate to see it marked up when it doesn't have to be." As he spoke, he drew soft circles on her skin with his thumb, smiling as bumps beaded beneath his touch. "Come on. I'll drive you to the hospital where they can take care of this properly."

He moved to touch her shoulder, but she scooted away, one hand raised up in front of him, the other still holding the gauze against her cut. "Don't."

Gil snatched his hand back but didn't remove the hurt from his eyes. "Don't what?"

"Don't come in here and suddenly start caring when you haven't so much as called me in the past six months." Her bottom lip quivered, but she continued. "I can't do this. I'm not a toy for you to play with whenever the feeling strikes you. I need more than a cock. Hell, if sex was the only thing I wanted, I wouldn't have spent the last half a year with only my hand to keep me company." She winced as a single tear cascaded down her cheek and puddled on the floor. "It's taken me a long time to move on. And I won't go through that again just because you need a distraction from the case." She held up her hand again when he went to speak. "Now if you'll excuse me, I need to take a shower and get changed. Jane invited me over for a barbeque, and if I don't show up, she'll send a squad car here to escort me." She motioned to the door. "And make sure you *lock* the door on your way out."

Gil's jaw tensed, the vein in his temple fluttering from the pressure. She thought for a moment he was going to argue with her, but then he simply turned and marched out, pulling the bathroom door closed behind him. More tears gathered behind her lashes, but she didn't try to stop them from trickling down her cheeks. The water from the shower would wash them away, as they'd done more times than she could count.

* * * *

Gil stood in Fallon's living room, trying to understand what had just happened. There'd been so much he'd needed to say, so many emotions swirling inside him he just couldn't get a handle on one long enough to put his feelings into words. He'd been scared. Scared he'd find her lying on the bathroom floor, her body sliced into decorative swirls, the beginnings of a cross carved into her chest. Scared that he'd never get a chance to tell her how much he still loved her, how he'd been an ass and wanted nothing more than to start over. Then he'd barged in and she'd turned the tables on him. Damn, she'd nearly broken his hand with the stupid toilet brush, let alone the welt humped on his forehead.

He smiled at the thought and couldn't help but chuckle. She was feisty, he'd give her that much. And based on the pain throbbing through his knuckles, more than capable of defending herself. Still…

He sighed and leaned back against the couch, wondering how everything he did turned out wrong. How his appearance had gone from rescue to raid without so much as a smile from her. Had she even realised the risk she'd taken? Hell, riding alone was crazy enough, but forgetting to lock her door was downright reckless. He had half a mind to march back in there and…

His phone jingled.

Gil flipped it open. "Something new, Wade?"

"You know, it might be more fun for you if you didn't know it was me until after you'd answered."

"I'm not one for surprises." Wade sighed and Gil felt his gut clench. "What?"

"I'm afraid I have some…disturbing news."

Oh God, had the bastard struck again? He closed his eyes and tried not to see the past seven crime scenes flash in his mind. "Another body?"

"Not exactly."

Wade made a weird huffing sound that chilled Gil's blood. "What then?"

Wade sighed again. "I just got a call from Trevor Watts. He said they had a break-in at the precinct last night. Seems someone took some files from the Human Resources office. Being Sunday, no one noticed until the cleaning staff found the door pried open."

Gil scowled. "And Trevor thought we'd be interested because?"

"Because the files the bastard took were the personnel records of the dispatch centre operators. He's got everyone's name, address and phone number, not to mention a whole bunch of other personal information."

"Son of a bitch."

"The only lucky break is that he doesn't know Fallon's name. There're at least a dozen ladies at the centre. He'll have a tough time narrowing down his search. Hopefully your girl can give us some more clues before he discovers it's her."

"So we're just supposed to sit around and see how long it takes him to figure out Fallon's his mystery girl? I don't think so."

"Trevor thought you'd feel that way. He offered to send a patrol car out to keep watch, but I told him you'd probably prefer to take care of Fallon's security yourself." Wade paused as if waiting for him to argue. "I'm sure we can secure a safe house for her if you want."

"Fallon would never agree to go. Since we have no proof that it was *the Priest* who stole the files, the Bureau won't give us the authority to take her against her will, even if it is to save her life." He cursed, hating the helpless feeling rising in his chest. "I don't suppose Trevor has any leads for us?"

"They haven't been able to get anything worthwhile off the security tapes. Looks like carving up women isn't this guy's only talent. Trevor said it was a madhouse Saturday night. And let's face it. The last place you'd think someone was going to break into is the police station."

Gil clenched the phone and suppressed the urge to toss it against the wall. He knew Wade was right. The police had too much on their plate already to worry about someone breaking into the file room. But that didn't help Fallon any. Based on the intelligence of *the Priest* so far, Gil doubted it'd take the man long to figure out Fallon's identity. He couldn't even bear to think what would happen then.

"Gil? Would you like me to call Trevor and have him send a unit over?"

"No. I'll keep an eye on Fallon. She's on her way to a barbeque at Jane's house anyway. Just tell Trevor I'll call him if I think she needs the added security."

"Sure thing, buddy." Wade paused and Gil was sure he could hear the man chuckling. "So do you think Fallon will mind you tagging along? She didn't seem to be angry with *me* this morning. I think she might like *me*."

"Right. You just keep telling yourself that, Junior." He stopped when he heard Fallon's door open. "Look, I'll call you later. Do me a favour and find out exactly what was in those files. I want to know how intimately our guy is going to know those ladies."

"Already on it. I'll call you later to see how everything's going. Oh, and Gil, try not to make her angry this time. I think your charm needs a bit of work."

Gil sneered at the phone and tucked it back in his pocket. He'd resisted working with Wade at first, but the man was proving to be more than just competent. He was becoming a friend. He sighed at the thought and looked up just as Fallon walked into the room. She stopped when she saw him, her hands curving around the sensual arc of her hips.

"You know, for a federal agent, you're not very good with orders."

Gil heard her voice bounce around in his head but was too distracted to understand the words. She was dressed in a fire-red shirt that skimmed her body, dipping down low in the front to reveal more than just a glimpse of creamy skin between her breasts. It looked like she had on a matching bra, the delicate lace edge peeking out at the bottom of the vee. Nestled in that beautiful valley was an emerald-coloured stone dangling from a green suede cord. The stone was shaped like an angel, the surface smooth and polished. When she breathed it almost looked as if the angel fluttered her wings, quivering gracefully between Fallon's breasts.

Gil forced himself to swallow as he followed the line of her body down to a mid-length black skirt, which accentuated the lovely curve of her ass. It looked like it was made out of some kind of silk, flowing from side to side with every movement Fallon made. She'd completed her outfit with a pair of black stockings, and it made Gil's mouth water wondering if they were thigh-highs. He felt his face kick up into an amused half-smile when he reminded himself he'd find out later, when he'd seduced her back into his bed.

Fallon cleared her throat, drawing his attention back to

her face. She looked anything but aroused and a sick feeling settled in his stomach.

"Is there a good reason why you're still standing in my living room?"

She shifted her weight to the other foot and Gil nearly creamed his pants at the way her skirt and top moved with her. Damn, she looked hot.

"I'm positive I told you to leave."

"Actually, you asked me to lock up on my way out." He took a step towards her. "As you can see, I'm not out yet."

Fallon huffed but didn't back down. "It was implied that you'd leave."

Gil shrugged. "Well, next time perhaps you should tell me what you want, instead of just implying it."

Fallon closed her eyes and Gil felt the sudden need to hold her. She looked lost again, and he couldn't help but feel responsible. It wasn't like he enjoyed fighting with her. He just wanted to talk to her, whatever the situation. But she definitely wasn't making things easy.

"Okay. Stay. I've got plans, so if you'll kindly move..."

"I'll drive you over to Jane's," he interrupted, grabbing her set of keys off the table before she had time to react. "My truck's just down the street."

Fallon's eyes went wide a moment before she crossed her arms over her chest and stared at him. "Excuse me?"

"You heard me. I'll drive. It's not safe for you to go alone."

Fallon snorted and stomped her foot. On anyone else it would've seemed childish, but on her it looked hot and sexy and he wanted nothing more than to push her against the wall and fuck her.

"I'm not a child. Besides, I'll be inside my car, and then far from alone at Jane's."

Gil lowered his eyebrows and looked at her. There'd been a strange tone to her voice when she'd mentioned Jane's house and it made him wonder if this barbeque was a cover for something else. He took another step towards her, using his full height to his advantage. "Are you going on a date?"

Fallon's face paled, then flushed, and Gil felt his own redden with anger. "It's not a date. It's a gathering."

"A gathering where there just happens to be single guys," he added.

Fallon shrugged and Gil wanted to pound the wall beside her.

"Jane thinks I don't get out enough, so she invited me over for dinner. I'm not sure who else is going. I think she mentioned something about a friend of Brad's being there."

"A firefighter."

She nodded. "A new guy at the station."

"And you're the appetiser for him."

Fallon glared at him and pushed him aside as she made for the door. "I'm only going to make Jane happy. If I skip out, she'll think I'm still sick and then I'll be banned from the office for another week. Besides, I like Jane and Brad."

"And this new guy from the station is just extra."

Fallon turned and looked back at him. "You know, if I didn't know better, I'd think you were jealous. Which seems kind of stupid since *you* were the one who left."

"Fallon, you know I…" He stopped. There was no sense explaining when he didn't have the answers. Besides, she was right. He had left. If he had any hope of getting her back, he was going to have to make up for that…and more. "Fine. You're going to a barbeque with your friends. But I'm still driving you."

"Why?"

Gil hesitated. He didn't want her to worry, but he also didn't want her to hear about the break-in from someone else. "Wade just called. Apparently someone broke into the precinct last night and took some personnel files from the Human Resources office."

Fallon frowned. "So? What has that got to do with you having to drive me?"

"The guy only took the files for the dispatch centre."

Her face paled as she worked it out in her mind. "Couldn't this be some weird kind of coincidence?"

"Maybe. But I'm not one to bet on a losing horse." He stepped over to her. "Just do me a favour and let me drive you there. I promise I'll behave myself and not make a scene at Jane's."

Fallon's lip seemed to quiver for a second, then she nodded and turned back to the door. She motioned him forward and followed him out, stopping at the side of his truck. "Just remember one thing. I have to work with these people. So don't do anything…"

"Stupid?" he suggested.

"Neanderthal."

Chapter Sixteen

Jane opened the door, a bottle of beer clutched in one hand. She was still talking to someone behind her when she finally turned her head. "Fallon. It's about bloody time! I was starting to get worried. Thought maybe you'd fallen into some kind of gorge or something." The woman stepped forward and smothered Fallon in a full-body hug. "Another twenty minutes, and I was going to have Brad and the guys go searching for you."

"Sorry. I, um, ran into a few obstacles along the way." Fallon pulled away from the woman and wrapped her arms around her chest as if she were cold. "But I'm here now, if you'll let me in."

Jane laughed and practically dragged Fallon over the threshold, spilling some of her beer on the porch. "You know better than to wait to be invited, girl," she quipped, stepping back inside before coming to a halt. Gil watched as the woman's eyes bulged wide, her gaze taking him in. She looked at Fallon, then back at him, rubbing one eye with the back of her hand as if expecting his image to disappear. Then she swallowed hard and locked her eyes on him.

"Gil?"

Gil nodded. "Hello, Jane. Nice to see you."

Jane snorted and crossed her arms. "I wish I could say the same." She turned to Fallon. "Want to tell me what *he's* doing here?"

Fallon's face paled further and her lips pulled tight. She looked from him back to Jane. "It's a long story I'd rather not discuss right now." She shrugged and turned away. "Just ignore him. That's what I intend to do." She walked inside, turning back to him as she toed off her shoes. "Remember what you promised. Behave."

Gil didn't have time to answer before she'd turned and all but sprinted down the short hall and around the corner. He sighed and looked over at Jane, wondering if she was going to let him through the door.

Jane looked him over, shaking her head. "You know, when you and Fallon were together, she was a force to be reckoned with. Now..." She sighed and looked down the hall where Fallon had disappeared. "Just do her a favour?" She gave Gil a stern look. "Finish up your...business...and leave her the hell alone. She hasn't picked up all the pieces from the last time you left. So don't fuck with her heart. She deserves to be happy." Jane turned and walked down the hall. "I doubt you can give her what she really needs," she tossed back over her shoulder.

"Great! I'm doing great, Jane. Thanks for asking," he mumbled, stepping inside as he pulled the door shut. Damn, was everyone pissed at him? Hell, all he'd done was show up with Fallon, and Jane seemed ready to persecute him. As far as he remembered, she used to like him!

Gil cursed and followed the women down the hall, stopping at the corner. Jane's house opened up into a grand living room, with a dining room and kitchen off to the left. It was the perfect house for entertaining, as one space flowed into the next with only the occasional half wall to separate each room.

Fallon had made her way over to the fireplace by a large expanse of windows near the far wall. She was talking to Brad, her back towards him. The man laughed at something she said and drew her close for a hug that rivalled Jane's. He was still smiling when he looked over her shoulder. Gil watched the man's demeanour change, his brows forming a distorted vee across his forehead. He leaned into Fallon's shoulder and whispered something. Fallon's body stiffened and her shoulders pulled up slightly as she shook her head, mumbled something and looked away. Brad gave her a sympathetic smile, patting her shoulder as he made his way over to where Gil was standing.

"Gil." He extended his hand. "Long time no see."

Gil shook the man's hand, his eyes still locked on Fallon's silhouette. "According to your wife, not long enough."

Brad chuckled and slapped Gil on the back in some age-old symbol of manhood. "I wouldn't take Jane too seriously. It's her *woman's time*." He waggled his eyebrows. "She gets pretty touchy, especially where her girlfriends are concerned." Brad followed Gil's gaze over to Fallon. She was talking quietly to two women by the door leading out to the back deck. "And Fallon seems to be her personal mission right now."

"So if Fallon's not happy, Jane isn't either?"

"Something like that." Brad took a swig of his beer, fingering the label with one hand as he spoke. "I think she was hoping Fallon might get out more. Give her something to do besides riding her damn bike." Brad snorted his disapproval. "She's insane, you know. I watched her compete in a cross-country race a couple of months ago. The stuff she does is crazy. And I don't scare easily."

Gil laughed and smiled with a sense of pride that caught him slightly off guard. It'd been a long time since he'd appreciated another person's accomplishments. "Fallon's always been good at what she does."

Brad nodded and turned towards him. "So does this mean you two are back together?"

Gil raised an eyebrow as he skirted his gaze over at Brad. "What did Fallon say when you asked her?" he countered.

Brad smiled. "She said you were working on a case together, plain and simple."

"It's plain, all right, but far from simple." He held the man's stare. "Let's just say the jury's still out."

Brad sighed and stepped over so he was facing Gil. "If I were you, I wouldn't let Jane hear you say that. As a matter of fact, I'd avoid her altogether. She kinda had some things arranged for Fallon today. And I dare say you're a huge clog in her works."

"You mean she set Fallon up with one of your friends from the station, and she's afraid I'll get all territorial on her."

"Won't you?" asked Brad with a raise of his eyebrows. "Or are you staring at Fallon because you're fond of the colour red?"

Gil pried his eyes off Fallon and locked them on Brad's. "As long as your pretty boy doesn't try to touch her, everything will be just fine."

Brad chuckled again and took two steps away. "Glad to see nothing's changed with you, Gil. Help yourself to a beer in the fridge if you want. There's soda too, if you're still on the clock."

"Thanks. A beer sounds good right about now."

Gil moved sideways, keeping Fallon in his peripheral vision. He didn't want everyone to catch him staring at her, but be damned if he was going to let her out of his sight, even for a moment. Something about the thought of her being 'set up' with another guy burned a hole in his stomach. Not that he had any right to be possessive. He'd walked out—or rather ran—as she'd so eloquently reminded him several times over the past two days, and had thus given up the right to stake his claim. She was free to see anyone she pleased.

As long as it's me!

He smiled at the thought, reminding himself how she'd assured him she hadn't allowed another man to touch her while they'd been apart. How no other cock had played in her pussy. And whether she wanted to believe it or not, she was still his. At least her body was. He wasn't convinced about her mind. She seemed to swing between wanting him close and pushing him away.

Gil cursed as he opened the fridge and pulled out a draft. He didn't intend to drink much, but he needed something to cool the raw nerves scratching at the surface of his flesh. He was too wired, and if he didn't get a hold of his feelings soon, he'd do exactly what he'd promised her he wouldn't…cause a scene.

"So. What dragged you out from underneath your rock?"

Gil cringed at the sarcastic tone wavering behind him and half considered making a run for the patio doors, before reining in his control and turning around. Jane was standing a few feet away, arms crossed, toe tapping the tile floor. Her face was slightly reddened, the colour fading into a dull pink as it crested her chest. Her lips were pulled into a distinct scowl and he could see the quick flutter of her pulse just below her neck.

She was pissed.

Gil raised one hand and took a step back. The last thing he wanted was to get into an argument with the hostess. "Easy, Jane. I promised Fallon I wouldn't make a scene, and I intend to hold true to that."

"Oh. So now your word is supposed to mean something?" She kept her voice hushed, but there was no missing the anger in it. Gil tensed as she moved forward, quickly closing the distance. "Do you have any idea what you did to her? How badly you hurt her?" She snorted and threw her hands up, bringing them back down on her hips. "You have some nerve stepping back into her life when she was just starting to move forward."

Gil forced himself to swallow past the lump lodged in his throat. Somehow hearing Jane say what he already knew hurt more than just saying it to himself. "I didn't step back into her life. You know damn well I'm on assignment. And for the record, I never meant to hurt her." He looked down at his feet, not able to meet Jane's eyes. "I just couldn't be around anyone for a while."

Jane tilted her head and snorted in that female way that made grown men flinch. "Save the sob story for someone who cares. You weren't the only one who lost someone that day. Fallon lost Charlie and you. Now she's going to have to go through all that again." Jane looked away, but not before Gil saw the hint of tears in her eyes. "She's still pining for you. Refusing to go out on dates. Holing herself up in that tidy little house, talking to the ghosts still haunting the halls. Hell, if she didn't go out on her damn bike, she'd never leave!"

Jane stopped and pulled herself back together. "Despite what she wants everyone to believe, she's fragile. And this whole serial killer thing proves it. She actually passed out at work, Gil." Jane shook her head. "The next thing you know, she'll be seeing things. I'm worried about her, and so should you be." She took a deep breath and turned away. "Why don't you do everyone a favour and finish this. Let Fallon find someone who isn't *afraid* to love her…before she's too afraid to even love herself."

"Did you ever stop to think that maybe I'm that someone?" he said, feeling the truth of the statement sink into his soul.

Jane looked back at him over her shoulder, her eyes sad, unyielding. "Yeah, I thought it. I just don't believe it."

* * * *

Fallon stood by the window, watching the first drops of rain darken the pavement. She'd been ambling around the party for twenty minutes but hadn't found the motivation to seek out the guy Jane had arranged for her to meet. It didn't help that Gil had shadowed her every move, staying just far enough away that no one would notice he was stalking her.

Great. It isn't enough there's a serial killer who's obsessed with talking to me. Now I have to deal with a man who doesn't love me but who doesn't want anyone else to either.

She sighed and turned around, when she nearly collided with Jane. "Sorry, Jane. I didn't see…"

She stopped, her voice fading into a muted gasp. Attached to Jane's arm was a man who could only be described as beautiful. He had short blond hair brushed back from his face, and crystal blue eyes that rivalled the sea for their brilliance. His skin was smooth and tanned, accentuating the strong, lean muscles poking out from beneath his tee. They rippled as he shifted his feet and eased his hand away from Jane's arm.

Jane grinned and Fallon felt the heat flush her face. She smiled awkwardly, wishing a hole would just open up and swallow her.

"Fallon. I'd like you to meet Jackson Brady." Jane motioned to the male god still standing beside her. "Jackson, this is Fallon Kinkade. The lady I've told you so much about."

Fallon nodded and extended her hand. Jackson smiled back, delicately taking her hand in his. Her breath hissed out through her teeth as he slowly raised it to his mouth, giving the back a soft kiss as he smiled up at her.

"Pleasure to meet you, ma'am."

"Now, Jackson, you're not in Memphis anymore. There's no need to be so formal," teased Jane, pushing Jackson over until his shoulders brushed against Fallon's chest. "Fallon's a simple girl, aren't you?"

Fallon coughed and drew her hand back. Jane was making her out to be some kind of country bumpkin. "Fallon's fine," she replied, glad her voice sounded stronger than she felt.

"Fallon it is," he said, with a deep voice that flowed out like thick maple syrup. "But from what I've heard, *simple* is the last word I'd use to describe you."

Fallon laughed and turned her attention towards Jane. "Well, if Jane's been your source, then you should be using words like stubborn or obsessive."

Jane rolled her eyes and stepped back. "Don't worry, girlfriend, he already knows all about your little quirks. Funny thing is...he's a lot like you." She gave Jackson a light pat on his massive shoulders. "I'll leave now, and let you two duke it out over which one of you can ride the farthest through the mud."

Fallon watched Jane go, a satisfied smile tilting her friend's lips. It was more than obvious Jane was pleased with her reaction, and Fallon was half surprised her friend wasn't whistling the wedding march as she wove her way back to the kitchen.

"Now why does Jane think we'd argue over that?" asked Jackson, poking her lightly in the ribs. "It's all too obvious."

Fallon looked at him, smiling at the hint of humour in his eyes. "Is it now?" she countered.

"Hey, they don't call me *the King*, for nothing."

"Well, I guess it all depends on your idea of riding, *King*."

Jackson flashed her a stunning smile that made her knees quiver. God, he was good-looking. "You know, Ms. Kinkade, that almost sounds like a challenge. Perhaps we should settle this dispute with a good old-fashioned mud-wrestling contest."

"Don't you mean riding contest?"

Jackson flicked his eyebrows and smiled. "Oh, did I say wrestling? Sorry. I was just thinking about you, covered in mud, and got a bit carried away." His smile widened when she laughed. "Seriously, judging by that bandage you're trying to hide with your stockings, I'd say you're the winner by a landslide." He edged closer. "Took a spill, did we?"

"I took a few of them," she answered, wondering when it had suddenly got so hot in the room. "I'm afraid I wasn't in the groove today."

"It looks pretty extensive. Maybe I should take a look at it? I am a trained medic, you know."

"Thanks, but I've cleaned enough of these things to know that time and tape cure most ills in this world."

"So they do," joked Jackson. "But if you change your mind, I promise I'll be gentle."

Fallon smiled but felt her face flush again. Was he being sincere or was he implying something else? A sexual something else that made the butterflies in her stomach take flight. But not in a good way. It felt more like fear than excitement. Sure, he was gorgeous and the slight southern drawl in his voice made her toes tingle. But compared to Gil…

Stop thinking about him!

The voice was loud and bitter in her head and she had to stop her hands from covering her ears in an attempt to quiet the sound. She knew the voice was right, but her heart wasn't listening. The only man *it* wanted was Gil.

Jackson cleared his throat, drawing her attention. "Look, Fallon. I'm not exactly sure what Jane told you, but I want you to understand something about me. I didn't come here looking to get lucky. Jane just mentioned you enjoyed riding as much as I do, and I thought it might be nice to talk to someone who doesn't think going thirty miles an hour down a steep trail overgrown with rocks and logs is crazy." He touched her hand again. "How about we start with a drink? Jane bought some of those coolers you like. Can I get you one?"

Fallon forced a smile, thinking about how the timing in her life sucked. Here was a guy she could actually see herself falling for, and there was nothing she could do to make it happen. Not as long as Gil was messing with her head. "Thanks, a drink sounds great. But I'd prefer a diet soda if it's all the same."

Jackson gave her a bewildered look but nodded and headed off in the direction Jane had gone. She did her best to ignore the way his back bunched and flexed as he sauntered across the floor, drawing every pair of female eyes in his wake. He was definitely all Jane had hinted at and more. But her heart wasn't looking…or listening.

"Now *that* is one good-looking guy."

Fallon cringed as the voice sounded behind her. She should've known Gil would be somewhere nearby. She straightened her shoulders and clenched her jaw, determined not to let him get to her. "Oh, he's far better than just *good-looking*." She crossed her arms beneath her breasts. "Much closer to drop-dead gorgeous."

Gil shrugged and moved around in front of her. "If you like the pretty boy thing he's got going." He gave her a gut-wrenching smile that flooded the heat between her legs. "I always figured you for more of the rough and tough kind."

"He's a fireman. I'm sure he's plenty tough," she bit out.

Gil nodded and looked across the room. "Maybe. Or maybe he spends more time in the bathroom getting ready than you do." He looked back at her. "Do you really want someone like that, darling?"

"Obviously you don't know what I want, or we wouldn't be standing here arguing!"

"Discussing, darling. We haven't yet escalated to arguing."

"Urgh..." Fallon threw up her hands and all but stomped her foot on the floor. "What do you want from me? Why don't you just bugger off and find yourself a big-breasted bimbo to be your sex buddy?"

"I've never treated you as my sex buddy, and you know it." He took a step closer and palmed her jaw. "I've always cared about you. And I always will."

"I don't want someone to *care* about me," she snapped, stepping away from his caress. She couldn't think straight when he touched her, and she needed her mind clear. "I want someone who *loves* me. Who isn't afraid to let me love them back." She bowed her head and concentrated on a small patch of flooring. "I'm thirty-two. I need more than just a man in my bed. I need a man in my life. One who's ready for the same things I am."

"Such as?" he challenged.

"Such as?" she repeated. "It's hardly rocket science. I just want the usual stuff...a home...a family."

She grazed her hand across her belly, wondering if her last wish was already coming true. Then she realised Gil was still watching her and quickly snatched her hand away. She looked over at where the other guests had gathered, their laughter ringing through the room. "I guess I want something more to show for my life than just a job."

"But I thought you loved your job?" His voice was strangely quiet, and Fallon turned to look at him, despite the voice warning her against it. His eyes were dark and brooding, and the edges of his lips were pulled tight.

"All I know for certain is that I'm not happy." She looked down at her feet again. "Sometimes I think it'd just be best if I started fresh. A new town. A new life..."

"Ah-hum."

Fallon jumped at the sudden deep voice behind her. She whirled around, nearly knocking two glasses out of Jackson's hands as she spun to a halt. He was standing just off to her left, looking awkward and out of place.

"Sorry. Did I interrupt something?"

Gil stepped forward, but Fallon stopped him with a quick glare over her shoulder. "No. We were just talking." She pulled at the hem of her shirt, flattening it across her skirt. "Thanks," she said, taking the drink he held out to her.

"No problem," replied Jackson, eyeing Gil with a look of apprehension. "So. Jane told me you're registering in the national cross-country race a couple of months from now." He shook his head and sighed. "Man. A friend of mine raced last year. He said it was the nastiest competition he'd ever been in. A lot of blood and tears." He nodded in the direction of her drink. "So that's why you're not drinking any alcohol. You're in training."

Fallon could almost hear the wheels spinning in Gil's head as his gaze levelled on her. He knew all too well she wasn't abstaining from alcohol because of her training. Not when she'd downed more than one cooler that first night, before she'd fully come to terms with the fact she might be pregnant. It wouldn't take much for him to come up with another alternative, especially if he'd seen her caress her stomach a few moments ago. She held back a curse and simply shrugged the question off. "Something like that." She stepped closer to Jackson, hoping Gil would get the hint and leave. "Do you race?"

Jackson opened his mouth but then closed it again as he looked over at Gil. He seemed uncertain of his next move with Gil just standing there, glaring at him. Fallon felt another curse form on her lips. Damn it if Gil didn't look like the possessive boyfriend right now. Hell, he all but had *she's mine* written across his forehead. She closed her eyes and wished she could just jump in her car and go home.

Jackson extended his hand. "The name's Jackson. I work with Brad."

Gil nodded and shook the man's hand, silently measuring his strength. It looked like the guy had a few pounds on him, but Gil suspected he'd come out ahead if things got ugly. "Brad mentioned it earlier. I'm Gil."

"Do you work at the dispatch centre too?" asked Jackson.

Gil hid his smile as he glanced over at Fallon. "No. I'm with the Bureau."

"Ah. A Fed. That suits you more." Jackson looked over at Fallon but seemed oblivious to the anxious twitch of her hands. "Have you two known each other long?" he asked with an arch of his brow.

"Nearly three years," answered Gil.

Jackson smiled and began to nod when his eyes widened. "Nearly… Oh. You're *that* Gil."

Gil couldn't help but chuckle as Fallon's face turned a deep shade of red, nearly matching the fiery tone of her shirt. "I see Jane told you about me. How sweet of her." He took a step back. "Good to have met you…Jackson." He knew he'd injected too much bite into the man's name, but hell, the bastard was all but caressing Fallon's arm. "I'll leave you two alone." He walked behind Fallon, stopping at her shoulder. "Just let me know when you're done, and I'll drive you home."

He heard Fallon mumble something under her breath and smiled. He'd made his position clear, and for now, that was enough.

Chapter Seventeen

Fallon walked into the kitchen, hoping no one would follow her. Between Jackson and Gil, she hadn't been able to sneak a moment alone since arriving at Jane's. And if the ache spreading across the bridge of her nose was any indication, she had a killer headache on the way.

"Hiding, are we?"

Fallon cursed and turned to face Jane. The woman was worse than Gil. "Just taking a break." She picked up a plate and spooned a few ribs onto it. "I am allowed to eat, right?"

"Of course, darling. But you could have asked Jackson to get you something."

"Now why would I ask a man to do something I'm quite capable of doing myself?" she countered, sinking her teeth into the soft meat. Damn, it'd been a while since she'd tasted anything so good—other than Gil, of course.

"It's called courting, Fallon. You should give it a try." Jane moved over beside her, picking a rib off her plate. "So what do you think?"

"I think Brad should come over and cook for me. These ribs are amazing."

Jane snorted and rolled her eyes. "Not the food, the man!"

"Oh." Fallon fumbled with one of the bones. "He's nice."

"Nice?" Jane grabbed her by the arm and twisted her around. "He's more than just *nice*. He's fucking hot!" She gave an exasperated sigh and shook her head. "I don't suppose this has anything to do with Gil?"

"Why would you say that?"

"Oh, I don't know? Maybe because he hasn't strayed more than ten feet away from you since you got here."

"He's on assignment. After the break-in, he's worried this creep may be following me." She tried to shrug Jane's concerns away. "You know how obsessive he is about his case."

"Nice try, but it's more than that. And I'd bet money that it's you he's obsessing over, not the case." She stepped back and gave Fallon a slow sweep. "Oh. My. God!"

"What?" Fallon's heart was racing as her friend surveyed her again. "Is something wrong?"

"You're sleeping with him!"

Fallon scowled at her. "Says who?"

"Says your body, girlfriend." Jane waved her hand up and down the front of Fallon's shirt. "Just look at you. You're all relaxed, and your skin is practically glowing."

"I just rode for five hours. My body is exhausted and my skin's always glowing. It's called sweat."

"Oh no. This is totally different. You've got that 'just fucked' look." She shook her head again and Fallon had to stop from smacking the knowing smile off her face. "You've been fucking him. And more than once."

Fallon sighed and put the plate down on the counter. "So? You were the one who told me to get laid so I didn't come across as needy."

"Yeah, but I didn't mean with Gil."

"I don't see how it matters who I get my sex with, *girlfriend!*"

Jane sighed and reached for her hand. "Hey. You know I've always liked Gil. But…he broke your heart. And after all you've been through, I just don't think he's the best person for you to get involved with right now. It's not like anything has changed. And you'll be the one who gets hurt when he walks away again." She gave her fingers a squeeze. "Don't you think it'd just be best to move on and put Gil and your past, behind you?"

Fallon pulled her hand away, doing her best not to cry. Hearing Jane say her deepest fears out loud was more than she could handle right now. "It's not that simple."

Jane moved forward and pulled her into a gentle hug. "I'm sorry. I didn't mean to upset you. It's just...you're still in love with him, aren't you?"

"So what if I am?" she snapped, pulling out of Jane's arms. God, her emotions were all over the place. If it weren't too early, she'd blame it on her hormones. "Look. I'm a big girl and I can take care of myself." She huffed at Jane's frown. "I know what I'm doing, okay?"

Jane threw her hands up just as Jackson walked into the kitchen. "Everything okay?" he asked, looking at Jane and then Fallon.

Fallon sighed and put the phony smile on her face. "Perfect." She grabbed a rib off her plate. "Hungry?"

Jackson flashed her a wicked grin and bent down, nibbling the edge of the rib as she held it out to him. Then he ran his tongue along her finger, licking away the drips of barbeque sauce. "Depends on what you're offering."

Fallon gasped and dropped the rib, pulling her hand back. She'd only meant to distract him and hadn't figured he'd take her offer as sexual. Not that he wasn't perfect sex material. His lean, impeccably honed muscles, the way his lips were soft and smooth. She could tell by the way he carried himself, he'd be a compassionate lover, with more stamina than a seasoned racehorse. The kind of man who could last all night, either in the bed or against a wall. But there was something missing. Maybe it was the sincerity in his eyes. She just couldn't imagine him tying her up or giving her a spanking. Not the way Gil had the other night.

Gil.

She stepped back and looked down at the floor. "Sorry, Jane. As I told Jackson earlier, I'm just not in the groove today."

Jackson laughed and seemed to miss the mild trembling of her hand as she tucked it against her waist. "I'll clean it up."

He bent down, but as he looked back up at her, his face faded, replaced by the glare of wet pavement. Fallon shook her head, watching as his image washed back into focus.

"Fallon? Are you okay? The colour just drained from your face."

"Huh? Oh, fine. Perfectly fine. Why wouldn't I be?" Damn, she sounded lame, but it was the first words she'd been able to form right. She felt off-kilter but wasn't sure why.

Jackson stood up and took her hand. "Are you sure your leg is the only injury from your ride today? Maybe you hit your head?" He rubbed his thumb across the back of her hand. "Why don't you go sit down and I'll bring you some more food?"

Fallon stared down at his hand, not sure why she couldn't pull hers away, when the scene changed and she was staring at another set of hands, clasped around a clean white cloth. They were older, with a few scars criss-crossing the back. She gasped and jerked away, snapping back to Jane's kitchen as her back collided with a stool.

"Jesus, Fallon. What the hell's gotten into you?" Jane was standing in front of her, waving her hand in front of her face. "Jackson was only trying to help."

Fallon pushed herself up and took a shaky step forward. "I'm sorry. I thought I saw a spider drop onto the floor beside my foot. You know how much I hate those things." Jane and Jackson looked down and Fallon sighed in relief. At least they wouldn't think she was completely crazy… yet.

"I don't see anything," said Jane. "Are you sure…"

Are you sure she's the one?

"What did you say?" gasped Fallon.

Jane arched her brow and gave Jackson a concerned look. "I asked if you were sure you saw a spider."

Fallon looked down, unable to process the words. Someone else was talking to her. A dark voice that seemed very far away.

She's the one. My next salvation.

"Damn it, Fallon, you're scaring me!"

Jane was practically screaming at her, but her voice didn't seem to register. Fallon looked up and forced a smile, knowing she had very little time left. "You know, come to think of it, I did bang my head when I tumbled over my handlebars. I guess it's got me a bit confused." She turned to Jackson and flashed him her best smile. "Would you do me a favour and grab me another bottle of soda? I'm just going to pay a quick visit to the ladies' room and then I'll meet you out on the deck."

"Sure thing. But are you sure you don't need to see a doctor or something?" He looked over at Jane as if seeking support. "You could have a concussion."

Fallon waved her hand, trying to ignore the way Jackson's body had become transparent. "Nah. I just need to sit down for a bit and rehydrate myself. But I'd love the company, if you don't mind babysitting me for a while."

Jackson chuckled and gave her a sweeping bow. "It would be my pleasure," he replied. "You go ahead to the bathroom, and I'll save a patio chair for you."

Fallon smiled and pushed past him, hoping her feet would carry her far enough away before the full force of the vision hit. She made for the doorway off the living room, knowing it led down a short hall to the bathroom.

The ground shifted and she stumbled, landing hard against the wall. Half of the room had faded away, leaving only a few feet ahead of her still solid. She lunged forward, grabbing the cold handle as she flung herself inside the room. She had just enough strength to close the door behind her, before her world disappeared and she fell to the ground in a crumpled heap.

* * * *

Gil stood on the corner of the deck, stunned. He'd done his best to leave Fallon to her new *friend*, but when she'd finally ditched the guy and made for the kitchen, he'd been unable to stop himself from following her. He'd lagged behind just long enough to give her a sense of freedom before weaving his way to the far door. What he'd heard had caught him completely off guard. She'd been arguing with Jane over her attraction—or should he say, lack of—for Jackson. Relief washed over him and he'd planned to walk away, when Jane had said his name. He'd stopped and listened, his chest tight, his pulse racing, as Fallon had admitted first her sexual relationship with him, and then her love.

Now he was standing on the deck, shaking. Though he'd assured himself she still wanted him, to hear her say it was more than he'd hoped for. Now he just had to find a way to get her to say it to him.

You're an idiot if you think she'll admit anything to you.

He snarled and pounded his fist on the railing. The voice was right. Fallon would keep her feelings a secret unless she had no doubts about his. And he didn't know how to tell her how he felt. How do you tell someone you love them, when you've spent the past six months hiding from them, from the truth?

Carefully.

He smiled at the thought and turned just as Jackson walked out of the door and headed over to one of the tables Brad had set up around the deck. He watched as the man set two drinks down on the table and pulled another chair over to his side. He was obviously expecting company.

Gil turned away and headed for the other door. The last thing he needed was for Fallon to catch him spying on her, even if he had ventured to the deck first. Knowing the kind of mood she was in, she'd only see it one way…her way. He wove his way into the dining room when Jane stomped to a halt in front of him.

"What the hell's going on?"

Gil looked the woman up and down, but it didn't look like she was drunk. "I'm sorry, but I have absolutely no idea what you're talking about."

Jane sneered at him and palmed her hips. "I'm talking

about Fallon. What is this case doing to her?"

The first inkling of fear prickled his skin as he quickly scanned the room. Fallon wasn't there. "Why? Did something happen?"

Jane flipped her head up and gave him one hell of a cold glare. "You mean besides you fucking her?" She sighed and motioned towards the kitchen. "We were talking in the kitchen and she completely zoned out on me. Like she was somewhere else. I'm worried. She's acting strange."

"Did she say anything, or tell you what was wrong?"

"No. She gave some lame-ass excuse about hitting her head while she was riding and then scurried off to the washroom like some frightened mouse." Jane shook her head. "I can understand her trying to ditch Jackson, but… she's never lied to *me* before."

Gil nodded and grabbed her arm. "Where is she now?"

Jane shrugged. "I don't know. I suppose either in the bathroom, or out on the deck with Jackson. Unless she decided to sneak away."

Gil shook his head and dropped his hand. "I just came from the deck and she knows better than to go out alone. Where's your closest washroom?"

Jane pointed to the hallway off to her left. "Through there, down the hall on the right." She stepped in front of him as he tried to walk by her. "Wait! What's wrong with her? Is it something to do with the case?"

Gil placed his hands on her shoulders and gently eased her out of the way. "Just do me a favour. Keep everyone away from here until I figure it out."

Jane nodded as Gil moved past her and down the hall. The door to the washroom was closed, but he could hear someone inside. He inched closer and pressed his back against the wall as he leaned over and listened. The noise was muffled, like someone breathing through a cloth over the phone. He reached under his arm and touched the grip of his gun, wanting to know it was close if he needed it.

"Fallon?" He tapped lightly on the door, hoping she'd

answer. But nothing inside the room seemed to change. "Fallon? Are you in there, baby?"

Gil cursed the silence that answered his plea and bolted over to the other side of the door. He waited just long enough to grab his Glock before twisting the knob open and swinging the door aside.

* * * *

Fallon stumbled across the pavement, finally slamming into a parked car. The images faded in and out of focus, making it hard to keep her balance. She glanced down at her hands, not surprised to see the glare of the road through them. She was trapped in the vision, but just barely.

"Sorry, Sue, but I'm going out with Steve tonight."

Fallon jumped at the sudden voice, the sound harsh and loud in her head. She looked across the road, only to realise it was a parking lot. Rows of cars were stacked across the pavement, spreading out in a kaleidoscope of colours. The rain was still light, making small dark circles on the asphalt. But like her vision, it was only beginning.

"I know Steve's still legally married. But he's promised me it's over."

The woman laughed and Fallon looked over to her right. The girl was young and blonde, and if not for the fatigue darkening her eyes, she could have been mistaken for a model. She was wearing a dull blue nursing uniform with plain white sneakers and a dark shoulder purse. Her hair was pulled back in a ponytail, and the makeup she'd applied this morning was smudged on her face.

"Don't worry, Sue. I'll double check everything. You know me better than that. Look, I gotta run. I'm a mess and I need to stop by the apartment before I meet Steve."

The woman clicked her phone shut and headed for a vehicle farther up the lot. It was a small red hatchback, but Fallon was too far away to see the make. The woman stopped at the back and slipped her purse off her shoulder.

"Damn it, where are you?"

Fallon watched the girl dig through her purse, tossing item after item back inside. She was obviously looking for something, but Fallon's head was too fuzzy to figure anything out. The rain was getting heavier, and a sudden gust of wind made the hairs on her arms and neck prickle.

"Salvation. Soon, it will be yours," the eerie voice whispered in her head just as a dark shadow moved across her. She turned as *the Priest* stepped in front of her, his long black jacket blowing in the breeze. She caught his scent on the wind. A heady pine musk mixed with a hint of cigar. There was another aroma mixed in as well. A sickly sweet scent that made her stomach turn and her head spin. He was standing too far ahead to see his face, but she'd come to recognise his silhouette. How he held his arrogance in the line of his back, and the way he cocked his head to one side as if listening to some hidden voice.

"Finally!"

The woman held up a set of keys and shook them once in victory, still oblivious to the man flowing towards her. *The Priest* didn't make a sound as he covered the wet pavement, stopping a breath away from the woman's back. Even as the girl stepped forward, he moved with her, slipping one hand over her mouth as another snaked around her waist. The girl's body stiffened in surprise before slumping against *the Priest*'s chest. Fallon tried to call out, but her voice was smothered by the distant sound of thunder. All she could do was watch the bastard lift the limp woman in his arms and carry her back to his car.

"Your altar awaits. Soon, your soul will be saved."

He was laying her in the back and covering her beneath a blanket, smoothing his hands along her side. Fallon cringed at the sensual way he touched her, like he was her lover, not her captor.

She pushed off the car and moved towards him, fighting the constant pitching of the scenery. Her name echoed off in the distance, but she kept moving, needing to see more, to memorise every detail. She stopped a few feet behind him, wondering what would happen if she reached out and touched his jacket. *The Priest* reached up for the hatch but froze as his fingers grazed the metal. He dipped his head slightly and twisted his shoulders. A chill ran down her spine as he stood poised behind his car, waiting. Then in one smooth movement, he turned.

* * * *

Gil slipped into the room, sweeping the small space with his gun. Fallon was sprawled on the floor, her hair covering her face. He took two steps in before toeing the door closed and clearing the space behind. As much as he wanted to go to her, he needed to make sure she was safe first.

He inched past her, peeking into the shower stall and closet before holstering his gun and kneeling down beside her. She was panting, gasping, her body twitching. She moaned and he wasn't sure if touching her would hurt her or bring her out of whatever she was going through.

"Look out! Behind you. Run!"

Her words were pushed out with a groan as she rolled on the floor. Gil reached out and gently brushed the hair back from her face. Sweat beaded her brow and her eyes were open, but dull. She looked scared but didn't react when he waved his hand in front of her.

"Fallon?"

"No. Don't. Stop."

Gil pulled his hand back when she flinched and gasped, breaking free from her trance as she bolted up with a soundless scream. He grabbed her shoulders, catching her before she fell back to the floor, her face white, her body shaking. Gil cradled her against his chest, smoothing her hair with his hands as she collapsed against him, her eyes drifting shut.

"Fallon?"

She mumbled a reply, whispering his name as she drifted

off again. Gil clenched his jaw to stave off a curse. He had no idea what to do next.

"Fallon? Can you hear me?"

Her eyes fluttered and she rolled her head back, swiping her lips with her tongue. "Help. Gil."

Gil nodded, though he knew she wasn't watching him. "Sure, baby. Just tell me how to help you."

Fallon coughed and whimpered. She shook her head. "No. Her."

Gil fought the helpless feeling surging through him. He hadn't felt this out of control since Charlie had died. "Fallon. You're not making any sense. Who's 'her'?"

She moaned again and slowly opened her eyes. "The woman…in the parking lot." She grimaced and grabbed her head. "Oh, God."

"What woman?" He gave her a small shake when she started to fade again. "Fallon. What woman?"

She squinted up at him and he cringed. She looked so weak he wondered how she managed to stay conscious. "A nurse…Harborview…he took her…black SUV…Mercedes, I think." She pressed her palm against her head, but he could tell it wasn't helping. "I tried to warn her…" She shook her head and sighed. "Couldn't help her…never…"

Her voice faded off as she slumped against his chest. Even unconscious she looked as if the images and pain were still with her. Gil hugged her close and reached for his phone. Wade answered on the third ring.

"What's wrong, Gil? Fallon decide I was her dream man after all?"

"He's struck again." Gil grunted as he tucked the phone under his chin and scooped Fallon off the floor. "Fallon says he took a nurse from the parking lot at Harborview and put her in the back of a black SUV. She thinks it was a Mercedes." He moved over to the door and nudged it open with his foot. "He's only got ten minutes on us. We need to move."

He heard Wade swear and a chair screech across the floor.

"I'm on it…hey? What do you mean 'Fallon says'? How does she know *the Priest* took another woman?"

"I don't have time to explain right now. Besides, I'm not sure I understand it all myself. Just get dispatch on it. We need a list of all the churches around the hospital." He stepped into the hall and cursed when he saw Jane peek around the corner.

"Do you have any idea how many churches there are in this town?"

"Lots. But he'll be going to one that's vacant. And since it's Sunday, that must narrow things down a little." He rolled his eyes as Jane stormed down the hall, Brad at her heels. "Do the best you can and call me as soon as you've got anything."

"You're not coming in?"

He could hear the uncertainty in Wade's voice, but he didn't have time to give a damn right now. Jane looked ready to tear more than a strip off him and Fallon's limp weight was a constant reminder of all he had to lose. "I need to take care of Fallon. I'll call you as soon as she's safe."

Gil balanced Fallon's body with one leg as he snapped the phone shut and shoved it in his pocket, Wade's voice still chattering on the other end. There wasn't time to explain. He needed to get Fallon out before he ended up fighting the entire house.

"Fallon! Damn it, Gil, what the hell have you done to her?"

Gil bit back a curse and turned to face Jane. "Fallon's fine. She just needs to rest. Now if you'll just calm down and lower your voice…"

"Calm down? She's unconscious! How the hell is that 'fine'?" Jane reached out and brushed a finger down Fallon's cheek. "What's wrong with her?"

"It's hard to explain. Let's just say she's having a few side effects from the case." He looked up at Brad and nodded towards the man's wife. "I'm sure Fallon can fill you in on everything once she's regained her strength. But for now, I need to get her home."

With that, he brushed past the couple, pleased to see Brad settle his hands on Jane's shoulders when the woman went to follow him. Now if he could just get out the side door before anyone else showed up.

"Hey, Jane? Have you seen Fallon? She hasn't…" Jackson's voice wavered into a strangled growl as he rounded the doorway and nearly collided with Gil. Gil snorted and tried to push past the man, but Jackson stepped forward and blocked his way. "What the hell's going on?" he demanded.

Gil all but stomped his foot on the floor as he sighed out his frustration and shifted Fallon in his arms. "I'm taking Fallon home. In case you haven't noticed, she's suffering from exhaustion and the sooner I can put her to bed, the better."

Jackson sneered at him and took another step forward, forcing Gil back a step. "She was fine just a few minutes ago." He gave Gil a once-over. "I don't suppose you had anything to do with her sudden illness?"

"You know, I'm getting awfully tired of being the scapegoat." Gil moved forward, this time forcing Jackson to back up. "Now, as I see it, we can play this two ways. Either you get out of my way and I walk out of here with Fallon, or I can put her down and we can take our differences outside." He drew himself up. "But either way, she's leaving here with me."

Jackson glanced over Gil's shoulder at Brad but didn't get out of the way. "And who are you to make decisions for Fallon?"

"I'm the guy she's going to be spending the rest of her life with," he bit out, making Jackson flinch. "So do us both a favour and get the hell out of my way."

Jackson looked at Fallon before stepping aside, his lips pulled into a thin line. Gil nodded as he walked out the door and headed for his truck.

Chapter Eighteen

Gil sat in the chair, watching Fallon twist and turn on the bed. She'd been unconscious since Jane's house, and he'd made the twenty-minute drive in ten, placing her on the bed while he paced the floor waiting for the men Trevor had agreed to send over. They'd pulled up fifteen minutes later and had stayed parked on the other side of the road ever since. And while that had eased some of the tension, Gil still couldn't seem to relax. Not until Fallon woke up and explained exactly what the hell was going on.

A jingle of music shattered his concentration.

"Talk to me, Wade."

"How's Fallon?"

"Unconscious. Any leads on our man?"

Wade sighed and Gil knew the answer before the man spoke. "It's harder than trying to find a virgin at a frat party. Do you have any idea the numbers we're up against?"

"There can't be that many once you eliminate all the churches having Mass or Sunday school today," countered Gil.

"Apparently you're not up on all the various religious sects in our fine city. Over half of them don't hold traditional services, not to mention the ones that don't associate anything with Sunday." Wade paused and Gil felt a shiver run down his spine.

"What?" he demanded.

"You know how much I like your girl, Gil…"

"But," he interrupted.

"We need more if we're going to stop this guy before he kills the woman." Wade sighed into the phone again. "I don't suppose she can connect or materialise or whatever she does again and tell us where the bastard is now?"

"She's fucking passed out on the bed. Exactly how do you expect me to get more information out of her?" He raked a shaky hand through his hair as he tried to calm his nerves. Shouting at Wade wasn't going to help anything. "I'm sorry. I just don't know what to do. I've never...let me see if I can wake her up. I'll call you back."

Wade mumbled a half-ass apology as Gil hung up the phone and looked over at Fallon. She was lying on her side, the blanket he'd tossed over her pulled up to her shoulders. Her skin was almost as white as the sheets and just the thought of trying to rouse her filled him with dread. The last thing he wanted to do was send her back into the nightmare.

"Fallon?" He touched her shoulder, caressing her skin gently with his thumb. "Baby, are you okay?"

Fallon moaned and rolled her head. Gil's voice was muffled, like he was speaking from another room. She felt his hand tighten on her shoulder as he called her name again. She took a deep breath and forced her eyes open, squinting from the brightness. Gil was sitting on the chair beside the bed, his face solemn, his lips pulled tight. She tried to smile, but the pounding in her head robbed her breath, and all she managed to get out was a muted whimper.

"Easy, darling. Don't try to move yet."

She tried to chuckle at the thought, but it only made her head hurt more. "Don't think I could," she said. She glanced over at the table but couldn't make out any of the numbers on the clock. "What time is it?"

"Five o'clock."

"Five?" she questioned, trying to sit up only to collapse back down, her palm pressed against her forehead. "How long have I been out?"

Gil's face paled. "About an hour." He brushed some hair back from her face. "How do you feel?"

"About as good as I look," she joked, hoping her small attempt at humour would ease some of the tension bunching his shoulders. "You okay?"

"Other than worrying Jane might take a contract out on me, I'm okay."

Fallon smiled, then frowned. "Oh, God. Jane!" She covered her face in her hands. "How am I ever going to convince her I'm fine now?"

"After what I witnessed, I'd say Jane is the least of your worries." He leant forward and she saw the fear come and go in his eyes. "Is it always like that?"

She eased back and pushed herself up, accepting the pillows he stacked behind her back. "It depends," she began, but then stopped when he levelled his stare at her. "Sometimes it's worse."

"Goddamn, Fallon." He looked away, but not before she saw the pain in his eyes. "Why didn't you tell me?"

His voice was soft and there was no mistaking the hurt in it. Fallon sat up straighter, ignoring the roaring sound in her head. "Because I knew nothing short of falling on my knees in front of you would've been enough to convince you. And I don't have that kind of control. At least I never did." She looked away. "This time's different."

She felt Gil's gaze on her, but she couldn't seem to meet his stare. "How?" When she didn't answer, he reached forward and placed his finger under her chin, raising her face to his. "How is this time different?" She tried to shrug it off but couldn't stop a tear from tracking down her cheek. Gil wiped the drop away with his thumb. "Come on, Fallon. It's me." He flashed her a smile that made her heart clench. "Talk to me."

Her bottom lip quivered and she tried to draw some strength from his touch. "It's stronger, more intense. The colours. The smells." She shook her head. "I still don't know how he connects with me before he calls."

"But I thought you said it only happened after?" She shrugged and he sighed, nodding his head. "What else?"

"What do you mean?" she asked.

He kicked half of his mouth into a sexy smile. "I mean you're holding something back. The real reason this vision was so different." He grazed her cheek again. "I need the truth, Fallon. Please."

She wanted to turn away but something in his voice stopped her. She looked into his eyes and saw more than just compassion and sincerity. She saw love. "He looked at me."

Gil's hand dropped from her face as he surged to his feet. "He did what?"

"He looked at me." She sighed out a long breath. "I was standing behind him, watching him tuck the woman in the back of his hatchback, wondering what would happen if I touched his jacket, when he reached up to close the hatch and stopped. Then he cocked his head as if he could hear me breathing and spun around and looked straight at me. That's never happened before."

Gil took a few heavy steps away before turning back. "So you've seen his face?"

"Not...exactly," she mumbled. "When he turned, his eyes locked on mine and it felt like something tossed me across the parking lot. The next thing I knew, I woke up in your arms."

Gil moved back beside the bed. "Do you remember anything about him?"

"Just his eyes. They were hazel. They reminded me..." She paused, not sure if she should say what she really thought.

"Reminded you of what?"

She bit at her bottom lip, wishing it didn't have to be like this. "They reminded me of Charlie." She looked up at Gil and saw the pain in his eyes. "I'm sorry, Gil, but it's not just his eyes that remind me of Charlie. It's the way he carries himself, the shape of his back, the colour of his hair. Hell, even his voice sounds similar." She shook her head as more tears dampened her skin. "Maybe I am going crazy."

Gil sighed and the bed dipped as he crowded the edge.

"You're not going crazy. And while we both know it can't be Charlie, maybe there's a connection we're missing. I'll check it out later."

Fallon nodded and leant against his shoulder. "So I guess this means you haven't had any luck finding the woman I saw?"

He shook his head. "Wade just called to inform me how daunting a task it was to narrow down the search. Apparently there're as many churches as there are coffee shops."

She pulled back and locked her eyes on his. Something in the way he talked about Wade's call made her believe the man had wanted more than just to update Gil. "And that's the only reason Wade called?" she pressed.

Gil's head lowered and Fallon knew what was coming next. "As a matter of fact, he was wondering if you could give us more information."

"Such as?"

"Such as where the bastard took the girl."

Fallon snorted and pulled back, wrapping her arms around her chest. "I told you. It's not like that. I can't just sit down and spy on people. The other person always initiates the connection." She looked down at her lap. "I'm just along for the ride."

"But you said it yourself…this time's different. Maybe the connection's always there, but you're able to hold it off some of the time." He knelt beside the bed and raised her chin again. "If you don't want to do this, darling, I'll understand. I can't even begin to imagine what it must be like."

"I can try, but…"

He silenced her with a warm finger across her lips. "That's more than I should ask." He waved at the bed. "Is there anything I can do to help?"

"Just be here when I come out," she said, then cursed the impetuousness of her tongue.

Gil merely smiled and brushed his lips softly across hers.

"Don't worry. I'm not going anywhere."

* * * *

Fallon twisted the covers in her fists, staring up at the ceiling as the clock ticked in the background. Nearly fifteen minutes had passed and still no contact with *the Priest*. Gil had stayed by her side until the tension had finally got to him and he'd taken to pacing the room, watching her as if she were suddenly going to sprout another head. She huffed in frustration and was just about to tell him the whole idea was ridiculous, when a wave of distortion rolled across the room. The ceiling wavered, faded into wooden beams, and then back. Fallon covered her mouth, trying to hold the bile down, as more of the room pitched and rolled, pulling her further into the vision. Gil called her name but she was already too far gone to reply. A heady floral scent assaulted her senses as the darkness finally gave way to light and the images steadied.

Fallon pushed herself up and grabbed a small table when the room swayed again. She waited for the feeling to pass, then surveyed what she could see. She was at the back of a rectangular room, by a set of large wooden doors. Off to her right was a doorway, which led to a brightly lit room. There were tall stands of roses lining the walls and a small book centred on a table by the doorway.

She moved forward, drawn to the light of the next room. She stopped just shy of the door, afraid of what she'd find but aware of the need to keep going. The other room seemed quiet, filled only with the distant sound of water. She peeked around the door and studied the room. A long aisle stretched out in front of her, flanked on each side by rows of pews. A stand of flowers had been placed along each row, the sweet fragrance filling the room. She moved through the doorway and down the aisle, staring at the beautiful view landscaped across the far windows. Water and hills streaked with orange as the sun dipped below the horizon.

Fallon walked to the end of the aisle, wondering why the chapel looked so familiar, when a soft scraping sound penetrated her haze. She looked off to her left and noticed another door shoved up against the back wall. It was hanging slightly ajar, a sliver of light reflecting on the opposite wall. She moved over to the opening and looked inside. *The Priest* was hunched over the woman, a small instrument clutched in his right hand.

"So pretty," he crooned, bending farther over the woman's chest. "Soon your soul will be beautiful too."

Fallon inched her way in, slowly pushing the door aside. The room was dark and cluttered with boxes, but she needed to see if the girl was still alive. She slid over to her left, hoping to get a better look, when he stopped and straightened. Fear punched through her stomach and she had to fight the urge to run.

He can't see you. You're not really here.

The argument sounded good in her head, but it did little to soothe her fears when *the Priest* cocked his head and sighed.

"I know you're there, Angel. I can feel you."

Fallon pressed her back against the wall, unsure of her next move. Would he hear her if she spoke to him?

"You've been with me before, haven't you? I knew there was a reason *you* answered my call."

He chuckled and Fallon cringed at the sound.

"What's the matter, Angel? Are you scared? Hoping to get a better look at my work?" He kept his back to her but shimmied sideways. "I'm not quite done, but then you already know what it's going to look like." He laughed again. "Aren't you going to talk to me, Angel?"

"Please. Don't do this," she whispered, edging back towards the door. How the hell did he know she was there?

"What's wrong? Don't you believe in me anymore? Aren't you here to watch me cleanse her soul?"

His voice was strong and laced with anger. Fallon braced

for what she knew was coming. "You don't have to do this. I can help you. Please. Just let her go and call me."

His roar pierced the silence. Fallon screamed and backed up, slamming against the door. His anger vibrated the air as he threw a box of tools across the room.

"I thought you understood!" he shouted, turning partway towards her. "I thought I could trust you!" He looked back at the woman lying on the table. "You were the only one who stayed the demons. You made me feel…human again."

His shoulders slumped and Fallon felt the world shift. "No. Wait! I can help you. I…"

He turned, his eyes locking with hers. She saw his pain, felt his regret, as his face disappeared on the whispered breath of her name.

"No!" Her voice cracked and she lurched forward, slamming hard into Gil's chest. His arms tightened around her back as she slumped against him, her body completely drained.

"Fallon. Damn it, baby, are you okay?"

She mumbled something into his shirt, wanting nothing more than to sleep, when he eased her back and lifted her face to his.

"What happened? You just zoned out on me. Then you screamed and I swear you aged me ten years." He shook his head. "Fuck. I never should've asked you to try…"

Fallon placed a trembling finger over his lips and flashed him a warm smile. "It's okay," she rasped.

"Do you know where we need to go?"

Fallon nodded, moaning at the increased pain in her head. "A chapel. Over by the ocean." She waved her hand in the air. "There were flowers and decorations. I think I've been there before."

"You've been to the church?"

"Not a church. A chapel. Where couples get married." She sighed and palmed her forehead. "Damn, my head hurts."

"Do you need to go to the hospital?"

Fallon laughed. "Only if you plan on committing me,"

she replied. "Don't worry. It'll go away once I rest." Her eyes fluttered shut and for a moment she felt her body drift.

"Whoa, darling. Is there anything else you can tell me? The colour of the chapel? An address?"

Fallon shook her head and forced her eyes open one last time. "I only saw the inside of it…" she started then gasped as an image flashed in her head. She was back in the chapel, only it was full of people. "Jane," she yelled.

"Jane what?"

"Jane's wedding. We went there when Jane got married two years ago." She grabbed her head as the pain flared. "He's in the back."

Gil nodded, already dialling his phone. "Wade. We've got a location. It's a little chapel down by Redondo. I can't remember the name, but it's right by the ocean."

"I know the place. A friend of mine got married there a few years back. I'm on my way." Gil heard him flip on the siren.

"Call Trevor and wait for backup."

"There's no time for backup. Don't worry, I'll be careful."

"Damn it, Wade! You'll wait for backup or I'll kick the shit outta ya the next time I see you."

"Go with him."

Gil turned and stared at Fallon. She was barely awake. "I'm not leaving you."

Fallon shook her head and closed her eyes. "I'll be fine. *The Priest* can't get to me now. Wade needs you and I need to sleep." She flicked a hand at him before tucking it beneath her head. "Go. You can wake me when you get back."

Gil watched her drift off to sleep, dark rings rimming her eyes. His heart flip-flopped in his chest and he knew he'd never be the same again. "I'm on my way." He glanced at his watch. "I'll be there in twenty minutes. And you'd damn well better be waiting for me."

"There's no need…"

"I said I'm on my way. Now you'll wait for me or I'll find myself a new partner, got it?"

Wade chuckled. "Guess we couldn't have that. Drive fast, old man, and I'll see you there."

Chapter Nineteen

Gil tiptoed into the room, his fatigue weighing heavy on his shoulders. It'd been nearly three hours since he'd left to meet Wade, but it felt like a lifetime ago since he'd seen Fallon's face. She was still sleeping on the bed, her hands tucked beneath her head, the blanket pooled at her feet. She looked like an angel lying on the sheets, her long dark eyelashes brushing the pale skin of her cheek and her hair fanned out across the pillow. He did his best to ignore the dark circles rimming her eyes—a testament to all she'd done to try to save the woman.

His chest tightened. She wasn't going to take the news lightly.

He walked over to the bed, unable to stop from reaching out and caressing her shoulder. She looked so fragile, so innocent curled up on the mattress, he couldn't fight the need to shelter her. She sighed as he slid his fingers down her side, smoothing out the fabric covering her hips. Damn, she still looked hot, and it was no surprise when he felt the firm press of his jeans against the hard length of his cock.

"Gil?"

Her voice was soft, husky with the sound of sleep. He leant closer, inhaling her warm, womanly scent as he dropped a gentle kiss on the top of her head. "Shhh, darling. Go back to sleep."

Fallon shook her head and he watched her fight to open her eyes. It was then he realised how exhausted she looked. "What happened?" she asked, licking her lips as if speaking had dried them. "Did you find her?"

Gil sighed and sat back in the chair he'd left beside the

bed. "Yeah, baby. We found her."

Tears glistened in Fallon's eyes as she pushed herself up and met his gaze. "And…" she prompted.

"And she's still alive," he answered, careful to keep his voice steady.

"But?"

He looked away. She knew him too damn well to fall for anything less than the truth. "He'd already done the damage." He returned his gaze to hers. "We found her in the back, just like you said."

Fallon's face paled as she threw herself off the bed and stumbled over to the window, her body trembling in the pale moonlight. She braced one hand against the wall as she turned to face him. "The cross?"

"Carved into her left breast, just like the others. It wasn't quite as intricate. I think he knew we were coming."

"Did he rape her?" she whispered, as if the sound of the words might change the outcome.

He could only nod as more tears slipped down her cheek.

"At least she has a chance to recover," he added, hoping to give her a reason to release the guilt he saw coiling up inside her.

"Recover?" she repeated, a hysterical cackle trembling across her lips. "How is she going to recover? Every time she looks in the mirror she'll see what he did to her."

"She's alive. That's more than any of his other victims can say."

Fallon merely shrugged, adding, "They were luckier," under her breath.

Gil growled and stalked across the room, grabbing her firmly by the shoulders. "This isn't your fault, so stop the guilty act. He's sick. And if it weren't for you, she'd be nothing more than a picture in a file right now." He pulled her closer, needing her to see the honesty in his face. "And despite what happened, alive beats dead any day of the week." He eased his grip slightly. "One day, she'll see that."

Fallon pulled herself free and pushed past him, making

her way over to the bed. When she turned to face him, her eyes gleamed with her pent-up anger. "When, Gil? When will she see how lucky she was?" She threw her hands up in the air. "When she's pushed everyone who means anything to her out of her life? When she's spent the better part of the next several years just existing, hiding from the world?" She shook her head. "No. She won't see the luck in her life until it's too late."

Gil met her accusations with a few quick strides, covering the distance between them before she could balk. "Just because I screwed up my life and hurt the only woman I'll ever love, doesn't mean she'll do the same. You've given her the chance to choose. What she does with that chance isn't your fault." He traced a single finger down her face. "It's never been your fault."

Fallon stared at him, her mouth open, her eyes wide. It was as if his words were still sinking in, still penetrating the haziness she'd woken to. He watched as understanding washed over her, and she dropped her eyes, unable to meet his gaze.

"Gil…"

"I want you, Fallon. Not just in my bed, but in my life. I want you beside me, sharing the good and the bad." He placed his hands on her waist and pulled her closer. "I wanted to hurt Jackson today for thinking he could touch you." He shook his head as Fallon looked up at him. "I know it was innocent, but damn, you're mine." He pulled her hard against his body, grinding his erection into her belly. "Mine, do you hear me? No other man is ever going to touch you, baby. No other man is going to get a chance to taste your sweet juice or hear you scream his name as you pulse around his cock. You're mine, now and always."

Fallon huffed and took a step back. Gil released his hold, allowing his hands to fall at his sides. "For always? Or until you've dealt with the past long enough and decide to hide away again?" Her bottom lip quivered. "What's so different this time?"

Gil took a deep breath, knowing his future hung in the balance. "This time, I'm not afraid to show the world how I feel." He took a step forward. "I love you, Fallon. I always have. And once we've taken care of your obsessive admirer, I'll show you just how serious I am."

Fallon placed her hand on his chest when he bent down to kiss her. "I don't need fancy words or shiny trinkets to trust in your devotion. I need action." She gave his body a long, slow sweep. "Prove it. Stake your claim right here, right now…or walk away."

Gil moved, pulling her tight against him, his tongue already demanding entrance to her mouth. She opened willingly, her tongue clashing with his, fighting for dominance of the kiss. He allowed her a few moments of triumph before sliding his hand behind her neck and arching her back, deepening the kiss in a way that told her he was in control. She'd wanted him to prove his claim, and he wouldn't stop until he'd done just that.

"Gil."

Her voice was breathless, husky with desire, and the sound of it surged more blood to his already swollen shaft, reducing what little room he still had left in his pants. He groaned at the increased pressure, hoping he didn't cream his shorts before he'd had a chance to strip her.

"Do you know how hot you look in this delightful scrap of fabric you have covering those beautiful breasts of yours?" He trailed a finger across her collarbone, lightly brushing her nipple. She moaned and arched further forward, pushing the distended pebble against his hand. "Every man at that party wanted to rip it off you and taste your pretty nipples." He chuckled, allowing her to undulate her chest against him. "I thought Jackson was going to die from that hard-on he was sporting since the moment Jane introduced you to him."

Fallon's eyes narrowed in confusion. "What?"

"You didn't notice the way he kept his shirt down over his jeans, darling? He wanted you…bad."

She smiled at the hint of jealousy he heard in his voice. "But you're the only one who gets me."

He nodded, happy she'd taken his words to heart. He'd meant every one. No other man was ever going to touch her. "Glad you see it my way, baby. 'Cause after tonight, you'll never question who you belong to again." He stepped back. "Now I'll give you two choices. Either you undress yourself, or I'm going to rip those clothes off you. Either way, I want you naked. Now!"

Fallon arched her brow in challenge. "Really. Isn't that just a bit barbaric? I mean…"

Her words disintegrated into a keening cry when he reached forward and grabbed the sides of her skirt. The bedroom echoed with the sound of the material ripping apart as he let the torn scraps fall. She stared at the black fabric puddled on the floor then slowly raised her face to his. Anger and astonishment flashed in her eyes before they glazed over with lust. He smiled, knowing she wanted his loss of control as much as he needed to lose it.

"Should I do that lovely red shirt next, or your panties?"

She crossed her arms as if protecting the material still covering her body. "I'll take it off," she whispered, reaching for the hem.

"Just make it quick, baby, if you still want to have it in one piece."

Fallon glared at him, but he could see the heat in her stare. She was more aroused than angry, and he knew she secretly craved his dominance.

"Very nice," he complimented as she placed the shirt on the chair. "Now for the rest of your garments."

He motioned to her bra and panty set as she reached for the front clasp. One flick and the cups separated, revealing the soft creamy skin of her breasts. Heat punched through his stomach and down his spine. God, she was beautiful. She didn't seem to notice the raw heat radiating off his body as she pushed her shoulders back and allowed the small scrap of lace to fall to the floor. Then she stood there, waiting.

Gil growled and took a step towards her. "Panties. Now."

Fallon raised her eyebrows, a seductive smile gracing her lips. "Those, you can rip."

"Fuck!"

The word was barely out of his mouth before he had his fingers rimmed around the lace. He paused just long enough for Fallon to see the carnal intent in his eyes before tearing the seams apart and throwing the remains over his shoulder. Fallon's giggle filled the room as he picked her up and tossed her onto the bed, his body coming down hard on hers. His mouth met hers and he twisted it open, pistoning his tongue inside. She tasted vaguely of Brad's chicken wings, and the slightly spicy flavour filled him with need. He wanted to erase the images he'd created of Jackson fucking her. Of imagining how her legs would be wrapped around the man's hips as he thrust inside her, making her scream out his name.

Only Gil's name would be torn from her chest with such force she'd feel hoarse after.

"Do you think that pretty boy could've fucked you like I do, sweetheart? Do you think he would've known how to take you to the edge of pain and pleasure without going over?"

She shook her head, screaming the word 'no' as he suckled her left nipple into his mouth. It was hard and thick, like a juicy berry waiting to be plucked off the vine. He burrowed harder into her flesh, plumping her other breast with his hand. She arched into him, rubbing her wet inner lips up and down his pants. He could feel the heat and moisture through the material and had to concentrate on something else for a moment before he spewed his sperm inside his jeans.

"Don't move," he said, putting enough authority into his voice so that he knew she'd obey him. He stood up and clawed at his zipper, amazed at how much his fingers trembled. Only Fallon had ever had this effect on him. No matter how strong he was, she reduced him to a trembling fool with only a look.

"Sure you don't need my help?" she asked, opening her legs a bit wider. His gaze snapped down and he moaned at the sight of her delicate pussy, plump and pink. He could see the glistening evidence of her arousal trailing down her inner thighs and practically ripped his own clothes off in the need to take her.

"You'll pay for that, darling," he promised, pulling her closer to the edge of the bed. He already knew how he was going to take her, but he wanted a taste of the sweet juice coating her skin. He leaned in, inhaling the musky scent of her arousal. It was so sweet and warm, he plunged his tongue through her slit without thinking. Fallon moaned and tilted her hips, pressing him harder into her flesh.

"So sweet, baby. God, I love the taste of you."

He dipped in for another lick, swirling the cream around her clit. She cried out and speared her fingers through his hair, anchoring his face against her mound. He chuckled and blew a hot breath across her clit, loving how it tightened in response.

"Don't worry, Fallon. I'm not going to tease you. I need you too badly."

And he did. After seeing the woman splayed out across the makeshift altar, her legs spread wide, the evidence of her suffering carved on her chest, he'd had to physically hold himself from running back to Fallon. To convince himself she was still safe, still his. More than once the nurse's face had blurred into hers and he knew he'd never be able to inspect another crime scene without seeing his lover's face.

Gil shook the unsettling thoughts from his head and sucked more of Fallon's juice into his mouth. He loved how wet she got when he touched her, and wondered how long he could lie there, licking her. An hour? A day? A week?

Fallon cried out and ground her pussy into him, drawing him from his thoughts. She wasn't going to last another minute at this pace and he needed to get her ready for the next event.

He pulled away, loving the huff of frustration that echoed his retreat. "Soon, darling. I just need to get you ready first."

"Ready for what?" she asked, pressing up onto her elbows.

He smiled and pulled the plug and lubrication out of the drawer. "For my grand entrance," he said. "There's only one way to really stake my claim. And I think you know what it is."

Fallon's eyes went wide as she watched him lubricate the toy, smearing a generous amount of gel along its length. She looked incredibly aroused, with just a hint of uncertainty flashing in and out of her expression. He knew she'd hoped he'd take her anally when she'd demanded he take action, but he also knew the thought of it left her feeling just a bit unsure. He hadn't been able to love her that way since Charlie had joined them, and he knew she was remembering that too.

"Ready, baby." It wasn't a question and he didn't wait for a reply. A shiver trembled through her as he placed the thick plug at her rear entrance, coating the tight pucker with a blob of gel he'd placed on the tip. "Relax for me."

Her muscles tensed then softened as she did her best to comply. A trail of juice had trickled down from her cunt, and he smiled when he thought of licking it all away. He eased forward, pulling her ass checks apart with his other hand as he slowly inserted the plug, not stopping until the base locked against her flesh. Fallon moaned and twisted, fisting the sheets in her hands.

"You're so tight, Fallon. Damn, I can't wait to feel you squeeze my cock."

"Then fuck me, already!" she screamed.

"Soon. But first I want to enjoy watching you squirm around the plug." He pulled it out, plunging it back in faster, harder. She bucked up but didn't ask him to stop. "That's it, baby. Let it stretch those tight muscles." He thrust it in again, loving the way her ass flowed around the toy in an effort to accommodate it. "Feel good?"

"So good. Please, Gil."

"As soon as I've eaten all this sweet cream you've made for me." He licked his way from her ass to her clit. "Delicious."

Fallon screamed her need, opening her legs wider, begging him to lick her until she came. He followed her wishes, lapping at her pussy, pushing her higher. He grunted when she twisted her hands in his hair, tugging on the ends with enough force to add a sharp sting. He smiled, wondering how she'd enjoy a quick spanking with the plug still in her ass when he flipped her over and prepared her for his final task.

"Now. Oh God. I need you to make me come. Now!"

Her fingers tightened around his hair as he increased the pressure against her clit. She was rocking with him, pushing the plug deeper into her ass as he licked her nub, nipping at it with his teeth. She gasped in one last raspy breath before wailing out his name, her body exploding beneath him. Gil growled into her flesh, drinking the juice that spilled from her cunt as her ass locked around the plug, refusing to let it move. Her fingers fell from his head, dropping on the bed beside him. A sense of male pride flooded his system and he smiled victoriously.

"Do you have any idea how wonderfully you orgasm, baby? God, it's better than any porn ever made." He nuzzled her bud and loved the moan that filled her lungs. "Now let's see if I can make you scream again."

With that, he rose from between her legs, dropping one last kiss on her mound as he straddled her body, rubbing his hands along her thighs. "Roll over, Fallon."

She snagged her bottom lip between her teeth as she stared at the engorged head of his cock. It was red and swollen, the tip shiny with his pre-cum. He could tell by the gleam in her eyes she wanted to suck him again.

"Next time," he whispered, loving how her mouth turned down into a disappointed pout. For a moment, he thought she might actually challenge him again, but then she lowered her eyes and turned slowly in the small confines of his body.

"Good girl," he praised, smoothing his hand over her buttocks. She cried out in surprise when he placed a firm whack across her cheeks.

"What was that for?" she demanded, glancing back at him over her shoulder.

He merely lifted an eyebrow. "For thinking about disobeying me, darling. I saw that look in your eyes."

Fallon's pout increased and he couldn't stop from placing another smack on her other side. She jerked against him and he saw her ass clench around the plug. A muscle twitched in his jaw at the sight and he couldn't help but spank her again.

"Damn, Fallon. Do you know how erotic it is to see you clench on that plug? You're killing me, girl."

"More," was all she seemed to be able to moan as she lifted her ass and tucked her knees under her. "More."

His heart swelled in his chest and he didn't try to stop the smile from lighting his face. He'd never imagined he'd ever find a woman who'd please him like she did. And he'd almost lost her.

Gil spanked her again, raining his hand down over her ass until her skin flushed a bright pink and she screamed out his name. Then he nudged her knees farther apart and grabbed the end of the plug.

"Take a breath, baby, and blow it out slowly."

Fallon complied and her breath hissed from her chest as he pulled the toy from her body, tossing it forgotten on the floor. Her hole was red and slick, slightly open from the pressure of the plug. He reached for the tube and smeared more gel along his cock, ensuring every inch was covered in a thick coat. Despite the preparations, he knew she'd be tight, and he didn't want to hurt her.

Fallon stilled as he placed his crown at her nether hole, gently splaying her cheeks apart as he pressed against her anus.

"Relax, baby. Relax so I can show you who truly possesses you."

His name hissed out with her breath as he slowly entered her, pressing through the tight ring of muscles until the bulbous head popped in. She let out a cry as her back bowed and her hips pressed back, sinking him all the way in. He grabbed her hips, trying to still her movement, but it was too late. The hot sensation of her ass clasping his over-aroused shaft was more than he could stand. His breath whooshed out of his chest in a sigh of defeat, and he gave in to the carnal need flowing through his body.

Fallon screamed as he powered into her, claiming her ass in one strong stroke then retreating just as quickly. She'd fisted the pillow beneath her chest as she met each thrust, angling him deeper, taking him farther into her body than he'd dreamed possible. She was howling in a deep, primitive voice that made the hairs on his neck stand up. If he hadn't known she was immersed in pleasure, he would've thought someone was killing her.

But then maybe he was.

With pleasure.

"Hold on. I'm going to come and I want to take you with me."

She cried out, the sound hushed by the pounding of his blood, so loud it made his head spin. He released one side of her hip and landed another smack on her ass, her scream the only indication he'd sent her even higher. Her anal muscles clenched around his invading cock, milking his release even as he fought to hold on. He came in one almighty spurt, filling her with seed until his toes tingled. Sometime during his release she'd locked him tight inside her ass, her body convulsing on the bed beneath him. He made one last attempt to pleasure her by reaching around and pinching her clit, rewarded by the wail that pierced the air. She gave another tilt of her hips, then collapsed on the bed.

Gil followed her down, dragging her over on her side as

he pulled her tight against his chest. His vision dimmed and his head rolled in dizzying waves as he waited for his orgasm to ease and his breathing to return to normal. Fallon was locked in his arms, her warm tears washing over his skin.

"I love you too, Gil," she whispered, her voice so soft he wasn't sure if he'd heard her.

He held her even tighter, loving how their bodies fit perfectly together. "Sleep now. We'll talk later. But know this. I'll never let you go again."

He thought he heard her sob once as she kissed his arm before sexual exhaustion won the fight and he drifted into the growing darkness.

Chapter Twenty

Fallon woke to the sound of rain on the window. It was hazy and distant, but just enough to ease some of the fuzziness from her head. She squinted at her surroundings, wondering why her body felt so hot. It wasn't until she tried to roll over that she realised she was pressed tight against Gil's chest. He'd looped one arm around her waist and the other under her head. Her heart clenched when she reran the events of last night, a small pinch in her ass confirming it wasn't her imagination. Gil had said he loved her…never wanted to leave her. And he'd certainly gone to extreme lengths to stake his claim.

She smiled at the images that filled her head, the feel of his cock tunnelling deep into her ass still vivid in her mind. It'd been so long since she'd experienced that form of pleasure, the intensity of her orgasms had nearly caused her to black out. But it'd been more than just the physical pleasure. There'd been a sensuality to his touch he'd never shown her before. It made her feel more confident than ever. She smiled and burrowed closer into him.

"You know, Fallon. You keep rubbing me with your ass, and I might forget what a pounding it's already taken tonight."

Fallon's smile widened. Gil's cock was already hardening against the small of her back and his voice was deep with lust. "Is that a threat? Or a promise?"

Gil rolled her over in his arms, covering her body with his. "Dangerous words, darling." Then his voice softened and a different emotion crossed his expression. "Are you sore?"

Tears pooled as he traced her jaw with his hands. He looked so sincere she thought her heart would pound out through her chest. "You could never hurt me."

A vein in his temple twitched as he clenched his jaw. "I already have," he whispered, climbing off of her and walking over to the window. "I pushed you away when all you wanted to do was help me."

Fallon's stomach dropped as she watched him stare out at the dreary night. She could see the pain in his reflection on the rain-streaked window. It was then she realised how much leaving had hurt him too. A calm settled in her heart and she pushed herself up and walked to the other side of the window. "It's taken me a long time to see that you didn't leave to hurt me. I think you left because it hurt you too much to stay." She looked down at her feet. "I never should've gone along that night. I knew it'd kill you inside."

She hadn't realised he'd moved until she felt his hands close around her shoulders as he turned her back towards the bed. "What?" His voice was harsh and the tone in it sent shivers down her spine. "You've spent all this time thinking I left because of the night we shared with Charlie?"

She nodded, unable to talk around the lump lodged in her throat.

Gil shook her once and moved away, stalking his way back to the bed. "That night is the only memory that's kept me sane these past six months." He met her gaze. "The only reason I didn't finish what those bastards started that day."

"But, I don't understand. If you weren't mad about sharing me with Charlie, then what? And why did you want to share in the first place?"

Gil sighed and sat down on the edge of the bed, pressing his head into his hands. "It started five years before I met you." He paused as if signalling her to sit down. She moved over, taking the chair across from him.

"Charlie and I used to work together out of the Reno office. We'd been stationed there since we'd left the academy, working extortion cases. I was pretty happy there, but..." He shrugged. "Charlie had met this beautiful young journalist and accepted a transfer to Seattle where she'd just been offered her own column. A couple of weeks before he was supposed to move, the three of us headed off for one last hurrah." He stopped and looked over at her. "And no, we didn't share her. It was just Charlie's way of saying goodbye.

"Anyway, we headed down to Central America for some cheap fun in the sun. Juliet, Charlie's fiancée, wanted..."

"Charlie's fiancée?" she interrupted lurching to her feet. "I never heard either of you mention any fiancée before." Gil merely nodded and motioned her back to the chair. She plopped down on the seat, not sure if she'd decided to sit or if her legs had given out.

"Juliet wanted to see this little town in the mountains her friends had told her about. And Charlie couldn't say no to her. We were nearly over the peak when some jackass trying to pass us on a blind corner barrelled into the car to avoid a head-on and sent us over the edge."

He looked down at his hands clenched in his lap. They were trembling. "What happened?"

Gil's jaw twitched and his eyes went distant, as if he was somewhere else. "I don't really remember much. Loud noises. Screaming. The next thing I knew I was lying on the ground beside the car, my head throbbing and my ribs so sore I could barely breathe. Somehow, we'd made it to the bottom of this crag and Charlie had pulled us both from the wreckage." Gil laughed, but it was hollow. "Charlie was the only one not hurt. I mean, not even a fucking scratch. To this day I don't know how he managed that."

"What about Juliet?"

Gil's face sobered and his skin paled. "She was pretty bad. In and out of consciousness...internal bleeding. We knew if we didn't get her some help fast, she wouldn't make it. Charlie tried climbing back up, but..." His voice trailed off and all Fallon could do was caress her fingers over his.

"We decided to walk it out. We'd passed another town

several miles back and figured we could reach it by nightfall. What we didn't know was how fucking slow it is traipsing through the jungle. Especially when one of you can barely move. I tried to keep up, but I was coughing up blood by sunset. Charlie decided to stop and did what he could to keep Juliet comfortable. But..."

His eyes filled with tears and his voice grew hoarse. Fallon felt her tears fall down her cheek but didn't release Gil's hand to wipe them away.

Gil took a deep breath. "She died in the night. We moved on the next day, Charlie still carrying her. He said he couldn't leave her there, alone. That he'd never forgive himself if he didn't bring her home to rest in peace. But that damn town never seemed to pop up and we ended up walking for hours again. By noon I was doubled over and so delirious I couldn't even remember where I was. I finally just collapsed. I told Charlie to go ahead and get help. That's the last I remember."

He stopped and looked like a man in need of a drink. Fallon thought about running to the kitchen, but he'd sandwiched her fingers between his and didn't seem able to let go. "Did Charlie go for help?"

He shook his head and tightened his hold on her. "I woke up a week later in a federal hospital in Reno. Apparently Charlie had carried me eight more miles before he stumbled upon the highway and was able to flag down some help. They'd flown us both stateside and..."

She nodded, her chest so tight she was fighting to take each breath. "What about Juliet?"

Gil closed his eyes and she saw the first tear ease down his cheek. "He had to leave her behind to save me."

"Oh God, Gil. I'm so sorry. Is that why he was always so...distant?"

"He never really came to terms with his decision. And I always felt like I'd made a part of him die that day. So I applied to transfer with him, and we continued on here as if things were the same."

"But they weren't."

"He'd changed. Never dated or showed any interest in women." He stopped and looked her straight in the eyes. "Not until I introduced him to you."

Fallon pulled back a bit, not sure what to say. Had she somehow made Charlie think she was attracted to him? Or worse, had she been, but been too ashamed to admit it? "Gil, I never meant..."

Gil patted her hand and forced a smile. "I know. It wasn't anything you did. It was just you. Your personality, your sense of humour. The easy way you accept people as if they're family. You were the only person who could make him smile...I mean really smile."

"So how does that translate into a threesome?"

Gil's lips tightened and he pulled his hands away. "We were working a very involved case. There was a new sect in town supplying weapons to American mercenaries abroad. We needed to know where and who, and to do that, we needed someone on the inside. Charlie volunteered. He was supposed to find out where the weapons came from and went so we could intercept a shipment. Everything seemed to be going smoothly until a few days before the raid. We were sitting at his place, drinking beer and going over the details, when he just out and confessed he was in love with you."

Fallon's stomach flip-flopped as she stared at Gil. But he didn't seem angry or jealous. "And you were okay with that?"

He shrugged again and sighed. "It's not like he was going to try and steal you away or anything. It was more a revelation. He hadn't cared about anyone for so long, and all I could think about was how he'd finally let Juliet go." He reached out and took her hand. "I wanted him to remember what it was like to be loved, so..."

Fallon nodded, all too aware of how the story ended.

"You saved him, Fallon. You gave him back that part of him he'd left in the jungle."

"So if that's true, then why did you leave?" Gil's face tightened at the question and she watched him fight against some inner demon. It was obvious there was more to his story than he'd told her. After a few minutes he stood up and once again walked over to the window. "What happened in the warehouse, Gil?"

Gil bowed his head as if holding it up took too much strength. "It involved this woman he'd had to *work* with during his undercover time." He waved his hand in the air. "It doesn't really matter. In the end, he got hurt and I didn't save him."

"That's not true." She stood up and padded over to him, stopping behind him. "You did everything you could."

Gil's face twisted with guilt as he shook his head. "I let him die, I..."

Fallon silenced him with a soft finger over his lips. He turned to look at her, tears staining his cheeks. "You didn't let him die. You carried him through that warehouse. You walked until you fell. I saw you try to keep him alive until you were lying beside him, unconscious." She ran her fingers over his cheeks, wiping away the light wash of tears. "You gave him your last breath. No one could ask for more than that."

Gil choked back a sob as he grabbed her and pulled her tight against him. She moved easily into his arms and surrounded him with her warmth. He burrowed his head into her hair, inhaling the fresh scent until the smell of blood and fear he'd always associated with that memory faded. A weight lifted off his heart, replaced by a new, deeper emotion.

"It kills me to think you saw that," he finally mumbled. Fallon merely held him tighter. "I wish you'd told me about this before." He pulled back and placed his hand under her chin. "Two years is a long time to keep a secret."

Fallon's expression changed as she pulled away and put her back to him. "It wasn't something you needed to know."

"Maybe not. But it was something you needed to tell me." He closed the distance. "I might have doubted your ability. But I never would've doubted you."

Fallon's shoulders hunched, tension bunching her muscles. "I couldn't risk it," she whispered.

"Risk what?"

A soft sob echoed in the room as she glanced back at him over her shoulder. "That you'd leave."

Gil's heart clenched at the sight of the fear in her eyes. "Why would I leave because of"—he waved his hand in the space between them—"what you can do?" He saw the hurt flash and the way she kicked up her chin spoke volumes. "Did someone else leave because of it?" She looked away. "Fallon?"

"Why do you think I grew up with my grandparents?"

A deep sinking feeling formed in his stomach. *Shit.* "I assumed your parents died or something. You never really said."

"They're alive and well and living in Florida. I haven't seen or spoken to them in twenty years. Not since…" Her voice trailed off and he knew the answer without her saying it.

"Not since your sister was murdered," he finished. Fallon whirled around to face him, anger glittering in her eyes. "I did a bit of research after you mentioned her the other day. I didn't know why you'd never told me about her." He gave her a soft smile. "After reading the report, I can see why." He took another step closer. "Did you see it all happen?"

Fallon's chin quivered and a single tear crept down her cheek. "She summoned me every day she was kept there. I tried to tell my parents, but… After the police found her body, they told me I was responsible. That it was my fault the police didn't find her in time. That I was helping the monster that took her. I guess they thought I'd actually been in the room."

Gil went to touch her, but she moved away, shaking her

head as she held up her hand. "They didn't speak to me for months, leaving food out on the counter so I wouldn't have to ask for it. Looking back, I guess I thought I deserved it. I probably would've stayed if my father hadn't..."

Shame filled her expression and Gil had to fight the urge to pound the nearest surface. "Until your father did what?"

She lowered her eyes and stared at the floor between her legs. "He started hitting me. He said it was my penance. Then one night he tried to..." She wrapped her arms around her chest. "I managed to get away and that was the last I ever saw of them. I took some money out of my mother's purse and hopped the next bus to Portland. My grandparents have a farm not far from there. I called them from the station and that's where I spent the rest of my life until I moved out on my own."

Gil moved before she could act, pulling her into his arms as he dropped kisses across her head. "You know it's not your fault, Fallon. You were only twelve years old. No one should have to live through that. Losing a sister. Seeing her tortured and raped, knowing you couldn't help her. And as for your parents, God help them if I ever lay eyes on them. I swear I'll kill the man for trying to hurt you like that." He pulled back just enough so she could look up at him. "None of that matters anymore, darling. You're mine now. And I'll never let you go, not for anything."

With that, he lowered his mouth and took her lips in his. They were warm and wet, and just the taste of her surged the blood in his veins, making his shaft stand at attention. He moaned as it brushed across her mound, pressing into the slick folds of her sex. Despite the situation, she was hot and wet, ready for him to pleasure her. He savoured the thought of loving her. Of spending hours worshipping her body. Moving inside her without needing to climax, but just revelling in the joining of their bodies. He thought of all he could say to her. How he could soothe her fears with his words and actions. She was giving herself to him, and he'd make sure she knew how much he treasured her.

Gil scooped her up in his arms and carried her the few steps back to the bed, careful to lay her down gently this time. He could tell by the way she clung to him she needed tenderness. Not a fast, hard fuck, but a long, gentle loving. He followed her down on the bed, covering her trembling body with his. She stilled when his shaft nudged at her entrance, asking for permission to enter.

He eased up on his elbows, alarmed by the sudden tension coursing through her body. "Are you too sore, baby?" he asked, wondering if he really had been too rough, despite her denial earlier.

She shook her head and more tears gathered in her eyes.

"Is something else wrong?"

She cringed and a thousand fears raced through his mind until she snagged her bottom lip and looked him in the eyes. "There's something I've been meaning to tell you..." she began, her voice barely a whisper. "Shortly after you left, I was having these bad headaches, so my doctor..."

Her voice vanished into the silence and Gil rethought the events of the day. The way she'd talked about settling down and starting a family. How she'd brushed her hand across her stomach with a dreamy look in her eyes. Then there'd been the no alcohol thing.

Pieces clicked into place and the truth settled on him like a warm blanket. Fallon must have seen the gleam in his eyes. Her face flushed a deep red that laced down across her chest. Her nipples hardened against him and he couldn't stop the contented moan from rumbling free.

"Maybe we should take precau..." she began, only to be silenced by his lips on hers. He kissed her softly, dipping his tongue into her mouth when she opened willingly.

He smiled at her when she finally opened her eyes. "I think it's already too late for that, don't you?" he said, shifting his gaze down their bodies towards her stomach. "And if it's not, then I want to try again."

Fallon cried into his mouth as he kissed her. He nudged his cock at her pussy and was rewarded by the warm heat of her sheath as she looped her legs around his hips and tilted his shaft inside.

"God, you feel so warm and tight. It's all I can do not to pump my cum inside you the moment you clench yourself around me." He slid deeper into her, loving the desperate moan that trembled from her lips. "Do you want me to come inside you, darling?"

"Yes." Her reply was a hiss of pleasure as he locked his sac against her flesh.

"Do you want to have my child, Fallon? 'Cause the thought of you all round with my baby makes my cock so hard I'm worried I'll split you in half."

"You won't hurt me. Please, I need more. I need to feel you pumping your seed inside me. I want your baby more than anything."

He smiled at her confession, drawing his shaft slowly out of her channel until just the tip was snugged inside her tight sex. He loved how her body flowed around him. Stretching as he pushed in, and closing behind the wake of his retreat. The sensation was amazing and he found himself moving faster, needing to feel the warm clasp of her pussy as he filled her. Wanting her to always remember what it felt like to have him inside her.

"Still need me to show you who possesses you, baby?"

She shook her head, tilting it back as he slammed home again. "Only you do," she gasped twisting beneath him. "Only you. Now please, Gil. Harder."

It was his turn to shake his head. "I want to show you how much I cherish you. How lucky I am to be the man who gets to love you. I want this to last a lifetime."

"You can have me again. As many times as you want. Just please. I'm so close."

"As many times as I need?" he teased, holding her orgasm at bay.

"Yes. Just make me come. Please."

Gil smiled down at her. Oh, how she'd eat those words later. Then he reached between her legs and plucked at her clit, sending her careening over the edge. She screamed his name as her head pushed into the pillow, arching her back off the mattress. He moved faster, knowing the hard strokes would drive the orgasm higher. She dug her nails into his back, meeting each thrust until her body gave out and she went limp beneath him. He roared in male approval, pumping into her until the fire in his spine exploded between his legs, and he released his seed, filling her until the excess seeped around his shaft and down their thighs.

"Sweet mercy," he moaned, holding his body rigidly above hers until the flashing in his head dissipated and he eased his body down, bridging some of his weight on his arms. He'd never come so hard in his life, except perhaps every other time he'd ever made love to her. And just knowing he'd have a lifetime of chances made his heart race.

"Sleep, baby," he soothed, pulling his weakening flesh from her sweet heat. She sighed out a soft breath, immediately turning into his chest. "Sleep, 'cause I plan on taking you up on your offer as soon as you open those beautiful baby blues."

Chapter Twenty-One

Fallon sighed, snuggling deeper into the covers. Her body ached in the most delicious ways, bringing a satisfied smile to her face. Gil had been masterful last night, taking her from one orgasm to another, filling her until she'd thought she might actually burst. And all the while, telling her how much he loved her…needed her.

"Someone certainly looks happy this morning."

Her eyes popped open even as she reached behind her, only to find Gil gone. She looked over at the doorway and felt her heart skip a beat. He was leaning against the doorframe, his massive shoulders wedged into the small space. He was naked from the waist up, the lean play of his muscles dancing in the morning light. His low-slung jeans hugged his legs, and the top button splayed open, exposing a light dusting of dark hair as it trailed from his chest down below his stomach. His feet were bare against the wood flooring and he was holding a tray in his hands.

"I'd be happier if you were still naked in the bed with me," she said, her gaze focused on the increasing bulge in his pants. She pushed up onto her elbow, allowing the blankets to slide down her arm, baring her breasts to him. His hiss of breath made her smile. "I don't suppose I could tempt you back?"

Gil kicked his mouth into a sexy smile as he made his way across the room. "I thought after all your exercise last night, you might be hungry." He chuckled as her stomach growled its agreement. "See anything you like?" he asked, lowering the tray onto the chair still sitting beside the bed.

Fallon gazed at the feast before her. He'd cut up a bowl of

fresh strawberries, topping them with a generous dollop of whipped cream. There was warm buttered bread, a plate of scrambled eggs, a basket full of muffins and two glasses of juice. "Think you brought enough?" she joked, eyeing the whipped cream with interest.

"I don't think either of us really ate yesterday," he said, popping a piece of muffin into his mouth. "And quite frankly, I'm famished."

Fallon smiled, loving how he watched her even as he stuffed more muffin into his mouth. He was hungry all right, but for more than just food. She raised an eyebrow and nodded towards his groin. "Take off your pants, and I'll show you exactly what I'm hungry for."

His eyes darkened as he looked back at the tray of food and then at her. He seemed to read her intentions as she sat up in the bed and motioned to his jeans. "Okay, baby. But remember. Turnabout is fair play."

"I'm counting on it," she purred, watching his fingers work the buttons on his jeans. He moved slowly, teasing her with glimpses of his cock as he slipped each one free, finally pushing the material down over his thighs. Then he was standing there, gloriously naked. She nodded and motioned him forward. "Stand in front of me."

He paused for just a moment, flashing her a look that was anything but submissive, and then stepped forward, stopping when his cock was inches from her face. She leaned in, inhaling the fresh clean scent of him.

"You grabbed a shower."

He shrugged, watching her through lowered lids. "I tried to wake you, darling. But sometimes you sleep like the dead." He smiled down at her, a mischievous gleam in his eyes. "Guess that'll have to change in nine months."

Fallon's stomach dropped hard, making her head spin. God, he'd said the words like he was discussing the weather. He didn't even look scared. "There's no guarantee I'm pregnant. I just wanted you to have a choice. One you should've had from the start."

"Well if you're not pregnant, it's sure not from lack of trying," he said. "And there was never a need for a choice." He touched her cheek softly then straightened. "Now I believe you mentioned something about being hungry. Or are you just enjoying the view?"

"Oh, I plan on enjoying more than just the view. Close your eyes."

"Careful, baby. You're moving onto thin ice."

"I'll take my chances. Now close your eyes. I promise you'll like my surprise."

Gil huffed but obeyed, squeezing his eyes shut. She knew he wasn't one to give in, and just the fact he was allowing her to lead showed her how deeply his feelings ran. She shifted on the bed, kicking back the covers as she knelt on the floor between him and the chair. She could tell by the tension in his thighs, he wouldn't last long, but she'd take every moment he gave her before she ended up back on the bed with him riding between her thighs.

"Mmm. What a delicious cock you have for me. I think it deserves a sweet treat." She reached over to the tray, swiping her finger through the whipped cream. "Did you picture me eating this cream off your cock when you prepared breakfast?"

Gil's mouth twitched and she could tell he was fighting not to open his eyes. "Actually, I picked all the things I wanted to eat off *your* body."

"And exactly what did you have in mind for the toast?" she asked, not able to picture anything in her mind.

Gil chuckled in a way that sent heat spiralling out from her core. "I have the perfect holding slot in mind, baby."

"You are wicked," she said, smearing more cream along his shaft. "Perhaps, if you behave, I'll save some cream for you."

"Darling, you already have all the cream I need. Now I suggest you get moving, or you'll find our positions reversed."

"I think you need to work on your patience," she teased,

distending her tongue to the tip of his shaft. She loved how his cock bobbed up at the sudden contact, nearly connecting with his stomach before descending again. "Tasty," she moaned, licking a small drop of cream off the hood. "I think we're going to need more cream."

Gil groaned as she lapped at his cock, licking every drop of cream off his shaft before pausing to smooth on a new layer. The mixture of tastes was intoxicating. Creamy sweetness. Salty musk. She bobbed forward, wrapping her lips around the crown and taking him deep, rubbing the tip against the back of her throat. His body tensed and his shaft thickened in her mouth, the head flaring as she eased back, sucking hard and swirling her tongue along the underside. She could feel the thick vein pulsing against the ridge of her tongue, pumping more blood to his already engorged head.

"You know, I never really liked whipped cream until this morning. But I think it's missing something."

Fallon reached for the bowl and picked out four plump berries. Gil had taken the time to cut them in half and she knew exactly where she wanted to balance them. "Now hold still, and let me enjoy some of my breakfast."

Gil's thighs clenched as she placed each one along the length of his shaft, smoothing a smear of whipped cream between each one. She wasn't sure how well they'd balance, but as long as he held still, they seemed able to stay on their perch.

"So good," she moaned, slowly engulfing his cock and sucking the first berry off his skin. She pulled back to eat her prize, watching the others bob as his erection strained against her assault.

"You'd better hurry, or I'll be digging those berries out of your sweet little pussy when I push you on your ass and shove my cock inside you."

His voice was strained with lust and she knew he meant every word. Her lips curved into a smile as she descended for another round, slurping the next strawberry off his shaft and into her mouth. But this time she didn't wait to enjoy the taste of it before bobbing back down for another one. "Damn. If I'd known you tasted so good all covered in cream, I would have done this two years ago."

"Fallon..."

She looked up at him, overwhelmed by the mixture of pleasure and pain on his face. He obviously loved her game, but the waiting was killing him. She held back a chuckle, knowing her next comment would push him over the edge, but unable to deny him any longer. "I don't suppose you have a banana I could use on another part of your anatomy?"

Gil's eyes popped open and he snapped his gaze down on her just as she surrounded his pulsing flesh with her velvet heat. His moan filled the room and he wasn't able to stop from punching his hip forward, fucking her mouth as she knew he longed to fuck her cunt.

"That's it, baby. Take it all."

Fallon moved faster, opening her jaw as wide as she could to accommodate his shaft. He was pumping her hard now, his hands locked in her hair, his hips undulating back and forth. She slipped one hand down and cupped his sac, adding another dimension of pleasure as she gently rubbed the small area between his balls. He groaned louder, increasing the pressure on her hair.

"Yes, that's it. Suck me hard, baby."

She complied, letting him plunge deep into her mouth and then hollowing her cheeks as he pulled out. She could feel his smooth skin rasping against her teeth, gently scraping the sensitive tissue under his hood. He managed to pound in three more times before he shouted her name and filled her throat with his seed. Fallon held on, sucking each spurt until his legs trembled and his grip loosened.

"Goddamn, Fallon. You've always been such a sweet mouth fuck. I don't know where you learned to give blow jobs, baby, but you could suck a man's eyes out through his cock if given the chance."

Fallon smiled up at his contented grin, finally allowing his weakening flesh to pull free from her mouth. "I'm not sure if that's a compliment or not, but I'll give you the benefit of the doubt." She rose to her feet and moved into his arms. "Now how about I feed you your breakfast?"

Gil shook his head and pushed her back on the bed, smiling at her surprised yelp. "I think I'd prefer to feed myself, baby. But don't worry, you're going to be my plate."

Fallon knew when she looked back at that morning, she'd blush about all the ways Gil had eaten his food off her body. How he'd covered her nipples in the last of the whipped cream and filled her belly button and pussy with scrambled eggs and crumbled muffin. He'd even used her smooth inner lips to hold his bread as he nibbled at it. Then he'd shoved a strawberry inside her and used his tongue to slowly extract it. By the time he was done, her body was humming, so close to climaxing she thought she might actually pass out from the strain.

"Please, Gil. I need to come. No more teasing."

Gil's breath whispered over her puckered clit, making it ache even more. "Oh, but you're so beautiful perched on the edge, darling. Your skin is flushed a pretty shade of pink, and your pussy is so aroused, it's dripping juice down your thighs. In fact, it's so creamy I think I'll have the other half of my toast now."

Fallon screamed and pushed up on her elbows, locking him between her thighs. "No more food, Gil. So unless you plan on fucking me with something from the refrigerator, I suggest you curb your appetite until you've made me scream."

The smile that formed on his lips sent hot waves of desire pouring out from her core. "Wait. Right. Here."

She stared in awe as he released her legs and bolted from the room, only to appear moments later carrying the largest banana she'd ever seen. He'd taken the time to cut off the rough end and was now busy encasing the fruit in a condom from his wallet.

"Now the trick with bananas is to keep the skin on so they stay hard inside you." He smiled down at her and moved back between her legs. "Ready?"

"You can't be serious. I mean…it's a banana!"

Gil frowned and looked down at his prize. "Now talk like that is just going to hurt his feelings." He gave the thing an affectionate pat. "Think of him as Mr. Pleasure. And I can assure you, you're going love what he can do for you." Gil leaned over and placed the end against her weeping sex. "Watch me, baby. Watch me pleasure you."

Fallon's gaze centred on the shiny banana, watching as Gil swiped it through her folds, moistening the surface with her juice. Then he nudged it against her entrance, pushing slowly but firmly until the first few inches slipped inside her. She gasped at the unusual sensation. The banana felt huge, and the coolness of it only made the stretching burn more. She lolled her head back, needing him to go faster but knowing anything more would shatter her.

"Oh no, Fallon. Don't look away." Gil's voice was low and gravelly, sending more shivers along her skin. "I want you to watch me, baby. I want to see the pleasure on your face."

She forced her eyes open and her head back up as he sank the banana completely inside her. She felt stretched to the limit, but it felt so good. Gil's face mirrored hers and she could see how much he was enjoying his game. Already his cock was hard and thick, more pre-cum beading the tip. "Please," she whispered.

"Okay, baby." He bent down over her, licking at her clit as he slowly eased the banana out of her, only to plunge it back in. She cried out, arching her mound upwards, grinding her clit into his lips, needing him to press harder. Gil chuckled once, blowing one last breath across her nub before suckling it into his mouth and devouring it.

Fallon held her breath, her body shattering into a million pieces as the orgasm pulsed through her, travelling down her body in endless waves that seemed to drain every ounce of strength from her. She opened her mouth to scream but only whimpered as she collapsed on the bed, Gil's mouth still latched around her clit, the banana still driving into her. More waves rolled over her and it wasn't until the light faded briefly into dark that she realised he'd finally stopped and was smoothing his hands over her skin, whispering sweet words in her ear. She focused on his voice, letting the low sexy tone ease her raw nerves, soothe her pleasured body back to life. She opened her eyes to find him staring down at her.

"I knew you'd like having breakfast in bed." He leaned down and kissed her nose. "Care for seconds?"

She laughed, knowing no matter how exhausted she was, she'd always want more. "Only if you plan on using your cock this time."

Gil smiled and rolled on top of her, stopping just long enough to wrap his arms around her body, before rolling again. She gasped as she flipped on top of him, her legs straddling his. "I want to watch you take me, Fallon. I want to see your face as you ride me."

She nodded, unable to speak. Gil didn't offer to relinquish control very often. He usually preferred to be the one driving into her, whether on her back, from behind, against a wall. She shifted her body, angling her hips more as she brushed his crown through her creamy honey. Gil's eyes narrowed and his lips pulled tight, but he kept still, waiting for her to sink down. She smiled at him, leaning over to brush a soft kiss across his lips as she lowered some of her weight and sank one full inch of his shaft inside her.

Fallon sighed out her breath, fighting the urge to plop down in one motion. She wanted to make the moment last. Savour every detail before her hormones took over and she rode him to completion. She stretched forward, placing a hand on each of his shoulders. They were broad and hard, barely giving way beneath her weight. She took the time to caress his skin, scratching her nails across his nipples and chest, loving his low growl of appreciation. He was perfection personified, and she couldn't wait to spend the rest of her life making love to him.

Gil's hands moved up to her hips, guiding her farther onto his cock. He was obviously trying to let her lead, but it appeared he had his limits. Fallon braced her hands back on his shoulders and rotated her hips, taking him halfway inside. Her pussy pulsed, pumping more juice along his cock, easing his way as she lowered herself, not stopping until her ass rested against his thighs.

"You're so big, Gil. So big and hard and all mine." She circled her hips, driving him slightly deeper, making him grunt with need. "I love feeling you inside me. Stretching me. Driving me crazy with want." She arched up, pulling him through her channel, moaning at the way his skin slid against hers, burning every nerve along the way. "I can't wait to feel you come inside me."

"I suggest you find a rhythm soon then, my love. Or you'll be feeling my cum very soon."

His words were forced through clenched teeth, and he tensed when she plunged again, taking him deep then pulling back. Every movement tightened his hold on her hips until she was sure she'd have small circular bruises. But the slight bite of pain only heightened her pleasure, and she moaned as the fire swept over her, heating her from the inside out. His cock was slick and thick, tunnelling into her with swift, hard strokes as she pumped her ass up and down, riding him like a stallion.

"Faster, Fallon. Pump me hard, baby."

She leant forward, bridging more of her weight on her hands, waving her breasts in front of his face. He didn't wait for an invitation before suckling the closest one into his mouth, nipping at it as she pounded onto him. Her head fell back, a cry of pure pleasure purging from her lips as the approaching orgasm slithered down her spine and into her groin. She had just enough time to scream out his name as his mouth latched on to her other nipple, before the world exploded, sending her body into climax.

"Fuck, yes."

Gil's roar followed hers and she was vaguely aware of the hot jets of sperm spurting from his cock, splashing against her womb as she arched back, her hair grazing his legs. His hands were wrapped around her waist, holding her up as the intensity of her orgasm dimmed the light and zapped her strength. She hadn't realised she'd collapsed on top of him until she felt his warm hands stroking her back, tracing small circles over her skin.

"You're so beautiful. God, I love you."

She kissed his chest, pulling herself tighter against him. "Good, because I can't lose you again. I love you too much."

He sighed against her hair, brushing a light kiss across the shell of her ear. "You're stuck with me now, baby. So stop worrying and rest. We've got a full day ahead of us."

"Anything specific in mind?" she asked.

"Yeah. Lunch and dinner."

* * * *

Two hours later, Fallon was sitting on the bed, trying to decide whether to even bother attempting to get dressed. She'd already made a trip out to the kitchen in one of her T's only to have Gil rip it to shreds before he threw her on the kitchen table and fucked her through three orgasms. She'd tried to be angry with him, but he'd silenced her protests with four firm whacks to her ass, with a promise of more if she tried to cover up her body from him again. Now she was perched on the edge of the bed, her ass still warm from his hand, wondering if she should just spend the day naked beneath the sheets.

"Good. You're still beautifully naked." He was standing at the doorway, watching her through lowered lids. "Now spread your legs wide, baby, and give me a nice view of that pretty little pussy."

Fallon blushed but opened her legs, giving him a full view of how wet he'd already made her. Gil's jaw twitched and the pulse in his neck quickened. She was just about to slip a finger between her lips to tease him when the harsh sound of music blared through the room.

Fallon jumped, falling off the bed as she tried to reach for the phone. She caught it on the third ring, staring at the shiny metal as Gil stopped at her feet. She looked up at him, unable to hide the fear in her eyes. "It's his ring."

Gil nodded, his phone already in his hand. He knelt down beside her, motioning her to answer it as he pressed his ear to hers.

"Nine-one-one. Do you need police, fire or ambulance?"

"I think you know the answer to that…Angel."

His voice was strange—a mixture of anger and exhaustion—and Fallon knew this conversation wasn't going to be like the others. "I wasn't sure you were going to call. It's been so long."

"So long since what, Angel? Since I've called you?" He paused, breathing heavily into the phone. "Or since we talked in person?"

Her body dissolved into tremors, making the phone shake in her hand. She bit down on her lip, wondering how she was going to keep talking, when Gil smoothed his hand down her back, silently soothing her fears. She chanced a quick glance his way, only to see him smiling back at her. "I'm not sure I understand what you mean," she replied, wanting him to explain what he'd seen.

"Oh, I think you do. Like I told you at the chapel, it's not the first time I've sensed your presence. You've been with me since my first salvation in Seattle, haven't you?" He waited, and when she didn't answer, he laughed. "What's wrong, Angel? Are you scared of me?"

"I'm not afraid," she lied, hoping her voice sounded stronger than she felt. "I want to help you. Please. If you'll just tell me where you are, I can get you some help."

"Like you helped me last night!" he shouted. "Bringing the cops and Feds like hungry little scavengers. You sent them to me when you knew I hadn't had enough time to fully cleanse her soul. I had to compromise on the cross, leaving out some of the more intricate details, and I barely had enough time to fuck her before I left." He sighed, making her hairs prickle. "You disappointed me, Angel. I thought you understood. I thought your soul was pure."

"I only wanted to help you. You seem so...tortured. I don't think kill—I mean purifying the women is helping you. I've seen the way you touch them. You don't really want to hurt them, do you?"

"What I want doesn't matter. I've been given a task and I intend to complete it. It's the only way to bring him back."

"Bring who back? Why are you doing this?"

"Enough!" The force of his voice made her jump back from the phone. The man was beyond reasoning with. "Tell me...Angel. Is your lover there with you?"

Fallon pulled the phone away and looked over at Gil. His lips were pulled tight and the expression on his face was pure hatred. He nodded, mouthing the word *yes*. "Yes."

"Good. Then you can tell the illustrious Agent Grant that I want to meet with him and his partner, Agent Davis."

"Where?" was all she could get out. How did he know Gil's name and that he was her lover?

The Priest laughed, building the bile burning her throat. "That's where you come in, Angel. I'll be waiting for you to pay me a visit. Once I give you the location, you can tell him where to go." He laughed again. "I'll see you soon... Angel."

Fallon listened to the connection go dead, her hand still clamped around the phone. It took a few moments before she was able to place it back on the table, forcing her fingers to open one by one. She stared at it, half expecting it to ring again, when she felt the familiar shuffle. The bedroom faded, blurring to black before materialising again. She turned and tried to focus on Gil, but his silhouette vanished, melding into a grey wall. She could hear a voice ringing through the empty room, but it wasn't Gil's that called to her.

"Are you there, Angel? I can feel your presence. You must

be near."

She scrambled to her feet and hid behind a bundle of boxes stacked along the wall. *The Priest* was somewhere off to her right, beyond the light. She inched forward, peeking around the edge. Dark shadows pocketed the space, giving the room a mottled appearance. She drew back, not quite sure what to do. Even if he could *see* her, it wasn't as if she were really there. He'd only see a ghost of her reflection. But the thought of facing him sent cold shivers up her spine. She'd never had to deal with this kind of connection before.

Minutes ticked by. She looked around the room again, a strange feeling prickling the hairs on her neck. It looked familiar, but the layout was wrong. Where she expected to see a row of windows, there was nothing but metal walls. And all the windows on the opposite side of the room had been boarded over. An image of Charlie's pale face wavered in her mind, but it faded into the sound of footsteps.

"What's it going to be, Angel? Are you going to hide from me forever?"

He was circling the room, waiting for her to make the first move. She took a deep breath and stepped out, walking to the centre. She stopped in a bright patch of light, and waited.

"Such a pretty face. Does it serve you well?"

His voice was behind her now and she spun in the hopes of catching a glimpse of him. He was moving through the shadows, keeping his body cloaked. "I'm here, just like you wanted. Now show yourself."

"Not yet. We both know you disappear whenever we look directly at each other, so our formal introduction will have to wait until later." He'd moved off to the left now. "Tell me. Do I appear transparent too?"

She looked down at her hands, but everything here was solid to her. "It depends on how strongly I'm summoned."

"So it's only you that shimmers in the light." He laughed, his voice stronger, closer. "You really do look like an angel."

"Are you going to tell me why you wanted me here?"

Fallon could almost hear his shoulders shrug as a soft sigh whispered across the air. "I thought we agreed you were going to tell your lover where to find me?"

"You could've done that over the phone. There's another reason you wanted to see me."

The Priest laughed. "Not only beautiful, but smart as well." He took a step forward and Fallon saw his boots emerge from the darkness. "Tell me, Angel. Do you use your gifts for good...or evil?"

"Please. Just let me help you. I can come to the meeting... we can talk."

"Don't worry, Angel. We'll meet soon. And then I'll tell you everything." He shuffled closer, revealing his waist and thighs. "Tell your man to meet me back at the chapel. And tell him not to bother searching for me. I'll find him."

Fallon took a step back just as *The Priest* stepped forward, baring himself to the grey light. Her body jolted backwards, the images around her beginning to fade. He smiled at her, the tilt of his lips so like another's that she felt the air purge from her chest, the faint echo of her name following her into the light.

"Fallon! Damn it, Fallon, talk to me!"

Gil's voice was urgent, and she could feel the firm grip of his hands on her shoulders. He was shaking her, his breath hot against her neck. She forced her eyes open, groaning as the room continued to shift. "Chapel."

Gil stilled at the sound of her voice, cupping her shoulders rather than squeezing them. "What about the chapel?"

She looked up at him, needing to tell him her hunch but unable to voice her concerns. She was fading again, falling back into the darkness.

"Darling, please."

She licked her lips, forcing the words through clenched teeth. "He's back at the chapel." She shook her head, wrapping her fingers around his arm. "Something...not right. Gil...don't." The rest of what she wanted to say got lost in the haze dragging her under. Too many visions in such a short time had exhausted her body, and she just couldn't seem to keep her eyes open. She focused on one last thought, putting all her energy into a single word. "Charlie."

Gil watched Fallon fade into unconsciousness, her head lolling off to one side. She'd lost all the colour in her face and she looked like she'd gone a week without sleep. He felt his chest tighten and his eyes sting. But even like this, she was beautiful. And so strong. He wanted to gather her up in his arms and hold her until the nightmare was over. But if he didn't stop *the Priest* now, he knew Fallon would never be free. And he loved her too much to watch her suffer.

Gil scoped her off the floor and placed her gently in the bed, brushing the hair from her face as he skimmed her forehead with his lips. Her skin was cool and clammy, and he reached for the blankets as he flipped open his phone and dialled the number.

"Wade Davis."

His partner's voice was deep and heavy, and Gil realised he'd probably woken the man. "Wade, Gil."

"Geez, Gil. Don't I get a chance to sleep? Not that I imagine you got much sleep last night." His friend chuckled. "Hope you two remembered to keep your voices down with a cruiser parked outside."

"We did our best. But it looks like the honeymoon's over. The bastard just called. He wants to meet us back at the chapel. I'm not sure what his intentions are, but it's worth the risk."

"Did he ask for us specifically?"

"By name. I was listening on the phone when he told Fallon the message. He seems to have discovered our relationship."

"I don't like the sound of that."

"Me neither. That's why I'm going to have Trevor send another unit over. I need to know she's safe before I leave."

"I'm on my way. I'll pick you up in say…ten."

"I'll be waiting, buddy. Let's make sure we nail him this time."

Gil hung up the phone and sat down on the edge of the bed, turning to watch Fallon sleep. She looked so fragile tucked beneath the white sheets, he had to force himself to stand up and fetch his clothes. He thought about what she'd tried to tell him and wondered why she always came back to Charlie. And how his dead partner could be the missing connection between her and *the Priest*.

He shook his head, stuffing his hands through his shirt, as he glanced back at her one last time. Soon the horror would be over, and he could only pray her visions would end with it.

* * * *

Fallon rolled to her side, keeping her eyes shut against the pain. Her head felt like someone was running a jackhammer inside it. Even her teeth hurt from the continual pounding. She pressed her palm against the bridge of her noise and released a shuddering breath. Maybe if she moved slowly…

Sparks pierced the darkness, but she forced herself up, feeling the room dip and sway as she swung her feet over the edge of the bed. Cool air caressed her skin, spreading goosebumps along her legs and arms. She cracked her eyes open and reached for Gil's T-shirt, still folded on the chair, slipping it over her head. The movement sent a wave of nausea churning through her stomach, but she ignored it, grabbing some socks off the floor. It took her three tries to stand up, but after the room stopped spinning, she found her balance and headed for the closet, emerging with a pair of sweats.

Images flip-flopped in her head as she opened the bedroom door and padded her way to the kitchen. She'd just flipped the kettle on when a hand tapped her on the shoulder.

Fallon screamed, grabbed the hand and turned, twisting the man's arm. Adrenaline pounded through her veins, giving her strength. She slammed the guy against her fridge, locking his arm behind his back. He cursed and tried to turn, but she had him pinned by the arm.

"Are you quite done now, Fallon? Or do I have to get Ken in here to pull you off me?"

Her eyes bulged wide. She knew that voice. "Jeff?"

"The one and only. Now, if you don't mind..." He grunted, tugging against her hold.

She gasped and released his arm, stepping back as he whirled to face her. "What are you doing here?"

Jeff shook out his arm, wiggling his fingers as if to ensure they still worked. "Protecting you, though I think your boyfriend underestimates your prowess with a fridge at your disposal. That was some move."

She shrugged, moving over to the chair. Now that her initial panic was gone, the pain in her head surged forward. She collapsed on one of the chairs, palming her head again. *Boyfriend.* Had Gil put it that way or had Jeff jumped to his own conclusions? Either way, she liked the sound of it. "Gil sent for you?"

"Apparently he and Trevor are worried you might be the next victim. So he asked Ken and me to keep an eye on you while another unit stays parked outside." He pulled out a chair and sat down beside her. "Hey, are you okay? You don't look so good."

"Headache," she mumbled. "I'll be okay." She glanced at the clock. "How long have you been here?"

"About an hour."

"Gil's been gone an hour?" she repeated, forcing her way over to the counter. She picked up the phone. "Has he called?"

"Nothing yet." He stood up and walked over to her. "I'm sure everything's fine. He could be quite a while if they managed to catch the creep."

Fallon nodded as Jeff sauntered back into the living room,

but it didn't stop the uneasy feeling crawling up her spine. She was still having trouble organising her thoughts from the last vision, but she trusted her instincts enough to know something was wrong. She dialled his cell, praying he'd pick up.

"Fallon? What's wrong? Are you okay?"

Gil's voice was a mixture of fear and anger, and she could only hope the latter wasn't directed at her. "I'm okay. Where are you?"

"I'm in Wade's truck. We're still at the chapel. Why?"

She shook her head, trying to clear it. "*The Priest*. Did you get him?"

"No. He never showed. At least we never saw him. There's a chance he's watching. Waiting to see if we came alone. But I think it's a waste of time. How's your head?"

"Feels like someone's playing the bongos inside. I don't think he was ever planning on meeting you there. That's where he told me to send you, but it's not where he summoned me from. He wasn't at the chapel in my vision."

"Do you know where he was?"

She moaned as another wave of pain rolled through her head. If it kept up, she'd pass out again. She tried to talk into the phone but only managed a whimper.

"Fallon? Darling, are you okay? Talk to me."

"My head. Damn. It's hard to think." She forced in a deep breath and tried to concentrate on the image of the room she'd been inside. "I went to a large room. I felt like I'd been there before, but not *really* been there. More like in a dream. Everything was the same, only in the wrong place. There was a long row of boarded-up windows and..."

Her voice cut into a keening cry as the kitchen shifted and dissolved into a dark room. She could see the faint gleam of light under a door at the far end, and there was the scent of oranges in the air.

"Fallon! Fallon! Damn it, what's going on? Fallon!" Gil yelled into the phone, his voice echoing in her ear as she sank to the floor, the phone still clutched in her hand.

"Gil." More images filled her head, but she tried to stay connected long enough to tell Gil what she was seeing. "Room. It's dark. He's opening a door." Pain flared through her head and it was all she could do not to scream. *The Priest* was moving down a hall, his attention focused on a man sitting on a couch. "He's coming up behind a man. There's a couch and…"

Her mouth opened into a soundless scream as she watched *the Priest* knock the other man over the head with a bat, tossing it aside as he turned towards another doorway. She recognised the colour of the walls and the feel of the floor. She closed her eyes, her consciousness slipping away as she spoke one last time into the phone.

"He's here."

Chapter Twenty-Two

Gil heard the phone clatter to the floor. He screamed her name, knowing she couldn't hear him but needing to try. A cold sweat erupted across his skin, stinging his eyes as it dripped down his forehead.

"Damn it, Gil. What's happening?"

"Punch it. Now!"

Wade didn't stop to question, but hit the accelerator, making the tires squeal as he jumped a kerb and screeched down the road. Horns blared in the background, drowned out by the wail of the siren.

Gil grabbed the mike and keyed up the radio. "Dispatch, I need you to connect me with the police unit stationed outside Fallon Kinkade's house." He thumbed the button, cursing with every breath. The truck shuddered as Wade threw the vehicle around a corner, nearly tipping it over.

"Delta three, go ahead."

"This is Special Agent Grant. I just received a distress call from inside the house. What the hell's going on?"

Static whined over the air before the officer's voice spoke again. "Everything looks good from here, Agent Grant. And the other two officers are still inside as you requested. But if you'd like, we'll head on in and check things out."

"Yes, I'd like," he sneered, checking his watch. "It's been three minutes. Stay together and check every door and window in the place. And whatever you do, don't kill anyone before you're sure they're on the other side."

The officer rumbled a big ten-four and Gil listened to the line go dead. "Fuck!"

"We're almost there, Gil. He couldn't have gotten far, not

with Fallon either fighting him or unconscious. We'll get her back."

"I'll kill him." Gil felt his partner nod in his direction, neither of them needing to say what was on both their minds.

* * * *

Ten more minutes had dragged by before Wade screeched to a halt in front of Fallon's house. Gil didn't even wait for the truck to stop rolling before jumping out and racing up to the door. An officer was standing on the porch, his hands stuffed in his pockets as Gil skidded to a stop. "Well?"

The man shook his head, pushing the door open. "We've checked the entire premise, sir. The two officers are still unconscious." He pointed over towards the couch. "One in the living room, the other in the bathroom at the end of the hallway. Paramedics are on the way."

"Where's Fallon?"

The man's face paled. "I'm sorry, Agent Grant. She's gone."

Gil felt the room sway as he ran into the kitchen and stared at the phone lying discarded on the floor. "Did you touch or move anything?"

"Nothing, sir. We only ensured both men were still alive before calling it in."

He nodded, but the words barely registered. She'd been here, standing in the kitchen, when the bastard had taken her. And he'd done nothing to stop him.

"Gil?"

He looked up. Wade was standing in front of him, his cell cradled in his hand. "I've got an ABP out on Fallon, and Trevor's sending more units this way. We'll canvass the neighbourhood. Someone must have seen something. If we can get a licence plate or a better description of the vehicle, we might be able to track him. Trevor said he'll send out the helicopter if it'll help."

"What fucking good will the chopper do when we don't even know which way the bastard went!"

Wade cringed at the tone of his voice, but he didn't care. Fallon was gone. And he didn't have a clue where to start looking. He cursed and headed back outside, needing some air to clear his thoughts.

"I'm sorry. I didn't mean..." Wade's voice trailed off into a sigh.

Gil turned to his friend, giving the man a pat on the back. "I know you're just trying to help. I just hate feeling so damn helpless. I should've known the chapel was a setup. He just wanted us out of the way so he could come after Fallon. She was his target all along."

"Did Fallon say anything on the phone before it went dead that might suggest she knew where he was taking her."

Gil ran a shaky hand through his hair, trying to remember Fallon's last words. "She was confused. Something about the chapel. How she didn't think he was planning on meeting us there. That she'd been somewhere else in her vision."

Wade stepped closer. "Did she know where? A street? A building? Anything?"

Gil sifted through the words tumbling around in his head. But all he could think about was how they really might be her *last words.*

"Gil?"

He looked up at his partner, wondering why the man was still bothering him. "What?" he snapped.

"We'll get her back. But right now you need to tell me what she said on the phone before *the Priest* arrived."

Gil turned to look at his truck parked in her driveway. He remembered carrying her into the bedroom, holding her like he never wanted to let go. She'd felt so fragile in his arms, but she'd never stopped trying to help the women she saw. And now she was one of them.

"Gil."

"She didn't know," he bit out, spinning to face Wade. "She just said it wasn't the chapel and that she felt like she'd been there before, but not really. I didn't understand what she meant. She was trying to describe it to me when she got drawn into another vision." He lowered his face so Wade wouldn't see the shame in his eyes. "She saw him stalking her but couldn't do anything to stop him."

Anger punched through his chest and kicked at the railing on the side of Fallon's porch. The wood cracked and heaved and it was all he could do not to rip the damn thing apart and toss it across the lawn.

"Easy, buddy. It's only been fifteen minutes. She's still okay."

"But for how long?" He sighed, the anger quickly replaced by fear. "How long before that bastard carves a cross into her chest? Before he rapes her?"

Wade took a deep breath, his lips pulled tight. "We're not going to let that happen." He stepped forward and placed a hand on Gil's shoulder. "I've been thinking about this whole vision thing with Fallon. You told me she only has them with people she's connected with."

Gil nodded, not sure what else to say.

"So, that means *the Priest* must be someone she knows or has had contact with. What we need to do is figure out that connection."

Gil cursed and was just about to tell Wade he'd been doing that for the past fucking day, when the answer slammed into his head. "Charlie!"

Wade dropped his hand and took a step back. "What?"

Gil ran to Wade's truck. "Come on," he yelled, jumping in the passenger seat.

Wade slid in beside him, revving the engine as he looked over at Gil. "Where to?"

"The office. I think I know where to start looking."

* * * *

"Care to tell me what we're looking for? Or is it only on a need-to-know basis."

Gil glanced over at Wade. The man was pacing the floor, trying to look over Gil's shoulder at the computer screen. They'd made the drive back to the office in a little over ten minutes, and it'd taken Gil another ten to pull up the information on the screen. Now he was stuck going line by line through the information in the hopes of finding what he needed.

"Sorry. The truth is, I'm not really sure what I'm looking for. I just remembered what Fallon kept saying these past few days. How this creep reminds her of Charlie. And then just before I left this morning, she said his name again before she passed out. I think Charlie's the connection. I just don't know how."

"Maybe it's someone you guys pissed off?"

"Maybe," said Gil, scrolling down the page. "But I think it's closer to home than that. It got me thinking about Charlie's family. He never mentioned having a brother, but then Fallon never told me she had a sister either. Maybe..." His voice keened into a growl as a new page flicked onto the screen. "Damn it!"

He pushed the chair back, cursing as Wade read the screen. "I don't get it. All it says is that Charlie's only surviving relative is a father."

"Keep reading. It gets better," he snarled pacing the floor. He had to figure out where *the Priest*—James—had taken Fallon.

"Holly, Shit. The guy's a colonel! Looks like he spent time in Iraq and Afghanistan." Gil heard Wade click down a few screens. "It doesn't say what his current status is?"

Gil growled and pounded a fist on the desk. "He was still active as of seven months ago. He missed Charlie's funeral because he was overseas." He looked Wade in the eyes. "The guy's a field medic."

"Damn. He's more than got the expertise to pull off these murders. But why the hell would he do it? It doesn't make sense. From what it says here, he's a fucking war hero."

"Yeah, in a war that's divided the country. Besides, I think his time in the military only planted his psychological unbalance. I have a feeling it was Charlie's death that pushed him over."

Wade raised an eyebrow at him. "I've read the report on the incident. There's nothing in there regarding Charlie's death that seems suspect."

"That's because there were a few details left out." He looked down at the floor, wondering why he hadn't seen it before. "What the report doesn't say is that everything was going smoothly until our informant ratted us out. Ratted Charlie out actually. He'd been sleeping with her as part of their cover. Charlie only saw it as necessary, but I guess she'd taken it as a long-term relationship. Seems she followed us home the night before the meeting, hoping to spend more time with Charlie. When things didn't go the way she planned, she lost it."

"By why would she kill him just because he went to your house? Surely he'd gone there before."

Gil shook his head. Why did it always come back to that night? He looked up at Wade, meeting the man's stare. "Because Charlie stayed the night."

"So?"

"No. I mean, he spent the night." He waved his hand in the air. "With Fallon and me."

Wade's eyes bulged for a moment before he settled his expression. "Ooohhh." A boyish grin crept into the lines of his mouth. "So you think she saw the…" It was his turn to wave his hand in the air. "The three of you. Together."

"Oh, she more than saw it. She yelled it back at him during the meeting. Then she added in the part about him being a Fed, and all hell broke loose."

"So why didn't that go into the report?" Wade cleared his throat when Gil glared at him. "I mean the part about her telling everyone he was a Fed?"

Gil sighed. "Because she was a daughter of a senator.

And the powers that be felt that dragging their family name through the ringer wasn't going to change anything. She died in the firefight too."

Wade nodded and looked back at the picture of James Cutter on the screen. "But you told Charlie's dad."

"He called one night about a month later. He wanted to know the truth. Said his boy would never blow his cover. I wasn't exactly thinking straight, so I told him everything with the assurance he'd keep it off the record. I never heard from him again, so I figured he'd gotten the closure he needed."

"Or just the right amount of stress to finish pushing him over the edge. I assume this lady was young, similar to our victims?"

"I think it's more that he's going for women he thinks are betraying the men in their lives. Look at our last victim. She was dating a married man. In his eyes, that's a sin."

Wade nodded. "Okay, so if James is *the Priest,* where would he take Fallon? Another church?"

Gil glanced over at the screen. The man looked so much like Charlie, he felt as if he were staring at a ghost. "Fallon's different. He doesn't see her as just a soul he needs to purify. To him, she's an angel sent to save him. I don't think he'll follow the usual pattern."

"That makes things more difficult. Without a starting place, we've got nothing to narrow down the search."

Gil paced across the room, running over what Fallon had said.

I went to a large room. I felt like I'd been there before, but not really been there.

"How can you be somewhere, but not really *be* there?" He hadn't realised he'd said the words aloud until Wade answered him.

"I'm not sure. Maybe you could dream you'd been there. Or have seen it on TV."

He spun around, nodding at Wade. "Or maybe you went there in a vision."

Wade stood up, already reaching for his coat. "One of the other crime scenes?" he asked, following Gil out the door and down the stairs.

"Not a church. The warehouse."

Wade paused as Gil ran across the parking lot and jumped in his truck before racing after him. "What are you talking about? What warehouse?"

Gil motioned to the ignition and Wade shoved the key in and turned it over. "The warehouse where we met the weapons dealers. The warehouse where Charlie died."

* * * *

"Wake up, Angel. I've been waiting for you."

Fallon heard the voice muttering in the distance but couldn't seem to open her eyes. Her body was cold and sore, the hard feel of concrete beneath her. She tried to turn, but her arms were locked behind her. She froze, shaking some of the fogginess away as the memory of what had happened returned.

"I know you're there, Angel. Open your eyes."

A set of strong hands wrapped around her shoulders, giving her a firm shake. She winced at the sudden burst of pain through her head and forced her eyes open, staring into the face of her captor. His eyes were hazel, his lips smooth and pink, and his hair a dappled mixture of blonde and grey. He looked down at her, a smile tugging at his lips as he cupped her chin in one hand. She stared at him, unable to believe who was standing before her.

"Charlie?"

She hadn't meant to say the name out loud and winced when *the Priest* tensed, squeezing her jaw between his fingers. "Not quite, my dear. But close."

He released his hold and she fell back, groaning as her head grazed the floor. Lights dazzled across her vision, blurring his face. When they finally faded she looked back up at him, seeing him more clearly this time. While he still looked like Charlie, she could tell he was much older than the other man would've been. Lines feathered out from his eyes, and his forehead was creased from years of hard work and worry. She scooted backwards when he bent down closer to her, pushing her against a wall. "Who are you?"

"Forgotten me already, Angel?"

"Your real name," she whispered.

His eyes narrowed and, for a moment, she thought he might strike her. "I no longer go by *that* name. That man is dead."

He stood up and stepped back, his eyes distant, haunted. She chanced a quick glance around. She was in the room she'd seen in her vision. "Where are we?" she asked, the overwhelming sense of déjà vu returning.

He looked around the room, sadness flickering in his eyes. "Back where it all started." He looked back at her. "Where it all will end."

* * * *

Wade pulled in front of the warehouse, steering the truck into the shadows. Gil shifted in his seat as the truck rolled to a halt. He didn't need to see the black Mercedes parked by a dumpster to know Fallon was inside. He could feel her.

"Should I call for backup?" asked Wade.

Gil stared at the Mercedes for a moment, then turned to face Wade. "He works alone. Besides, the last thing we need is to make him panic with the sound of sirens." He stepped out and closed the door, drawing his Glock. "I'll go in here. You circle around the building and see if you can flank me. I'll try to keep his attention. With any luck, you might get a clean shot at him."

Wade shifted uneasily as he looked at the large building. "Are you sure you should go in first? Maybe I should take the main entrance, just in case…"

Wade didn't finish his sentence, but Gil knew what the

man was thinking. Just in case Fallon was already dead. Just in case he was walking into another crime scene with her on centre stage. "No. She's still alive."

"We both know…"

"I'm not going to let her down," he interrupted, clenching his fists to still the sudden trembling. "I can't lose her." He waved his hand when Wade moved to speak. "I know. But no matter what's waiting for me in there, I owe it to Fallon to be the one to confront him."

Wade lifted half his mouth into a cocky grin. "Then I guess I've got your back, *partner*."

Wade took off, disappearing behind the building's far wall. Gil turned back to the hinged doors off to his right. He hadn't been through those doors since that fateful day with Charlie. He'd lost his best friend that day, and he'd be damned if he'd lose Fallon too.

He moved to the door, careful to open it slowly. The first area was cold and dark. There were several rows of stacked pallets off to his left, their presence nothing more than shadowy ghosts in the shifting light. Another doorway wavered to his right, the pale light of the next room glowing beneath the steel slab.

Gil stared at the door, unable to move. That's where it'd all fallen apart. Where the blood of his partner still stained the floor. He'd managed to carry him several rooms over, away from the spray of bullets, but it hadn't been enough. Charlie had died. And then he'd lost Fallon to his own foolish pride.

The faint whisper of voices crept through the stillness, shattering the memories. Gil inched his way to the threshold, his back pressed into the wall. He could hear the mumble of a man's voice. *The Priest* was in there, but he couldn't tell if Fallon was alive or dead. He took a deep breath, clenched his jaw and opened the door.

Chapter Twenty-Three

The Priest moved back towards a small pack. He kept his eyes locked on hers, his lips pulled tight. She knew he was waiting for her to make a move, but she knew better than to try and run. With her arms bound behind her back and her head still spinning, she'd be an easy target. Better to wait until he was close. One strong knee to the groin followed by a few strategic kicks might be enough to give her the time she needed to make an escape.

He smiled at her, as if he could read her thoughts. She looked away, trying not to think about what would happen if she never got the chance.

"Don't worry, Angel. I'm not going to treat you like all the others. You're special."

He rummaged through his bag, removing a large knife. It was longer and thicker than the small precision instrument she'd seen him use on the other woman, but much more intimidating. There was only one purpose for a blade that big.

"I thought you were going to tell me everything?" she parried, hoping to keep him distracted.

"Why tell you, my dear, when you already know?" He flicked his thumb across the edge of the knife. "There's a reason you called me Charlie."

"You look just like him," she whispered.

"Or perhaps he looks just like me."

"Oh my God." The words flowed from her lips just as the image hit her. She'd mixed it up. "You're his father."

The Priest smiled at her. "See. I knew you'd figure it out." He turned and looked around the room. "Now we just have to see if lover boy can figure it out too." He looked back at her over his shoulder. "A fitting ending, don't you think?"

Fallon glanced around. She could've sworn she'd been there before, but it still felt wrong. She looked down beside her, her breath leaving her lungs in one quick hiss as she stared at the blood stain on the floor. "The warehouse."

She hadn't realised he'd heard her until his voice broke the stillness. "Right again, Angel. The very place where evil took my son from me. But not for long. Soon, he'll be back with us."

"No matter what happens here, it won't bring Charlie back. Please. If you'll just let me, I can get you the help you need."

The Priest laughed, but it was hollow, empty. "I'm not crazy, Angel. I don't need *that* kind of help." He took a step closer. "Your power is all the help I'll need."

Fallon shook her head as he moved slowly towards her. "But I don't have any power. I'm not really an angel."

"Now, now. We both know that's not true. Or do you think I've forgotten our previous meeting? Though I must say, you're much more alluring in the flesh." He stopped at her feet. "Don't worry. I'm not going to hurt you. I'm only sending you home."

Fallon tried to scoot away as he knelt down and pulled her up, holding her tight to his chest, the cool metal of the blade touching her skin. She closed her eyes, knowing her only chance was to launch an attack, when his body tensed and he wrapped his other arm around her waist.

"I wouldn't try anything if I were you, Angel. Besides, we've got company…and right on schedule."

The Priest turned and pressed his back to the wall, holding her in front of him as he faced a doorway off to their left.

"Smile, Angel. Our moment of glory has arrived."

* * * *

Gil stood in the doorway, his muscles tensed, his Glock

pointing straight out. *The Priest* had Fallon tight to his chest, a knife wavering by her throat. But it didn't matter. At least she was still alive. And nothing the bastard had done to her was going to change the way he felt. He loved her, and he'd spend a lifetime showing her just how much.

The man smiled at him, as if he'd been waiting for him to arrive. Gil shuffled forward, his eyes fixed on the knife. If the creep gave him any indication he was going to use it, he'd take the shot, even if it meant clipping Fallon's shoulder in the process.

"Hello, Gil. How nice of you to drop by. I was starting to think you hadn't figured it all out yet."

"Put the gun down, James, and no one will get hurt."

The Priest cringed at the sound of his name, a firm scowl etching across his face. "James Cutter no longer lives in this body," he snarled, shifting Fallon in his arms, covering more of his body with hers. "I've been reborn."

Gil took a step forward, his focus still locked on the knife. Fallon gasped as the point nicked her skin. "Fine. Whatever you say. Just please, don't hurt her." A single drop of blood welled at the wound and he felt his chest squeeze. He couldn't lose her. Not when he'd finally got her back. "Tell me what you want. I'm sure we can make a deal."

The Priest laughed, stroking the ends of Fallon's hair with his other hand. "I don't want anything from you. I've got everything I need right here." He ran a finger down Fallon's arm. "You're only here to witness the miracle I have in store." He flashed Gil a knowing smile. "I think you'll like it."

Gil held back the growl in his chest, as he watched the man caress *his* woman. He could tell the mere touch of the bastard's hand sickened her, but he could only hope she'd hang on. James was obviously too worked up to try anything fancy. "And what miracle is that?"

James smiled a toothy grin at him. "This is where I raise the dead," he said, his voice cold and calm.

"Nothing you do here can bring Charlie back. Believe me.

If there were a way, I'd have found it. He was more than just my partner. He was like a brother to me. But he's gone."

James snarled and pulled his arm back, scratching Fallon's skin. She stiffened and it was all Gil could do not to empty his clip into the man. But he didn't have a clear shot, and he wasn't about to take a shot through her. "That's where you're wrong. Charlie's still with us. His spirit hasn't left yet. He wants to come back."

"Even if that's true, killing Fallon won't bring him back."

James laughed like a man with a secret. "Oh, but it will. Didn't you know that whenever a fallen angel is returned to heaven, a single soul is released?" He gazed at Fallon's head. "She's so lovely. I've been waiting for her for a long time. I knew the moment she appeared in the church, she was the answer to my prayers. The others were a test. A show of my commitment. Now God has graced me with the power to bring back my son."

Gil felt the heat rise in the room. There was no way he'd be able to reason with the man, but maybe he could keep him talking long enough for Wade to find them and get off a shot. "I thought angels were pure? You know Fallon and I are lovers. How can she be an angel?"

"That's why she's a *fallen* angel." James looked at him with confusion. "Don't you see? I'm saving her, just like all the rest. Without me, her soul would go to Hell. But I can purify her. Send her back to Heaven where she belongs."

"She belongs here…with me."

The Priest sneered at him, waving the knife around before settling it back against her neck. "If you care so much for her, then you would've married her before taking her to your bed."

Gil smiled, easing forward another step. "Hand her over, and I'll marry her now." He met the man's glare. "You're a man of the cloth. You could officiate for us."

The Priest faltered, his gaze darting between Fallon and Gil. He knew the man could see the honesty in his eyes, and the stark truth seemed to unnerve him. "No. I need her to bring Charlie back."

"So you'll kill the one woman Charlie loved in order to resurrect him?" Gil shook his head. "How do you think Charlie will feel when he learns what happened? Do you really think he'll be thankful?"

The Priest shook his head. "She's your lover, not his!"

"That's where you're wrong. Charlie joined us the night before he died. I wanted to give him a gift...something to show him how much he meant to me...to us. Fallon loved him as surely as I did."

The Priest's eyes clouded over with doubt and his hand dropped slightly. "Is this true?" he asked, shaking Fallon.

Fallon nodded.

"Say it!" he yelled.

"Yes. Charlie and I were lovers. He stayed with us the night before he died." She sobbed and Gil fought the urge to go to her.

The Priest snarled and shook his head. "Did you love him?"

For the first time since he'd arrived, Fallon locked her gaze on his. Gil could see the pain in her expression as she was forced to tell another secret she'd been keeping from him. He smiled back and nodded.

"Yes," she whispered, and he knew it was the truth. He'd always known, but the jealousy he'd expected to slam into him didn't. Instead, he felt relief. A sense of pride at her ability to open her heart and give the greatest gift to the man he'd loved himself.

Gil took one last step closer. "Can you do it, James? Can you kill her knowing Charlie would've died for her? That with a single touch, she'd eased his demons and cured him in a way no one else could? In a way even you couldn't?"

James sighed, and for a moment Gil thought he'd lower the knife. But then he smiled and raised it back to her throat. "It wasn't a true love. It was tainted. The three of you shared that night. Together. I know Charlie will forgive me."

"Will he?" yelled Gil, distracting the man once again. "Not that it matters, 'cause in the end, he'll blame himself. And that will kill him more than any bullet could."

James looked him, pausing just long enough that Gil chanced a glance at Fallon. Her eyes were wide and glassy, her brow furrowed. He could see a slight twitch in her jaw. She forced a weak smile, her love for him evident in the curve of her lips. Gil held her stare, praying she could read his thoughts.

"This isn't going to work, James. We both know Fallon's not really an angel. Yes, she's been given a gift, but nothing you do here will bring Charlie back." He reached out his other hand to the man. "Please. Let her go. We'll talk."

James looked down at Fallon. "I suppose in the end, it all comes down to faith." He met Gil's gaze for the last time. "And I, for one, believe."

With that, James moved, pressing the tip into her skin. Gil screamed her name, willing her to step back. Fallon moved with the man, twisting her head away, driving the knife back. Gil lined James up just as the report of a gun echoed through the air. *The Priest* jerked sideways, the knife dropping from his hand as his body collapsed on the floor, covering Fallon's. Gil ran to her, beating Wade to the scene by three steps. James was bleeding from the side of his chest, his breath wheezy and laboured.

Gil rolled the man over, pulling Fallon out from underneath. Blood was splattered across her shirt and a steady trickle ran down her neck. Gil's heart stopped. He grabbed her neck, pressing the small laceration closed with his thumb as he fought to tear a piece of cloth from his shirt.

"Just hold still, darling. I need to stop the bleeding."

Fallon moaned and reached her hand up to cover his. Her skin was cold and clammy, and just the feel of it sent his adrenaline into overdrive. Gil took her hand and used it to hold the wad of fabric as he tore off his jacket and laid it across her. "She's in shock, Wade."

"EMT's are already on their way. Trevor's got a few units

coming too."

Gil nodded, his focus aimed on Fallon. Her face was pale and her breathing seemed sporadic. He longed to gather her in his arms but knew it was more important for her to stay still until some of the colour returned to her cheeks. He smiled at her, caressing her jaw with his fingers. "Nice move."

She nuzzled her face into his hand. "I had a good teacher." She nodded towards *the Priest*. "Is he going to make it?"

Gil looked over at James. The bullet had lodged somewhere inside his chest, but Wade had seemed to get the bleeding under control. "Looks like it." Gil turned away, trying to ignore the patches of dried blood staining the floor. Charlie had got shot in that same spot before Gil had set off a smoke grenade and carried him to safety. He jumped when Fallon touched his hand.

"Gil?"

He leant closer, not wanting her to have to strain. "Yes, darling?"

"I'm sorry. What I said about Charlie..."

Gil stopped her with a gentle finger across her lips. "There's nothing to be sorry about, Fallon. And there's nothing to explain. I loved him too. How could I expect anything less from you?"

She smiled as the sound of sirens filled the air. Soft, then louder, until the very room seemed to vibrate with the noise. The bleeding beneath his hand had slowed and he could see a faint tinge of pink in her cheeks. "How did you know?" she asked.

"You kept insisting Charlie was the key, so I finally went back and looked into his file. I never imagined James would be behind this." He nodded towards the man. "You were right all along."

"So does this mean you're a believer?"

Gil smiled. "I've always believed in you, darling. But we do have one problem."

Fallon's eyes widened slightly and he could tell she was

holding in her fear. "What's that?"

"Well, with your admirer unconscious on the floor, we don't have anyone to officiate. I guess this means we'll have to do it the old-fashioned way and have a real wedding."

Fallon's mouth fell open and the stunned look on her face made him smile. "A real…" Her voice trailed off, replaced by an impish smile. "Oh, I don't know. We might be able to get to city hall before it closes and grab a marriage licence. But isn't there some sort of waiting period?"

Gil pulled out a folded sheet from his pocket. "Already took care of that the other day when I went out with Wade." He handed her the paper. "I hope you don't mind. I took the liberty of signing your name for you." He bent over and kissed the tip of her nose. "Just say the when, baby, and I'm all yours."

Fallon smiled up at him, a single tear fading down her cheek. "When."

Chapter Twenty-Four

"Well?" Gil stood outside the bathroom door. He'd been pacing the floor for the past five minutes and the anticipation was killing him. "What does it say?"

Fallon turned towards him, her pale eyes flashing in the early morning sunlight. "It says we're going to need a bigger house."

"It's positive? Are you sure?"

She giggled and rolled her eyes. "It's pretty easy to read, Gil. A plus sign means positive and a line means negative." She handed him the small applicator. "What do you see?"

Gil scanned the tiny window. "It's definitely a plus sign." He looked back into her eyes. "You're really pregnant."

Her lips pulled tight and he could see the tension move through her muscles. "It's still early, Gil. If you're not sure about this, I can..."

Her voice carried into a delighted shriek as he picked her up and twirled her around the room.

"Are you kidding? I'm just not sure I can wait another nine months for it all to happen." He carried her over to the bed. "How soon before you can get an ultrasound so we can see my son?"

"Or daughter," she warned.

He smiled and kissed the tip of her nose as he laid her gently on the bed. "I'd love to have a little girl, Fallon. One that looks just like her mother." He brushed her hair back as he watched her face. "But I suppose in the end, it doesn't really matter. We'll put more stock in it with our second child."

Fallon's eyes bulged wide as they welled up with tears.

"Our second child? Just how many do you want?"

He shrugged. "I don't know. Three or four."

"Three or four?"

"We can have more if that's not enough for you. I'm flexible."

Fallon's smile made his heart swell. She'd not only agreed to marry him but had insisted they stop on the way home from the warehouse. It hadn't mattered that only Wade and Trevor were there to witness the ceremony, or that both of them looked like they'd just been rescued off the street. All she'd wanted was to seal her love with a kiss. He was secretly planning another wedding for her. One with all her friends and her grandparents. The kind of day girls dreamt of from the time they were told their first fairy tale. It seemed the least he could do for all she'd given him without ever asking for anything in return but his love.

"You know, just because I got pregnant so easily this time, doesn't mean it'll be that way every time."

"Who cares? I just want to keep trying, darling."

With that, he followed her down on the bed, taking her lips in his. He kept his kiss soft and loving, teasing her just long enough for her to take charge and deepen the kiss, plunging her tongue into his mouth as if she needed his taste to live. He met her attack with one just as strong, jousting his tongue with hers until she finally pulled back. Her eyes sparkled as she watched him from behind a veil of lashes. He could tell she was up to something, but he wanted her to have the illusion she was in control.

"I bought you something," she said, reaching for the bedside table.

"Flavoured oil for me to lick off various parts of your body?" he guessed, raising his eyebrow in question.

Fallon smiled and threw him a quick glance over her shoulder. "Well, I did get some oil, but it's not for you to lick off me. As a matter of fact, it's for me to use on you."

Gil narrowed his eyes as he watched her pull out a bag from the small drawer. "That sounds…dangerous."

She laughed and his heart skipped a beat. He'd been so afraid she'd distance herself and fade into a deep depression after the warehouse, that now her outward display of humour eased the worry he'd been hiding. And as he watched her remove a toy from the bag, he realised she was more than okay.

Fallon held up the device, rotating it as she smiled at him. "Well, what do you think?"

"Why don't you tell me what it is first?"

She huffed and he couldn't help but smile. "It's an anal plug, silly."

"It's not like the ones I've seen at the store." He nodded towards the drawer. "Is there something wrong with the one you have?"

"No. Besides, this isn't for me." She met his heated stare. "It's for you. It's supposed to drive men wild. Something about an anal G-spot and the prostate gland." She matched his raised eyebrow. "I got a narrow one so it won't hurt you. Don't tell me you're nervous?"

Gil shook his head. Now she was trying to goad him into allowing her to fuck his ass with a plug. The girl had definitely got more courageous during their separation. But he had to admit he liked the new cockiness. It made his cock stand at attention and his imagination run wild. And if this was what married life had in store for him, then he was more than up to the next fifty years.

"Careful, darling. Pregnant or not, I'll still spank you."

She tilted her head as if considering his threat. "Let's see. A spanking in exchange for watching you take the plug and mounting you while it's still deep inside you." She sealed her eyes to his. "Sounds like a fair deal."

Fallon moved across the bed, holding her prize in one hand, a bottle of scented oil in the other. She could see the uncertainty in Gil's eyes as he watched her approach, his gaze flicking between her and the plug. She'd known the instant she'd spied it on the shelf, she had to buy it, but she hadn't been sure whether Gil would let her use it on him. He'd never been one to let her lead, and just the fact he hadn't tossed her down and ripped off her clothes spoke volumes.

She met him in the centre of the mattress, her body easing against his. His muscles strained as he fought to keep the contact light. An internal battle raged in his eyes as he stared down at her, his lips slightly parted, his eyes heavy lidded. She leaned in to kiss him, but he stopped her with a firm hand across her chest. Something raw rippled across his expression as his gaze, once again, centred on the plug.

"Fallon."

He spoke her name as part warning, part plea. A sense of power surged through her and she fought to keep from smiling. He wanted to play but wasn't sure how to accept the rules of the game.

"We both know you're not gay. And just because you let me try this, doesn't mean I'll suddenly start worrying when you call me to tell me you're working late with Wade." She tilted her head again in a way she knew drove him crazy. "Unless you're planning on teaming up on me with your new partner?"

Gil growled a moment before his lips covered hers, his kiss hard and urgent. She opened when he nipped at her lips and felt his heat spear into her mouth. He plunged inside, licking and teasing until his scent was all she could taste. It wasn't until she whimpered in need that he released her, his eyes burning down on hers again.

"Never again." His voice was a dark curse. "You're mine and mine alone. So if you have any fantasies about Wade, I suggest you forget about them."

"You're the only man I've ever fantasised about. And that will never change."

Her response seemed to ease some of the tension in his body, and the fine lines around his eyes diminished. He nodded at her and moved back, stripping his shirt off as he relaxed on the bed. "Then by all means…"

He waved at the toy still perched in her hands and a new wave of heat rolled through her. Only this time, it culminated in her groin, making her juices spill out along her plump lips. She was hot and wet, and so damn horny she wondered if she'd climax simply by burying the plug up his ass.

The image filled her head and she heard her low groan fill the room. Gil grinned as she knelt over him, fingering the waistband of his jeans. "I'm afraid these will have to go, darling."

Gil didn't have time to nod before she'd jerked open the buttons and pulled the denim apart. The stark white of his briefs wavered between the two sides as his cock head pulsed beneath the thin fabric. She moaned at the sight, knowing she'd have to taste him before she prepared him for her game.

"Ease up for me."

He paused just long enough to show her his acceptance to the game, but also to emphasise his choice in the matter. He'd play as long as he decided, and not because she commanded him.

Fallon nodded, waiting until he raised his hips to slip his jeans and briefs down his thighs, pulling them off his legs and tossing them behind her. She didn't turn to see where they landed on the floor, just content to get the damn things off him. Now he was perfectly naked.

Her purr of approval vibrated in the air and Gil smiled at her feminine response. He liked to know she appreciated his body as much as he did hers. She leant forward, inhaling his scent. It was clean and spicy and she couldn't seem to stop her tongue from dancing along his shaft, teasing the thin slit with just a hint of penetration.

"Oh God."

His gravelly voice echoed in her head as she dipped in for another taste. A splash of salty musk coated her tongue and she lapped at the head in hopes of getting another taste.

"You taste divine. I hope you'll give me more."

"Keep talking and you'll drink my cum before you get anywhere near my ass."

Fallon smiled against his skin, suckling one testicle into her mouth. Today was all about him. A chance for her to show him how much she truly loved him, and how seriously she took her oath to give, only to him. Of course, he wouldn't let her go without at least one orgasm, but the need to pleasure him was more intense.

"Then I guess I'll have to get started," she breathed, nuzzling the base of his cock with her nose. "Why don't you roll over and let me rub some of the tension out of your shoulders?"

Gil's heated stare met hers before he kicked his mouth into a sexy smile and rolled onto his stomach. The move was strong and masculine, an indication of his dominance. Fallon took a moment to savour the sight of his long, lean body stretched beneath her. The way his shoulders seemed to fill the bed before dipping into his tight waist. From there his hips gave way to a firm set of muscles layered across his ass, making his buttocks perfectly shaped. She'd often longed to touch him the way she was going to now, and couldn't stem a moan from feathering from her lips.

"You have the perfect ass, darling. All tight and strong. God, I can't wait to watch you take the plug."

Gil mumbled something into the pillow, but he didn't try to stop her as she ran her fingers down the sensual cleft of his butt, circling his anus with a solitary finger.

"Now remember to relax, darling. I can tell you from experience it feels so good any pinching will soon be forgotten."

Gil turned as if to look at her but then stopped and rolled back. She took that as her signal to move, rubbing her hands down his back, dancing them across his muscles. Every swirl sank him further into the bed until she thought he might fall asleep. Then she switched gears, teasing each inch with a light scrape of her nails, reviving every muscle she'd soothed, until his hips punched forward and his breath came in deep pants. His body was primed again, but this time for pleasure.

She reached for the oil, dribbling some on her hands before smearing it across his back. "Just relax, Gil. The oil is just what you need to help you along."

He moaned his reply, obviously aroused by the slick feel of her hands across his flesh. She waited until his back had a nice thin covering before moving to his buttocks. The muscles flexed as she ran her hands along his cheeks, covering every inch of skin. She stopped to reload and then eased her fingers down the valley, pausing to rim his anus. A low guttural sound floated out from the pillow, but he didn't move. Instead, she felt his hips pressing back ever so slowly, as if seeking a deeper penetration.

Fallon responded with another pass of his pucker, this time sinking a single finger inside. He gasped at the intrusion, punching his hips forward as a low growl broke the silence.

"Feel good?"

"Fuck, yes."

His voice was edged with a mix of pleasure and pain, a feeling she was all too familiar with. "Good. Now try to keep your muscles relaxed as I go a bit deeper."

She felt him physically try to release the tension as she poured more oil on her hand and sank her finger completely inside him. She could feel the tight knot of his prostate gland up towards the back of his channel and arched her finger so she could rub it. The sharp jerk of his hips and low growl of his voice told her she'd found her mark.

"Okay, Gil. Now for the plug."

Fallon picked up the toy, smoothing more oil along its length before lining it up with his nether hole. Her breath lodged tight in her chest as she watched his small pucker merge around the thin, bulbous head, stretching to accommodate the width of the plug. Never had she witnessed such an erotic act as she slowly pushed the toy into Gil's body, mindful to keep the penetration slow and easy. The breath she'd been holding hissed out through her teeth as the base of the curved toy locked against Gil's sac, adding another layer of sensation.

"Oh God, Gil. Now I know why you love watching me take the plug so much. I've never seen anything so sexy."

"I love watching my cock fill your ass even more," he countered through clenched teeth. "And if you don't hurry up, I'll be pounding your ass before you can scream my name."

"And miss watching this?" she said, slowly pulling the plug out before pushing it back in, this time slightly faster, harder.

"Fuck."

Gil's hips punched forward, grinding his cock into the bed. He cried out when she pulled the plug out again, leaving just the first inch clamped inside his anal ring, his voice keening into a sharp hiss as she plunged it in, taking his ass in a firm, steady stroke. Instead of pausing at the end, she kept the rhythm up, surging and retreating until he threw his head back and shouted her name.

She stopped, holding him on the edge.

Gil's body erupted into beads of sweat as his cock pulsed and flared, moments from exploding. Fallon lifted up, whispering for him to roll over. The muscles in his back bunched as he fought to lift his body, finally just collapsing on the bed, his jaw clenched, his cock standing straight up. She moved quickly, sheathing herself on the hard length of flesh in a single motion.

"Now. Ride me hard and fast, baby, or I swear…"

His threat was replaced by a growl of pleasure as she set up a torturing cycle, taking his cock deep then rising quickly. Over and over she plunged, feeling his crown flare across her womb, building her orgasm until her need matched his. She heard him beg, gripping her hips as he added his thrusts to hers. He seemed locked on the edge of release, unable to cross over. Fallon pulled one hand from his shoulder and reached behind her, grabbing the end of the plug. Using the last of her sanity, she matched her rhythm, fucking his ass as she claimed his cock. In. Out. Back. Forth. Filling his body then leaving it all but empty.

Gil's breath caught once, stalling in his chest before he shouted her name and flexed up, purging a full stream of sperm into her channel, as his body jerked beneath her. A second spurt erupted inside her sex before the world exploded and she collapsed on top of him, her shaky breath matching his. Dots flared across the darkness, words floated around in her head as she fell back to earth, her body completely sated. It wasn't until his arms tightened around her that she realised he was whispering to her.

"God, I love you."

She smiled at the honesty in his voice, so overwhelmed with her love that tears welled in her eyes again. She raised her head, meeting his gaze just long enough to place a chaste kiss on the tip of his nose before falling back down.

"Right back atcha," she breathed, feeling her courage bloom in her stomach. "So does that mean I'm excused from my punishment?"

Gil's chuckle sent more juice coursing to her cunt, and it was all she could do not to start moving again. "Nice try, sweetheart. But not only are you going to be spanked, I intend to use the cuffs."

Butterflies fluttered through her core. She'd always wanted him to handcuff her. "Just when do you intend to do this, Gil? Correct me if I'm wrong, but I think I just drained you."

Gil kissed her hair as he smoothed his hand down her back, patting her ass once before cinching his arm around her waist and rolling on top of her. Her gasp filled the room as he stared down at her, his eyes glowing. "Just the tip of the iceberg, baby," he said, thrusting his thickening cock deeper inside her. "Best take a deep breath, Fallon. 'Cause the ride's about to get bumpy."

"Just as long as I get to ride," she added, arching her hips, taking him even deeper.

"Forever, baby. You're one fallen angel that's going to stay right here on earth with me."

Deadly Obsession

Excerpt

Chapter One

March 12th—Seattle—Quill and Ink Bookstore

Brooklyn Matthews sat behind the table, pen poised between her fingers, brushing a stray lock of hair behind her ear. She stared at the crisp, blank page, listening to the woman ramble on about her sister and how much they loved reading her books.

"We're your biggest fans," the woman said in a heated rush, threading all the words together in her haste. "We've read all your books. I like *Sarah's Secret* the best, but Marg, the sister I was telling you about, she thought *Badge of Honour* was better. Don't get me wrong, I liked it too, but I still think this is your best work." She paused to gulp down a large breath of air. "Do you have a favourite, Ms. Matthews?"

Brooklyn looked up from the flap of the book. She'd tuned the lady out ten minutes ago, and other than her name, hadn't heard enough to even hazard a guess at an exceptional answer. She smiled, twirling the pen around her fingers. "Am I making the dedication out to you?" she asked. "Or did you say this was for your sister?"

The woman hesitated, giving Brooklyn a puzzled look, before flashing another exuberant smile. "For me...please. As I was saying, *Sarah's Secret* is my favourite novel of yours."

"That's very kind of you to say," replied Brooklyn, scribbling the same, sentimental words across the white paper. She signed her name, closing the book as she handed it back across the table.

The woman giggled with joy, clutching the treasured pages to her chest, as she rose from the seat and headed for the door. Brooklyn looked around the small store, relieved the steady stream of eager fans had dissipated. She sighed and glanced at her watch. Only half an hour before she was scheduled to meet Gage at the lawyer's office, and she definitely needed a breather before she'd be ready to face him. She rose from the padded, wooden chair, fidgeting with her hair again, before heading towards the back of the store. At least, she could steal a few moments of quiet in the woman's restroom, even if it meant listening to the steady drone of elevator music playing across the intercom.

She ducked down a small hallway, skirting a discarded bucket and mop. She turned left at the end, but stopped at the entrance, staring at the muck splattered across the floor and the large, yellow sign blocking the doorway.

Out of Service.

She stepped back, reading the black, block letters with a sigh. She backtracked to the hallway, opening the door to the men's room. The only male employee had scampered off on a break, and she doubted the manager would care which restroom she hid in.

"Hello?" She stepped inside, ignoring the predominately

male scent lingering in the air, and headed for the sink, eager to spray a handful of cool water across her face. Of all the days to have a book signing, today was by far the worst. She never would've agreed if her agent hadn't conned her into it, subtly reminding her how well her books did when she mingled amidst her fans. While it was usually one of her favourite activities, her heart just wasn't in it today. She looked down at her left hand, noticing how bare it looked. She feigned a smile, telling herself it was all for the best... Gage didn't love her, so why make them both suffer?

She wiped a tear from her cheek, feeling others sting her eyes. She hadn't seen Gage in the past three weeks, and it'd been over six months since they'd made love. She lowered her head, remembering their last encounter. He'd been angry, and had touched her in a way she'd never forgotten. Her heart clenched wishing the memory was one to cherish rather than forget. It marked the beginning of the end.

She stifled a sob, biting her bottom lip for strength, when something cold brushed against her back. She looked in the mirror just as the blade pierced her shirt, sinking into her flesh until the hilt locked against her skin. Her chest constricted as her throat clamped around a scream. She locked her fingers around the porcelain rim as an arm reached around her chest, pulling her backwards. She slammed into a man's chest, feeling the knife twist in his grip.

"Did you think you could escape me, Sarah?" he slurred, brushing the side of his woollen mask against her neck. "Did you really think I wouldn't find you?" He slid his hand under her shirt, cupping her breast as he gazed at her reflection, inhaling deeply. "What an intoxicating scent," he mused, plumping her flesh, rubbing his erection against the cleft of her buttocks. "You smell good enough to eat, precious."

Brooklyn stared at the mirror, her body frozen, as the pain buckled her knees, leaving her sagging in his arms, the shaft of the knife holding her up. He was a full head taller than she was, with large shoulders and strong arms. He was covered in black, from the ski mask on his face to the sweater and pants hugging his body. They were tight, clinging to every inch of his muscular frame. She looked into his eyes, watching the brown colour turn black with desire. And though she couldn't see his mouth, she knew he was smiling.

"This is only the beginning, Sarah. And if you survive, you'll prove you're worthy of my love." He pulled the knife free laughing as she fell to the floor. "Don't disappoint me, Sarah. I'll be waiting."

More books from Kris Norris

Book three in the Til Death series

Another dead body – another victim.

Book one in the Dark Prophecy series

After roaming the earth for five hundred years, Rafe's life is about to begin.

Book two in the Dark Prophecy series

Despising the sight of blood isn't a desirable quality for a vampire.

Enchanted Love

Mira has only five days to lose her virginity, or face certain death…and only one man is up for the job.

About the Author

Kris Norris

Author, single mother, slave to chaos—she's a jack-of-all-trades who's constantly looking for her ever elusive clone.

Kris started writing some years back, and it took her a while to realize she wasn't destined for the padded room, and that the voices chattering away in her head were really other characters trying to take shape—and since they weren't telling her to conquer the human race, she went with it. Though she supposes if they had…insert evil laugh.

Kris loves writing erotic novels. She loves heroines who kick butt, heroes who are larger than life and sizzling sex scenes that leave you feeling just a bit breathless.

Kris Norris loves to hear from readers. You can find contact information, website details and an author profile page at https://www.totallybound.com/